TREATIES, TRAITORS AND PATRIOTS

G.A.CREWS

D1518974

THUNDERBORE BOOKS

TREATIES, TRAITORS AND PATRIOTS
Text and cover graphics copyright ©2014 Gregory A. Crews

Second Edition
Published by: THUNDERBORE BOOKS

This book is a work of fiction and is provided as such: excepting Appendices
I, III, IV, V, VI and VII, which comprise public domain documented history.

Available from Amazon.com, CreateSpace.com, and other retail outlets.

For my fellow Americans

TO CHUCK & DOTTIE
Greg
8-15-18

CONTENTS

PART 1

PART 2

PART 3

APPENDICES

PART 1

1. The DoP

The white stone gravel was playing a noisy tune on the steel wheel wells. As Grover considered the silencing effect of plastic in the newer vehicles he suddenly straightened, noting that he'd been cringing in the seat as if THEY might be zeroing on the racket. As speculation intensified in his mind, his thoughts were becoming a first and second person debate: ("You don't even know that was THEM, or even that it was your place THEY were moving on... and knock off the THEY and THEM crap.")

He steered the old pickup around a red faded barn and into a bone yard of farm implements; shutting off the engine, he coasted to a stop behind a combine of flaked green, yellow and mostly rust.

Grover released a long breath, eyes moving from his white knuckles to focus on a distant figure ripping equidistant slices along a downed tree just within the shaded wood. Relaxing his death grip on the wheel, some color returned as he popped the door and slipped down onto the soft earth. The drone and zing-zing of the chainsaw had a calming "business as usual" note; but he still rushed off like a man on a mission.

Ben saw him making straight for the woods, but moved back to the downwind end and began dropping short logs from his tree. Benjamin Franklin was a grizzled old character with shoulder length hair held back from his face with a St. Louis Browns ball cap. His Carhartts were rags; but they kept the sawdust off him, capturing wood chips on all the frayed tips. His lovable grin would disarm the most timid of children.

"Whatcha in such a hurry 'bout?" shouts Ben, slowing the chain speed but still sawing away.

He knew from Grover's demeanor that something was up and he just wanted it out. Outwardly, Grover Henry was usually one of Ben's more laid-back buddies. That beeline across the field and the way he sidled right up beside him was a dead giveaway.

"Hmm…" Grover waved him on and backed off upwind, to sit down on the stump of the downed tree.

Ben knew he'd get nothing out of him now and pushed the saw back to ripping wood at full power.

Grover's mind was racing in every direction at once. ("What's my hurry is right… You got to mellow. Game plan, straighten up… OK, cool it. You're sweating, but it is warming up today, so that's OK; don't want Benjy thinking you're losing it. Get up and drag some of those limbs out of the way so he's not tripping his way down the line.")

After clearing a nice work area, he moved back to the stump. The zing-zing-drone of the 2-stroke chainsaw reminded him of a hare scrambles or motocross race. They both knew that it was powwow time when Ben finished lopping off the last log from the base of the trunk. Grover counted seven index slices and knew that Ben's saw sounded like a race because he was anxious to get on with the dialogue.

("Alright think: THEY… there I go again… they didn't know that was you in Ben's old Dodge, so nobody followed you here.")

Ben had asked to borrow Grover's Avalanche to pick up a stack of 4X8 plasterboard the day before. It had been storming to the north and he needed the enclosed bed to keep his load from getting soaked on the road home. It wasn't the first time they'd swapped trucks, as Grover liked using Ben's old beater to haul compost to the Hancock garden. Being a microwave bachelor, Grover always appreciated a good meal with family or friends. John usually sent him home with some garden vegetables to nuke and his wife Dorothy might top the sack with some delicious leftovers.

("Six: So, I have to get my truck and get the hell out of town… no, you haven't got anything but the shirt on your back… you've got to go home. Then what? If that was THEM: they won't let me in. They'll just haul me off. There are already stories going around about harassments and confiscations; but it is easy to write that off as just some city boys rolling over. You might eat crow if the same story plays out at home. What do you do when you're not home and they've already got the drop on you?")

("Five: Maybe I shouldn't have spammed out the DoP on Facebook, Twitter and another couple dozen of the social networking sites. You could have tested the water with the email spam while you got dug in. Didn't expect the black helicopters without emailing the President himself though.")

("Four…")

Grover caught a whiff of burned 2-stroke oil from the saw when the wind back gusted for a moment. His mind drifted back to a gentler, simpler time… riding through cool autumn forests with brothers and friends…

("Pistols in our pockets for fun, campsites or pit stops, plinking at targets. I didn't even know they were making gun laws back then. This is America, land of the free; we've got the Second Amendment… Yeah, ripping along on the Bighorn, free as a bird. If you got behind, you always knew you were on the right trail from the scent of Full-Bore wafting on the breeze.")

Zing-zing; another log rolls clear and Grover snaps back to the present.

("Three: You haven't got any of your laptops with you, but you have got your cell. You can take video for the record, and if they've just come to harass you, an audition on YouTube might curb their enthusiasm… So that's it… I play it cool and go home.")

("Two: So, do you stir Benjy up or just get your keys and go? But then… he's not going to let me run off without a story either way…")

Grover's eyes leveled on *GOMER*: Ben's '66 Dodge. Across the field he could just make out the name on the door, or maybe it was only focused in his mind's eye. Five central letters remained after portions of the original white lettering had been sanded away. The red finish was doubly faded where *MONT* and *Y COUNTY* were nearly rubbed out: remnants of another age.

("One…")

Zing-zing-zing… Ben looked up at Grover with a "*you ready?*" expression, and then ripped through the last cut. Zing-zing-clink-clink-clink; the saw choked to a stop as Ben set it down. He upended the base log and plopped himself down facing Grover. They stared each other down for a long moment.

"I need my truck," Grover started, with a wink.

"Yeah, yeah, told you I was done with it yesterday."

"I know," Grover replied. "I just figured I'd do a last load this morning. Driving around in Gomer kind of makes me feel like a good ole boy."

"You are a good ole boy. But… you'll never be a classic like me if ya keep buyin' those shiny new trucks every few years."

"Well, somebody's got to make those factory payrolls, and shiny doesn't seem to bother you when it's raining."

Ben ignored the ribbing. Grover knew Ben's great-nephew had made the plasterboard run anyway.

"Now, your ole '53…" Ben slowly nodded his head "-classic."

"And I made NAPA's payroll with that one."

Ben was leaning forward with his forearms across his knees, eyes on his feet. He rotated his head 45-degrees and peered up at Grover through one eye.

"So, what's eatin' ya anyhow? C'mon, let's have it."

"Yeah… You looked at your email this morning?"

"No, I been out here with this tree," Ben replied. "What'd you do now?"

"I sent out the DoP, but not just email. It's all over Facebook and the rest of them."

"Your Declaration of Patriotism; you and your bros talked about that way back. Always thought it was Cleve stirring the pot, but now it's you finally whipped up a few lines, huh. I'da figured you'd be savin' it 'til they started knockin' down doors."

"I was… then studying that damned UN arms treaty in light of these new Executive Orders; by the time I rolled out this morning I was so pissed off I just figured what the hell. This is bullshit. You know they're just going to pick us off one by one. Anyway, they *are* knocking on doors. You think just because they started in the city that they're going to leave us alone? Divide and conquer. Those city boys are our neighbors too, our countrymen… *AMERICAN CITIZENS*. We're not the criminals here. Anyone who tries to break the Constitution and turn the Republic to socialism is guilty of treason. Ronnie's rolling over in his grave; after all he did to help the Soviet Union boot the Communist Party, now the Pinks have come to roost in DC."

"Take it easy, Grover. OK, so now you're thinkin' bring it on; but it's not like they already launched a drone with your name on it… You didn't spam the President, did ya?"

"No, but listen: I was headed home from Johnny's and there's several black SUVs headed south on my street. So, I just kept going east and here I am. But then, maybe it was just some yuppies from up north, come down to chase coyotes."

"Shoor, sure it was. Shoulda run that last loada shit last night, huh. What the heyull were you theenking?"

"Yeah, yeah… twenty-twenty."

"Duh, thenk owl light a bonfire on my front porch and then go for a Sonday crooz," Ben drawled in a thickened tone, dripping with sarcasm.

"Yeah, yeah."

"You better hang here and I'll go check it out for ya."

"No." Grover stood up. "Doesn't matter if they are there or not. I am going home anyway."

"You're sure?"

"Yep, already thought it out. You might stop over and let Cleve or Gerry know what I'm up to. I don't know if our phones are secure anymore, not if… you know, shit's already hitting the fan."

"Your AV's in the barn," said Ben as they started across the field. "Hey… don't do anything… crazy."

"Benjamin…" Grover began, then halfway to the gravel he sighed: "Keys are in Gomer. Thanks." With a shrug, he turned and made for the barn.

"You are very welcome my friend," Ben whispered softly to the wind.

Ben navigated old Gomer through the smoke screen of limestone dust drifting up the road after Grover's hasty exit. He decided to make it a quick trip and headed for Cleve's place.

A few minutes later Ben turned onto gravel and passed a "DEAD END" sign. At the first 2-track stood a pump jack: classic Churchill black with orange horse head. A large mailbox hanging from three heavy bridle cables accentuated the overkill. In bold black letters "CLEVELAND P. HENRY" was emblazoned on the orange box.

Ben drove on by as he spotted Cleve's SUV up the road. Turning around at the dead end, he pulled up behind the dusty dirt tinted Navigator and leaned out the window.

Cleve was stretching barbed wire with a come-along and had it tight enough with a few more click-click-clicks. He looked up at his visitor with a smile.

"What's up Benjy?"

"Oh- Grover ask me to come see you or Gerry. You're right here and I haven't been up there in years."

"You in a hurry?" Cleve asked, thinking Ben was a little too anxious.

"No. No, not really, it's just…"

"Good. You head on over to Gerry's. I'll just clamp a patch in this wire and be right behind you. I was- I was headed that way anyhow."

"OK," Ben mumbled as he fired the engine.

"I know what this is about. Did Grove phone you?"

"No, I had his pickup. He didn't wanna use the phone yet this morning."

"Heh, heh. Yeah… right behind you."

Cleve caught Ben just as they reached the foothills. After a quarter hour of winding up and down, they turned off the blacktop where a switchback turned away from a low ridge that had been running parallel to the road. A cattle guard set in granite outcrop made the entrance obvious; the track from there crossed the same smooth outcrop surface. On closer inspection the local rock (commonly labeled granite by the industry) was in fact mostly fine-grained rhyolite with streaks of granite rippling through it.

The route over the ridge was a "driver's choice" affair: making it difficult to determine the traffic load or how recently a vehicle had passed. Beyond the ridge was a maze of tracks through terrain that varied from prairie like glades to steep wooded slopes. Several more subtle links to the blacktop joined with the primary track that Ben and Cleve were following through the backcountry.

Turning east down a straight gravel drive, Ben squinted at the mirror. All but Cleve's windshield seemed to blend into the dust cloud. Everyone knew Cleve to be a little eccentric, but Ben knew the big angular SUV to be a step beyond. That flat finish was actually glass blasted titanium plate, thick enough to weigh in heavy, even for a 1-ton. He would have beefed up the V-10 anyway, but with the extra weight: Cleve figured a beefed-up Allison aircraft engine to be more appropriate.

They passed through half a mile of pine forest that ended abruptly at an entryway and bridged stream. Things were looking different than Ben remembered. Ben was the good-natured sort of old-timer that everyone loved to drop in on; so, he didn't get out much. He was thinking he hadn't been up here since Patrick died, and that was almost two decades ago.

Ben idled up to the entrance gateway and stopped; he rolled down both windows as the dust cloud filtered off through the trees. Nostalgia took him with recognition of the two massive logs that traversed the 30-foot span. Ben had helped raise those logs atop the support posts more than half a century ago. He'd notched the upper log to slightly overlap the lower. The lower log had a broad flat surface, into which Patrick had burned: "LEATHERWOOD". Ben fondly recalled the project. Patrick's boy, Grover, had needed a leash to keep him from under foot. Cleve was still a toddler, safe with Momma Henry, and Gerry a twinkle in her eye.

Coming up the drive Ben hadn't realized the entire original gateway was still planted there. From out front, it appeared as if granite had grown up around it. A standing grizzly was sculpted into the right pillar and a reclining bison on the left. The rock additions didn't just strengthen the aged wood pillars; they enhanced the aesthetic power of the ensemble.

Cleve blipped his horn to wake the old-timer from his reverie. Moving along, Ben smiled as Gomer rocked with a toggle-toggle-whump crossing the oak plank bridge.

The drive continued straight ahead to a dense wood where it swept north before a granite-based Quonset hut. The track north was mostly shielded by blue spruce in short rows at a 45-degree angle to the drive. The manor house was mostly visible behind oak and elm trees just beginning to leaf out. The old ranch style log home had the same granite base overgrowth that seemed to have afflicted most of the structures at Leatherwood. The original logs were visible beyond a rock veranda, which now surrounded the sturdy wood house. Silos of various sizes were associated with most of the outbuildings on the property; all built of the earthy red-brown granite. A one-hundred-foot silo with a 20-foot tall rectangular base rose from the back of the manor, which appeared to be transitional to a parapet surrounding a castle turret. The turret silo hosted a 20X38 foot version of the Stars and Stripes furling in the gentle breeze.

Most of a 320-acre clearing was encompassed by the drive and stream. The stream entered the dell from the northern tree line, passing beneath the westernmost of several outbuildings in the northeast corner of the estate. Meandering its way south then west through small irregular orchards and glades, it reached the western tree line about half a mile north of the bridge. At that point it flowed into a broad straight canal, running under the bridge and disappearing in the woods to the south.

The northwest corner of the dell was dominated by a deep blue lake overflowing into the canal at a rate similar to the adjacent stream. Located on the stream bank was a massive tri-nozzle fountain feeding the lake from the southeast. One of the high angle discharge nozzles dumped a heavy load of water near the northwest shore; in conjunction with the southerly and easterly discharge targets, they created a triangular interference pattern of waves between the three. The inevitable rainbow mist overshadowing the entire lake complemented the composition.

It was unclear where the cumulative flow of water originated. The northern border of the dell was an obvious 3-row plantation of white pine, backed by a vertical rock face. There was no waterfall down the face and the geography made it clear that the densely forested slope east of the dell could provide no more than its own meager runoff: meager relative to the perennial flow in the waterways. Entering the dell south of the estate manor, the slope's runoff would provide adequate irrigation for the gardens and crops below.

From the south half of the northeast eighty, the landscape formed a broad gentle hollow that dipped southwest. The manor house overlooked diverse fruit and vegetable gardens flourishing along en echelon terraces down the flanks of the hollow. In the south one-sixty, the dip of the hollow diminished while trending due south. The terraced gardens gave way to a mingling of orchards and vineyards, then pasture and row crops scattered with windbreaks and wildlife food plots.

Ben found himself mesmerized by the intrinsic beauty of Gerry's Leatherwood; then, in the blink of an eye he was gaping at a Kawasaki doing hang time over his hood. The dirt bike had launched off the bridge embankment from the south, crossed up in the air, and landed north of the drive in the east-west corn furrows. The bike made a pivoting landing then shot down the plowed furrows, giving the impression that the machine had ricocheted to the east. Though mechanically precise in its execution, Ben thought the entire maneuver conveyed the fluid grace of a deer jumping a fence and silently springing away.

"Silently..." Ben thought aloud.

That's how he had been caught by surprise. The motorcycle had not made a sound; it was quiet as a mountain bike. But nobody had legs with power like that. While considering the implications, Ben was again yanked from his musings as the roar of over two thousand super charged horsepower shocked his eardrums through the passenger window.

Cleve had launched off to the right and the paddle like lugs on his Goodyear farm tires were shoveling slabs of sod and earth onto Gomer's hood and roof. Ben instinctively swerved left, but Cleve stayed in the prairie grass south of the drive. Mass notwithstanding, Ben watched the big Lincoln pull the front wheels in the air several times as it leapt across the half mile stretch. Actually, Cleve was intentionally tagging the ground to maintain directional stability and could have flipped it anytime with the accessible traction.

A quarter mile from the bridge, the dirt bike was flat out on the north shoulder when the Lincoln thundered by. The bike's track diverged north up the hollow shortly before Cleve's brake lights lit up. The SUV snaked onto the gravel but would surely slide into the shrubberies or slam the Quonset hut if he tried to stop. So, he dove back into the earthy traction on the right; then turned left between the Quonset hut and the east woods.

Ripping through the hollow, the bike popped in and out of view through the orchards. Ben puttered up the drive (smiling now) as the biker took air on terrace after terrace, ultimately disappearing on the manor grounds above.

Up ahead, Ben spotted the Lincoln slipping out from behind the Quonset hut and edging north along the woods, back to the gravel. The performance was reminiscent of a puppy that just dug the wrong plant. The grounds around the building were groomed with flowers and shrubberies; Cleve had dug up enough wild plants already. He still sprayed the Quonset hut with gravel as he shot on up to the house.

As Ben shut off his engine he heard Cleve justifying: "-no crops along there."

Gerry's voice reprimanded: "The fescue just came back from the last time you did that. Now we'll have to blade those ruts in."

"You got a mouse in your pocket?"

"I oughta whoop your ass," Gerry was shaking Cleve's hand with a crooked smile on his face as Ben ambled up.

"Mr. Franklin: Greetings," said Gerry, extending his hand.

"Back atcha, *MR.* Henry," replied Ben, gripping Gerry's vice-like paw and adding: "You boys are trying to give an old man a heart attack."

"You're not an old man Ben; you work too hard to be old. You just get more leathery."

"*It is the working man who is the happy man. It is the idle man who is the miserable man.*[1] Aren't *you* gettin' a little leathery to be ridin' like that? I thought that was one of your kids out there wildin'.""

"Open face helmet; the kids all wear the full coverage jobs," Cleve quipped.

"Where did you get a silencer like that?" asked Ben, grabbing Gerry's arm.

Gerry chuckled: "Huh-huh- show you later. Come on inside."

"So did you check your email this morning?" asked Cleve, heading for the garage, "I'm sure that's what Ben's here to tell us about."

"No, I like to get out early in this spring weather. I just get more work done in the morning; let the emails season until lunch. Lately it's just you or Grover trying to rally me anyway," Gerry waved them to the front door, "but you can leave the sawmill out here Ben."

Ben frowned and wiggled out of his Carhartts.

"Ann celled me down in the south extension when you guys were coming up the drive; said she had something I should come check out," he continued, closing the door behind them, "That way Ben: Ann'll have us some coffee in the kitchen."

Ben knew his way around because the core layout hadn't changed like the exterior of the building had. He rounded a corner and found himself wrapped in a gentle bear hug.

"Benjamin, it's been sooo long," said Ann in a soft, possibly incriminating tone; Ben heard it as: "*why don't you ever come visit?*"

"Well, come visit me sometime," said Ben.

Ann straightened, then declared: "Maybe I will," as she slid to the side and walked Ben to the table.

"You're lucky you took that monkey suit off, Ben. She wouldn't have touched you," Cleve teased, as he sauntered into the room, "see how she shies away from me."

"Don't start with me Cleveland Patrick."

He started toward her, but she skipped away.

"Grease monkey," she chided affectionately.

Gerry brought three cups of hot coffee and sat down with Ben and Cleve.

"I know Grove was really wound up with that UN task force rumor." Gerry added: "Ann's printing copies of his email right now."

"I saw it," said Cleve, "I mean, I didn't open the dot-doc, but Grover told me about what he wanted to say- if and when."

"So, nobody's actually read it yet."

Ann laid a printed copy of Grover's DoP in front of each of the three men; then left the room.

"Drink up boys. There's more coffee where that came from. Let's see what Grover has to say."

***

DECLARATION OF PATRIOTISM TO THE REPUBLIC

IN GRASSROOTS.

By Declaration of the free patriots of the United States of America,

When in the Course of human events, it becomes necessary for a patriotic people to reject the heinous demands of a political regime intent on fracturing the very foundations of the Republic in their contempt for the ideals set forth by the Founding Fathers in the Constitution for the United States of America, and to assume among the powers of the earth, the Freedom guaranteed by said Constitution, and all Freedoms to which the Laws of Nature and of Nature's God entitle them; a decent respect for the opinions of mankind requires that they should declare the causes which impel them to disregard the unconstitutional demands and illegitimate laws presented by the Executive traitors, Judicial perjurers and Legislative incompetents.

We hold these truths to be self-evident, that all men are created equal, that they are endowed by their Creator with certain unalienable Rights, that among these are Life, Liberty and the pursuit of Happiness.— That to secure these rights, Governments are instituted among Men, deriving their just powers from the consent of the governed,— That whenever any Form of Government becomes destructive of these ends, it is the Right of the People to alter or to abolish it,— Or, in the case of the Republic, to re-establish The Constitution as "the law of the land", and to remove those whom have attained office through perjury in a conspiracy to subvert the national sovereignty of the Republic. Prudence, indeed, will dictate that Governments long established should not be abolished for light and transient causes; and accordingly all experience hath shown, that mankind are more disposed to suffer, while evils are sufferable, than to right themselves by abolishing the forms to which they have been pacified. But when a long train of abuses and usurpations, pursuing invariably a new world order based in Socialism and Communism, evinces a design to reduce the Republic under absolute Despotism.— It is their right, it is their duty, to throw off such Government, and to provide the old Guards for their future security.— Such has been the patient sufferance of these United States; and such is now the necessity which constrains the Patriots who live by the Laws of the Republic, to oust the traitors who would make war on the peaceable citizens of this great Nation in defiance of the 2nd Amendment to the Constitution for the United States of America.

The history of the current President of the United States is a history of repeated injuries and usurpations, all having in direct object the destruction of the sovereignty of these United States.

To prove this, let Facts be submitted to a candid world:

He has excited domestic insurrections amongst us, is guilty of sedition by inciting class and racial bigotry; and by attacking our right to bear arms has endeavored to bring on the inhabitants of our cities, the merciless criminal element, whose known rule of warfare is to prey on the weak.
(Amendment II. A well regulated Militia, being necessary to the security of a free State, the right of the people to keep and bear Arms, shall not be infringed. _US Constitution)

He has attacked and invaded our homes, depriving us in many cases, the benefits of Trial by Jury. *(Amendment IV. The right of the people to be secure in their persons, houses, papers, and effects, against unreasonable searches and seizures, shall not be violated, and no Warrants shall issue, but upon probable cause, supported by Oath or affirmation, and particularly describing the place to be searched, and the persons or things to be seized. Amendment V. ...nor shall any person be subject for the same offence to be twice put in jeopardy of life or limb, nor shall be compelled in any criminal case to be a witness against himself, nor be deprived of life, liberty, or property, without due process of law... Amendment VI. In all criminal prosecutions, the accused shall enjoy the right to a speedy and public trial, by an impartial jury of the State and district wherein the crime shall have been committed... _US Constitution)*

He has instituted multitudes of Agencies, and sent hither swarms of Officers to harass our people, and eat out their substance.
(Amendment IX. The enumeration in the Constitution of certain rights shall not be construed to deny or disparage others retained by the people. Amendment X. The powers not delegated to the United States by the Constitution, nor prohibited by it to the States, are reserved to the States respectively, or to the people. _US Constitution)

He has combined with the United Nations to subject us to a jurisdiction foreign to our Constitution, and unacknowledged by our laws; by enacting International gun treaties and giving his Assent to their Acts of pretended Legislation: he thereby levies war against us. *(Article. III. [Section 3.] Treason against the United States shall consist only in levying War against them... Article. II. [Section 1.] The executive Power shall be vested in a President of the United States of America... Before he enter on the Execution of his Office, he shall take the following Oath or Affirmation: -- "I do solemnly swear (or affirm) that I will faithfully execute the Office of President of the United States, and will to the best of my Ability, preserve, protect and defend the Constitution of the United States." Article. II. [Section 4.] The President, Vice President and all civil Officers of the United States, shall be removed from Office on Impeachment for, and Conviction of, Treason, Bribery, or other high Crimes and Misdemeanors. _US Constitution)*

He has affected to render our Military, Federal and Local Police independent of and superior to the Civil power, in contempt of his Oath, by Executive Action and usurpation of the 2nd Amendment, he has constrained our fellow Citizens to become the executioners of their friends and Brethren, or to fall themselves by their Hands;

If and when they too are deaf to the voice of justice, and we have conjured them by the ties of our common kindred to disavow these usurpations: We must, therefore, acquiesce in the necessity to hold them, as we hold the rest of mankind, Enemies in War, in Peace: Friends.

We, therefore, the Patriots of the United States of America, in Grassroots, Internet, appealing to the Supreme Judge of the world for the rectitude of our intentions, do, in the Name, and by Authority of the good People of these States, solemnly publish and declare: That these United States are, and of Right ought to be Free and Independent States; that they are Absolved from all Allegiance to the current President's treasonous regime, and that all political connection between them and said regime, is and ought to be totally dissolved; and that as Free and Independent States, if the US Senate fails in its duty to impeach all officials party to the treachery delineated hereto, they have full Power to levy War, conclude Peace and replace the traitors with elected officials whom in good faith do not perjure their oath to uphold The Constitution, and to do all other Acts and Things which Independent States may of right do. And for the support of this Declaration, with a firm reliance on the protection of divine Providence, we mutually pledge to each other our Lives, our Fortunes and our sacred Honor.

*G.T.Henry*_____

GROVER T. HENRY

***

2. Grover's Stand

Cleve had gone to the kitchen window and was staring out at the shimmering lake. When Gerry finished reading, he found Ben studying him from across the table.

"Grove didn't pull any punches," Gerry stated flatly.

"No... his analyses- the DoP: that's laid out," Ben agreed. "Kind of redundant though: cloning so much of the Declaration of Independence."

"I like it," Cleve turned from the window, "what's sad is that there are people out there who will think that entire document is radical new text. The idea is to get people to think about the words and why they are so familiar. It's like a number of years back when Kentucky's Senator Rand Paul did a thirteen-hour filibuster: from what I heard, when he was running out of steam, he'd go to reading and quoting from the Constitution. He got hassled by some of his own party later on. They didn't have a clue; his point was: *Do you recognize this? You do remember reading this? Maybe you need to hear this again.* If civil servants hear it over and over, maybe they will acknowledge some of what they took an oath to uphold."

"OK," Gerry cut in. "Who all did Grover spam this to?"

"Undisclosed recipients- that's all I know," Cleve replied. "Ben?"

"That's why he wanted me to talk to you. He sent it to his whole address book and posted it on every account he had, for those Internet social medias.

"That was before breakfast," Ben continued, recapping the events of the morning and adding that Grover intended to use his phone to send live video from home to a YouTube account.

"I was going to try phoning him for an update, but let's just check YouTube first," Gerry suggested, retrieving a laptop and pointing at the screen: "This must be the file; it was delivered this morning, real time. I'll pipe it to the big screen in the den."

Ann joined them as Gerry was starting the "untitled" video. The clip began with a view of a gray door panel and quickly moved past a dashboard to a driveway over the hood of a Chevy pickup.

"That's Grover's drive and I don't see any SUVs," Gerry commented.

Cleve chimed in: "No black helicopters-"

"Just listen," Ben cut him off, "Grover's narrating; turn it up."

The video had been panning the area from garage to house, to pond, reversing the sequence, then repeating. Grover was saying: "-thing out of the ordinary. Don't see anybody; no vehicles anyway."

After exiting the truck, the view moved along a walkway to the house. The modest home was clad in cedar shingle siding, but most of the front was glass. The covered porch was a pine deck extending the width of the building.

Moving up the walk, Grover whispered, "There can't be much going on out here because the bullfrogs are happy."

The brup-bruup-bruuup of dozens of frogs was audible in the background. The porch steps creaked under Grover's weight and the tone of the song changed slightly as frogs on the near side of the pond quieted. He opened the screen door and scanned the door jam.

Focusing on a dent opposite the latch he said: "Looks like somebody jacked the frame to pop the door; but then maybe some punk did that."

The bullfrogs had resumed their full-chorused chant as the door swung open. Kitchen, dining and living rooms were combined across the front half of the house. The video swept to the center of the large room; Grover's shotgun lay on the floor beside his 1911 style Colt .45; a set of decorative black powder guns (from a wall display) were on the couch.

"And that ain't right... I don't leave guns out on the floor. Looks like a photo op for a setup."

Grover was positioning the camera somewhere along the front wall, shooting back toward the couch, when his face filled the screen with a goofy grin: "Hi Mom."

Backing slowly his smile faded. "Hear that? The bullfrogs just went silent... and I can feel engines firing up."

Grover stepped off screen.

Coming back into view, he held a straight double-edged sword. With a flash of his right wrist, he cut a double twirl and raised the blade horizontal overhead as he moved to the center of the room.

Raising his left hand to the hilt, Grover rotated the sword to vertical as he lowered his hands to waist level. Shirtsleeves could not mask the bulge of his biceps. With both fists firmly gripping the sword, the rippling sinews of his forearms seemed to indicate he was intent on crushing the hilt to dust.

Any softness of image was lost to the scene, as Grover stood firm and shouted: ***"Give me Liberty, or give me Death!"***[2]

The request was immediately capitulated with the crash of shattering glass, splintering wood and the rat-tat-tat of fully automatic weapons fire. Grover stood like a statue for almost two full seconds before several large splats of red struck the wall behind the couch, followed by his mutilated corpse. Before the body could fall back onto the shredded rag of furniture, the video crackled out.

B ack in the den at Leatherwood spirits were devastated. Ann was sobbing softly; her face against her husband's shoulder. His head was bowed over her; he was running his palm along her long brown tresses, stroking her back from neck to waist. Gerry's hand moved with mechanical precision, but an occasional droplet splattered from his wrist or rolled off to be gently petted into Ann's soft locks.

Cleve was standing as if frozen in place, still staring at the blank screen. His steely gray eyes were welling red, but the grit of his underbite made it debatable whether he was predominantly struck with loss or anger.

Ben broke the long silence, his own emotion betrayed by the crack in his voice: "Nobody shows that clip to Momma."

A s some semblance of composure eventually returned to the group, Gerry pulled a bottle of black label Kahlua from under the bar along with four short stocky glasses. Running her fingertips down his arm to a light squeeze and release of his hand, Ann excused herself from the company.

"I'm going to find Patrick and Angela to warn them that… things have changed."

Gerry stowed the extra glass as he poured double shots into two glasses; he pushed one to Ben and tipped the bottle toward his brother.

"Whiskey," Cleve growled.

Retrieving a bottle of Devil's Cut Beam, Gerry sloshed a heavy double into the third glass and began pouring Beam over his own Kahlua. Cleve snatched his glass, knocked it back and snapped it back down before Gerry could set the bottle down.

"Whoa big fella. How about holding this one for a toast?" Gerry sloshed him another.

Ben raised his glass: "To Grover."

"To Grover," the brothers echoed.

Gerry topped up all three glasses with 50/50 Devil's Cut Kahlua. Cleve rolled his eyes but waved him on.

Cleve was the first to cut loose: "So that's it. That's the answer from our new socialist dictator. Declare allegiance to the Constitution and you will be massacred. You are a political dissident: send the goon squad and machinegun the whole lot of 'em."

"Grover figured they couldn't get a warrant and he hoped that video would keep them civil," explained Ben.

Gerry concurred: "They won't get any warrants from *our* Judges. Probable cause? Just because the Pinks in DC are shredding the Constitution, doesn't mean local Justices will scrap the Fifth Amendment. Those goons were acting under Executive Orders. What we don't know yet, is if they were just Executive cronies or a UN task force. I'd like to know if the UN rumors are true."

"***Tricks and treachery are the practice of fools that don't have enough brains to be honest.***[1] But Grover ain't comin' back whether it was UN, ATF, or KGB," Ben sighed.

"I think we can rule out the KGB, partner; but Gerry is correct sir: we need to know." Cleve continued: "Grover spelled it out too. If UN troops- foreign troops -are being quartered on American soil and have been used to slaughter U.S. citizens: the Administration is levying war against the United States. That is the constitutional definition of treason; and when Executive Orders constitute treason: impeachment proceedings must be addressed by the Senate."

"Good luck. Most of those boys have been using the Constitution as a boot scraper for so long, they'd feel guilty reprimanding the President if he was kicking a copy around on the House floor. Do we have enough real Americans left in the Senate? And party be damned; I mean enough honest men with the balls to draw the line: *dismantling of the Republic stops here*."

The conversation moved from one topic to another, always returning to the state of the Union as a centerpiece. Ben frequently steered the conversation off with questions about the mysterious modifications at Leatherwood. Too many of his questions were answered: "be easier to show you."

"Where has Momma been keeping herself?" asked Ben, "I can talk with her about Grover, if you think that's right."

"That would be perfect Ben," said Gerry thankfully, "we need to let her know, but I can't picture myself telling her just yet. Grover used to say I was her favorite, but I think that was just because I was the baby. I know she totally respected Grove because he was so much like Dad... Unless you want to tell her, Cleve?"

"It's going to break her heart. I couldn't have asked, but thanks, Ben. You're the stoic; and Dad always gave her strength like that."

Gerry waved his hand northward: "She'll be out in Number Two; said she'd be pulling taps and using up the last of the maple sap today."

3. Routine Confiscation

When the team of federally funded hit men finished with the Grover T. Henry operation they had made another stop for reconnaissance, then departed on the road north as they got their units loaded. By the time they reached the county line the five SUVs were spread over several miles. After just passing into neighboring Montgomery County, the sub-commander in the lead vehicle keyed his radio.

"Benny, uh, Chief, you copy?"

"This is Benny. Go ahead, Bud."

"We just passed a tall black man in blue bib overalls and a blaze orange ball cap with a scoped varmint rifle in his hands. You want us to come back for him?"

"No. No- all of you head on home. I'm bringing up the tail here. The five of us can take care of this one, if he's right out in the open."

"He was at the north edge of his yard; first house on the right after the county line," replied Bud.

"We'll get him. It should be a *routine confiscation*."

Henry Knox was a kind-hearted man of modest, but independent means. He and his wife had built their old house into a fine modern home with determination and grit. He'd worked at a factory south of the big city for almost a decade until it shut down when production moved to China. He was only thirty-four when he lost his job, but it didn't bother him much as his workday gained a few hours without the commute. Henry could always find local work with his tractor and meager farm implements: mowing or baling all day long when he was on a roll. Finances without a weekly paycheck were difficult at first, but a few years after the factory closed he was doing better as a small contractor and had more quality time with his family. He was also a competent dirt farmer and mostly fed the family with his crops and gardens.

Henry was as proud as a man could be of his wife Virginia. He thought she was too pretty a girl for him to hope for when they met, but Virginia knew a real man from a fancy Dan. She had Henry roped and tied before his head had stopped spinning. Virginia was five years his junior and they had enjoyed eleven years of marriage. Henry knew his wife always had enough to do in the house, but Virginia loved working the gardens; she kept track of what was ripe-when and where. Henry didn't think her cooking could be beat by a gourmet chef.

The Knox family included their nine-year-old boy Henry and three-year-old Monica. Little Henry wanted to be just like Dad and came along wherever his little legs could follow. Henry taught the boy all the common-sense knowledge that his own father had imparted to him. He felt closest to his son in the fields, where little Henry learned about the land and conservation of the resources to which all Americans are stewards. He learned that just as the wild animals in the natural world have every right to these resources, we too are animals natural to our world; it is our right, it is our legacy to utilize these resources to the benefit of man, with the understanding that our renewable resources require the give and take of ethical stewardship.

This day: little Henry was not home from school yet and Virginia had left for shopping and groceries when her husband came in for lunch. The nearest town was south of the Montgomery County line and they considered that to be their hometown. Henry was delighted to have an excuse to stay home and play with his favorite angel this afternoon. He couldn't spend enough time with his little Monica and she had him wrapped around her little finger. Monica was looking out the living room window on the north side of the house while Henry cleaned up their lunch mess.

"Daddy, Daddy, there's a black and white striped puppy out there."

"Hold on Darlin', the only way we got any pups out here is if somebody dropped one off at the road again," said Henry as he joined Monica at the window. "That's not a puppy, that's a smelly ole skunk."

"There's a skunk in my bunk!" Monica recited the title of a book her cousin Eleanor had read to her.

"Oh, you don't want this skunk in your bunk. He's probably the vermin that's been gettin' our chickens."

"What's vermin?"

"Vermin is critters that are no good for farms or people. We need our chickens and their eggs. You want to always stay away from vermin like skunks."

"Where do they keep all the friendly skunks Daddy?"

"Skunks aren't friendly Darlin'; they're mostly scared of people. They're not generally mean: unless they're sick, or hurt, or cornered. They're just wild animals."

"But the skunk in the bunk was friendly."

Henry was standing squarely behind Monica. She didn't have a care in the world, leaning back against her father's strong legs with her little arms wrapped as far around his knees as she could reach. Henry had his hands curled around Monica's pigtail braids, holding them loosely in the air, like handlebars steering his 4-wheeler through the woods. They were both watching placidly while the skunk continued its digging and rooting around a small bush.

"Baby, the animals all talk in cartoons and kid's books: but you know real animals don't talk, right?"

"Daddy... I *know* real animals don't talk."

"Well, whenever they do talk, that story is not about animals; that one is about people. Nobody that tells those stories wants you to get bit playing with wild animals. What they're saying is that you should not treat someone like a skunk just because he looks like a skunk. Now, if he starts acting like a skunk, then you can start treatin' him like a skunk... But you always start off showing people the same respect whether they be white, or black, or black with two white stripes."

"Like Uncle George?"

"Huh?"

"Uncle George- he's got white hair on the sides of his head and doesn't have any on top."

"Heh-ha-ha," Henry chuckled, "that's right Baby, Uncle George don't have much hair left, but he's just as good a man as your daddy."

"Are the city skunks vermin too?"

"Well, there aren't many skunks in the city or any other wild animals either. When the cities were built most of the animals cleared out. The big predators were hunted down to make it safer for people and domestic animals."

"What's predators?"

"Predators are animals that eat other animals and some of the big ones can eat people too. Now part of the problem is that man has upset the balance of nature to make it safer for little girls like you. As stewards of the land we try to help Mother Nature restore the balance by filling in those gaps that we have created."

"What's suewards?"

"Oh Baby, I'm sorry, I been teaching your brother about conservation and I forgot you're too young to understand these things."

"Teach me too Daddy. I'm not too young. Teach me about suewards and conservation; I want to know everything that you know Daddy."

"Now that could take a while. But some day Baby, smart as you are, you'll know as much as I do and lots more."

"So you'll teach me about suewards and… conservation? Pleeease…"

Henry took a deep breath and sighed: "Ooookay… With regards to nature: conservation is protecting our environment from destruction-protecting the plants, animals, lands and waters from disappearing -that's not to say we are trying to prevent any changes to our world. The earth has been changing for billions of years; it always has and always will. The challenge of conservation is to maintain a balance whereas the widest variety of plants and animals can share the earth with us. With regards to nature: STEWards are those of us who practice conservation. Now, there is a lot of foolishness in the cities where people have forgotten that they too are animals. They think conservation is making a museum of the wild domain and freezing nature in some historical configuration that they deem correct."

"Configuration?"

"Form, style, layout… pattern?"

"Ohh-K…"

"They have no understanding of the balance you and I learn from living on the land. And many fools believe that we should not have guns. As stewards, we hunt the animal populations that predators no longer control. Even the graceful deer, that most everyone find delightful to watch, would be considered vermin if hunters did not control their population. And with less predators out there: there are so many rabbits to eat, that there's not so many of God's creatures want to catch a smelly skunk for dinner. The skunk population is too big around here already and they're the worst critter for carrying rabies."

"What's rabies?"

"Rabies is a horrible disease that vermin can pass to dogs and people, 'specially when they go crazy and bite ya."

"Why do they go crazy?"

"That's what rabies does. Makes 'em froth at the mouth too. If you ever see a dog frothing at the mouth: you stay away from that one, even if it's ole Tracker."

"What's-?"

"Hold on, Baby. I *gotta* go take care of that skunk or it's gonna be up to no good."

"Can I go with you Daddy?"

"No, now I told you: you need to stay away from that kind of vermin. It could run right up and bite you before you could say *Chicken Little*."

"Because it's crazy?"

"Because it might be, Baby. Because it might be... and there's no reason to take the chance. Now how about you put away some of these toys and then find us a good book to read. I'll be back in just a few minutes."

Henry slipped four .22-250 shells in his pocket, pulled his Savage BVSS from the gun rack and clicked the lock bar back in place. Monica had been taught to never touch one of Daddy's rifles, but of course she was still too young to be trusted with unlocked weapons, even for a minute.

Henry had made short work of the skunk and was strolling back to the house when a black SUV whipped into his drive and stopped by the mailbox. He reckoned they were just turning around, until four camoed men stepped out on the lawn. He noted they each carried a SCAR-H assault rifle pointed unthreateningly at the ground, although their stance and formation were anything but unthreatening.

("Military? What is this? Are these guys for real? Or a boatload of survivalists out practicing for an invasion?") Henry was thinking as he approached his front porch steps. ("I've only got three rounds left in the magazine and an empty shell in the chamber, so I'm shit outa luck if these're crazies.")

Henry was a crack shot and he knew it; he'd been to local competitions where he'd taken home his share of pies and ribbons. However, he was still outgunned even if he had another live one in the chamber. He was thinking about how fast his archrival Ethan Allen could chamber rounds with a lever action: not fast enough to take out four keen soldiers and certainly not with bolt action. ("Though I wouldn't bet money against Ethan puttin' these bozos down with semi-auto.")

As Henry reached for the handrail with his left hand, a voice from a loudspeaker commanded: "Sir, place your weapon on the ground and step away."

Reaching across the steps to the right handrail, Henry turned toward the vehicle and backed slowly up the steps.

"This here is private property and we don't want no trouble," Henry hollered back.

"I am a federal agent and you are in violation of a federal gun ban under the UN Arms Treaty. Place your weapon on the ground," Benny repeated.

"I don't know about any UN treaties. And I don't know how you boys got here: but this is the United States of America. You come back with a warrant."

"I repeat: drop your weapon and stand down," Benny continued with agitation.

Henry still held his rifle in his right hand, the receiver across his thigh and barrel pointed at the floor between his feet. He grasped the doorknob behind his back and slowly swung the storm door open with his left hand.

Benny set the mic down and spoke to his Number One man who was kneeling beside his partner, with Number Three and Number Four standing at the ready behind them: "Gil, don't let him get inside; wing'im."

The men knew that when Benny said "wing'im", he wanted a bullet through the flesh of a thigh, clear of the femur. Gil had a clear line to Henry's left leg and took his shot as the rest of the fireteam shouldered their weapons. As he squeezed the trigger, Gil glimpsed movement in the slice of view between the target's knee and the partially opened door.

"No…" whispered Gil.

Henry was moving his leg to clear the door as the bullet grazed his thigh and ripped through Monica's throat. The child was thrown against the door jam and rebounded against the back of Henry's legs. As Monica's little body buckled his knees, he knew... and Henry's senses exploded. He chambered a round as he straightened and shouldered the Savage.

"NO!" screamed Gil as a tight group of NATO rounds tore through Henry's chest.

His first odd thought as his body banged against the wall was: ("No ribbon today Henry, didn't even show. Wonder if Ethan woulda got a round off? -Nah...")

The tough dirt farmer realized he was dead when he felt no pain as he slid to the floor. He sensed a distant shouting that faded into an obscure static of no further significance. Straining for focus: a golden crystalline pattern flickered on the borders of his vision. Henry's broken body had come to rest slumped over Monica, his legs across her neck and waist. At the edge of his focus, though spattered with blood, he divined the face of a sleeping angel.

Through the fuzzy pattern of golden haze, he fought to hold his focus. Despite Henry's efforts, his field of view was shrinking as if he were backing into a shimmering crystalline tunnel. As the vision of his angel dissolved into the encroaching haze, his last perception of the corporal world was the image of his own calloused palm alongside Monica's tiny hand. Though his life on earth was done, Henry longed to give that little hand one last squeeze-

He thought of little Henry and hoped in those nine short years he had imparted the same values to his son that his own father had passed to him. His pride in the boy made his spirit soar and he prayed young Henry would continue the Knox legacy in wise stewardship of the land. He reflected on his loving wife... and was saddened at the thought of her raising their son alone. He pictured her vivacious smile and considered her indomitable fortitude. To be widowed so young... so tragic...

The image of Monica's tiny hand was quickly fading into a shimmering haze at the distant end of the tunnel... and Henry imagined that hand growing into the hand of a beautiful young woman, as proud and strong as Virginia... and he would have passed that hand to a fine young man one day... and... and his dreams faded into the shimmering haze of mist and static as he passed away.

Benny strolled onto the porch and kicked the bodies. Two of the soldiers had entered the residence to check for survivors and pilfer the rest of the target's guns. Number Two was checking around back and Gil was standing in the yard with his back to Benny.

Benny noted his slumped shoulders and remarked: "Hey Gil, don't take it so hard. Shit happens. If it makes you feel better, we'll fill out an EO document for this guy, we've got plenty of blanks. That kid's just collateral damage."

"Shut up Benny… That's a little girl we just- I just killed."

"You didn't kill that kid, Gil. That dumb son of a bitch there did. If he'd have obeyed orders, this wouldn't have happened."

"He wasn't *under* orders: he was a civilian; one of *your* countrymen. This whole business is getting out of hand and I didn't sign up for this shit. I joined the UN to fight terrorists and fanatics, not farmers and families."

"These are just common criminals Gil. Wackos that won't let go of the Wild West. We've got a gun ban to enforce… and you did sign up. You take orders from me," added Benny.

Number Two was back and stood quietly at the side of the porch listening to the discourse.

"Yeah, we take orders," replied Gil, "but you're not even military and there's only so much of your shit we've gotta take. And yeah: I signed up, but that was before I read your Declaration of Independence, your Constitution and your Bill of Rights. Have you ever read those?"

"Of course, we read them in grammar school."

"You ever read them since? You remember what they say?"

"We the People, blah, blah, blah. I don't need a history lesson from you," Benny smiled: "We've got new laws now."

"I don't think this guy even knew about your new laws. Look around: they don't even have a satellite dish."

"Then him not knowing got his kid shot," Benny kicked Monica's body again. "Let's bag 'em up boys."

Gil grit his teeth and continued: "We shouldn't even be here Jackass. Your own military wouldn't join your witch hunt and the UN shouldn't have gotten involved either."

"Hey, you better lose that attitude honcho. You've had a rough day, so just head on back to the SUV and cool off. Tomorrow you start on a few days of R&R. Hold on; grab a couple of those body bags first. Or no, just one, and bring one of those lawn and leaf trash bags. No use wasting one of the big zippered bags on this little one," added Benny as he kicked Monica's body again.

Gil snapped.

"YOU KICK THAT LITTLE GIRL AGAIN YOU FUCKING PRICK AND I'M GONNA KICK YOUR ASS SO HARD YOU'LL BE SHITTIN' OUT YOUR EARS!"

"Yeah, I've heard that before Pal... and you are bordering on insubordination."

"I'M BORDERING ON RIPPING YOU A NEW-" Gil exhaled a deep low growl that *bordered* on threatening to chew Benny's head clean off; then he pivoted and paced off to the SUV.

Gil returned a little later with two body bags. Number Three and Number Four loaded the bags and carried them to the vehicle. Benny was running strips of yellow "crime scene" tape across the door when Number Two picked up a little book that had been lying beneath the bodies.

"*Go Dogs Go*: theis eis my favoreite Doctor Seuss book of all time. Eit eis pure classeic: *Beig dog. Leittle dog.* Here, leisten to theis: *Dogs driving around ein cars. Go dogs. Go.*"

"PUT IT DOWN PIERRE- NO -give it to me."

"Sorry Geil."

Gil walked back to the SUV with the little book clutched against his chest.

4. Sarah

Ben found the number two building easy enough; aside from several small cottages, it was one of the few original outbuildings still standing. Most of the new additions at Leatherwood were of Quonset hut design. Number Two still fit right in aesthetically, with its granite base and heavy log walls that matched the manor house. It was an exceptionally solid barn even before the basal reinforcement. A walk led to the southeast corner of the building where Ben pushed open a heavy 4X8 foot door, which swung quiet and easy on roller bearings. Ben noted the door and jam was two logs thick now and thought: ("That door was a bitch to open when it was half as thick.")

An overhead deck extending along the south wall comprised the ceiling of rooms along either side of a long corridor. Beyond the deck to the right was the central main chamber. Proceeding down the corridor past everything from tack room to electronics labs, Ben stepped out into the open southwest corner of the main chamber.

He stood gazing at the back of a lone figure in a yellow, red and black streaked silky-thin gown. She stood before a 50-gallon stainless cauldron over crisp blue flame. Her pure white hair was gathered into a loose dangling ponytail. Posture and grace of movement challenged the knowledge that she was a woman in her seventies. She held a long wooden spoon, occasionally stirring the great pot.

After a time, the woman spoke: "Well, what is it? You're not going to sneak up on me."

"No, I'm not gonna do that. How have you been Momma?"

She cocked her head to the side, still not looking back; dipping the spoon again she quipped: "I ain't your Momma you grisly old coot."

"Good to see you again too, Sarah," said Ben, moving up beside her.

She turned her head and looked Ben square in the eyes: "Haven't seen you since…" Her olive eyes went slightly glassy as she looked back to the pot and finished: "-in a long time."

She steeled herself and challenged: "Is your skin getting as thin as your hair, or are you going to give me a hug?"

Ben immediately wrapped his arms around hers and felt a spoonful of hot syrup running down his pant leg. She dropped the big spoon into a bucket at her feet and pulled Ben closer, forgetting the ladle had been full. Anyone watching the scene would have thought they had just stepped into a nuthouse. Ben started leaning left, slowly dragging Sarah along in a clockwise spiral of choppy irregular steps.

She only held on for one rotation, then stepped on his foot and fell back: "What in Sam's valley do you call that?"

Ben held her up straight, then with an: "Ouch," he stumbled back and to his left; he straightened: "Ow," then leaned left; straightened: "Ow…"

By the third ow, Sarah had clamped a Vice-Grip at the wet spot on Ben's pant leg: "Now hold that away from your skin while the syrup cools. Sorry Ben. I was about to ask if you were doing a rain dance, or the sap around the pot: ya silly sap. Men… you'd give up a leg before you'd miss a good squeeze."

Ben cracked a smile and she warmed him with a light laugh: "What brings you out here old man?"

His smile staggered for a moment, but he didn't want to lose the nostalgia of the moment and commented: "It's beautiful up here this time of year."

"You once told me: *a man is blind if he can't find beauty in every season and every corner of this great country.*"

"You remember that…"

Ben was intrigued with her recall of a phrase uttered on their single date, so many years ago; her beauty and wit had enchanted him, but not to be tied down: he had set her up with his colleague shortly thereafter. Patrick had chased his last rainbow when he met Sarah.

"You were a romantic back then," Sarah smiled.

"Maybe," Ben countered, "but a romantic with a master plan: that's a paradox."

"I've still got the card you painted to ask me out."

"Thank you."

"Thank you?" she eyed him curiously.

"That painting was a nice piece and you clearly appreciated the gesture. I think that kind of romantic went out with the deluge of movies, TV and tech. Modern women all saw the one about a psychopath artist who chops 'em up and buries 'em in the back yard."

"Oh Ben, stop."

"I wonder how many innocent little paintings are rotting away in an official file labeled: *Artists and Psychos – The Usual Suspects*."

"Are you finished?"

"OK, I'm off the soapbox," Ben laughed, "but just imagine a true romantic in a society where the only socially acceptable means of impressing a young lady is money. You would not have gone out with me and hence never would have met Patrick."

"You know he told me that you were so taken, he thought you were going to say you were in love; then you suddenly went into some Humphrey Bogart scene and made him promise he would meet me, if you could arrange it." Sarah lowered her voice in a satirical attempt at Bogart: *"Where I'm going, she can't follow. What I've got to do, she can't be any part of."*

"Memory lane… Sarah: they got Grover."

"What?"

"Grover; he's dead."

Sarah was shocked and dumbfounded that a man she had just called romantic could be so blunt.

"I'm so sorry Sarah. I… I wanted to ease the blow, but all I was doing was babbling on."

She did not move a muscle, so Ben shuffled closer. She locked her hands behind his neck and hung her head against his chest. She wept silently as a spot grew on the front of Ben's shirt. He patted her back as she was racked with an occasional sob.

A long while after the sobbing had subsided, still not moving, Sarah whispered: "You're sure?"

"The coroner's office called. Gerry gave Ethan permission to release him to Adams Funeral Home."

"No investigation?" Sarah's eyes were still red and glassy, but the strength was coming back to her voice, "I'm guessing, but you just tell me what you know right now, Benjamin."

Again, Ben recapped what he knew, but leaving out the YouTube video.

Sarah pulled away from Ben and squared her shoulders. She pulled her hair back from her face and knotted her ponytail. Circling around the cauldron of maple sap, she leaned down by a workbench at the wall and rotated a gas valve.

Ben watched as the flame shrunk, vanishing with a pop, and then looking up found Sarah toting a stainless 12-gauge Ithaca.

"I'm going down there to set things right," Sarah exclaimed.

"No, no, not yet," Ben argued, "Cleve and Gerry are inside making plans right now."

"The boy's have been making plans for years and look at where it got Grover. Damned commies. I'm taking the Terex down there and I'm going to crush anything that looks military or Fed," Sarah countered.

"Just calm down a minute; don't sell yourself cheap. You go attacking the wrong people, they'll just make you out to be a lone crazy," Ben continued: "A lot of people know Grover was a good man; and he was just protecting his own when they attacked him. Grover will be remembered well. You should take advantage of what the boys have built here; this whole estate is a stronghold. Even this old barn– it used to be a single log thick."

"You don't know the half of it Ben. There's three quarter inch plate between those logs, and one inch in the door. This is the heaviest building at Leatherwood, and you can be sure none of the Quonset huts are tin cans either. The boys have been having fun all right. Everything is built like… well; they never built 'em like that. And the Terex, sheesh: you don't want to know."

"I haven't seen that one yet," admitted Ben.

"Well, I'll take a pickup, but I'm still going right now."

"I understand; but let me drive. Best if you don't go charging in there with the tires spinning."

They headed out in a white F250, but weren't past the gate when a phone rang in the console. Ben dug it out, while Sarah complained: "They've got a couple disposables in every vehicle. Like damned umbilicals; you just can't get away from them."

"It'll be alright," Ben flipped it open, "Hello."

"Where you going?" Cleve's voice demanded.

"Momma wants to see Ethan Allen about why he's omitting the investigation," Ben explained, "Actually she wants to raise hell with the assassins too; but I'll keep her out of trouble. We'll just be a couple old folks puttering around town."

"Don't take her by Grover's house Ben. We're going to do a night op there tomorrow and we don't need her stirring the hive tonight."

"Sure. See you this evening," Ben clapped the phone shut.

At the first 4-way on the edge of town, Sheriff Jefferson's truck was parked in the shade of an old oak tree by the city limits sign. With the semblance that he was busy watching traffic: it was his favorite "get some air and think" place, and he had been doing a lot of thinking today. When Ethan had shown him the body, he had driven out to Grover's place to find the collateral destruction. Seeing the 2nd, 4th, 5th and 6th Amendments overridden by Executive Order in one fell swoop just stuck in his craw. He felt like a festering plague had commenced the subjugation of his county. His sulk was interrupted by the approach of the Henry's F250.

Ben and Sarah spotted the sheriff's truck across the intersection and noted he was subtly waving them in. Ben eased his passenger door up alongside the driver's door; he wanted to keep their friendly sheriff in his truck so he wouldn't get nervous about the shotgun tucked under Sarah's right arm.

"Hello *Thomas*," Sarah glared at him with narrowed eyes.

"Hello Mrs. Henry, and… Benjamin?" responded Sheriff Jefferson, "I thought it would be Gerry; I wanted to talk to you all about – well, I was hoping him or Cleve wouldn't do anything… rash."

"Anything *rash*?" Sarah was getting red in the face, "You mean like barbequing a pack of commie assassins?"

"Sarah: I didn't have anything to do with that. A UN task force was at my office first thing this morning. I told them they needed a warrant from Judge Adams, but they claimed jurisdiction by Executive Order. Said any interference would be obstruction of justice. Justice my ass… I called the house anyway, but Grover didn't answer."

"You say it was the UN; the boys wanted verification about that," said Ben.

"There were five BATFE SUVs; each with a third of a dozen UN troops," Sheriff Jefferson replied. "There was a BATFE agent commanding each fireteam and one of them took the lead- the one flashing the EO documents. I'm thinking they want to maintain the image of U.S. Feds handling these gun heists and assassinations, but they don't have enough paid cronies to pull it off; they need the UN backup. Federal agents are civil servants just like me; we've sworn an oath to uphold the Constitution. There will be dissent among the ranks throughout the Republic – patriots will emerge in resistance to these unconstitutional orders. *The tree of liberty must from time to time be refreshed with the blood of patriots and tyrants.*[3] *And what country can preserve its liberties, if the rulers are not warned from time to time, that this people preserve the spirit of resistance? Let them take arms.*[4] I believe the silent majority of men are morally sound, and will ultimately fight for the inalienable rights of all Americans. But the weak and greedy, who have seen promotion and perks for the morally deficient, will sell their souls for a position in the new socialist tyranny. That would be this morning's task force commanders. I think they called the leader Benny; yeah, that was his name: Benedict Arnold."

Ben changed the subject: "How'd you know it was us? Half the trucks in town are white Fords."

"Gerry makes that same bumper and headache rack for all the Henry pickups; but the secret's safe with me," the sheriff smiled. "That fella, Benny, was asking about Cleve: told him Cleveland is out of town most of the time... You be careful in town; and you should go see Ethan. He's quite distraught about having his investigation stymied."

"Thanks Tommy."

It was late afternoon when Sarah asked the receptionist: "Would you inform Mr. Allen that Sarah Henry is here to see him?"

When Ethan entered the room, Ben immediately felt that he would himself be identified as "the thing seen stepping from the swamp". Ethan was a tall, lean man with an intense gaze. He wore a fine black suit, reminding Ben that his own day had begun in the woods. Sarah, on the other hand, carried herself with a grace that would camouflage her sap stained gown if they had crashed a formal ball.

The perfect gentleman, Ethan knew this was not a social visit. He nodded to the office girl: "You can go home now dear, I'll see you in the morning."

Ethan locked the door and took Sarah's arm; leading her to an inner office he offered: "My deepest condolence for the loss of your son, Mrs. Henry."

He led her to a chair in front and seated himself at his desk. As Sarah sat down the Ithaca slipped out from the folds of her dress. She frowned and laid the shotgun across her thighs.

Ben just rolled his eyes when Ethan said: "My, what a big gun you have, dear."

"The better to blast commies with," said Sarah.

Ethan appeared to be straining to keep a straight face; in fact, he would have broken out in laughter if he had not just written the death certificate for Sarah's first born.

"You are quite safe here, dear lady, I can assure you," said Ethan, purposely pulling his perfectly tailored coat tight against his chest, outlining a 1911 beneath the material as he stood.

He reached back to what appeared to be a large decorative cigar box on a small shelf beneath a rifle display. He tipped the lid to expose a tight pack of .30-30 ammo. The crossed rifle display featured finely engraved Winchesters with mahogany stocks. Between the twin Winchesters was a small placard with an Eagle Scout "BE PREPARED" emblem; beneath that was engraved "ALWAYS LOADED". Higher on the wall to the right was a golden eagle. Beneath the taxidermy piece was four fully loaded bandolier bullet slings that appeared to be hanging from the claws.

"What are you going to do when they knock your door down with an Executive Order young man?" questioned Sarah.

"That shall be their undoing," Ethan's eyes snapped from Sarah to Ben and back again three times in a fraction of a second.

Ben had to wonder if those hawkish eyes couldn't actually acquire and eliminate half a dozen threats in a matter of seconds. He had heard tell that Ethan had won every acquisition and accuracy competition he had ever competed in; though he always qualified, he never attended a national competition. He was proficient with any tool at hand, but favored a lever action with iron sights. Even so, given a choice between a truckload of yahoos spraying ammo in full-auto mode and a man who can make every bullet count: you'd want this gunner on your side.

"The funeral home already has Grover's body," Ethan started. "I am embarrassed to admit that I dispensed with the investigation as per protocol delineated in the Executive Order document. I spoke with Judge Adams first. He was outraged that a *dead or alive* EO document be delivered with a body to the coroner's office, as if it were a deer tag and harvested animal. They included a photo of the deceased; face down with several guns on the floor beside him. The implication is deplorably obvious: however, I know for a fact that Grover had never loaded those old black powder cowboy pistols, so it is ludicrous to infer he was firing them.

"Judge Adams told me to fill out the death certificate as I see fit and follow the EO protocol for now. I will keep my own private file on the matter, nonetheless. The Judge indicated the need for a town hall meeting to discuss options. Sheriff Jefferson is not physically capable of jailing a BATFE led task force of two dozen troops, to be tried for: *crimes against the Republic*."

"Samuel Adams is a good man," Sarah began. "I understand your predicament now, and I am comforted to know this infraction is being taken seriously."

"Quite so my dear, in fact, Judge Adams believes the sheriff will need a local militia to scuttle future… *infractions*. There is also the need to forecast a potential mobilization. This morning, when Thomas saw that email, he phoned me and said: *Grover sure believes in that First Amendment*. Mayhap we should thank God and Grover for the wake-up call."

The dapper coroner slipped a copy of the death certificate into a manila envelope and passed it to Ben as they all got to their feet.

"I was about town several times today and I am confident the task force has returned to the city," his earnest smile assured them the town was safe for now.

Sarah exited the front door first and as Ben stepped out behind her he quietly stuck a yellow sticky to the doorframe.

Taking Sarah's arm, Ethan walked them to the street and opening the passenger door he helped her into the truck.

"Mrs. Henry, no one in this town will remember Grover as anything but a fine and respected citizen, and I for one, will always honor him as the Patriot of patriots," with a bow, Ethan kissed Sarah's hand, pivoted and paced back to the building.

"Kinda cheeky, idn't he?"

"Ben." Sarah squinted at him through one eye.

As Ethan closed the door he pulled the sticky note. It read: "For your private file: YouTube, untitled, 8:53 this morning."

B en turned the truck down Main Street toward the Square as Sarah's eyes combed alleys and parking for anything… suspicious.

"Pull over up here and let's just have a walk around the Square," instructed Sarah.

"OK, but only if you leave the shotgun in the pickup," Ben countered.

Sarah's eyes narrowed: "Spoilsport."

The old couple walked a half block to the northwest corner of the Square and crossed to the central park area. They had passed several pedestrians; two of which had looked Sarah in the eye and said: "*Liberty or Death.*" Both times she had looked questioningly to Ben, who had walked on expressionless.

They did a lap around the perimeter then strolled to the honored veteran memorial and cannon monument. A boy of 13 or 14 years was kicked back on a park bench, thumbing a Gameboy.

"Howdy partner," Ben saluted, "Hooked on the game, huh? At least you're not keeping yourself holed up in the dark somewhere."

"Fresh air. I figure if there was ever any action around here this might be the best seat in town; and my uncle's name is on that stone tablet right there," said the boy, pointing.

"Where did he serve?"

"Iraq."

"**Rebellion to Tyrants is Obedience to God.**[1] I'm sure he was a fine soldier," Ben acknowledged, and then Sarah grabbed his hand and towed him to the northwest corner.

Their truck was north; she pointed up 1st Avenue to the west: "A black SUV."

"That could be anyone Sarah."

"Come on," she took his arm and pulled him along.

As they window shopped their way up the north side of the avenue, Ben was arguing: "Doesn't look big enough… the plate's not right," as they came alongside, "look at the junk on the dash- kid's toys -it ain't right."

At the same moment they both spotted another suspect vehicle coming east down the avenue, only this one did look right. The suspect parked just up the street on the south side and two men exited the SUV. The driver pulled off a jacket with BATFE across the back and left it in the vehicle. They started across the road angling straight toward the old couple.

"I can't believe I left my shotgun," Sarah scolded Ben in a whisper.

"Don't be so paranoid; keep your face to the shop window," advised Ben. "Look at 'em: they're probably just headed to dinner at Gino's."

The men's track hooked into the entrance of the café next door. Sarah turned and stared at the black SUV across the street.

"What are you thinkin' now, ole girl? Ethan said the hit squad was gone; you know these guys may have nothing to do with this morning," Ben advised.

"Doesn't matter. Maybe those boys don't know they're wearing the wrong team colors; but they're about to be educated."

"Momma, don't ya know these guys'll have a nose for trouble."

"Then we'll have to distract them, won't we, *Grampa*? They're just lucky you talked me out of coming down here in the Terex or they might be like ground sardines in a flattened SUV tin about now."

They hurried back down to the Square and turned left to their pickup. Ben U-turned the Ford and was parked in the Morris Hardware lot a few minutes later. Leaning a thin 4X8 sheet of plywood against the headache rack, Ben strung a length of monofilament fishing line from the plywood through a loop at the tailgate and back through the passenger door. In the meantime, Sarah pulled a long snatch strap from the toolbox and coiled it at her feet in the cab.

Ben circled west then turned down 1st Avenue toward the black SUV. As they neared their target, Sarah pulled the fishing line; the plywood stood up and the wind flipped it back onto the tailgate. Ben slowed to a stop with their front bumper just forward of the SUV's rear bumper. He eased himself out of the truck; his slow-motion demeanor was more indicative of an arthritic couch potato than healthy old Ben. With slow deliberation he got the sheet of plywood back in place and tied down.

Meanwhile, Sarah had dropped the coiled snatch strap on the walk. There was a thick 2X6 foot slotted cast iron grating in front of a sewer slot in the curb. The grating acted as both manhole cover and gutter drainage. She secured one end of the strap to the grating and looped the other to the tow hook in the SUV's bumper. Running some slack forward along the frame, she tucked it against the inside of the tire and along a crack in the gutter back to the sewer where she stowed the rest of the slack. The filthy grease and dirt toned snatch strap was perfect camo with the pavement.

Sarah was already seated in the truck when Ben climbed in and puttered off down the steep avenue. They passed along the north side of the Square, waving to the boy at the memorial monument. Ben turned left, circled back past their former spot on Main Street and parked two car lengths from the corner. Main was a two-way stop at 1ˢᵗ Avenue.

Francis opened the door for Gunther and followed him into the little café. The two BATFE agents managed to plan their routine such that they rarely missed the Thursday special at Gino's Café. Besides, Francis kind of had a thing for the waitress, Jenny, who gave a little wave as the men slid into their usual booth. Francis always sat with his back to the wall and a view out front, as well as the grill and cash register. Gunther was happy with a view of the TV monitor.

There were only half a dozen tables taken, but when the agents sat down: four parties stood up and left. Jenny brought two cups of coffee and looked at Francis with a frown.

"I'm sorry guys, yall're not gonna be too popular round these parts this evenin'," Jenny drawled apologetically. "And I know yall don't even work round here, an' ya just stopped in for the special- ya do want the special? I didn't bring ya menus -but some of yall's partners done real bad this mornin'… and well… Gunther, I reckon ya best roll up that jacket o' yourn 'fore ya head back outside."

"We never see any action Jenny," Gunther assured her. "We get to travel a lot, makin' our rounds; but we're not much more than alcohol and tobacco inspectors. Are we Francis?"

While tapping two fingers against the little "SPECIAL" placard on the table, Francis huffed a bit: "We're more than that Jenny. It's just that we mostly only deal with good people."

"That man yall's friends *dealt* with this mornin' *was good people,*" she snapped, spun, and stomped off.

"Jenny, I didn't mean…" Francis' voice trailed off as he bit his lip.

Having consumed most of their meal in silence, Gunther suddenly perked up: "What the hell is this?"

A home movie with the YouTube logo in the corner had started up at commercial break. Jenny strolled over and topped up their coffees.

"Our local cable provider has played that clip several times this afternoon with no explanation and no apology," said Jenny, turning away. "I reckon it's about yall's friends out *dealin',*" she added, over her shoulder.

"Jenny, they're not our *friends*," Francis protested.

Looking over his shoulder, Francis watched the video through. The Henry pickup had stopped on the avenue, but Jenny didn't give it a thought as the old man adjusted his load. Engrossed in the video clip, both agents totally missed the performance out front.

Silently sipping his coffee, Francis' unfocused eyes were pointed at their SUV when he was roused by something splattering against the driver's window, then sliding down the door to the running board.

"C'mon," he headed for the cash register.

"What about dessert?" Gunther complained.

The little café was known for their homemade pies and Gunther never missed a dessert.

"No pie?" Jenny questioned.

"Not tonight," Francis dropped cash for both of them and headed for the door.

"Got the cherry today?" Gunther licked his lips.

"Yeah."

"Ohooo…" Gunther moaned, as he followed his partner out.

Ben and Sarah had been sitting on the corner bench straight down the sidewalk from Gino's Café. They weren't there long when the taller BATFE agent rushed out the door. The old couple jumped up and hurried to the pickup. Ben pulled up to the crosswalk and stopped; they looked up 1st Avenue. The shorter agent was shouting at a small group that was milling about the entrance to an alley just downhill of the black SUV. A tomato sailed from amongst the group of protesters. The taller agent slapped the tomato down and pulled the other toward the SUV; his partner seemed reluctant, but followed.

"Looks like your distraction has been taken care of," Ben pointed. Sarah smiled and lowered the 12-gauge to the floor.

"What the hell's the matter with you people?" Gunther was shouting as he reached into his jacket.

Francis blocked a tomato and grabbed his partner's sleeve: "No Gunther, let it go. Get in the truck."

They slammed their doors as more fruit splattered on the hood.

"Just burn like hell outa here Francis," Gunther instructed. "We've got the right of way onto the Square, so just launch down the hill and maybe you'll catch them off guard. They're going to unload on us when we pass that alley and if they start throwing eggs too: this truck's going to stink like hell. It's a bitch getting that slime out of the window jams."

Francis thought his partner was making good sense and he had already clicked the transaxle into 4-wheel drive. He did a little brake-torque off the line so Gunther wouldn't think he'd wimped about the launch suggestion. The SUV bit the road hard and shot down the avenue. Feeling like a kid again, Francis was taking everything the big V8 could deliver.

The snatch strap slack had fed out perfectly and the stretch factor had reached its limit when the grating was ripped from its concrete setting. Francis felt the drag and lurch as the grating leapt after them. Thinking it was a traction fluctuation; he kept the pedal to the floor as he checked the rearview mirror. His eyes froze on the cast iron projectile overtaking the SUV.

"DUCK!" Francis screamed as he slammed the brake, throwing his torso to the right and down.

Gunther leaned forward, not knowing what to expect. The iron grating obliterated the rear window, tumbled through the van section and stabbed a couple feet through the windshield; finally rocking back down against the steering wheel. The SUV slid through the intersection, skidding to a stop against the parking curb in front of the old cannon.

Staring across the intersection, Ben admitted: "I thought it would fly right over 'em and they'd run over it; you know, comin' down the hill like that."

"I thought it would just bash into their tailgate," Sarah countered.

They looked each other in the eye and echoed in unison: "Perfect."

Ben crossed the intersection and pulled up next to the SUV. Sarah looked in the window to see that the driver had in fact ducked against the bench seat. The passenger was sitting upright.

She hollered over: "You boys having trouble with your car? Can we give you a lift somewhere?"

Gunther hollered back: "No ma'am – we're just fine… but thanks for asking."

The old couple puttered away as Francis was still fighting to reach his seat belt release. When he freed himself, he rolled onto his back and looked up at Gunther.

"We're just fine?"

His partner was glancing all around: "I wonder if we could get a job with the FBI?"

Francis started with a muffled chuckle that Gunther followed with shallow laughter, and that developed into an infectious deep rolling laughter that both continued for half a minute. His eyes were still watering as Francis pushed his door open with a foot and wiggled his way out under the grating. Standing up, he looked back at his partner.

"I'm going back for a piece of pie," he giggled.

Gunther jumped out and followed his partner across the intersection. As they started back up 1st Avenue, he said: "You know who that was?"

"Huh?"

"That was Patrick Henry's widow. I met her at a fundraiser awhile back. She had just donated a new fire truck to the district. She's just about the sweetest old girl you could possibly imagine."

A little later, Jenny informed them that the man in the YouTube video was Sarah's son, Grover.

As Ben puttered down 1st Avenue north of the Square, the boy from the memorial was standing on the curb; Sarah waved and declared: "Best seat in the house."

When they'd reached the foothills with the sun setting behind them, Ben asked: "Are ya happy now?"

"No."

Ben mentally kicked himself for his insensitivity.

5. Leatherwood

Back at the house, Sarah turned in and Ben returned to the den where Cleve and Gerry were still at it.

"I wonder if the Pinks have got the numbers to attempt a coup?" Ben mused. "They've been pushing socialist bills for years."

"Are you kidding? This *is* a coup; but it's the dictator that's pulling it off," insisted Gerry. "He turned traitor when he broke his oath to **preserve, protect and defend the Constitution⁵** by supporting that international arms treaty. Even the *Pinks* in the Senate don't want to see it ratified because it is a clear breach of the Constitution. So, the dictator's cronies just drag their feet and do their best to tie up our more patriotic Senators, while their master does an end run with these Executive Actions."

"Yeah, and the socialist media plays down the assassination of patriotic citizens as a few radical crazies getting their just deserts," added Cleve. "The Pinks have really got a handle on the First Amendment; media lies and half-truths go a long way toward what they like to call *opinion focusing*."

"**Half a truth is often a great lie**,"¹ Ben quipped.

"More divide and conquer," continued Cleve. "But, if the Senate blatantly overrides too much of the Constitution, with ratification of unconstitutional bills and treaties: they wouldn't be able to cover the fact that the Constitution has been effectively abolished. People would wake up *before* we've lost our Republic; and then there'd be hell to pay."

"Your ass. There is hell to pay: right now. True, there are some saps out there who wouldn't recognize the socialist agenda even if the Administration announced: O*h, by the way, the* **Declaration of Independence**,ᴵᴵᴵ *the* **Constitution**ᴵⱽ *and* **Bill of Rights**ⱽ *are all history*. But that will never happen. The media will just start subtly referring to the United States as a *progressive nation in a new world order of economic unity*; and those same saps will say: *Dude, party time... burn another doob*. Seriously though, you don't give people enough credit. I don't know anybody who voted for that Pink SOB in the White House."

"Birds of a feather; you probably have a natural aversion to pea-brains *and* subversives," countered Cleve, "and you are correct: I do not give credit or respect to any milquetoast who knew the Republic dourly needed honest leadership, but contributed a consolatory vote anyway."

"True; when our last black president was assassinated they fabricated the *ethnic martyr* scenario by playing the race card. We still have no idea who was responsible for taking out Air Force One; it was probably a Taliban terrorist cell, but the media Pinks couldn't resist pushing the white supremacist theory. They knew if they stirred up enough racial tension they'd get a consolation vote for someone who could follow in their new martyr's footsteps."

"More like use his carcass as a springboard. That was the same ploy they used every time there was a school shooting: offer a wrong choice with an emotional feel-good kickback. They knew they could offer up the pinkest socialist available and as long as he was black: he was headed to the White House."

"Then why didn't the Republicans run a good honest man against him? Maybe... Clarence Thomas."

"I knew you were gonna say that," returned Cleve. "I have to liken ole Clarence to Grover Cleveland: whom Dad always said had good common sense, and a lot more of it than most people."

"They just couldn't get Clarence *in the water*."

"I liked Dr. Ben Carson. I would have voted for him again in a heartbeat."

"They got him in the water and look at what happened."

"Too bad we couldn't get our buddy George Washington into politics: coulda run him. It's just that he loves life too much to put his family through all that media abuse."

"I think Martha would fit right in as First Lady."

"Sure... But now: we have a dictator."

"If you remember back when Obama was Prez, I told you we could do a lot worse. True, his economic programs were ultimately a death spiral to hell, but I'd like to believe he meant well. He was intelligent enough to know that to abrogate the Constitution would be a slap in the face that would wake up too many patriots. Obama knew that only a fool would incite civil war by infringing God given rights expressly acknowledged by The Declaration of Independence and confirmed in our Bill of Rights. Now, years down the road, we've got a Pink doing exactly that; out of stupidity? Nay: I say it is a demented desire to provoke civil strife and economic collapse. With the Republic incapacitated in chaos, he hopes to institute stability by subjugating our nation under a new world order of socialism and communism."

"That theory explains why Grove was hit, no questions asked," said Cleve. "The sooner they stir up the patriots; the sooner our ersatz dictator can try to overthrow the Republic with his little revolution. They must be setting up hit squads all over the country."

"If you boys are done saving the world; it's after my bedtime," Ben yawned.

The powwow session had gone on all afternoon: plans and speculation. Gerry tipped the bottle to Cleve.

"Might as well. You know I wanted to hit my house tonight, but you done tanked me."

"Nobody's been twisting your arm," Gerry demurred.

"Well, I'd appreciate you being my pit crew tomorrow, or support driver anyway. I'm going to pick up a few things and I don't want to walk in my front door. And Ben: you should stay here tonight."

"Yeah, I meant to say that earlier," echoed Gerry. "But come on out to the garage before you turn in."

"Oh, I got my second wind already, not having another drive in front of me," Ben replied.

"So how did it go down there?" asked Cleve.

"Oh, Momma reprimanded a couple of ATF boys for wearing the wrong colors," Ben related, "and Sheriff Jefferson confirmed the task force that hit Grover was ATF led UN troops. Judge Adams wants a militia to help Thomas bag the task force if they come stomping on the rights of any more local patriots. And Ethan Allen: That guy's a time bomb waiting to explode."

Cleve smiled: "And hence the war is begun."

As they followed Gerry out the side door, directly into the garage, he was explaining to Ben that Leatherwood had become a menagerie of energy storage. They had been supplying surplus electricity to the local grid for years.

Ben walked straight over to a row of team green dirt bikes and asked: "So, what is this? These aren't Kawasakis."

Gerry chuckled: "We got tired of waiting for electric. So, we just hacked the engines and: modifa-caish-e-own. They're a little heavy because of the batteries, but the silent running is so cool. We've got kilowatts to burn here and the LFP batteries charge up pretty quick."

"LFP?" Ben questioned.

"Lithium ferrophosphate: battery tech is going all different directions, but we've got our money on LFP for now," Cleve explained.

"You've got one of these bikes too?"

"Who do you think designed the mods for these babies?" Cleve went on: "The Kaw gear boxes are not right for the torque band of these motors, but you can't have everything. Gerry likes a granny low for puttering around on logs and such; whereas I use sprockets that get me a lot more mileage on a charge, with a high gear that could have whooped the Lincoln in the quarter. Then again, Gerry's bike topping out like that is not a bad idea, 'cause a hundred plus MPH on a dirt bike can get a little squirrely."

Gerry cut in: "We've got charging stations all over the place at Leatherwood, so I'm not worried about mileage for around here. But I've got a couple high-gear flat tracker designs for off campus operations... You figured out where all this electric power comes from Ben?"

"Hydro: I realized something wasn't right 'cause the flow volume to the canal was 'bout what used to come down the north canyon. Duh, hello... where is the canyon?" Ben rapped his palm against the side of his head. "You're an industrious clan of beavers, in a technological sorta way. How'd you blend the dam into the bluff?"

"Stained the cement and crushed local granite for the sand and gravel. A little artistic license with the concrete forms and we finished up sand blasting the surface to bring out the feldspars. It looks better every year with the weathering and lichen growth," Gerry explained proudly.

"Oh, it could keep a person guessing if they hadn't known about the canyon."

Gerry and Cleve were tag teaming as they continued pointing to the north and west from the back of the garage: explaining the interior workings of the Quonset huts and various smaller outbuildings.

"So, all the power is generated at the base of the bluff," muttered Ben, absentmindedly.

"No, there are turbines at the base of the south gorge as well; the canal is a secondary reservoir. It's actually cut a lot deeper than you would imagine. We quarried most of the masonry granite around here in the excavation of the channel."

"And you sell most of the power…"

"We sell the surplus," Gerry interrupted. "We use as much as possible. Another energy reserve at Leatherwood is hydrogen; and you can suck quite a few kilowatt-hours down the tube in the decomposition of water. The Quonset hut that straddles the stream produces hydrogen and oxygen twenty-four/seven from a complex of electrolysis cells. We call that one the Hydrogen Hut. It's the heaviest of the Q-huts, with the exception of the 24-gauge west end wall. If the unthinkable happens: everything would blow out over the lake."

"I thought it was cheaper to crack hydrogen from petroleum."

"From an oil refinery's standpoint: yes; but we haven't got significant oil production, nor a refinery. Different economics: we would pay market for crude, but we can't sell surplus electricity at market. Also, our pure hydrogen is perfect for fuel cells; whereas petroleum sourced hydrogen is contaminated with carbon monoxide to some degree. So, there is a specialty market for our surplus hydrogen. We pipe the surplus out as compressed gas; and utilize it thus for fuel cell power in most of our *big toys*."

"Like the Terex?" Ben speculated.

"The SARAH," Cleve cut in, "we call her the SARAH. Momma's the only one calls her the Terex: 'cause we cannibalized so many TR-one-hundreds in the creation."

"She's got a certain respect for that one: wanted to take it out wildin'," Ben admitted.

"The real power storage at Leatherwood is liquid hydrogen; massive tanks deep in the bluff," Gerry finished.

"Now, now; total kilowatt-hours of energy storage: yes. But for instant EM pulse discharges: the capacitance silos are the *real power*," argued Cleve.

"If it was anyone but the Henry bros talkin': I'd think you boys were LSD loadies. I'm turnin' in," Ben added, heading for the door.

"He hasn't heard anything about the subterranean layout yet," Cleve whispered.

Gerry laughed: "He'll find out soon enough, if he winds up coming back to hole up at Leatherwood."

6. Cleve's Place

"**S**hould have brought that whole pot of coffee along," complained Cleve, his head still pounding as they clunked along through the backcountry.

"You'd already emptied the pot before we headed out," Gerry corrected. "The ride wouldn't be so rough if you weren't dragging ass through every pothole. You usually float the washboard and fly over everything else."

"You wanna drive?"

"Yes- you said I was your driver."

They had left the house early: too early for Cleve, who didn't like to "hurry up and wait". Before leaving they had loaded the Lincoln: turning Gerry's bike on its side to slide it in, they then inverted Cleve's bike and stacked it like a 2nd layer sardine; another advantage to dry cell power. Gerry took one of the flat trackers so his brother wouldn't have the edge in range or speed.

Cleve had been grumbling since he got up and didn't stop when Gerry took the wheel: "There's no big hurry; I'm not ridin' until I can see the trail without a headlight."

"That's fine," replied Gerry, "I've got the perfect spot to tuck this Lincoln away while I'm waiting for you, but it will take a little maneuvering. And, I want to get the scope set up so I can watch your twenty."

When the bluffs and ridges were giving way to rolling hills, Gerry slowed and slipped off the highway between guardrails. He shut off the lights as Cleve flipped a brake light toggle and handed him the night vision optics. They wove through a copse of scrub pine on a trail that was not so much a 2-track as a braided wildlife trail. The slope steepened at a ponderosa grove around an outcrop face where Gerry started jockeying the Lincoln back and forth in an attempt to make a one-eighty.

"You roll this puppy down the hill and I'm gonna have to whoop *your* ass," Cleve warned.

"Well, get out and spot me, muscle-head." Gerry retorted.

Cleve hopped out; they soon had the big SUV turned and tucked in alongside the low face amongst the pine. They got Cleve's bike out and set up a tripod for the scope. He couldn't see his ranch down on the rolling plains, but knew it would be visible at first light.

Cleve pulled out a couple lawn chairs, sat down and leaned back against the side of the Lincoln. Gerry pulled out a thermos and retrieved their mugs, topping them up with coffee.

"I lied... I made a pot before you got up." said Gerry, passing him a sack of Ann's homemade donuts as well.

"Ain't that sweet. Guess I won't have to whoop your ass after all, little brother."

"Just eat your donuts so I don't have to listen to your grumbling. How long are you going to wait?"

"Just until I can get a little peek at the house," replied Cleve. "The moon's already set and I'm not riding down that slope with night optics on my head. I don't expect anyone else has a scope on the place, so I should be able to slip in the back way at first light."

"How about another swig of whiskey before you go?" asked Gerry, with a laugh.

"Yeah-heh, right; I think I'm done drinking until after the war. I didn't want to get up this morning and this thing my head is doing could almost be called a hangover."

"We should stay on top of our game from here on out, but I'm not going to rule out the occasional shot: Grover may not be the last patriot we toast before it's over," sighed Gerry, banging his mug up against Cleve's.

The first glow of daybreak was half an hour off. A chill morning breeze carrying the fresh scent of pine needles wafted through the grove. Backs against the side panel, sipping coffee in silence, the brothers gazed out over a landscape faintly lit by stars twinkling through wispy clouds. Reminiscences of a gentler, simpler time... The bond between them was strong, maybe stronger in the knowledge that they would never again share such a moment with their big brother.

The shroud of darkness had just begun to lift when Cleve wolfed another donut, set his mug down, and walked over to the scope.

"What do you think Benjy meant about Momma *reprimanding a couple BATF boys*?" Cleve mused.

"That went in one ear and out the other at the time," Gerry chuckled, "guess we should ask them this evening."

"It's going to take me fifteen or twenty minutes to get there, so I'm moving out now. I'm going to try to find their trip wire first, and trip it last," Cleve explained, "from their response time we can determine if they're coming from the big city or if they've got a staging outpost."

"What makes you so sure they would target you so soon: you hadn't autographed the DoP when Grove spammed it out."

"Hellow-oh... You've seen Grove's place: he's got all those hunting pics on the wall," reminded Cleve. "They probably figure they can make their confiscation quota for next week with the assortment of rifles they saw in my hands alone. Fortunately, everything but a .30-06 is already out at Leatherwood."

Cleve didn't keep much of value at the house because he travelled so much. As a geologist, he mostly took out of state and international contracts. With the Pinks coalescing into a self-righteous political class; their socialist agenda bent on despotism for the Republic, including government control of education and finance, along with the destruction of free-market capitalism: Cleve didn't want to come home and find his most prized possessions confiscated when they abrogate the 4th Amendment. Gerry fully agreed with him moving most of his valuables back to Leatherwood over the last few years.

Cleve was away with a quiet whoosh of earth and pine needles that landed on Gerry's boots. Down the slope, his cursing and grumbling was audible over the sliding of rocks and tires as Cleve worked to slow the bike to a manageable speed in the dim light. Gerry checked the time when Cleve reached bottom and silently rode off down the ravine.

Leaving the scope aimed at the house, Gerry moved to a better view of the foothills. There was a long knoll that Cleve would have to cross before a final dip to the tree and bush dotted prairie. He spotted a faint line of dust and put the binoculars to his eyes. The bike was just visible through the haze. Gerry checked the time, thinking Cleve's ETA would be pretty close. He walked back to the scope and checked out the house: the gate was closed and the drive was clear.

A short time later, Gerry was scanning the ranch with the binoculars when he noticed Cleve leaning his bike up against a tree at the back fence. Moving up to the house, he seemed to be digging at the foundation, then suddenly disappeared into a hole. Cleve had utilized a coal chute in the old foundation to slip into the basement.

He was inside for some time and finally walked straight out the back door. Gerry was watching through the scope now as Cleve carried two duffels to the bike and strapped them down. Leaving a backpack on the seat, he returned to the house and disappeared in the tall shrubbery. He eventually emerged beyond the trees in the front yard, striding to the entrance gate. He carefully inspected the hinges and found the device he had expected to find in the house.

Gerry watched him jog back to his bike. Cleve opened and closed the gate with his remote. He pulled the pack onto his back as the gate cycled, then headed out.

G erry checked with the binoculars to find Cleve crossing the knoll right on time.

As Cleve proceeded over hill and dale he kept reaching behind to check the duffels that loosened with every bump. He worked his way up the ravine, thinking about the slope where he had come down from the SUV. He would probably loop the bike on that slope, so he continued along the outcrop surface and exited the ravine on a gentler grade to intersect the trail above the SUV.

Cleve shoved his bike between the boughs of a pine and headed off toward the rocky overhang. He crept up to the edge, peeked at the roof of the Lincoln and visualized Gerry leaned up against the opposite panel. He lowered himself from roots to rock and rock to rock, always careful to pick clean outcrop. Silently lowering himself to the earth beside the vehicle, Cleve knelt to peer beneath.

A pebble whacked him on the back.

"Bang," said Gerry from atop the overhang.

With several quick moves Gerry dropped to the ground beside Cleve and leveled a banana at his head.

"Now go get that gear and let's get packed, Master Splinter," Gerry chided.

They got the SUV loaded up and scanned the prairie.

"OK, they're not here yet," noted Cleve, "so they'll be one and a half to two hours from the city, depending on speed and whether or not they stopped for Egg MacMuffins."

Cleve had a sip of coffee.

"So you heard me in the ravine or coming down through the woods on foot?"

"Neither."

Cleve looked at him curiously.

"Actually, I was impressed," admitted Gerry. "But I knew you were up to something when you came off the prairie right on time, then missed the boat in the ravine."

Cleve pointed to a line of gravel dust extending toward his ranch, then checked through the binoculars.

"It's them."

Gerry watched through the scope as five black SUVs turned towards them one by one, crossing the cattle guard at Cleve's pump jack mailbox. The 2-track drive ran east between barbwire fences for a quarter mile to the gate before the house. At the gate, the fences turned north and south for a hundred feet, then back east to ultimately surround the house. The north fence was truncated at a timber barn in the northeast corner of the enclosed yard.

Halfway up the drive the first and second SUVs cut north and south to rip through the barbwire, pulling up or snapping off several fence posts in the process. The third and fourth SUVs followed suit, but tore back through the hundred-foot sections to the front yard, whereas the first two circled and ripped back through the north and south fences to reach the back yard.

"That's high tensile wire, but lucky for them I was too stingy to put up real fence," Cleve chuckled. "If that was Stay-Tuff 1561-3, like it oughta be: those boys would be wrapped up right now."

"Doesn't look like they plan on serving you any warrants either."

Their comments came as they watched the fifth SUV slam the gate open and skid to a broadside stop in front of the house. A man in black with four sage and brown camoed soldiers poured from each unit; the soldiers spread into formation around the house and dropped to one knee.

Cleve snickered: *"Boys, boys, boys... Ya nehva shoulda been doin' this."*

He roused Gerry and pointed north of the scope's field of view. The slight rise in the landscape beyond the barn gave way to a long gentle grade down to a broad meandering river. A dark mass was flowing from the groves and thickets south of the river.

With a "cat that ate the canary" look on his face, Cleve shrugged: "They musta woke up the herd."

Gerry lowered his eyebrows and frowned. Looking back in the scope, the soldiers were still in position, but the men in black were all looking north and pointing.

B enny was sure he had another rat trapped in his hole. The gate had only opened once this morning, so he figured his rat should still be inside. In his mind these gun rights wackos were just common criminals. He'd heard all the hype from his elders about the United States being a republic. But he wasn't interested in ancient texts; the public school system had taught him since childhood that the United States is a democracy. The President had been elected in a democratic election, so the Commander in Chief can run the country as he damn well pleases. The fact that he and his sub-commanders had been guaranteed promotions and big bonuses to carry out these Executive Orders was only proof that they were doing good; and he'd heard somewhere that *there ain't no end ta doin' good*.

Benny's mind was racing through a review of the operation. After yesterday's recognizance, he'd made a tentative plan for the raid, but hoped it would not be for another few days. Still, everything had gone so smoothly; the UN fireteams were in perfect formation. But now his net had begun to unravel: two of his commanders had shouted "*STAMPEDE*" and they all recommended a retreat to the road. Benny didn't want his rat sneaking off while they were groveling behind a cattle guard. But then the rumble was building to an intensity that hinted of a crescendo where an earthquake would lift the hillside and throw it on top of his little task force.

"Everybody back in the trucks… Back in the trucks," Benny found himself repeating and signaling to be sure he was understood. He got right onto the radio and said: "Hold your ground, they can go around us."

The agents all turned their radios up to hear over the rumble and one started to protest: "But Chief…" he trailed off as the crest of the hill went black in a wooly wall of thundering hooves and thrashing horns on two-thousand-pound engines of churning organic locomotion.

"Chief, it's not cattle: they're bison…"

The northwest SUV was hit broadside and nearly thrown in the air, it tumbled over twice before spinning around a tree and wedging against another. The SUV to the northeast suffered a similar fate as it was rolled over and over until it slammed into the southeast unit; wherefore the bison being forced past the two units oddly rotated and commenced hammering the vehicles from the south.

The deluge of animals broadsided the southwest SUV and rolled it fifty yards through half a dozen rotations; wherefore the bison that had passed on the west strangely circled back north to pound this unit from all sides as well. It was as if the metallic newcomers were the focus of the herd's rage.

Benny's command unit was the only SUV aligned with the initial tide of the stampede. The first few glancing blows only moved them forward slightly, but dragged the rear end toward the house. The bison started hitting the passenger side, but this unit did not roll, as there were already animals on the driver side. Every impact viciously ratcheted the SUV another few feet closer to the house, sliding Benny's unit in downstream of the trees constraining the wedged SUV. The impacts subsided as the bison flow was forced around the passenger side, pushing the lead animals on south.

When he'd seen the herd bearing down on the first SUV, Benny knew he had made the wrong call. The unit was scrap before it hit the trees. He started to reach for his seatbelt; then grabbed the wheel instead. At the first jolt he closed his eyes as gravel-like window debris scattered through the vehicle. He clenched the wheel tighter. Like a turtle he tried to draw his head into his shoulders, in resistance to the side action whiplash that was wrenching his neck with each and every impact. Just as he was about to try holding his head with his hands to keep it from snapping off: the jackhammer impacts subsided.

Benny snatched up the radio mic, screaming: "SHOOT THEM! SHOOT THEM! KILL THEM ALL…"

He turned to check the status of his fireteam. There were four seats in the van section, offset with space between for each soldier's equipment. The passenger side panel was crushed up against both seats: one soldier appeared groggy and the other unconscious in his seatbelt. Benny heard distant gunfire from the southeast, but now realized that the unit to his north quite possibly contained five unconscious men.

The soldiers on the driver's side had turned in their seats with their backs against the side panel and were positioning their boots on the crushed panel with their assault rifles aimed out between their legs. Both men emptied a magazine indiscriminately into the wall of fur pushing past the window. They cycled mags and emptied another.

In the southeastern SUV the five men were prepared to weather the stampede. The team was feeling less shellshock from bison impacts than the rest of the task force: not having been hit directly by the first wave. They were concerned for the condition of the team in the unit that had been rolled up against them, but hoped it would shield them somewhat as the bison continued south. To their bewilderment, as the first wave passed: they watched the lead animals turn and charge back at them. The return assault had less momentum and the other unit backed them up against the impacts. Still, the side panel was soon hammered past the frame rail; crowding the soldiers in a rapidly shrinking van. Also, the traffic jam initiated by bison turning back north was transforming the stampede into a stockyard of angry engines of destruction: and the animals seemed to have a relentless desire to obliterate the SUVs.

When Benny's voice came over the radio: "*SHOOT THEM*" was exactly what the UN fireteam was thinking. They cut loose as if Benny had a finger on their triggers.

Their acting commander yelled: "NO! NO! BAD IDEA!"

One of the soldiers had shoved his rifle through the north window to shoot bison through the other van. The concussion from the ensuing explosion blew him backwards against a massive skull that slammed him back into the van, where he no longer felt a thing as their own leaking fuel tank exploded as well.

In the command unit, Benny understood the implications of the double explosion and was considering the consequences of a bullet ricochet or flash ignition if their own fuel tank integrity were compromised.

The southward flow of bison had devolved into a struggle to get at the SUV and a number of dead animals lay alongside the vehicle, diminishing the momentum of the charge. Several bulls were plowing tenaciously into the crushed panel, pumping their heads as they commenced with a slow roll of the SUV.

Benny was already scrambling through the passenger door window as he watched the groggy soldier jerk upright, then fall back, spraying bullets into the west panel. As the window reached twelve o'clock: Benny twisted and sprang from the door. He jumped over two bison in the direction of the SUV's roll, grabbing a hold in the mane of the second as he slid over its shoulders.

He hadn't known if disorientation from the roll would elicit a spray of stray bullets, or if the gasoline would be ignited after the bulls ruptured the tank: he just knew he didn't want to burn. Like clockwork, he felt the concussion of the blast he had predicted, although he had hoped he would be wrong. He felt the wave of heat pass overhead as he dug all ten fingers into the matted wool of his bison's thick mane. The beast hardly noticed its clinging passenger as it leapt forward. The man hung on, bouncing along for several long strides, but the bison bucked him loose as it passed the stone and mortar steps to the front porch.

Benny crawled under the stone overhang and pushed his back into the corner, then checked the right foot he'd been dragging along. The boot maintained the form of a foot, but he knew the bison had shattered his ankle under hoof during his Wild West rodeo show. He tried wiggling his fingers and figured three on the right were either jammed or broken.

Several burning bison galloped past, bucking and kicking. Fire was one thing the mob gave way to. Benny figured they were dousing themselves in the little pond south of the yard.

The herd had lost interest in the little man-thing under the porch, which somehow aggravated Benny. Out of spite, he emptied his forty-five into the mob. ("That was dumb: now I'm out of ammo. But at least they can't get at me here.)

("How could such a simple operation have gone so wrong?") Benny pondered. ("These buffalo shouldn't have been so... mean. But then, I've never seen a real stampede before. Damned outlaws: and this one might still be inside. Waiting to finish us all off, the stinking little rat. Probably trained these buffalo to attack, and now he's sneaking around in there.")

Benny noticed the crackle of wood burning, over the squeaking of the metal expansion in the gasoline fire, and realized the house was on fire.

("At least the wind is out of the southwest or I'd have to move right now.")

There was a strong low pitched: whoooooump, accompanied by a flash and flutter of burning branches and leaves floating to the ground, then a weak pop-poom. Benny assumed the fire had reached the other SUV; the gasoline had already drained out and then ignited without a major explosion.

The throng of bison had been thinning out since the explosions and fires had commenced. The southwest SUV was visible from the porch now. It was the only one that wasn't burning. Eventually the bison were all pushing their way north.

Benny was piecing together what had happened in the last SUV. From their angle they'd have seen flames from the other four units; at least any of them who were still conscious. As the view cleared, Benny noted a downed bison with a long jagged gash visible along a bloody matted line in its mane. A heavy knife hilt still protruded from the animal's neck. One or more of the men had sold their lives dearly, but to no avail: they'd killed the beast by hand to avoid sparking the fuel, only to be mauled by the mob.

The human bodies were in and around the vehicle. The roof of the SUV was peeled back and laid over the hood like a sardine tin. The bison had torn through the tailgate, bucked the roof free and stomped their way out over the dash, trampling everything along the way.

As far as Benny could tell, the only bison still around were those that were dead or dying. ("I've got to get to that last unit to get some ammo or a rifle, if they haven't all been trampled. If that filthy outlaw didn't already sneak away: I've got to be ready for him. The fire will smoke him out eventually. I'm just going to have to hope he's not watching out the front window.")

Benny couldn't walk, but found he could crawl fairly well. Holding his ruined foot in the air was rough on his right knee; even so, he managed to scramble the distance on all fours.

"You gonna just leave that wreck out on the Square?" the waitress asked contentiously.

"I kinda like it there, Heidi Jo. Thought I might lower the cannon sights and let the kids fire a couple cannonballs at it," retorted Sheriff Jefferson, with mock belligerence.

The sheriff was seated at the window in Gino's Café and had just finished his bacon and eggs. He had stopped by early at the office and everything seemed quiet in town. All he wanted now was a coffee refill, but Heidi wasn't done teasing. He was trying to keep his eyes on his cup as his mind wandered: ("-just the cutest thing in town... and she's got those hips that won't quit... won't quit knockin' me out anyway...") Heidi had a figure that could run a man into a lamppost doing a double take.

She stood with the coffee pot in her right hand, but shifted her weight left and rested the other hand on her hip: "I thought you were supposed to investigate rebellious stunts like that."

"I'm going to leave that one for the BATFE to clean up. That SUV is a message to DC. *I hold it that a little rebellion now and then is a good thing, and as necessary in the political world as storms in the physical... -It is a medecine necessary for the sound health of government.*"[6]

Heidi laughed and topped up his coffee: "That's what I like about you, Tommy: you've always got an answer with a message."

The sheriff's phone rang and he scooped it off the table. His expression went instantly serious, although his eyes remained on Heidi as she turned slowly and sashayed across the room. He followed her to the cash register.

"Not going to finish your coffee?" Heidi frowned.

He noted the disappointment in her voice and responded: "No. It sounds like trouble up north."

"Trouble?"

"The office got a call about earth tremors, so I'm thinking someone stirred up the herd on the Henry ranch."

"You better hope Cleveland is not out of the country if them buffalos ran over the fence again," Heidi laughed.

He gave her a wink as he pulled the door wide and let it glide closed.

Sheriff Jefferson was still thinking about Heidi when he spotted the trails of black and gray smoke blowing northeast. Actually, he was thinking about whether or not at his age he *should* be thinking about such a sweet young thing: ("but then, she could do a lot worse with a pea-brained pretty boy.") He came over a rise to see that the smoke was definitely coming from Cleve's place. When he reached the highway, he doglegged left then right onto the dead-end gravel road.

The sheriff keyed his mic then released it. He could distinguish at least two automotive fires and the house engulfed in flames. His first thought was to call it in: ("but then hosing down the house would turn the whole scene to slop; we'd be investigating with a soup spoon. The house will soon be too far gone to save anything and the fire hasn't got anywhere to go, here on the prairie… this time of year.")

He keyed the mic again: "Betty, you copy?"

"Go ahead Sheriff."

"Call the firehouse and let them know I'm watching a fire on the Henry ranch that's going to burn itself out. If they get any calls about it: tell them to finish their breakfast and I'll let them know when I need them. Better send the EMS now though. Thanks. Oh, and call Ethan: tell him he'll probably need to round up a crew for his little CSI routine, but have him come on out by himself right now."

"Copy that, Boss."

He keyed his mic twice and shut the radio off. Betty knew Sheriff Jefferson had gone into investigative mode; she was not to bother him until he came back on the radio. He would answer his cell phone if she had reason to call, but it better be good.

He turned down the drive scanning the scene intently. There was a demolished shell of an SUV to his right with three trampled bodies visible nearby: two in camo around back and one in black up front. Four other steel shells were pouring carbon black smoke from viscously swirling furnaces of gasoline and vinyl/plastic/rubber fueled fire. He slipped his cell phone headset on and thumbed a speed dial. Two downed bison were thrashing about and would have to be euthanized before he could feel safe studying the scene on foot. He parked between the wounded animals, grabbing his Browning BPS 10-gauge as he slid from the truck.

"Betty, revise that message to the firehouse: tell them to pack up the donuts and come on out with the dry chem truck. I've got four automotive fires and it doesn't look like anyone got out. Oh, and I guess they'll need the water trucks for the house. We've got bodies in there, so we'll have to kill the whole damn thing or the vehicles could reignite. I didn't expect them to be up against the house like that, or that the men wouldn't have bailed out. Well, I've got a couple wounded bison to put down and more to check: don't want one to jump up on our firemen. Maybe I can piece the story together before they make a hog wallow of the place."

The sheriff had worked his way up behind one of the wounded and put a 10-gauge slug in the back of its head as quick as he'd clicked the phone off. He heard the other jump to its feet behind him, but it was already slumping back down as he turned. As he put the second one down, he heard a snort and moved along to finish another one off as well.

A voice from behind said: "Drop it Jefferson."

The sheriff kept his shotgun pointed unthreateningly at the ground and turned very slowly to look straight into the back of the demolished SUV.

"I SAID DROP IT!" screamed Benny.

"Just take it easy. You're not going to shoot me or that vehicle's going up like the rest of them."

"Maybe and maybe not, you and that pool of gasoline are downwind. And if you don't drop that shotgun: we're going to find out."

Sheriff Jefferson bent down and carefully deposited the weapon on the ground at his side. He noted his adversary was perched in a peculiar fashion on the broken console. The seat backs were stomped down to the seat level on either side. The differential was broken from the shackles and shoved up under the back seats. The rear deck hung in the air, the bumper three feet off the ground with a pool of gasoline growing beneath.

"What's the matter with you, Special Agent Arnold? The fire fighters will be here and we should do a safety assessment. We may have more wounded animals to put down."

"What about *my men*? You didn't do a safety assessment for them. You knew about these trained buffalos and never said a thing."

"What are you talking about? You can't train bison. Anyway, this time you charged out here without notifying me of intent."

"I had an EO document, so I don't have to notify you of anything. And: I *saw* a trained bison in an old National Geographic."

"That animal was one in a million. Bison are low-stress animals; you thought you could start shooting without pissing them off?"

"There was someone here early this morning and we had to move," snarled Benny.

"I told you Mr. Henry is out of state most of the time."

Sheriff Jefferson knew Cleve was around, as he'd had lunch with him a few days before; they were not best buddies, but had been on hunting trips together and shared a mutual respect. His opinion of

Benny was far from respect since the moment they met and had been going downhill ever since. While looking down a gun barrel, he would be happy to volunteer as much baloney about Cleve as Benny could stomach.

"Someone was here," insisted Benny.

"Maybe he was asphyxiated when you burned his house down."

"We didn't start that fire, the buffalo did."

"Sure, I see: they brought matches with them, did they?"

"DAMN YOU! I'LL KILL YOU! I'll KILL you I tell you!"

Sheriff Jefferson was suddenly disgusted as he realized this whining punk was just trying to intimidate him while waiting for EMS to arrive. Noting the anemic skin tone and blood overflowing from the agent's boot: he also realized the punk was in worse condition than his frenzied exuberance indicated.

The sheriff was about to pick up his shotgun and walk away when he was chilled by Benny's crazed laughter. He still had a handgun trained on the sheriff but was pointing north. Following the indicator to its objective, Sheriff Jefferson found himself staring down an enormous bull. The animal had a broken left horn and an old scar that parted his mane from horn to shoulder. The big bull broke into a trot straight toward him.

Benny continued laughing hysterically, but Sheriff Jefferson had lost all interest in the crazed agent. He recognized the approaching beast as the alpha bull; Cleve had pointed him out on a tour of his "low-stress" grazing glades by the river. He considered whether he could side step at the last moment, but unlike a matador he had no cape to distract the animal and bison were known for turning on a dime.

He decided to go for the 10-gauge. The bull was already charging at full gallop, which left less than two seconds to impact. He would probably still be crushed even if he managed to put a slug through its brain. Seizing the shotgun, he pumped a shell into the chamber as he waggled it to the side, hoping the glimmer of the barrel would attract the bull's attention. He would attempt to step aside and then take his shot.

The sheriff was astonished when the huge bull pivoted in full charge, bounding to the back of the SUV.

As the massive beast landed on the deck, the entire unit rocked on the rear wheels like a seesaw, launching Benny into the air from the console. Firing wildly, he sparked the fuel with a frame ricochet through the deck, but not before he was skewered on a bison horn. The bull's charge carried them right over the vehicle as it was rocking back down in front.

Sheriff Jefferson was running for his truck before the bull had reached the SUV. He heard the shots as he leapt behind the cab. What came next was not so much an explosion as an open-air ignition. Diving into his truck he pulled clear, parking north of the entrance drive. He gaped out the windshield on a scene that smacked of blood and gore theater at a live action drive-in. The bison was trotting around the freshly lit SUV. Benny's pitiful carcass was still dangling from its good horn; hooked through the ribcage and bobbing about like a puppet. It appeared as if the old bull wanted to charge back in at the SUV, but the fire was holding him off as he circled.

Suddenly the bison stopped, turning to face a little copse of trees south of the house. He began shaking his head and backing slowly. The bull pumped his head up and down: with flailing arms his Benny puppet bounced in the air twice, then crumpled to the ground beside him. The old bull turned and trotted off to the north.

The Henry brothers had watched the entire episode from the hills. Gerry had kept his eye to the scope in silence, while Cleve had watched through binoculars, occasionally thumbing his cellphone. Whenever the beeping was audible over the whooshing of the wind, Gerry had noted the annoying keypad punching out the corner of his eye and had started putting two and two together.

"What the hell was that?" asked Gerry.

"What?"

"The stampede- and old half horn… That was your alpha checking the dead this side of the fires when Tommy arrived."

"Magnus… Yeah, he doesn't scare easily," replied Cleve, ambiguously.

"Is that what all that shaking his head was about, when the rest of the herd had already moved north? Think I didn't correlate your phone games? C'mon, what the hell?"

"Later," Cleve waved him off while making a call on another phone. "Sheriff, this is Cleve Henry."

"Speak of the Devil. Where are you at?"

"I'm- out of town. I hear that I had a stampede."

"You hear? Did you *hear* that your house is on fire? Did you *hear* that your bison killed a- *massacred* an entire federal task force?"

64 G.A.CREWS

"No, no I didn't. I guess news doesn't travel *that* fast."

"It doesn't, huh?" The sheriff went on: "Well, this Benedict Arnold, their chief, was raving about trained bison; and then that one horned monster-"

"-Magnus."

"-*Magnus*... Anyway, I figured my life was a toss of a coin and then that son-of-a-bitch made a right hand turn in mid-charge. Explain that."

"He's a wise old bull: maybe he saw your badge-"

"Cut the crap, Smartass! He went after that prick like he had a target painted on him."

"I don't know Tommy: maybe he smelled blood. Maybe it was the gasoline-"

"What do you know about the gasoline? How many fingers am I holding up?"

"Dammit Tommy. Trucks are like big metal animals to those bison and they smell like gasoline."

"Alright, alright... We'll talk about this later," the sheriff was waving fire trucks into the yard: "Here comes Ethan now. I'm going to let him clean up this mess and bag the bodies for the Feds. You're going to have to take care of these dead animals though."

"How many?"

"Must be a couple dozen at the house."

"I'll contract the processing plant to pick them up," said Cleve. "If they get right on it, that meat will fill a lot of hungry mouths."

"You'll have quite a few more wounded down at the river."

"I'll have to cull them out myself."

"You be careful. The Feds have got an Executive Order on you-"

"And that means?"

"I think they're carte blanche, fill in a name. If it reads like Grover's: it's not much more than a license to assassinate."

"Thanks Tommy."

"Don't thank me."

7. Mementos

Cleve was still making phone calls as Gerry turned onto the highway.

"-get Barry on the line?" he was saying, then pressing the phone against his leg, he looked up, "Stick to the backcountry and just get close enough so the batteries will go the distance."

"Yes Mother."

"-Barry, it's Cleve, hey, I'm hoping you can put things on ice and do me a favor which I will pay top dollar for."

"Put things on ice? This isn't some crazy scheme, is it?" Barry questioned.

"It's like this," Cleve continued, "I've got twenty or thirty dead bison, just went down an hour or so ago. You round up enough help to get them hung before the meat goes to hell and I'll pay for the trucks, helpers and all your time and processing costs. Distribute the meat to locals that need it or could use it, but don't insult or embarrass anyone who won't accept charity. Let them know they are doing me a personal favor by not letting so many of these majestic animals go to waste."

"I guess I can cut back to a skeleton crew and send some of the boys out right now. We'll run three shifts until we get caught up."

"Well, don't send them right out. I didn't mention it's a helluva mess out there. Contact Sheriff Jefferson and coordinate your operation with him. There are fires and... well, you don't want to tangle with the firemen. Some of the carcasses may be ruined by the fire and some may have too much lead in them: the bastards machine gunned the poor devils."

"Assassins?"

"Talk to the sheriff," Cleve replied. "There'll be maybe a dozen more wounded that will take some time to separate from the herd. I'll have them delivered to the plant as you finish up this first batch. I want you to make money on this job, Barry. I really appreciate you getting right on it and I don't want you taking a hit on my account."

"OK, I'll take it from here. And Cleveland: I was real sorry to hear about Grover."

They bounced along in silence with only the occasional clunk of a rock hitting the undercarriage to break the monotony. Eventually the trees tightened up around them and started slapping the sides of the Lincoln.

Cleve finally spoke up: "Where the hell are we?"

"Ha. I knew I could find a 2-track that's off your grid."

"We're in my grid, you just rolled into the trees while I wasn't payin' attention."

"We can bury the truck in these pine. There's a trail to Buzzard Creek at the bottom of the hill."

"OK, I know where we're at now. My bike could take some more charge, but it'll make it, so let's blast."

"Relax: have another donut," Gerry teased. "The action's at your place today; we can raid Grove's place at our leisure."

A short while later the two bikes were quietly ripping along, crisscrossing Buzzard Creek and riding gravel beds on long dry stretches.

They'd been cruising along for a few hundred yards in a mostly dry section of creek bed with Cleve leading the way. Passing between stream cut earth banks about five feet high, they came to a fallen pin oak. Its branches were stuck into the creek bottom like jail bars. Cleve stopped and pondered the best way around. On the right bank the log had no branches, but he was down in the channel.

Out of the corner of his eye he noted that Gerry was not slowing his approach. Turning on his seat he watched Gerry swing left then whip to the right. Climbing at a 45-degree angle along the near-vertical bank with his momentum holding him against the face: Gerry crested the bank, tagging the log with his front tire and shaving some bark with the rear as he launched into the air. Swinging his tail end in a counterclockwise arc, he nosed back down the bank into the creek bed. Cleve sat captivated by the beautiful execution of the traverse. The bike and rider were out of sight in another few heartbeats.

"That son-ova…"

Cleve jumped off his bike and started kicking branches until he managed to make a hole he could partially stuff the bike through. He crawled through another gap and dragged it the rest of the way by the front wheel.

"Damned creek bed cul-de-sac son-ova…" Cleve continued grumble cursing as he hopped back on the bike and shot off after his brother.

He knew he couldn't catch up unless Gerry crashed, and Gerry rarely crashed, especially with the confidence of such a lead.

Cleve's mind was racing with the challenge: ("Along with the consistency of Gerr's ability comes predictability. He's going to stick to the Buzzard trail all the way down because he knows what to expect and probably has a countdown to ETA clicking in his head right now. He reckons he's got me whooped and won't take any chances. So: I'm going to cut some big switchbacks off my route by blazing over this ridge to the right as soon as… I spot… an opening… like… right… here.")

Cleve was zinging along the earthen trail by the creek when he swerved into the brush on an obscure deer trail. The slope steepened immediately and the trail zigzagged its way upward in tight switchbacks. He dropped down a couple gears to get into the groove.

The underbrush started to thin as Cleve left the creek behind. He'd begun cutting across the switchbacks and had soon turned his route into a straight hill climb. His path had ceased crossing the wildlife trail and he didn't know if the trail had dissipated or turned away. As he neared the ridge crest he found more and more ledges cropping out that he couldn't find his way around.

Cleve was bouncing or digging his way over the stair step outcrops; purposely weaving to reduce his angle of attack. Carefully maintaining his momentum: Cleve knew that from this point on he would have to keep climbing or turn back for another run. Ahead was the last trial to the summit. It was a triple ledge affair with loose shaly-looking tuffs between. The trees were scrub and sparse. The outcrop ledges were about a foot thick, with a few feet of material between the first and second. It was about ten feet from the second to the top ledge; which looked like the face of a miniature butte from below.

There would be no more tacking. Cleve would have to muster enough speed to take him straight over the top. He managed to accelerate slightly on the flat tops of the first two ledges and was stretched over the front wheel as the rear tire chewed its way up the last pitch. Just short of the summit, Cleve knew he was running out of steam.

("We ain't gonna make it… not both of us anyways…")

Cleve dropped to where he was literally hanging from the handlebars, his belly against the back of the seat. The slight increase in traction kept the bike moving, but he was pulling it past vertical. Using up the last bit of his own inertia: Cleve shoved the bars forward and dropped off the back. He hit the curved base of the face on all fours and slid the last few feet to the ledge.

("Now dive right, in case the bike comes back down to beat the hell out of me.")

He sprang clear, but the bike had stuck where he had delivered it. Finding some roots for aid he scrambled back up to the top. Cleve jumped on the bike- and then jumped back off. Holding the front wheel between his legs, he straightened the forks; then he was off down the other side of the ridge. Starting out, the ledge configuration was almost a mirror of the upside; but he was having no trouble negotiating the downside.

From the ridge, Buzzard Creek was clearly delineated by geomorphology as well as vegetation density: its meandering route through the valley was expansive, though Gerry's track would not follow every oxbow. Cleve had cut a lot of distance off with his own track, but it wasn't over yet. His plan was to continue perpendicular to the ridge and over the next low hill into the sand flats past the old mine.

("Gerry will abandon the creek trail at the mine and I'll already be out on the flats when he comes out past the last tailings cone at the highwall.")

Cleve was coming down the hill to a haul road he planned on following west, where it made a wide circle down to the sand flats. He stopped for the view and looking southeast: there was Gerry, shooting up the ramp from Buzzard Creek to the base of the highwall.

("Damn him. Musta been flat out. He shoulda been taking it easy. But he knew I knew he had too much lead and he figured I'd try something.")

Cleve was eyeing the westernmost tailings mound, which was as tall as the highwall and banked into it. Gerry had already passed from view at the east end of the wall as Cleve swooped down toward the western mound.

The mine had not been disturbed by heavy equipment since it was abandoned; so, the little flat above the highwall was still as smooth and level as the day the mine closed. Cleve kicked it into 4th gear as he reached the flat and accelerated across the surface. He streaked toward a drainage notch in the lip at the edge, using it like a gun sight to aim just left of the mound's peak. His plan was to touch down near the peak on the far side of the cone. Just after taking air: Cleve wondered if maybe he was going just a little too fast.

Gerry glanced up the last little valley before the ramp to the mine. No sign of Cleve: but he didn't let up as he ripped on down the creek.

("Thought he might jump that ridge and come down this way. He might be right behind me, just ahead, or he might still be up to something. We'll meet up on the flats one way or another. And then creep on in to the edge of town.")

Gerry turned up the ramp to the mine. He was passing between the highwall and numerous irregularly spaced and overlapping mounds on his left. Up ahead a last cone of tailings blocked the way along the face and Gerry was busy scanning left for the best route over the eroded surface of the broad span separating the final mound. Out of the corner of his eye he detected movement from the top of the highwall. By the time he had slowed enough to glance up; he only caught the impression that something had streaked across the gap, passing beyond the last mound.

("What the hell was that? Drones? No... It couldn't have been... No. Could it have been?")

Gerry ripped on around to the far side of the mound to find Cleve shaking tailings sand out of his helmet. His bike was stuck in the sand halfway up the mound. Cleve looked up and leaned drunkenly, stumbling a couple steps, his head still spinning from the tumble.

"Shiiiiiiit..." Cleve drawled, "I... I overshot."

"You crazy fool. Never learn, do you? You can't land in sand at that speed. Maybe Rich Willey could have, or some other legendary motorcycle man of steel. But *you've* never pulled it off."

"If I'd of landed just past the peak-"

"Or you could have smacked right into the peak: that would have left a mark-"

"Kiss my butt."

"From those iron stain streaks on your knees: looks like this wasn't your first tumble either, Wildman," Gerry continued to ride him, "those leathers look like they're twenty years old."

"They are twenty years old."

"Eggs-zactly. While you get your bike down, I'm going to check out the plant. Haven't been here for an age."

After digging his bike free, Cleve joined Gerry in the "ghost town" that was the remains of the processing plant. The lesser entrance doors had been violated years ago and sign of various wild critters taking up residence was evident, but otherwise the layout had not changed much. Both were thinking it couldn't hurt to know the ropes around some off-grid theaters for the bushwhacker's art. They did a bit of climbing around the inner structure, while reminiscing on friendly rock fights between teams of youngsters in days of yore. Leaping from the rail of a high steel catwalk, the Henry boys took fat delays on a pair of rusty chain hoists and slapped the floor simultaneously to conclude their sojourn at a childhood playground.

The brothers crossed the flats in formation. If viewed from the air: their 2-track drawing in the sand would look like a long snake with a rodent in its belly wherever their tracks diverged around islands of vegetation. As they neared the south forest, the flats had become rolling dunes with rooted vegetation that had migrated over the years. They split up in search of the old trail that would take them west and then northwest. Cleve found the familiar trail and turned back for Gerry.

Soon they were both ripping through the trees again. The trail had turned west just inside the border of the old forest and tracked northwest after the tree line turned north. When they reached the south edge of town the trail meandered along just inside the border of the forest. In areas where they would be exposed to a view from the road: they slowed and worked their way through the thick brush deeper in the forest. A short while later they were leaning the bikes up against trees behind Grover's place.

"So... How do you want to do this?" asked Gerry.

"Like I said before; and you didn't have a better idea. We do a cursory check for a trip wire and then take turns watching for trouble."

They walked around front and stepped onto the porch. The usual yellow tape was strung all over the doors and windows. The wooden door and walls were still standing.

"I knew there wouldn't be any glass, but I kinda thought the wall would be gone as well. It doesn't look as bad from out here as I expected. Apparently, a fox or coon couldn't wait to get in there either," noted Gerry, pointing.

He cut the rest of the tape loose from the sliding glass door above the varmint's hole. They stepped inside through the open frame.

"If they'd have set up a couple mini-guns, the roof would be down here on the floor," Cleve speculated, as he scanned the room. "They put enough three-oh-eights in the walls as it is and Grove had enough glass up front: they didn't have to take the front wall out. But just look at the wall over the..."

Cleve's voice trailed off as he noticed the scraps of wood still dangling from the shattered 2X4 studs behind the couch. They were stained a dark reddish brown, as opposed to the off-white painted paneling of the surrounding walls.

"Those bloody bastards," Cleve muttered. "You know I didn't actually expect the herd to take them out, but they received exactly what they deserved."

"Yeah... I'm still waiting to hear the rest of that story... Seven-sixty-two."

"What?"

"Those H-rifles use seven-point-six-two NATO."

"Same difference."

"No... I'll go check the safe while you collect your mementos; and keep an eye out front."

"Don't think you'll find a safe," countered Cleve. "I think you'll find a hole under that plywood there, where they winched it through the floor."

"You are correct sir. So, I'll go see what they left behind."

Cleve collected up a number of photos that hadn't been shredded. He loaded a duffel with various small electronic devices, GPS and laser, some particularly nice mineral and fossil specimens, as well as numerous other knick-knacks and G.T.Henry original sculpture.

"I got several hundred good arrows from the false-wall closet down there," announced Gerry, coming up the steps. "Got his backup drive and his favorite Hoyt bow too. No stray bullets down there, hopefully nothing got hit in the attic either. He liked this Carbon Element G3 so well he bought another in camo and stocked it away up there. I know there's at least two fine swords there too, but I've never been up there."

"I know where they're at, you take the watch."

Cleve climbed onto the countertop and pushed the attic panel aside. He pulled himself up and disappeared from view.

"Not much up here," Cleve reported, as he lowered the swords and bow through the opening. "No ammo, but another couple hundred arrows."

"Yeah, there were only a couple boxes of 12-gauge slugs and a box of double-aught down in the closet. He kept his ammo in the safe."

"One thing about losing the safe: we should be able to haul this stuff in one trip without dropping anything, as long as you don't go racing off again."

"Me? You're the one jumped off a cliff."

"Let's get the hell outa here."

B ack in Benedict Arnold's office another little red light was flashing on a panel.

"Sir: Benny's got another detector lit up; and he hasn't called in yet today."

"He's probably too busy raking in more bonus money with all those weapons he brings in. Leave him be: it's not like he's working alone. He can take care of himself *and* his little idiot lights."

8. Family and Friends

Cleve and Gerry unloaded the Lincoln onto the garage floor and traipsed into the kitchen to sit down at the table.

"Gerry Elbridge: you are a mess," Ann scolded, looking up from her cutting board. "You expecting service?"

"Yes, please," responded Gerry. "I could probably drain a 55-gallon drum of iced tea."

"You too?"

"Orange juice, thanks."

She brought tall glasses to the table and looked at the men disgustedly.

"You are a shining angel, my dear," avowed Cleve, waxing eloquent.

"Yeah... when you boys finish those drinks: you're going to march right back into that garage and peal those filthy clothes or you'll be facing an *avenging* angel."

When Ann returned to her work, Cleve looked at Gerry and whispered: "I gotta get me one of those."

After showering, Cleve entered the great room via the den, where he stopped at the bar fridge for a glass of grapefruit juice. The den was a loft in an immense room of A-frame design. The first-floor master bedroom was situated beyond the south wall of the "A", with the kitchen located beyond the north wall. Above the master bedroom was a second-floor clone. Above the kitchen was a second-floor mirror to the clone: which Cleve had long ago claimed as his "home away from home back home at Leatherwood". The den looked out past small balconies from the mirrored bedrooms. A multitude of hanging plants from the balconies and walls added ambiance and a fresh garden scent. At the back of the den was a door to the second-floor hallway, which ran north-south with four bedrooms and a staircase along the east wall. The first floor had 12-foot ceilings with the dining room directly beneath the den. On either end of the dining room were steps to the living room (the split-level base of the great room).

The great room window afforded an unobstructed view to the west. Thick triple pane panels (up to 8X8 foot square) started at the floor of the living room and peaked well above the second-floor ceiling. The inner and outer panes of each panel were set rigidly, while a sandwiched central pane floated on an array of guide rods in the panel frames. A tinted fluid filled the inner gap; a clear fluid filled the outer. Pumping in tinted fluid darkened the view; pumping in clear fluid squeezed the tint right out of the window.

As the sun dropped to the western treetops its last rays were scattered through sparkling refractions in the cascading fountains; finales dancing in the shimmering mist. Cleve turned a knob and the room brightened with scattered rays flickering through the glass like a laser light show. As the tint ran out of the window, the unmitigated magnificence of the spectacle over the lake flowed into the great room.

"That view never gets old," muttered Cleve to himself.

"That you up there, Cleve?"

"George?"

"Quit your sneakin' around and come on down here."

Cleve moved to the railing and glanced over; none of the arriving guests had made it past the dining room.

("I wouldn't have either if Ann's put some of her appetizers out,") thought Cleve as he reached for the pole.

The north end of the den railing semi-circled around a hole in the floor, where an age-tarnished brass pole extended from the great room ceiling to the living room floor. The natural patina of the brass was mostly polished away from the level of the den rail down, but just enough to bring out the metallic crystal structure. When the county built the new firehouse and put in a stainless pole, Grover had tried to buy the pole from the old building. The fire chief would have nothing of it and presented the old brass pole to the Henrys in honor of everything their family had done for the district over the years. Patrick had always wanted a firehouse pole in the great room; of course, his wife Sarah had said he was just being silly. When Grover and Cleve encouraged Gerry to install the pole: Momma had protested, but it was an honorary gift after all. The old brass pole was too short to reach the central peak, but then its less prominent setting was more aesthetically tolerable for the home application.

Cleve spiraled down the pole with drink in hand to alight facing the dining room. A visit from George and Martha Washington wasn't a surprise; seeing George's sister Virginia sitting at the table with young Henry Knox standing beside her was. Not so much a surprise that they were here- but that young Henry was not his rambunctious self, outside playing until dinner call with the rest of the kids, and that his father was not here with the adults. Cleve's usual MO would be to grab little Henry and ask: *"what's the long face about big guy?"* But then with the somber demeanor of the two women seated alongside, he was expecting the worst.

"Hello Virginia… Martha…" said Cleve, then turned and gripped George's hand, "and how's George doing?"

George Washington was a well-educated gentleman, stout of build, standing a few inches taller than Cleve. He'd worked in a law office and served two terms as a district judge. Having been the first black American to take the local bench, George had also been their youngest judge ever elected, and he was still one of the most widely respected men in the community. He loved to hate politics and retired early with a healthy *"Green Acres- fresh air"* attitude. Of course, Martha preferred *"town square"*, but they got along fine with a little of both.

"George is doing well enough old man. I see you've still got the spring in your step, making an unorthodox entrance as usual," George bantered as he turned his back to the others and lowered his voice, "Can we step out somewhere and kick a few things around?"

"Sure George," said Cleve as he headed for the kitchen.

Ann was still busy at a countertop; Gerry was leaning lightly against her back with his arms around her waist, watching over her shoulder with his cheek against her neck. Cleve stepped over to Momma who was sitting at the kitchen table. He dropped to one knee and hugged her close.

After a long moment they stood together. Cleve gave her a squeeze and turned to the door; he couldn't quite look her in the eye just now. George laid his hand on her shoulder as he passed and gave her a comforting smile.

"Why don't you show us the garage Gerry?" suggested Cleve as he pulled the door open.

"George: I know you've heard about what happened to Grove yesterday morning, but Gerry and me have been out all day. What did we miss here? Where's Henry at?"

"Henry Knox is dead… and little Monica too. And we don't know what happened Cleveland."

After a moment of silence, Gerry questioned: "What *do* you know, George?"

"Well, yesterday afternoon Virginia shows up at the door crying and calling out: *George, go get George.* So, Martha was trying to calm her down and sends John and little Henry out to find me. I saw the boys coming and got down off the tractor. Henry runs up, grabs me around the waist: *Help us Uncle George*, he says, and just holds on for a while. I told him it would be all right and asked what happened. The boy's a real trooper; that first bit of emotion was all he showed. He explained that his mother had picked him up at the bus stop, that their house was locked up with yellow tape, and his father and sister were missing.

"Back at the house Virginia wanted to call Ethan Allen straight away, but I reminded her she was under Montgomery County jurisdiction. She trusts Ethan because he's a friend of Henry's. Most folks see the two of them at a tournament and think they'd be mortal enemies because they were so competitive. Henry knew the backcountry like the back of his hand and could show even Ethan a thing or two. They appeared to be exact opposites, but they shared a passion… Sorry, I went off there on account of we didn't get satisfaction from Montgomery County and called Ethan anyway. He said he'd check it out, but today he didn't have time to talk about it."

"Yeah… I imagine he was tied up at the ranch today… Shoulda invited him out here this evening," added Cleve.

"Oh, I'm glad to hear you say that little buddy: because I did. I was meaning to say something and it just slipped my mind. I don't know how well you know the man, however I can guarantee he *is* good people."

"Grover knew him well and *he* liked him. I know enough about him to know he's a man you can trust; that's the best credentials for a friend of a friend. And times being what they are: a good man who can shoot like Ethan is certainly welcome at my dinner table. Oh, and I ain't *that* little, big bud."

"Hello? Nice of you guys to be making all these dinner plans without clueing in me or the wife," Gerry admonished.

"Sorry Gerr," said Cleve, "he'll probably show up late if he makes it at all."

"No, I'm just riding you. Ann and I figured no telling who might show up with all the shit that's going down. She's got it under control. Some folks will bring dishes anyway, times being what they are. Go on George: what did you get out of the Montgomery authorities?"

"OK, so I phoned the sheriff's office up there and was transferred to the coroner who had the worst possible news. Well, he apologized that he didn't really know what happened: he was instructed to issue death certificates and release the bodies, nothing more."

"That's cold," said Cleve.

"Hmm. He already had a positive ID on the deceased, but needed a family signature to release the bodies to Adams Funeral Home since they're from another county. Of course, Virginia will be having the service at St. Albert Church."

"Momma's already talked to Monsignor Lincoln about having Grover's service Monday afternoon," Gerry interjected. "We'll have to speak with Virginia; perhaps she would consider one service for the three of them. The logistics of tandem services would multiply the stress for a lot of people. Also: a single service may promote bonding and local unity, in resistance to the Godless oppression that they fell prey to."

"Mm-hmm..." George looked Gerry in the eye and gave him a compassionate smile, then his eyes refocused somewhere at their feet as he resumed: "Moving on: so, the coroner met me at the Knox farm, cleared it from crime scene status and gave me a copy of the death certificates along with the incident report. He wouldn't talk about the report; said it was BATF bullshit and belonged with the garbage."

George looked up at the sound of the door, nodding as Ben and Ethan Allen joined the garage party.

"Speak of the Devil," Cleve piped up.

"I've been called worse: but not this day. Presuming you reference myself rather than my respected companion, albeit reluctant transporter," responded Ethan, glancing at Ben.

"You just looked too damn clean to ride in my old Dodge; but the dirt on the passenger side is courtesy of Cleve dumping a load on old Gomer with his tractor tires," grumbled Ben.

"Nonetheless, my appreciation of the lift to Leatherwood is undiminished Mr. Franklin. Dirt is of little concern as there is an entire profession that specializes in the cleansing of clothing. I'm assuming your vehicle is not infested with ants at any rate?"

"Yeah, well, I hosed *them* out awhile back…"

"You boys make a fine couple," teased Cleve. "We wondered if you would show, Ethan. I was afraid you might get tied up in that little… ruckus out at the ranch."

"Ahh… and from which side of the Dark Gate does a man draw the power to bring a stampede of wild animals down upon his tormentors?"

"Speak of the Devil," echoed Gerry, "I've been waiting for the rest of that story all day long."

"Not before dinner," Cleve demurred. "Though you should know: those are full-blooded bison; I hand picked that herd and there's no mellow ever been bred into a one of 'em. The bulls are bolt lightning and the cows are thunder. Sorry George: you were saying that the Montgomery County Coroner called the incident report *BATF bullshit that belonged in the garbage?*"

George resumed: "Yes… he said if we want some semblance of honest closure we should get a private investigator to piece together a more likely scenario. He didn't know Henry personally: but accurately assumed he had better sense than to storm out the door with his little girl at his heels- gun blazing -for a face off with a truckload of soldiers. Oh, the Special Agent providing the report did request that CSI dust the hands for gunpowder corroboration that Henry had fired the cartridge they left as evidence. The BATF report claimed Henry had fired a wild shot over one soldier's shoulder, disrupting his aim and causing him to hit the girl-"

"That is a lie!" Ethan proclaimed firmly.

George held up his hand and continued: "The coroner said he was delivered an Executive Order document that forbid him to investigate-"

Ethan cut in again: "That was their modus operandi with Grover as well; the good coroner's hands are tied- until he recognizes his moral obligation to sever the bonds. Pardon the interruption Mr. Washington; please go on."

"No, that's all I have to say. Virginia has not read the BATF report, and quite frankly, I would shit-can it rather than infuriate her with its contents. I am quite ready to hear what knowledge you may have gleaned from your visit to the Knox farm, Mr. Allen."

"Ethan."

"And you may call me George."

In the past the two had often crossed paths at the courthouse, but George looked at Ethan as if he had never seen the man before, and offered his hand. Perhaps he hoped to find a bit of his brother-in-law in this man who had been closer to Henry than he had ever been; moreover, George felt his former position as Judge had kept him at arm's length from many a good man. Conflict of interest: one of the things he hated about politics. If you are not guilty of cronyism you will probably be labeled an anarchist. Ethan offered a strong grip but the big man attempted to crush his hand anyway; which only elicited a wry smile from the wiry weapons master, whose own hand seemed to solidify into what felt like an iron bar from George's perspective.

George clapped him on the shoulder with his left and laughed: "We are going to get along just fine, my friend. Now tell us your take on the last stand of Henry Knox."

Gerry had broken up the garage party and asked that Ethan tell his story after dinner, as everyone would want to hear. Back inside Gerry began greeting guests who were already seated at the dining room table. Martha and Virginia hadn't moved from their chairs, so George took a seat by his wife.

John and Dorothy Hancock were seated across from the Washingtons, while little Henry was standing at the end of the table letting John enthrall him with some slight-of-hand tricks. John was running out of tricks and turned to his wife with a muted sigh of relief as Ethan strode up and stood beside the boy.

Henry was used to adults upstaging him and started to turn away; turning with him, Ethan placed a hand on his shoulder, then guided him toward the south stairs asking: "May I have a few minutes Henry?"

"Uh-huh."

The steps to the living room were broad carpeted winders that curled toward the center of the great room. They seemed to waste floor space, however they were like extra seating for down-home folk and wide enough not to block traffic. Henry sat down near the center of the stairs and Ethan seated himself two steps lower, on the shallow treads at the inside of the curl. Both were comfortable with a view out the window, nevertheless, the tall man was on eye level with the boy.

"The sunset from here must have been beautiful," Ethan started.

"I think it was," said Henry.

"You *think* it was?"

"I wasn't really watching, Mr. Allen."

"Ah… I understand… Henry, your father was an extraordinary man and a good friend."

"He said something like that about you too, sir."

"Hmm… We shared many a good hunt. You came along quail hunting once: remember?"

"I remember. I remember you were mad at me because Dad wanted only one of you shooting at a time, while the other held onto my hand."

"I wasn't mad at you Henry. I wasn't mad at all; I was just disappointed to see half of our dinner flying away when Tracker kept pointing those big coveys. I'm sorry I gave you the wrong impression that day; apparently, I was too intent on the birds to discern your perspective. Your father was wise to keep you in hand."

"Dad has been taking me with him and only asked that I stay behind him when he's got his gun up."

"You *are* safer behind a lone shooter; and, you are older now as well."

They took a moment to regard the fountain spray still visible against the evening sky above the treetops.

"Henry, I was out at your farm last night to determine the sequence of events that led to the loss of your father and sister. After dinner I will explain my findings to the entire company here. I want you to know that although I'm only ninety percent certain of the accuracy of my assessment, I am one hundred percent certain that the report made by those responsible is a fabrication. If you watch any major media reports or are confronted with any claims that Henry Knox was the aggressor responsible for the shooting: I want you to pay them no heed, as I can assure you that your father was the victim here. You should always be proud of him and I want you to hold your head high whenever you hear his name. Will you do that young man?"

"I am proud of him… and I will, Mr. Allen," Henry proclaimed with glassy eyes.

"You are the man of the family now, Henry. I want you to call me Ethan, and I hope we shall be friends as your father and I were."

"Yes sir, Mr. Al- Ethan."

Ethan offered his hand and the little man gripped it as firmly as he could manage with his short fingers.

Cleve paused in the kitchen to say hi to a couple of neighbor women who had apparently usurped the dinner preparations from Ann. As he entered the great room and turned right to the north living room stairs he noted Ann descending the east stairs to join Gerry with the guests at the table.

Momma was in an easy chair on the opposite end of the dining room. Ben moseyed up to Momma, who stood and wrapped her hands around Ben's throat in a mock effort to strangle him.

"What do you think I saw on cable last night?" asked Sarah.

"What-?"

"Maybe a YouTube clip?"

"Sorry Sarah, I…"

She released her grip and gave him a hug, "It's alright Ben. You did right; if I'd have seen that video before we left for town, I would have taken the Terex for sure."

Once Cleve noted that Momma and Ben were sharing a good hug he moved down the stairs, spotting Egbert Benson and Gouverneur Morris seated in the living room; it was their wives Maria and Nancy Anne who had taken over in the kitchen.

Cleve jumped the last three steps to thump down on the floor in a satirical attempt to startle Joe Martin from his reverie at the window. Of course, Joe had known it was Cleve coming down the steps and slowly rotated his head to eye him over his left shoulder. Joe was responsible for security on the grounds at and around Leatherwood. Nobody really new how much of Joe's blood was Native American. He wore a ZZ Top beard, but he was too proud of his Cherokee heritage to admit to any other ancestry.

"I've got something for you, partner," Cleve whispered. "Remind me before you pull out tonight."

Cleve strolled over to a collection of sofas. The two men lounging there stood and nodded.

"Howdy Egg… Goober," Cleve smiled. "So you put the girls straight to work in the kitchen, huh?"

"Oh, they insisted that Ann had done quite enough today already and should visit with the guests. How are you Cleve?" asked Egbert.

"Well enough Egg; and you?" countered Cleve, turning to shake Egbert's hand while noting that Gouverneur was stewing over the crude greeting.

"I'm doing fine, though Maria and I have been distraught with the news about Grover."

"Yes, the clip that played over cable was appalling; despicable treatment of a respected citizen. Nancy Anne and I were quite disturbed as well," added Gouverneur, with a quick bow of his head. "You have our deepest sympathy for your loss, good sir."

"I appreciate the sentiment," said Cleve, tipping his head in turn.

"Though I do take exception to your unequivocal disfigurement of my name. I have previously granted sanction that you address me as Gouvér."

"Alright… whatever you say Goov. Always got to act so prim and proper, don'tcha? But I know you're just a country boy at heart," Cleve laughed and offered his hand.

Smiling, they shared a warm handshake; then Cleve clapped his left palm under Gouvér's elbow and sighted down his forearm as if it were a shotgun aimed at the sofa. Egbert slapped Cleve on the shoulder and chortled.

Gouvér pulled away in protest: "Alright knock it off you hooligan. Next you would have me climbing trees."

"It could only do you good Goov."

"You *are* a little too prim Gouvér," Egbert grinned, "nevertheless, that's not why Cleve rides you so hard… you old socialist."

Gouvér grit his teeth: "I have told you before that I am not *a socialist*. I only expound the virtues of socialism as a universal government in an idealized world society."

Egbert continued the ribbing: "Ah… the old planet-wide Shangri-La theory. I suppose you'd be a flower child if only good and evil would all get together and *love one another right now*… So, you admit to being a utopian idealist?"

"That would be my mother and her mentor/spouse: Mr. Smith. Now *there* are a couple of Pinks for you. It is bad enough that we have federal intervention in the public education system; I certainly don't want her and William indoctrinating our children with their pink fantasies as well. We bought Mother that holiday villa in Florida so they could preach their *flower power* theories to a lot of benign retirees and leave us be."

"Didn't your step-father used to be *your* mentor before he took to your momma?" asked Egbert, with a sly grin.

"I was but a growing child at the time: chasing dreams and hungry for knowledge, naïvely asking questions for which William Smith seemed to have the answers."

"I guess some of those *love the one you're with* answers are what put you in the market for a six-million-dollar leg, huh?"

"Hmnph…"

"You've got so much pink in your family history, we just can't help riding you," Cleve interjected. "You're still a socialist in the sense of your belief in the utopian concept. But you're *our* socialist, so we still love ya Goov- heh heh heh -and the flowers ya rode in on: right Egg?"

"Wouldn't have you any other way Gouvér," Egbert grinned.

"Touché -as you bask in your own self-righteousness, I bring forth Exhibit A: an icy night of February and a year ago. The Broken Bottle Tavern is a wretched little roadhouse: not my preferred choice of cocktail lounges, but a welcome sight for any traveler caught in a mountain ice storm with no tire chains. Long story short; I was pleasantly surprised to find Cleveland engaged in a conversation wherefore he suggested- nay, promoted -the concept of a world government to facilitate commerce with extraterrestrial alien cultures; if and when we become a space-faring society. Yes, my friend, you even acknowledged that a pure form of socialism *could* work, if we created some computerized form of politicians that were incapable of greed, corruption or cronyism."

"Ha -ha, ha -ha. How many had I put away at that point Goov? I do recall, with the prospect of sleeping in a chair or on the floor, there was no last call that night. But yeah… if we're going to fantasize about interplanetary commerce, we can fantasize that only honest men will run for political office as well. Seriously though, to maintain perspective, note that a monarchy or dictatorship would be the most efficient form of government if you were blessed with a wise and benevolent leader. There are multitudes with such potential; nonetheless, my guess is that twenty to one would fall to the corruption cultivated by absolute power. So mankind may experience fifty years of utopia followed by a thousand years of torment at the hands of tyrants."

With hardly a breath Cleve continued: "Make no mistake, the shared power of a socialistic political party cultivates the same corruption that inclines the tyrant to force his will upon the people. The history of socialism and communism across the planet comprises a plethora of tyrannical regimes. Just look at recent history: human rights in China are a sick joke; and the single-party communist control of the Union of Soviet Socialist Republics similarly strangled the people with their power grab for world domination in the late twentieth century. But then Gorby knew he couldn't squeeze any more blood from his people without an economic implosion; his good fortune was that Ronnie had the balls to show the Soviet Politibureau- and the entire world -that slave labor cannot beat capitalism in an arms race.

"And anotha thing," Cleve was on a roll, "back here in twenty-first century U.S.A.: Both political parties have been fostering government bureaucracies that are choking good ole American capitalism to death through cronyism and feel-good regulations. *Free capitalism* is dead or dying. But it's hard enough to get anyone to vote for a third party, much less an independent. The two-party system has devolved into a party of Pinks versus a party besieged with bargain basement Pinks. It's like Coke making New Coke because Pepsi got an edge on them; what the heyull were they theenking? Maybe there should be a new *Classic* Republican Party: or is that what a Libertarian Republican is? Or would it take the crossbreeding of the Republican Party with the Libertarian Party, the Constitution Party, the American Conservative Party, the America First Party, the Reform Party, the Independent American Party, and the Tea Party Party? No... what we need is an unchained independent like good ole number one President George Wash-"

Cleve felt a heavy hand on his shoulder and turned to find his buddy George smiling at him.

Egbert took advantage of the interruption to say: "Hey, wasn't ole George the first a Federalist?"

"No, he was not. He favored their policies and they tried to claim him as one of their own, but he never joined the Federalist Party," responded George. ***"Let me now take a more comprehensive view, & warn you in the most solemn manner against the baneful effects of the Spirit of Party, generally.***

This spirit, unfortunately, is inseparable from our nature, having its root in the strongest passions of the human mind. ___It exists under different shapes in all Governments, more or less stifled, controlled, or repressed; but in those of the popular form it is seen in its greatest rankness and is truly their worst enemy. ___

The alternate domination of one faction over another, sharpened by the spirit of revenge natural to party dissension, which in different ages & countries has perpetrated the most horrid enormities, is itself a frightful despotism. ___ But this leads at length to a more formal and permanent despotism. ___ The disorders & miseries, which result, gradually incline the minds of men to seek security & repose in the absolute power of an Individual: and sooner or later the chief of some prevailing faction more able or more fortunate than his competitors, turns this disposition to the purposes of his own elevation, on the ruins of Public Liberty. ___

Without looking forward to an extremity of this kind (which nevertheless ought not to be entirely out of sight) the common & continual mischiefs of the spirit of Party are sufficient to make it the interest and the duty of a wise People to discourage and restrain it."[VI]

Little Henry nudged Ethan on the shoulder and asked: "Are those guys for real? Dad always said if I had any political questions to save them for Uncle George, but I don't think I could get a word in with that group."

"What you see there is called: *preaching to the choir*," Ethan responded. "You could say they are practicing for a debate with a mainstream socialist. Did you notice how Cleveland and Egbert tried to force Gouverneur into a defensive posture, wherefore they could storm his platform?"

"Uh-huh."

"Look at Joe Martin, over at the window. He would clearly agree with *your* assessment. Joe lives by the poker face; nonetheless, if you look close, you will discern his smirk. That guy would be right at home on the spoor of a dinosaur in a primordial rainforest... Not sure why I said that; envy of the man, I suppose. After all, I would love to join such a safari myself."

"Me too," whispered Henry.

Ethan waggled his palm atop Henry's head, "Just like your father."

A pillow landed between the four men by the sofas. Gerry was leaning over the dining room rail saying: "You politicians want to close down the convention and come get some of this chow?"

George cocked his head to a 45-degree angle and leaned back to give Gerry the evil eye, as he muttered: "Politicians?"

Back on the stairs Ethan said, "Henry, let's go eat."

As they finished their meals a few of the guests had made their way to the living room, although most had just pushed their chairs back from the table to enjoy an after-dinner coffee or wine. Several detached conversations were silenced by the ding-ding-ding that rang from George Washington's wine glass as he tapped his spoon thrice.

"Come; let us all listen to Mr. Allen's account of what took place at the Knox farm yesterday afternoon," advised George.

Ethan waited for everyone to top off their beverages and find a seat within earshot. The group was of moderate size for the big dining room, so the children had been seated with the adults rather than being demoted to smaller tables as was common with large gatherings. The Washington children: John and Eleanor were there, as well as the two Morris boys. Before dinner they had been chaperoned by Pat and Angela Henry who, at nineteen and twenty years, enjoyed entertaining the younger kids in the field. Of course, little Henry Knox had been with the adults all evening.

"Do the children need to be present for this, Ethan?" asked Nancy Anne.

"I believe so," he responded. "Henry is the youngest and he definitely needs to hear the truth; or at least a far more accurate version than the one fabricated by those responsible for the incident."

"Fabricated by who?" asked Maria Benson.

"It was the BATFE that taped and posted the house-" Virginia started.

Gerry broke in: "George, some of the group need a summary of what you told us in the garage earlier. Everyone needs to be up to speed to understand why Ethan's report is so important."

George finished his summary with a "light" version of the "official" report, shrugged, and gave Virginia an apologetic smile for trashing the hard copy.

"Let me start with a little background information as well," Ethan began, "-to give you an idea of what we are dealing with in the guise of BATFE task forces. My opinion is that these are really Executive task forces: like the President's own personal hit men. A BATFE agent is contracted to lead each 4-man UN fireteam; giving them the air of regular federal authorities. BATFE agents have sworn an oath to uphold the Constitution, as have all civil servants; but perhaps many of them are so used to being tempted by drug lords that they actually feel legitimate obeying un-Constitutional orders from their superiors.

"I suppose most of you have seen the YouTube clip of the ruthless attack on Grover. Their contemptible treatment of the remains, and the demeanor of the task force commander made my skin crawl; and then came word that they had followed up on the Knox farm. We know why they came for Grover; though the extreme prejudice of the assault was unjustified. Henry Knox was a private man who had not made a public *Declaration of Patriotism*, as his wife may attest. It is my belief that Grover's assassins chanced upon Henry as they passed the Knox farm on the road north and the command team opted to stop.

"The official report states that Henry took a wild shot at the fireteam. Let me just say that I have hunted and competed with the man enough to know that if Henry Knox pulled the trigger: Henry Knox hit his mark. If you were to follow him at the same target: about the best you could hope for was to put a bullet through the hole Henry had left behind. I disputed the validity of the official report as I read it; for if Henry had fired on the assassins there would surely have been another body.

"The report indicated that they had retrieved one .22-250 shell that was verified to have been fired by Henry. Searching for an imaginary bullet across the road to the west would have been a fool's errand. By my judgment, the fact that Henry was alone with Monica precludes the possibility that he would precipitate a confrontation with a superior force; nor is it likely that he would leave the child alone for the mere pursuit of target practice. Subsequent investigation along the edge of a furrowed field north of the yard revealed the man's fresh tracks in the soft earth. Being very familiar with Henry's target stance, I was able to pinpoint his direction of fire. In the brush across the field was a skunk that had been shot in the appropriate timeframe.

"My assessment is that, as fate would have it, the attack force happened upon Henry returning from an errand in pest control. Why they shot the man remains subjective speculation; though I have to believe that they would not maliciously shoot an innocent child. Henry was hit by four NATO rounds: three were kill shots to the chest. The fourth bullet grazed Henry's thigh, passed through

Monica's neck and is imbedded in the front doorframe thirty-three inches above the porch deck."

The room was silent and a few in the company were looking at Ethan with indignation for being so technically explicit in the presence of children. Virginia had both arms around Henry, but her chin was up and her tear-streaked face was turned toward Ethan in a bid for him to continue. As Ethan glanced around at the group, Nancy Anne lowered her brows, while John then George gave him the nod.

Ethan gave Virginia a commiserative bow and resumed: "My conclusion is that there was no *wild shot* disrupting the shooter's aim. I believe that the shot to Henry's leg was meant to drop him to the deck; hence the child was taken by accident. Generally, I would never have expected Henry to attempt a shot he could not make; nevertheless, under the circumstances, Henry's instinctive reaction to the shooting may have been a precipitant to the discharge of the barrage that finished him. This is my most objective conjecture.

"On a more emotional level, having developed a personal loathing for the late task force commander: I do not discount the possibility that he ordained Henry's execution to obscure a botched operation."

"The *late* task force commander?" questioned Sarah, "There's more to his story?"

"YouTube, Mr. Washington and myself have recounted most of the atrocities implemented Thursday by Special Agent Benedict Arnold," Ethan answered. "He met his demise this morning when a bison stampede resulted in the annihilation of his entire task force. Arnold had been treated with extreme prejudice by the animal responsible for the culmination of his story. Nonetheless, his were the only recognizable remains of the 25-man force. Perhaps Cleveland may now relate *the rest of the story*?"

Cleve demurred again: "How about Momma and Ben tell us about the black SUV parked in front of the old cannon on the Square? That story might go down better before dessert."

"Actually, cake and ice cream would be good right now," Ann broke in. "Afterwards the kids can get ready for bed. Everyone is welcome to spend the night, so please do. There are plenty of rooms and we expected no less tonight."

After some argument the children had settled into acceptable sleeping arrangements, while back in the dining room, Ben and Sarah related yesterday's "operation SUV on the Square".

Gerry had continued badgering Cleve about the stampede, to which he finally began answering questions.

"OK, so several years back I started experimenting with recordings of various buzzing insects, digitally processed to higher frequencies which bison are sensitive to, in the hopes of finding a means of stopping a stampede. Turned out initiating a stampede was pretty damn easy; stopping one: not so much."

"And that's why you put all those loudspeakers in the glades on the north bank of the river a few years back," John Hancock speculated.

"No, I actually *did* put those up for the harvest festival," corrected Cleve, "just playing music kept the bison south of the river during the festivities, but didn't bother them from that distance. Some of the folks watching the herd from lawn chairs probably thought the river was a game barrier and didn't know the bison could have crossed any time. But they don't really like rock an' roll *or* country, so I never worried about them joining the festivities. And yes, I did use those loudspeakers to spook the herd this morning."

"So, you left a CD player in the glades, rigged to go off?" Dorothy queried.

"The speakers in the glades and the trees south of the pond only need coded receivers; the base system was in the house," said Cleve. "Anyways, I seemed to get the best response with the hum from a variety of dragonfly. I don't know what the bison are hearing once it's altered to a frequency above the human threshold. Maybe they interpret the sound to be an eight-hundred-pound bumblebee; maybe it's just painful to their ears. It won't stop them, but at continuous high volume they will run.

"However, split-second bursts alternating with intervals of silence doesn't seem to hurt their ears; but I guess the *threat* of pain makes it a target to charge. So my third set of speakers was the 2-way radios in the vehicles. I sent that one out on a full range of probable channels. Not something the FCC would approve of, but who's going to hear?

"Now I just want to say: I didn't plan things going down like they did. I figured I'd just get the herd moving south and the assault force would back off or wind up needing some bodywork on their vehicles. But the sons-of-bitches started shooting dumb animals- well, not so dumb -and I made a target of the SUVs."

"Those boys weren't thinking of your bison as dumb animals," said Joe. "Bison are native Americana; they were patriots defending the Fourth Amendment."

"Well…" Cleve began thoughtfully, "Eventually UN and domestic Pinks will all understand that by backing un-Constitutional programs they wage war on the American people and may well die for their crimes against the Republic. The Administration probably led the UN boys to believe they were just playing backup for a legitimate gun collection program. I'm not altogether proud to have had a hand in slaughtering UN troops who may or may not have known what they had gotten themselves into."

"Don't you lose any sleep over it Cleveland," Sarah cut in, "Soldiers are not illiterate; if those boys failed to research their assignment, count them as collateral damage by their own hands. The war commenced when Grover was assassinated for stating his intent to remain true to the Republic. So be it.

"Let us hope that a clear message is not lost in the irony that, though they come for ours guns: *we* have not yet returned fire in spite of their recent losses. Let it be known that those who come to rob us of our freedom shall find our wrath to be manifest in every tool at our disposal. The Republic shall not fall."

It was a new day before the entire company had found a bed in the house or one of the cottages. The Bensons had opted to head home. They left around midnight and Egbert offered to run Ethan into town, so Ben could stay on. Cleve wanted Ethan to leave Sheriff Jefferson in the dark about the stampede, but only asked that he wait until the time was right. Ethan had explained that Tommy previously proclaimed: "*when an Administration wages war on its citizens, it is war they shall garner*".

Joe Martin was the last man standing and waited patiently at the back door. Cleve returned to the kitchen with the camo Hoyt bow he'd retrieved from Grover's attic.

"Carbon Element G3," Joe drooled, "she's a beauty."

"It's yours Joe."

"No Cleve, Grove would want you to have it."

"I've got his black one that he'd decked out for hunting. He hadn't set this one up yet, so you can make it your way. Gerry is happy with his own bow and all that matters is we want you to have that one."

"I was gonna own one of these," claimed Joe, holding the bow overhead in his left as they clenched their right hands in an arm-wrestler's grip.

"I know that," Cleve assured him, clipping a plump quiver of arrows at Joe's side.

"Its arrows shall be as true as the spirit of he who has passed," Joe vowed. "It is an honor holding this memento to the memory of Grover T."

Releasing his grip, he melted into the shadows.

PART 2

9. Easy Pickin's

Gil Lafayette and his partner, Pierre Charles, had taken a 3-day weekend off as per Benedict Arnold's orders. Gil had never considered himself particularly lucky, but when he heard the news Monday morning, he thought maybe he should have spent the weekend at the casino. They were told that Benny's entire task force had been lost to some freak accident. The incident was under investigation and the details were on a need to know basis. All Gil and Pierre needed to know was that they had dodged a bullet and were flying out in half an hour to round out a fireteam that had two men down with food poisoning. They were to be back by noon as the operation involved an elderly couple described as "geriatric". Special Agent Burr (who was to be CO for the operation) claimed they'd be finished before breakfast. "It'll be *easy pickin's*," he'd said on the phone.

The morning was still young when Gil and his partner hopped into the SUV with Aaron Burr and the rest of his team. Gil had been studying the dossier for George and Mary Mason on the plane and he had some questions for Agent Burr.

"OK, you researched this assignment Saturday, then knowing the Mason's ride their electric wheelchairs to church and breakfast every Sunday morning: you opted to request cooperation from behind closed doors on Monday?" Gil sounded as cynical as he felt. "What were you thinking?"

"Never do today what you can do tomorrow. Something may occur to make you regret your premature action,"[7] said Aaron, with a wink: "and something did occur; a couple of the boys got food poisoning, so we had to borrow you two. Ain't that a bitch? Anyway, this Mason couple will be puttering around the apartment behind walkers; so, what are *you* thinking?"

Pierre answered first: "My grandma uses a walkaer and eit doesn't seem to slow *haer* down…"

George Mason could make a round trip to the local diners with a cane and he still drove his car when necessary. Mary had gotten to where she was using an electric wheelchair whenever she went out and it wasn't long before George had bought one for himself because she was wearing him down; he wasn't good enough with the cane to stay up with her chair. With plenty of restaurants in range: the chairs were actually less hassle than the car. They left the chairs in ground floor storage while using walkers around the third-floor apartment. Their eldest daughter kept them stocked with groceries, so they didn't have to go out much anyway.

George had not been hunting in years, since his knees could no longer go the distance. Mary still argued that he should have at least kept the old hunting cabin, so she wouldn't have to put up with wall displays of antlers and bear traps in the apartment. He'd long since pulled the 2-shot rod out of his Remington and had it standing in the corner loaded with half a dozen 12-gauge slugs led by a couple rounds of 00-buckshot. He had clamped a yoke-like clip to the underside of the magazine that would latch securely to the crossbar of his walker by firmly snapping it in place. George could use the walker for stability while targeting his shotgun if confronted by intruders.

Mary had enjoyed her twenty-two for plinking cans while growing up in the country and later to knock down starlings in the pole barn. Until recently she hadn't kept any of her own guns since they'd moved to the big city. Local crime had increased over the years and she had become concerned when a woman was shot in the back at the corner ATM. Replacement costs for wheelchair batteries and the crowbarred door to their storage room was the last straw. She had told George to go buy her *"one of those big pistols that holds a dozen bullets or so; and make it fifty caliber or better."*

George had chuckled: "You're going to have to stop taking advice from Jeremiah Johnson, Ma. You'd be lucky to keep a nine-millimeter on target. But don't worry; I'll get you something you can handle."

A friendly shop owner had had a good laugh when George related his wife's enthusiasm, then looked him in the eye and said: "What your little lady needs is this AR-15. Seriously… it don't kick like a hog leg and she can raise hell with that motha, smooth as silk. You just slip that strap over her shoulder and hang the little darling at her side… she'll know your heart's in the right place."

George thought: ("What the hell? She'll either like it or have a good laugh.")

She loved it. In fact, the very next weekend Mary got George to load her into the car and they headed out to the family farm for a little target practice.

The old homestead had been abandoned for years and the sharecroppers had taken over so much of the yard that George was surprised not to find scratches from the plow along the foundation. It didn't matter though, because the plows couldn't make the turn between the house and the woods, so they had the backyard for their plinking picnic. Mary would have no problem negotiating the walkway to the patio as the grass and weeds had recently been mowed.

This trip was quite a break from their routine and Mary was excited enough to get out and drag her walker off the back seat on her own. George was just standing by the car looking the place over, reminiscing, while she popped the trunk and transferred a sack of laptops onto the seat of her walker. Then she slipped her AR-15 into the holster-like mount that George had fabricated for her and headed out back.

"Come on, Pa," called Mary, "set these targets up for me on the old cedar table under the tree."

"That table's not five yards off the patio, Ma."

"Yeah, and if somebody busts the apartment door down back home, they won't be any farther away."

George lined up a couple Gateways and a Dell across the table as he asked Mary: "You want to turn these on?"

"The batteries for the Gateways are dead; in fact, I already disposed of them. So, we can shoot the hell out of those two," Mary grinned, "you can bring up a picture of Hillary on that Dell though, if you'd like."

George laughed and pulled the last target from the sack.

"Mare-eee… Nancy just gave you this MAC for Christmas. You can't trash it *already*."

"Think not? That's the most disobedient piece of electronic arrogance I've ever owned; and if she gives me the new Windows next year it'll follow that MAC as the next addition to my reality sculpture."

Mary's sculpture was a collage of laptops with component appendages she had hammered, sawed and twisted. Each addition to the almost organically snake-like construct were coated and brushed into the mass with thick clear polyurethane, fostering the impression of vertebrae within a translucent alien creature that grew longer every year. She calls it her "reality sculpture" because she claims that the slow demise of the computer as an obedient servant and concurrent rise as a bludgeon for the gamer/programmer (to beat us with) has created a monster bent on destroying the productivity of the American worker.

"I'd like to know what possessed Bill to let Microsoft hire a boatload of Apple refugees to make Windows more MACish," Mary went on.

"APPish too," added George. "I don't use them like you do, but what was wrong with a good old dot-EXE?"

"All that APPishness escalated with those wretched iPhones. Then the saps with more money than sense were Jobbed by Steve's incredible salesmanship; not knowing the difference between a PC and a giant iPhone. I mean, you buy a MacBook and you're stuck with the settings some crazy geek wanted," Mary continued relentlessly, "not that a loyal MACaroid cares, because that's all they really wanted was a giant iPhone anyway. They must feel there's some prestige in paying twice the price; and that's just the initial layout. Buy a Windows program and you continue tweaking the settings- at your leisure -until you reach a configuration that maximizes your personal efficiency. Buy a MAC APP; then go back surfing for another APP to beat the first one into submission, and maybe buy another to hammer it some more. It's a gaming platform; the programmers think we're all gamers. But you don't pay game points for APPs: you buy them with hard earned greenbacks."

"You finished Ma?"

"No," Mary glared as she took a breath, "and not just disobedient; Apple's got to be the most blatant spy network on the planet. You leave a MAC online and we're talkin' data whore: Windows sends and receives data when you upload or download; walk away from a MAC and it just sucks it up and gives it away shamelessly. To be fair... a real geek can do a heckuva lot with daddy's credit card and a MAC; but don't try to lure me into geekville. Apple is for hard-core geeks or iPhone MACaroids. As for us mainstream American workers getting the job done: leave our classic Windows alone Microsoft."

"So, who's picture do you want on the MAC?"

"Turn it around and that little white apple on the back will do just fine."

When George had hobbled back to the patio he clipped his 12-gauge onto his walker and set his cane aside. By the time he got himself into a stable shooting stance, Mary had already rung off half a dozen shots with her AR-15 that had gone high or wide, leaving just one clean .223 hole in the top right corner of the Dell's screen. George felt he'd been upstaged by a rookie and pumped off successive rounds before he realized he'd blasted a Gateway out into the grass and blown a leg off the table with the second shot. The table did a slow tip toward the missing leg and the other three laptops slid to the ground.

"What have ya done now Pa? You shredded the screen with one shot. Now that Gateway's already played; except I'll do a little additional sculpting on the keyboard with a fork and hatchet."

"Sorry Ma, I meant to pocket those rounds of double-aught buck."

George propped up the low corner with a tree branch and set the other three computers back up on the tabletop. Back on the patio the old couple agreed to "sculpt" on the Gateway first then the Dell. Mary started out off target again and George's first 12-gauge slug hit the edge of the screen, spinning it sideways; then a shot through the body popped the keyboard up and knocked the second Gateway off the table.

"You're shootin' low again Pa. You know I wanted to do some forking sculpture on that keyboard back home."

"Maybe I'm overcompensating for you shooting high," George parried.

"Maybe I'm shootin' wide," Mary quipped.

George waited while Mary took a dozen shots at the Dell, walking it back a few inches as five small surgical holes appeared across the screen. He smacked another laptop off the table as a big slug splintered a shatter pattern and ripped a ragged hole through the Dell's screen.

"All right, that's enough," said Mary. "I'm taking the MAC inside to set up in front of the cupboard door where it'll have back up and I can see where my wild shots are going. We don't want to stay out here in the rain anyway."

"What rain?" George queried as a raindrop tocked against his hat.

He retrieved the other three "sculpture" pieces and deposited them in the car trunk. Meanwhile, Mary worked her walker into the kitchen, shoved a bar stool up against the cupboard door and set the MAC in place. The pitter-patter of rain on the roof had become a steady drone as George shoved his walker through the back door. He hung his dripping hat on a dusty chair back and sat down.

"Reminds me of the times we were snowed in here," George smiled. "You remember?"

"Every moment… It was about the only thing that slowed you down back then."

The old couple sat at the kitchen window enjoying the moment as the rain dripped and flowed from the roof in little sparkling waterfalls.

Breaking the long silence, George declared: "It's about time we tear this old shack down before some kid gets bit by a rat in here, or whatever."

"Good Lord, you're still as romantic as ever. The old place takes you back to warm memories of yesteryear and your next thought is to tear it down. Well, stand up and start blastin'."

Mary turned her walker toward the cupboard and cut loose with her AR-15. This time she could see every bullet hole as it appeared on the wooden door and she hooked the perforations right into the MAC. She kept firing until the little white Apple icon was obliterated. George intentionally avoided disrupting his wife's artistic license with the last laptop. He cut the door in half with a horizontal line of holes across the center. Stuffing rounds into the magazine and firing 12-gauge slugs as quickly as he could pump shells into the chamber, he proceeded with blasting the hinges from the doorframe. When the remains of the door's upper half fell away and knocked the laptop to the floor, Mary went from "sculpting" the Apple to targeting the door latch and lower hinge; wherefore the last scraps of the door scattered into the remains of the cupboard shelves along with the shattered bar stool that George had finished off with a last few rounds of 00-buckshot.

"I think we're done here Pa."

"If the damned heathens crowbar our apartment door now: they better hope you're not home, Ma."

L ater that spring on a Monday morning, George and Mary Mason were languishing in their living room after a breakfast of Belgian waffles soaked with a stick of melted butter and buried beneath a pound of brown sugar.

"The only improvement you could have made to those waffles would have been some pure maple syrup on top."

"And a few scoops of ice cream," added Mary.

A firm aggressive rapping came from the front door followed by the doorbell. For practice Mary reached behind the couch to lift her AR-15 from the rifle rack affixed there and slipped it into the holster mount on her walker. George grabbed a cane and clicked his way over to his walker by the wall. He turned to see Mary with her rifle and smiled as he snatched up his Remington, snapping it onto the crossbar to complete the drill.

As George moved closer to the door he responded to more knocking by hollering: "Who's there?"

"May I have a word with Mr. George Mason please?" asked Special Agent Burr in a friendly tone.

"Who are you? Who are you with? And what are you selling?" George shouted back.

"I'd just like to ask you some questions Mr. Mason," the agent's soft voice implored.

"You'll have to speak up; no, better yet, go home and write us a letter," George was shaking his head and waving Mary to stand up.

He glanced at the back door and was reassured by the thought of the steel bars and shades he'd installed between them and the fire escape staircase.

The agent's voice came back authoritatively clear and demanding: "I am Special Agent Aaron Burr; we are here by the authority of the federal Bureau of Alcohol, Tobacco, Firearms and Explosives. We have a record of your recent purchase of an AR-15 assault rifle in violation of a UN Arms Treaty. We ask that you surrender the rifle or sign an affidavit as to who currently holds the weapon. Either way we will be searching your apartment by Executive Order. Don't make this difficult sir, and we will be done in a few minutes."

George's eyes popped open like he'd been stuck in the butt with an icepick, though he responded with amazing cool for his surprise: "Oh, I'm sorry sir, I thought you were a salesman. Just let me get my pants back on and I'll come open the door and tell you who's holding that gun."

Agent Burr glanced at the two soldiers backing him up and rolled his eyes, muttering: "Disgusting old man."

Inside George was whispering to Mary: "Do we go through with this; or turn 'em in and wait for the jungle to close in and rob us?"

Mary was shaking her head: "George... Dear George... It's just the last month, in the frailty of old age, that I have experienced a transcendent strength in the knowledge that my property, my body, my very spirit cannot be easily plundered by any malevolent entity. Though evil may be embodied with the physical strength of youth, these withered hands hold the power to repel such evil with equal force. They say it was Sam Colt made men equal, well, Armalite made me more equal. Pa, we've lived an honest and happy life together for the better part of a century. What example will we be to our children if we bow to social subjugation beneath the lash of a corrupt political elite? We raised six proud Americans in the land of the free and home of the brave. Are they to watch as we are raped of our liberty? No, my love: you tell that boy at the door to just move along."

With tears in his eyes George gave his wife an awkward hug and whispered: "That's my girl. *If I can only... _leave to my children but a Crust of Bread, & Liberty, I shall die satisfied...*"[8]

George adjusted telescopic extensions on his homemade walker to bring the crossbar to chest level, then silently rolled it up and positioned himself at a 45-degree angle to the hinged side of the door. He waited quietly for the inevitable, impatient knocking.

At the first rap, a 6-inch gap slammed open and George's Remington was aimed point blank at the side of Agent Burr's head. Mary had pushed a button on a remote that activated three solenoid cylinder rams in the hinges, opening a gap opposite the doorknob where a potential intruder's attention is focused.

"Now I can assure you that that AR-15 will be pried from the cold dead fingers of the one who currently holds the weapon," George began. "Don't make this difficult son, and we will be done in a few minutes. We are peaceable citizens and mean you no harm. You can leave that pistol on your hip, but just slip your hands behind your head. I already know you fellas come in fives; so, you just instruct the rest of your boys to move into that elevator behind you. Have them step into view holding their rifles in one hand, by the end of the barrel. I want to see the rifles first. Warn them not to try shooting through this bulletproof wall, because if I get nervous... well, you don't want to find out if that helmet shield will keep this point-blank 12-gauge from spreading your face across that wall."

Aaron Burr's face could probably get no paler had he donated ten pints of blood. He waved his men toward the elevator and hoped neither of them wanted to play hero on his behalf this morning. Two camoed soldiers stepped into view with their rifles out front.

"The others are out back watching the fire-exit," said Burr.

"You two hold it right there," George demanded, raising his voice. "Use that radio on your hip to explain the situation and have them come on up in the elevator."

Agent Burr interrupted: "They are fully aware of the situation; we're all wired for continuous communication," he looked questioningly at his captor, "May I?"

George nodded and cocking his finger toward the soldier across the hall, added: "I want to hear."

"Copy Gil?" Burr's eyes rolled back to focus on the ceiling for a moment.

"Yes," Gil's voice crackled across the hall as the soldier trimmed his radio.

"Will you and Pierre take the elevator up here?" Burr implored.

"No."

"What do you mean, no?" Burr looked apologetically at George.

"I mean N-O," Gil repeated.

Pierre could be heard chuckling softly in the background and George's eyes narrowed on the man he had taken as the team's CO.

Gil continued: "We *will not* surrender our weapons. If we ride up in that elevator: when the doors open, people will be shot- and it won't be us."

"It will be me and your boss," said George.

"He's not our boss. He's just acting commander for these… operations."

"Fair enough, sir. Your wisdom is above and beyond the rest of us today. My desire was only that you all hear what I have to say and clearly you copy." George continued: "I would like to propose to you and your colleagues that you have all been diabolically deceived by your superiors. You have been led to believe you serve the cause of justice, when in fact your cause is a trespass against the laws of the Republic of the United States of America."

Pierre could be heard uttering a low aside to Gil: "There eis that proud patrioteism to the Republeic again; eit makes you wondaer eif a corrupt democracy has not opened the door to leynch mob reign ein the United States."

Agent Burr blustered: ***"Law is whatever is boldly asserted and plausibly maintained."***[7]

"Well spoken," commended George. "The laws of the Republic *are* boldly asserted in our Declaration of Independence, our Constitution and Bill of Rights; and *we the people* shall maintain those laws."

"The United States has signed arms treaties with the United Nations and now *those* are your laws," Burr argued.

"You err," said George. "The United States did not sign those treaties. The treacherous politicians who champion un-Constitutional treaties are traitors to the Republic. *We the people are the United States of America.*"

Noting the agent's smirk had not abated, George began again in earnest: "In the late seventeen hundreds, ***when the resolution of enslaving America was formed in Great-Britain, the British Parliament was advised by an artful man, who was governor of Pennsylvania, to disarm the people. That it was the best and most effectual way to enslave them; but that they should not do it openly; but weaken them and let them sink gradually...***[9] He who would be dictator studies his lessons well: and seeks to enslave us, one by one."

"No one is trying to enslave you; the Administration just wants the U.S. to be more civilized," said Burr.

"And how civilized will you look when the news comes out that you are attacking senior citizens in their homes?"

"The Administration won't let the media blame a federal agency: ***Slander has slain more than the sword.***[7] We will be heroes and you will be labeled a radical extremist."

"That would be a tragedy indeed," George replied sadly, "because ***the freedom of the press is one of the great bulwarks of liberty and can never be restrained but by despotic governments.***"[10]

Agent Burr grit his teeth and stared into George's eyes with an intensity that suggested he was considering an attempt to outdraw George's trigger finger.

George broke Burr's concentration with a last word: "Well, you best back off into that elevator with your buddies. I can see you don't take your lessons seriously while looking down the barrel of a shotgun. You boys could take more pride in your work and you would probably sleep better at night if you expend your energy taking guns from criminals."

Aaron Burr matched George's stare as he backed into the elevator and growled: "You *are* a criminal."

The door hinges snapped closed before Burr could draw.

The soldier nearest the control panel hit the open button before the door was half closed.

"Let it go," his CO barked. "We get the battering ram first and then knock that wall down."

"You think he's lying about the armor plate?"

"Of course he's lying," snapped Burr. "It's a rental unit- OK, dammit; bring the metal detector too."

When they reached the ground floor, Burr's men went for the equipment in the SUV and he stood scrutinizing his two substitute soldiers for a long moment.

His gaze had been locked on Gil for half a minute before he spoke: "All right wise guy, we don't have the equipment to get through those bars, so take your partner up on that rooftop opposite the fire-exit and see if you can get a bead on the geriatrics from there. But don't snipe him until I have a chance to talk him down. Got it?"

Gil nodded, then the two men jogged to the SUV to swap out one of their assault weapons for a sniper rifle. Gil stowed his SCAR-L, grabbed their cased FR-F2 and headed for the rooftops. They were climbing a secluded staircase in a building on the other side of the parking lot when Pierre broke the silence.

"Heis plan eis not to be talking weith anyone," Pierre stated flatly.

"No," Gil returned.

"He eis going to shoot that poor bastaerd fairst chance he gets."

"Yes."

George cycled the double-aught shells out of his shotgun, topping it up with a couple slugs and then lowered the crossbar on his walker to a more usable level. He backed up to sit down on the couch beside his wife, where he wrapped his arms around her in a warm and tender hug.

"It's been a long time since you wanted to cuddle," teased Mary, smiling.

"No Ma, time's running out. We need to be getting ready."

"You think they're coming back?" Mary queried. "I thought you were pretty convincing."

"You didn't see his eyes Mary," George sighed. "He'll be back; he didn't like being lectured to and was seething about being caught. I expect we'll be treated with extreme prejudice this time."

"Bring me the apple cider vinegar, a 3M filter mask and my Speedo offshore goggles, will you George?"

"Going homemade, huh? Sure you don't want one of these Israeli masks?" George asked as he adjusted the gasmask straps against his head, "How do I look?"

"You look real cute, Qweedo," Mary teased. "You know, I don't think we'd last long in prison. Do you think they'd let us keep our walkers? Bet they don't serve Alden's organic ice cream at bedtime."

George's tone went somber: ***"Our All is at Stake, & the little Conveniencys & Comforts of Life, when set in Competition with our Liberty, ought to be rejected not with reluctance but with Pleasure."*** [11]

"Lighten up Pa," she gave him a little smile and glancing at his hip added: "Serious enough to strap on the old Smith & Wesson. I thought you gave that to William?"

"I'd always felt it was an inevitable fact of life that ultimately a son would own his father's gun… I just don't know anymore…" sadly he turned away. "Alright Ma; you better get yourself situated in your little cubby-hole."

The front door was in the south wall of the living/dining room. A curtain ran the length of the west wall to where the kitchen met the dining room in the back of the apartment. The curtain was patterned with a rendition of trees and landscapes that embodied a false wall backing up the couch. Five-inch breaks in the curtain at either end of the couch displayed ornate door handles to walk in closets, without revealing the alcove between them. The curtains had been drawn to exhibit Mary's snakelike reality sculpture until it had grown too large for the alcove.

The master bedroom was to the northeast and a guest room to the southeast. George planned on making his stand from a short hallway to the bedrooms. The master bedroom extended a few feet farther west than the little hall's south wall, which was riddled with numerous small shelves shared by the living room. They were loaded with plants and knick-knacks that George's shotgun barrel would blend right in with.

What George didn't know was that with the open master bedroom door behind him: Gil had spotted his hideout and already had a bead on him through the window. George had only considered the kitchen door and window to be security issues, due to accessibility from the small fire-exit porch.

"Ma, I can see you through the curtain," said George, "the light from the lamps goes right through that thin material. I'm going to shut the lights off and open the blinds in the dining room. It'll light the material up from that angle, instead of shining through. I want you to just sit tight Love; let me try to talk them down with my Remington. You'll know if I need you."

Agent Burr was maneuvering the battering ram out of the elevator with a remote. The electric monstrosity was a modified forklift, designed to accelerate to ramming speed in a short distance. One of his team was checking the apartment wall with a metal detector and the other soldier was carrying a hand-held specialty ram for punching fist size holes.

Gil's voice came over their earphones: "The target will probably be in the hallway halfway up the east wall. I've got a poor view of the living room, but the little slice of the front wall that I can see has a tall piece of furniture- maybe a china cabinet -against it. That would be west of the door, so east of the door is probably your best bet."

"There's no more metal bracing than some little cylinders in the doorframe, so I'm going to just knock the whole thing out of the wall for a clean entry," Burr returned. "We're punching a hole now and going to take a peek with the video snake. We'll toss a canister in when I say *gas*, then forty seconds and I knock the door down."

The soldier stuck the snake through the fresh hole at the baseboard, felt a jerk and the monitor went blue screen. He pulled the snake out to find it truncated where George had chopped it off with a machete. Agent Burr looked from the useless video camera to the soldier and shook his head. A few seconds later he softly reported: "Gas," as the soldier kicked the canister through the hole.

Inside: George picked the canister up with his hot dog tongs, tossed it into the bedroom and closed the door. He shoved his shotgun through a hole in the wall and got ready for the end.

George was waiting to see portions of the wall crumbling inward or an axe blade splitting through the door. He was shocked to watch the entire door and frame slammed from a vertical panel to a debris-covered ramp onto their coffee table. One soldier dove over the door from the right, in an attempt to do a log roll left to the east wall. A debris-covered sheet came alive as a hidden bear trap snapped shut with a sickening crunch; shattering his cervical spine at the number three vertebrae.

From left to right, the second soldier had run past the heels of the first, and the other trap seized his left leg. His face impacted the corner of an end table as he went down; his gasmask was already half off when he face planted the floor. The angular velocity had banged him to the floor with a whiplash that knocked him silly. He was down, but not out. His eyes were already burning, so he pushed his mask aside as he got to his knees. He knew he had bones broken in his calf and it felt like the trap was chewing on his leg as he struggled to turn. His vision was blurred but the tear-gas was not as bad as he expected; he could make out the door beside him, so pointing his SCAR-L generally northeast, he cut loose with a spray of bullets that perforated the east wall in arc to the south. Realization that his head was spinning came when he glimpsed Agent Burr charging onto the door from his right. Aware that his aim was drifting away from his target, he swung his weapon back to the north.

George was expecting more dialogue after the initial incursion and had hoped the exchange would not go down so viciously, but he could see the writing on the wall. Or rather: he could see the bullet holes on the wall, which appeared to be tracing an infinity sign as they arced back his way. George dropped the second soldier to the deck with a 12-gauge slug to the head.

He was pumping another shell into the Remington's chamber as Agent Burr charged up the door-ramp shouting: "SNIPE! SNIPE!"

Gil had lost his target when the bedroom door was closed. When George cracked the blinds, Pierre had moved over for a view with his binoculars through the dining room window. Gil set up the FR-F2 next to Pierre, but would have no line on George. None of the team was yet aware of Mary's whereabouts. By the time Gil had his sights on the living room, both of Burr's soldiers were down. The sniper team watched the BATFE agent standing on the coffee table yelling: "snipe" and blazing away at the east hallway with his HK-UMP40.

"Target lost," replied Gil as he watched Burr empty a magazine in the direction of the old man's refuge.

At the finish of his barrage Agent Burr watched as George's body slumped into view from the hallway. Before Burr could reload, he was hit from the left with a barrage from Mary's AR-15. Feeling the burn of a .223 slug passing through his left buttock, he dropped to the right, hoping to find cover behind the ramped door. Burr felt at least one rib crack as a trio of bullets hammered his vest and the *whack-whack* of two more glancing off his helmet dazed him; then he hit the floor hard.

Agent Burr lay still; his head was turned to where he could just see the old man through the corner of his mask. The room seemed to be spinning but he was sure he had not lost consciousness. He found himself retroactively tallying the number of times he'd heard his name- *Agent Burr... Agent Burr... Aaron... Aaron Burr, are you conscious?* -("Four... four times...")

The agent whispered: "Target, west, snipe."

When Mary had seen Burr charging up the ramp with gun blazing she knew George would need help. Unfortunately, in the excitement she had forgotten to release her safety. By the time she overcame her frantic frustration and found the little lever, Burr had already hammered George's position. Mary fired a dozen rounds at the agent and counted a number of sure hits. She figured he was down for the count, not realizing that not much lead had gotten past his armor. With her rifle still slung at her side, Mary walked her way hand over hand along the back of the couch to the north end, then got down on her hands and knees and crawled over to her husband.

"George, oh George," the tears were fogging Mary's goggles as she straightened his torso against the wall. Pushing his mask aside, she wrapped her arms around his neck, "Oh my darling George."

George's pants and midsection were totally blood-soaked and Mary thought he was gone. Agent Burr thought he was finished as well, but what Burr didn't know was that George actually *had* installed shielding when he fabricated the shelved wall. His upper body had not taken any lead, but he was gut-shot with several bullets; his spine had been fractured, leaving him numb and paralyzed from the waist down.

Mary's heart skipped a beat when George whispered in her ear: "Don't move, just hold me. The man in black is not dead. You put him down, but not out. We were both playing possum; he didn't know I could see him, but he was looking around: he's conscious. I'm real proud of you coming to my rescue like that-"

"Oh George... I-" she was sobbing as she gently rocked her cheek against his forehead.

"It's alright Mary, you did your best. Now you keep blocking his view while I ease this forty-four out. I can't feel my legs, so you just keep holding me upright." When his revolver wouldn't slip free, he grit his teeth and added: "You're going to have to slide over a little, dear. You must have the holster pinned against my leg."

Mary could feel the holster against her thigh and loosened her grip to shift her weight slightly. She heard the impact of a scrap of plasterboard falling to the floor and instinctively turned to identify the source, but found herself looking directly into Agent Burr's steely eyes. He had been silently rolling his body whereupon he could comfortably draw his sidearm.

Mary grabbed for the AR-15 at her side, attempting to turn her weapon and body at once, but she would not out-draw the seasoned agent. In one exquisitely fluid motion: Burr pulled his knees into his chest and spun on his right cheek; drawing his weapon while straightening his legs, he sighted his Glock 27 between his toes, directly at Mary's heart.

Mary's senses were in denial as she lightly reasoned: ("That boy could be a ballet dancer.")

Then, between the WHAM-WHAM of two .40 caliber discharges and the encroaching darkness, the rest of Mary's life passed from her mind.

A gent Burr was contemplating the ethics of what he had just done. He slowly pivoted his torso to a vertical position with his weapon still leveled in the old woman's direction. He released his two-handed grip and propped his aching left cheek off the floor. Lowering the Glock to his right thigh, the agent was re-assessing the importance of collecting guns if you have to kill senior citizens to get them. His eyes scanned to the body of the woman's husband, still propped against the wall. The eyes were still cracked open as they had been beneath the mask, but there were streams of tears on his face.

Reality snapped Burr from the sojourn with his conscience. The tip of Mary's gown lay across George's leg and a wheel-gun had just poked its way out from under the material draped between them; the barrel was centered just above Burr's armor.

("Model 29 Smith,") he thought as he said: "Wait…"

The agent slowly raised his hand from the floor and proceeded pointing and waving toward the door, saying: "We can still get an ambulance in here to help you-"

George had slumped a little to the right, to where his eye was right in line with his gun barrel and Agent Burr's head, so he was thinking: ("OK George, you've got one shot, centerline's dead on, you might know your gun well enough to get the elevation right, but you don't want to miss high and a little low should still take him...")

Agent Burr was waving with his left hand and ranting something that was meant to distract George while he made his move with the Glock in his right. George didn't wait for the move; he cracked a quarter-smile and put a bullet through Burr's Adam's apple that just about blew his head clean off.

George let out a long breath and then choked a little on the residual tear gas that was irritating his sinuses. He fell to the side as he tried to pull Mary to him, then laid his head on her chest for some... much needed... rest...

When Gil and Pierre had heard Burr say: "*Target, west, snipe,*" they knew they were to take out the shooter who had just hammered their CO from the west.

"See that?" Pierre prodded, "The old gairl was behind that caertein all along."

Gil already had a bead on Mary as she worked her way along the couch. His partner watched silently as Gil backed his eye from the scope and bowed his head. He slowly got to his feet and backed away from the FR-F2.

"You're going to have to do it Pierre," Gil demurred, "I can't shoot a woman in the back; not for defending her home... her husband."

"I have been waiting for you to stand up; stand up for what eis right. Baerr could have waited the old couple out once he had trashed their front wall, but he sent the troops straight ein: and for what? Theis entire buseiness eis just wrong. My fameily tree eincludes an offeicaer who fought the Breits ein the Amareican Revolution-"

"Yes, yes, mine as well," Gil interjected.

"Well, my fathaer always spoke weith pride of owaer heistoreic einvolvement ein the Amareican fight for freedom," Pierre continued. "France has always supported the people of the United States; for God's sake, we gave them the Lady on Leibaerty Island to celebrate the centennial of their Eindependence Day. Are we to asseist an Admeineistration- that by their own laws eis obviously corrupt -ein an attempt to subjugate these proud patriots who only fight to maintain the leibaerty that we helped them to wein? I say thee nay. Eit would have been propaer to resign owaer commeissions when they ordaered us to the States, but now that we are here, I say we fight for what eis right."

Gil felt as though a massive weight had been lifted from his shoulders as he clasped Pierre's hand and vowed: "I am with you my friend. Now let's get down there and see if we can defuse this situation."

The two proud Frenchmen feared the worst when they heard gunshots on the way back to the apartment. They carefully entered the room and checked for life signs.

"What a waste," Pierre sighed.

"I don't want to report on any of this," Gil stated flatly. "We'll let forensics sort it out. Close those blinds; we lost our view when the old man closed the bedroom door."

When they made their report to Agent Burr's superiors they were instructed to wait for CSI, then take the SUV to the airport.

"We'll do best riding along for now," Gil advised, while Pierre nodded his head.

Their original flight had been cancelled as they were now booked on an earlier private flight to meet up directly with their new team. They would return to their delegated district; and the afternoon op they were already slated for when they joined Aaron Burr for- *"easy pickin's"*.

10. Memorial Services

The weekend at Leatherwood had gone as well as could be expected; comings and goings and phone calls aplenty. A cloudless sky held all weekend long and the intensity of the deep blue vastness seemed to amplify the sense of freshness in the crisp spring air. The peaceful country setting helped attenuate the sense of loss that hung over the company.

The Washington and Knox families stayed with the Henrys through Sunday. It was decided that visitations at Adams Funeral Home would be Monday from 10:00AM to 2:00PM. The memorial mass for their loved ones would be at St. Albert Church at 3:00PM, followed by a late afternoon interment for the three, with full military honors for Grover.

Sarah had asked Virginia to bury her husband next to Grover with little Monica between them. Grover had not married and thus would never use his allotment of the family plot. Virginia had a very special place in Sarah's heart. She and her brothers had lost their parents to a car accident when she was twelve. Being so much older than his little sister, George became a father figure to her. George had worked for Patrick Henry when he was young, spending summers in the fields with Grover and Cleve; he had also enjoyed helping Sarah with her beehives when she was short-handed. That was where he developed his love for the land and George knew that time spent at Leatherwood could only be a good influence on a maturing teenager. He would leave Virginia to help tend hives for weeks at a time in the summer and she had spent numerous spring weekends with Sarah for the maple sugaring. It was a lonely time for Sarah; when she lost her husband and her grandchildren were just babies, so she looked forward to every minute in the company of the ambitious young Virginia Washington.

Virginia was not ready to return home yet with little Henry. She planned on staying at the Washington's home Sunday night and George had asked them to stay as long as they'd like. Cleve rode along with George to the Knox farm on Saturday to collect clothes and necessities for Virginia and Henry. They checked on the chickens and arranged for the animals to be fed by a neighbor boy, who was glad to make a little extra money on his way home from school.

When they returned to Leatherwood it cheered up the group on the patio to see little Henry smiling when he was surprised by a wet tongue on his ear and Tracker jumping all over him.

Everyone had left for home by Sunday evening, leaving it all quiet at the manor house. Preparations were in order for the next day and to each his own; the Henry family was immersed in the solitude of thought.

Adams Funeral Home was a fine establishment of exceptional size for a small town. Monday morning it seemed as if the entire town, maybe the entire county, showed up to pay their respects. Adams wisely opened their empty parlors to keep the crowds off the street. The funeral home was a block off the Square with the main entrance facing south. There were three parlors on either side of a broad central hall. Henry, Monica and Grover were in the parlors on the west side with open egress between them.

Before noon it was very slow negotiating a path through the building and there was a line outside waiting to get in. Afternoon the hall had cleared enough for a short person to see twenty or thirty feet down the line, but the parlors were still packed.

Cleve and Gerry had been in and out of the various parlors all morning though they'd spent most of their time talking with Grover's visitors. Ann had stayed with Momma and as the day wore on Gerry curtailed his drifting, adding his support alongside them.

Cleve couldn't say if the open casket had been a good idea or not. The mortician had known Grover, and created a fine rendition from what was left of his face, but it still had the look of a wax sculpture.

Not long before the procession to the church, Cleve worked his way through the central parlor to get a last look at Monica. He hadn't gotten right up to the casket all day with folks stopping him to talk. He noted a little Dr. Seuss book tucked under her arm. To see the spark of such sweet innocence snuffed out so young was the hardest to bear. There were more tears shed in view of Monica that morning than the community would see for some time.

As Cleve turned away he caught the eye of a young woman who worked part-time with the mortician. She was near the parlor entrance and Cleve held her attention as he made his way to where she was standing.

"Hello Cynthia. The Dr. Seuss book-" Cleve started, but paused to scrutinize a man he did not recognize.

The man marched straight past him and the girl without a glance. His jaw was set with a commanding cast and there was a marked precision to his manner. His crisp new suit was obviously a rush fit as it failed to do justice to his broad shoulders. And then his boots…

("Military…") Cleve surmised as he realized Cynthia was already explaining about the book.

"Cleveland?"

"Yes, sorry, go ahead."

"Well," Cynthia began again, "I was working when Monica arrived and a copy of that book was with her. It was very… soiled; so, Mr. Adams charged me with locating another copy and paid me to make the four-hour round trip to pick it up. He assumed there was some significance to *Go Dogs, Go* and insisted on a new copy for Monica. People wouldn't know it, but Mr. Adams has a very sentimental streak. Why, I remember the time when…"

Cleve patiently listened to Cynthia going on and on as he slowly reversed their positions so he was facing back into the parlor. The stranger suddenly pivoted and retreated with the same precision with which he had entered. However, his eyes and expression had softened, whereas he looked to Cleve as if he had just been gazing upon his own daughter in a coffin.

When Cynthia finally paused for a breath, Cleve interposed: "Thank you, Cynthia. It was very nice seeing you again."

Cynthia grabbed his hand and added a last word: "Cleveland, my sincerest condolences for the loss of your brother. You know everyone loved him, everyone in town, and-"

"Thank you, Cynthia," said Cleve, gently pulling his hand free, "Thanks."

Cleve tried not to hurry to the hall, where the stranger was nowhere to be seen. Across the hall he spotted Ethan scanning the crowd with equal intensity and moved toward him. Ethan saw him coming and stepped into one of the empty parlors where the crowd had dissipated.

Ethan spoke immediately: "Two of Benedict Arnold's fireteam were here. I had assumed they were amongst the remains from your ranch, but I am certain these were his men. One did a recon of Henry Knox and the other checked on Monica."

"Stern looking fella, wearing a new suit that he borrowed from his little brother?" Cleve quipped.

Ethan tipped his head to the side: "Yes."

"Where'd they go?"

"To the east, out the front door ten seconds apart," answered Ethan. "You and Gerry had best not stray in the open; remain within the crowd when you proceed outside."

"We've got Joe and his boys keeping an eye on the town," said Cleve. "It's only a few blocks to the church and I don't think anyone would attack a funeral procession. We'll be the most vulnerable at the cemetery."

"I will keep an eye out for the soldiers' return."

"Thanks Ethan."

The procession to the church was uneventful. Monsignor Lincoln presided at the requiem mass, blessing and incensing the dead. After reading the gospel he stepped down from the pulpit and conveyed his accolades for each of the three, with formal yet personal eulogies.

Pausing, the priest looked about and suggested: "There are those of you who would also speak for these beloved souls today. Please, please come forward."

There was movement and murmuring as several persons near the front started to rise, then relaxed back into the pews. They were exonerated by the firm clack-clack of footsteps as someone more decisive had already made his move. Ethan Allen strode up to the sanctuary; at the altar he crossed himself and genuflected, then stepped up to the lectern.

Ethan's hawkish eyes scanned the entire congregation before he began: "Having had the honor of calling each of the deceased *friend*, I ask that you grant me the honor of speaking on their behalf.

"In sharing many a good hunt with Henry Knox, I found him to be an honorable woodsman and a true conservationist. A hard working and devoted provider to his family; he was a peaceable man with a proud respect for nature as well as his fellow man. Most of us will remember Henry wearing his indomitable smile: at a local festival or county fair, so proud of his family, his wife and son at his side with little Monica riding on his shoulders…

"Young Monica: such precious innocence. To any who has found himself captivated by her vivacious radiance; clearly as bright and beautiful as her mother... what wonders she would have achieved in the life she will never know-"

The last word caught in Ethan's throat as he momentarily bowed his head.

Taking a deep breath, he continued: "And lastly the Patriot of patriots: Grover T. Henry; a world traveler who has set foot to each of the seven continents of the earth. Is there another present who could possibly recount the multitudes of wondrous tales that the man had to offer? Fireman, swordsman, adventurer, storyteller, master craftsman and sculptor extraordinaire: Grover rose to the challenge and excelled wherever he set his mind. A proud veteran of the United States Army: he was the embodiment of Airborne Ranger. He fought the Vietnam War: a quest to obstruct the tide of communism in the Far East; never dreaming the quest to eradicate freedom and individualism would one day come knocking at his own door, in the United States of America."

Ethan once again scanned the congregation, this time locking his stare for several seconds on Gil Lafayette then Pierre Charles before addressing the deceased: "God's peace my friends."

Cleve rose and offered Ethan an appreciative quarter-smile as they passed in the aisle. At the podium he took two deep breaths as he gazed across the room.

"Grover T. was my big brother; Gerry's big brother. Big brothers don't have to be taller than you, only older; but to Gerry and me, Grover was always bigger than life. There is so much to be said-"

Cleve's voice broke and he took a breath: "Hoo... Didn't think this would be so hard. Ethan is the better orator and I thank him for that...

"Henry Knox was a quiet man who I regret not knowing better; though I've known Virginia all her life and am quite certain she would never have married any but the finest of men."

Having regained his composure, Cleve digressed slightly: "As for Grover, he did have a good life and saw more than his share of it; but Henry had a family to raise... and Monica the most tragic of all..."

Cleve made the sign of the cross then held his palm out to the deceased, spreading his fingers wide in a last farewell before returning to his seat.

When the mass was ended, Monsignor Lincoln led the caskets to the northern entrance at the back of the church and the congregation began moving to the center aisle behind them.

Cleve circled to the west aisle and moved back toward the northwest corner where he had spotted Gil from the podium. Gil was still seated in the pew, but rose when he saw Cleve coming. He stepped into an open antechamber separated from the aisle by a flowered marble rail and waited. Cleve watched him remove a wire and hang it from the rail where it would receive clear audio from the choir. He rounded the rail and strode up to the stranger. They stood staring into each other's eyes for a long moment.

Gil was first to break the silence: "So, your brother was a Ranger."

"Seventy-Fifth Infantry, as was his father in World War II. Yeah," Cleve nodded, "Dad was one of Merrill's Marauders."

"I would have expected him to put up a fight," Gil ventured.

Cleve grit his teeth: "He was not challenged..." he shuffled closer; the toes of his shoes bumped up against the stranger's, "he was assassinated."

"Yes, he was... I am ashamed to admit to that... though neither my partner nor I partook in the slaughter."

By this time most of the congregation had passed into the vestibule. Another stranger was still sitting in a pew near the center aisle: his gaze was frozen in a southwesterly direction; making it obvious to Cleve that he was watching them peripherally. It was also obvious to Cleve that Ethan had positioned himself on the east side of the church where two different pillars blocked his right hand from the view of the soldiers, if either should glance his way. Cleve had kept himself away from Ethan's line. Holy ground notwithstanding, he knew that if either soldier made a wrong move: each would drop with a hole through the heart.

"Listen," Gil began again, "we- I know you spotted my partner over there -we are not here to, as you Americans would say: *stir the pot*. There are three snipers out there and that does not sit well with either of us."

Cleve immediately pulled out a phone and began dialing.

Gil continued: "Do what you must; the BATFE agent is your countryman. But the UN soldiers, as you would say: are between a rock and a hard place. We prefer that you would take them alive."

Cleve cracked a dry smile: "Our plan was to start with that MO. We haven't got any of your fancy instant knockout juice, but a little livestock tranquilizer will do the trick. We are still working on the plan for dealing with prisoners."

He heard the ringing stop on the other end of the line, held his phone up and said: "Listen," then nodded for Gil to continue.

"There's a sniper in the bell tower, one on the water tower, and the third is on the tall knoll five kilometers southeast."

Cleve put the phone to his ear: "Did you hear that? What have you got? Where you at?"

Joe Martin answered: "Little Joe bagged one at the water tower. I haven't heard from Billy for a while, but he's on the one in the bell tower. I'm in a tree over the lake. I've covered all the little knobs to the south, but we never considered the overlook... way out there."

"I know-" Cleve lowered the phone, "What the hell Mister-nobody makes a shot like that. If they did try lobbing one in here, they could hit anyone."

"Not once I'd planted this little microchip targeting device on you; he only needs you in the general vicinity of his viewfinder and the projectile will find its target. My job was to plant this one on you and Pierre was to plant one on your brother."

"Whudda you have against Gerry?"

"Orders," Gil turned his hands up and shrugged.

"Gerry's a family man, just like Henry Knox was," Cleve went to gritting his teeth again.

"Yes... That was a tragic event... which *I* must learn to live with," Gil frowned as his eyes glazed slightly.

Cleve sensed the sincerity in the man and softened his tone: "Well, you'd best keep that story to yourself till a lot of hearts have cooled down. In fact, there's a man with his sights on you right now who will never forgive anyone involved in that Knox scandal."

"I am aware of Mr. Allen," Gil returned. "Whatever else he may be, I am confident he is an honorable man. His intensity toward me is his statement that I *am* in his sights *and* that he will not take me without further cause."

"Well, *what else he may be* was a close friend of Henry Knox... and he loved that kid too-"

The whites of Gil's eyes went pinkish as Cleve watched the blood vessels swell; he again softened his tone: "Mr. Allen may one day find you worthy of his respect, but don't push him."

When Cleve tried to get Joe back on the phone, he'd lost him and couldn't get an answer on redial.

Joe Martin had repositioned himself to scope in on the far knoll with his high power tactical binoculars and recognized the evidence of a blind amongst the bushes. Joe was perched in a tree on the south bank of the lake at the south border of the graveyard.

It was a quaint old cemetery that bordered the church grounds on the south and east in an "L" pattern. The top of the "L" extended far to the west; St. Albert Church still owned the grounds west of the church and north of the graveyard. They originally owned the entire block and the graveyard was in fact still called St. Albert Cemetery.

When Joe hadn't heard back from Cleve for a full minute: he down climbed and jumped the last ten feet from the tree. Rolling to his feet, he was off and running through the woods. What Joe didn't know was the impact of his roll had popped the cover off the phone in his pocket, disengaging the battery contacts. His primary concern was reaching the third sniper as quickly as possible.

Joe's eldest son had bagged the soldier who was assigned to the water tower. Joe Jr. had been trying to come up with a plan to disable the soldier's radio connection as he crept around a tower leg searching for access. When the man caught his wire on some shrubbery (ripping it from the transceiver) Joey immediately hit him with a tranquilizer arrow and waited for him to drop. Then he zip tied him spread-eagle to the security fence where it passed through the cover of the shrubbery; the soldier was already dressed in camouflage, but Joey added a piece of camo net to give him the outline of a shrub and stuck a few sprigs in it. Having taken his man out early, Joey headed off to help his father scour the landscape south of the graveyard.

Joe's younger son, Bill, hadn't been so lucky. He'd kept an eye on the bell tower, but didn't think anyone would be so obvious. He had checked every other tall building in town with a clear line to the cemetery. When he had stealth accessed the last reasonable rooftop without locating a sniper, he proceeded to scope out the rest of the town. While scanning the bell tower the second time around, he realized he'd been passing right over a camouflaged rifle setup. Studying the scene closely he spotted a thin wisp of smoke from behind the northeast corner post.

("There he is, dammit,") thought Bill, ("Now I've got to take him out with him already in position. And none of these rooftops are close enough for me to chance getting a tranq-arrow through a chink in his armor. Dad might make the shot from over there, but I can't chance it. I'll have to get in close enough for the dart gun.")

Bill picked up some gear on his way to the bell tower and crept up the stairs to a windowed room near the top. The last twenty feet to the belfry floor was accessed by ladder rungs of one-inch steel rod set in the stone wall; he silently slipped a pin through the latch on the trapdoor and climbed back down the ladder.

He strapped on his climbing harness and anchored his rope with a double figure eight tie-in to the bottom ladder rung. The anchor looked like a bomber, but he backed it up on the second and third rungs anyway, just in case he ripped the first rung out of the setting. He hung the loose end of his rope through a sling near the north window, lapping it with each length shorter than the last, so it would feed out with no tangles. After removing the window panels, he pulled up the slack from the anchor, slipped his Yates Rocker onto the rope and then he stepped up onto the windowsill.

The old bell tower was constructed of large limestone blocks; the small percentage of original mortar that had crumbled out left adequate crevices for purchase. The original belfry had been a wooden affair that was removed a couple decades back. The new belfry extended the cylindrical tower at a 20-degree taper with four pillars of 12-inch angle iron and an outer veneer of lighter toned limestone. The new 4-foot wall from the belfry floor followed the inward slope of the pillars. The younger stone matched the raw surface texture of the darker horizontal block construction, but in contrast: was set along the vertical slope, in half block widths. The bells hung twelve feet from the belfry floor, where the pillars met the underside of the roof. The steeple roof was a cone, shingled with white enameled tile. The glazed tiles were half-width and twice as long as the new stone construction. The overall effect was a shining beacon in the semblance of an arrow pointing to heaven.

Bill began scaling the outer wall. It was an easy climb for an experienced climber, so he didn't set any protection as he ascended the old tower to the base of the new stone belfry. He hadn't taken much gear along, as hanging more than one piece on each loop of his harness would risk the telltale click of metallic contact. Neither did he carry more than one item in each pocket.

He looked down at the church roof and speculated: ("I *probably* wouldn't hit the deck from here if my anchor holds. That'd be a helluva fall though, and I might tag it in the rope stretch. Alright, cut the sightseeing tour and find a bomber set for this top pro.")

He only found two useable crevices in a vertical line from the window. The joint in the top row of blocks had more taper than he had hoped for; he set a number one Friend SLCD and moved to the crack two rows down. To no avail he probed the joint with a nut in search of a solid wedge; but the crack had nearly parallel faces, so he set a single-aught Friend and smiled.

("Thank *you*, Wild Country, though I'd rather have had the bomber on top.")

Bill traversed right until he could just see the top of the soldier's hat. The man was slouched against the inner corner of the pillar, still smoking a cigarette.

("If I climb high enough to target his neck, he might spot me before I could shoot and he'd probably get a message off anyway. I'm gonna have to get 'im from behind.")

He traversed back left to the northeast pillar and found firm toeholds in the old stone while his knees rested against the sloping new surface. He pulled the rope from the anchor tight through the pro, held it to his waist and then pulled an additional measure of slack through the Yates Rocker. Sliding his Trango Cinch onto the rope, he clipped it to his harness; then removed the Rocker and slipped it into the pocket where the Cinch had come from.

Bill scanned the 70-degree, 4-foot belfry wall and thanked the Lord he didn't have to free climb that surface. The new stonework had thin, shallow joints that would provide minimal purchase. He would keep his left toe in the better of the two joints he was currently supported by and move his right foot to the best smear he could find up on the belfry wall; that would put his shoulders a little above the top of the wall when he stood up, and at an angle where he could get a glimpse of the soldier's position as he made his move.

("This isn't going to be easy: got to be totally silent while I pounce, and only one little toehold that I've got any confidence in… Buck up you wimp. Frank Sanders would be standing on two smears with a cigarette in one hand and no pro. Now get on with it.")

Still crouching, Bill pulled a glove onto his right hand and removed the dart from his gun.

("OK, now I take this wire clipper in my left, and I've got one chance to snip that wire while I stick the tranq-dart into his neck. Then I pray he instinctively goes for the needle before the gun, giving me the few seconds I need to get clear.")

He stood up and wrapped both arms around the pillar. The soldier started to look left as he pulled away, but then the needle in his neck sent him diving forward. Bill jabbed at the wire with the clipper and missed. He dropped the tool, grabbed the pillar and pulled his feet to the top of the wall; turning to the right he grabbed the rope on both sides of the Cinch: the anchored side in his left hand, the free slack in his right. Then he took one falling step toward the SLCDs and landed at the edge of the old structure. His feet held the smear as he folded to a crouch and allowed his body to rotate to horizontal.

From the belfry floor, the soldier stumbled to his feet and yelled: "SONOFA BITCH-" as Bill sprang from the tower.

He launched himself toward an imaginary point on a radial from the window. Once his feet were clear of the tower he dropped the slack and grabbed the rope with his right hand just below his left. At maximum extension, Bill felt a double jerk and knew his top pro had blown out of the crack.

("Hold on baby, it's just you and me now... and we're comin' in low-")

Bill pulled his body as high as he could; his fists gripped the rope at his chest, but the centrifugal force was too much for him to lift his torso above his hands. He had set his rope length to place him near the top of the window, so that he would still clear the opening if his primary pro failed.

("Must have miscalculated the stretch,") thought Bill.

His feet cleared the windowsill and he immediately arched his back, but banged his butt anyway. With the new window-top pivot point, his trajectory turned upward, wherefore he slid his right hand down the rope to the lever on the Trango Cinch. He fed slack through the Cinch and his momentum took him across the room as he dropped to the floor. Bill arched his back again and slapped his soles against the deck. Concurrently, he released the Cinch lever and as it locked on the rope he fell back to the floor, banging his butt again.

"Ouch again," grunted Bill. ("Guess I should have used a static rope for this op. Dynamic rope stretch is a plus if you fall, but that is an *if*. This little stunt was the *plan*.")

He turned his head slightly to the right to identify a "whoosh-sh-sh-SH-SH…" Then came a "WHACK-Thump" that stung his ear and thumped his chest as the number one Friend slid home.

Bill grabbed his ear: "AOWWW…"

Joe Martin had been running through the forest for near fifteen minutes as he approached the target knoll. He slowed to a jog when he reached the base, due west of the peak. His plan was to circle ninety degrees counterclockwise while spiraling up the hillside. He wanted to make his final approach to the peak of the knoll from the south. The vegetation was thicker on the south slope and closer to the rocky knob that was the high point. More importantly it was behind the sniper's blind. The bald knob was in fact a scenic overlook with trail access from a parking area, and was actually the best view of the town; it was just too far away for a sniper's rifle.

When Joe got close enough for a look with his binoculars he could see why they'd set up so far out. The BATFE sniper stood behind a bodacious high-tech cannon mounted on a trailer. It could have been a Star Wars rocket launcher for all Joe could tell; he had never seen anything like it. Parked in the trees down the trail was the truck that had towed it in.

Joe worked his way in closer while the black-garbed agent paced back and forth with a phone in his hand that was wired to the headset in his helmet. The agent had lost radio contact with two of his team and two seemed to have signed on with the church choir; he continued punching the phone, letting it ring half a minute and then repeating the routine.

Joe had been crawling and duck-walking to stay under cover of the rapidly thinning scrub. He was still out of range, but checked again with the binoculars. The agent was facing Joe when he snapped bolt upright, pulled his sidearm and rang off a few wild shots as he ran to the cannon. The first instant Joe thought he had been spotted, but then something falling away from the agent's shoulder made Joe pan back to the tranquilizer arrow that had probably had its needle broken off against the agent's armor.

The BATFE agent snatched up an HK-MP5 from the trailer, then spun to the southeast and emptied the magazine in a sweep to the northeast. He cycled magazines for another full load as he moved closer to the enemy in the bush. Blazing away as he walked forward he concentrated his fire in a tight barrage to the northeast. Cycling mags again, he commenced firing three round bursts intermittently at three distinct targets: one directly northeast and the other two at thirty degrees to either side.

By the time the BATFE agent had cut loose with his second barrage, Joe was up and sprinting straight for the shooter.

When Joey reported the soldier immobilized on the water tower fence, his father told him to do a secondary sweep south of the graveyard.

Joe had added: "You know I didn't miss any possible sniping locales; so, don't be shy about exploring any impossible locales."

Joey took his father's words as fact; he'd never known anything to escape those eagle eyes. After doubling back over the most likely knobs, he gazed off to the southeast where a lone knob poked up out of the surrounding forest.

("There's an impossible shot,") thought Joey as he jogged off through the woods.

Joey knew the southeast region well. The road signs identified the knoll simply as: "SCENIC OVERLOOK", but the locals all knew it as "Lover's Lookout". West of town, the scenic overlook sign on the north-south highway tended to discourage tourists when they noted the little "5 MI" sign next to the arrow. The east-west road south of town was barricaded at the overlook's parking area; which was situated on the southwest flank in an abandoned 19th century pilot quarry. Beyond the barricade the road broke south-southeast, rounded the knoll in a sweeping arc and continued east to the old mine. The trail to the overlook left the parking area ascending in an arc to the east, but zigzagged through the trees on the southeast flank to enter the clearing through the scrub. The hiking trail was marked "AUTHORIZED VEHICLES ONLY"; pickups could make the corners with a little jockeying and even cars made the climb if they didn't mind losing a muffler now and then.

Joey made straight for the parking area; then shadowed the trail through the switchbacks. He mopped up at the truck and duct taped the driver to a tree. At the edge of the woods he circled east to a boulder garden hidden amongst the scrub. There was a stand of forsythia that would provide better cover than the rest of the scrub bushes, so Joey edged his way up behind the thick shrubs. He knew there was a park bench on the other side that had been planted along with the shrubs; the high point of the overlook was just beyond.

He had seen the trailer tracks back at the truck; peeking out under the bench he was shocked to see the abomination it carried. Joey could see beneath the trailer and the bustle of boots indicated the man on the other side of the weapon was still setting it up.

As he backed off Joey was thinking: ("What the- is that guy planning to blow up the whole funeral party or what?")

He chose a 3-foot boulder that was due east of the trailer. It was behind the forsythia screen, but from the lower edge of the boulder Joey had a view through a thin break in the thick shrubbery, with a little additional cover from some scrub sprigs. He set his pack down and removed a tiny roll of string, a half dozen black nitrile gloves and a small gas cylinder; then he backtracked a little to the southeast.

("This should be out of earshot of that sniper… or bombardier… or whatever.")

Joey filled the gloves with helium and tied them off with 6-foot lengths of string. He tried phoning his father as he had before taking out the truck driver, and left another quick message; then returned to the boulder. He pulled three Cobra CXR 825s out of the pack; set them to consecutive sub-channels and stuffed them into his pockets. Joey crawled about ten yards north and set one of the Cobras face up on the dirt in front of a small boulder, with a few rocks stacked in front of the radio. He tied two gloves off so the fingers would reach just above the scrub if they were released.

("And that's a big *if*: hope I don't need 'em… and if I do- be lucky if he doesn't pop 'em before they get up,") Joey was thinking, as he placed some leafy sprigs of scrub on the rock above the radio with their heavier stalks set to slide off of the swollen helium gloves if disturbed.

He crawled another twenty yards north and rigged a similar skit; then moved twenty yards west and set up another.

When Joey got back to his pack he matched the far walkie-talkie's channel on the fourth Cobra; this one had a short length of 2-inch PVC pipe duct-taped over a jacked-in microphone. He sat on the earth with his back to the boulder and adjusted a mirror on the ground to his left.

Joey had to take this gunner out before he fired the cannon. He figured he could take his best shot when the man settled down to sight his weapon. He watched his target in the little mirror and waited.

("With that helmet on it'll be riskier trying to get one in his neck from here. I'd best put one in his arm: right where a shot belongs. It'll take longer to bring him down, but then I can play him for a while.")

The agent had been pacing back and forth and Joey decided to move while he was out in the open. In an instant he was crouching on his boulder and nocked an arrow. He straightened enough to see over the forsythia.

("OK, he just dialed, thirty seconds and he'll dial again, his left arm is looking straight at me; I'm gonna *git 'im while the gittin's good*.")

He drew the bow to his shooting posture with slow precision, then straightened and fired. The agent went for a redial prematurely, rotating his left arm slightly to the right, wherefore the tranquilizer needle narrowly missed his shoulder pad and only remained lodged in his arm for a moment before being wrenched out against the edge of the armor. Joey could only guess the dosage he'd delivered.

He immediately dropped behind the boulder after observing the arrow hit. He heard a few warning shots and was thinking that if the shooter didn't go down, he probably had enough in him that he'd make an easy target. Then bullets started hitting to his right, scattering brush and earth as they blasted their way past his cover, then continued mowing away to the north. Joey covered his face as the barrage passed by, but a stray shard of rock from a ricochet cracked him on the skull. He shook his head and then felt the notch in his scalp with his fingers.

("That left a mark,") he thought as he pushed his mouth into the PVC on the Cobra mic.

"*Hehayyyy, I'm a victim of SOYcumstance*," Joey complained over the far walkie-talkie; then switched channels to the center radio: "*Whoy... I oughta pouwwnd yooo-*"

The full automatic weapons fire started back up after an apparent magazine change and just hammered away at the center location this time. Joey was looking to see if any of his gloves had gone up and figured that full load barrage must have shot them up before they could get off the ground.

"*Hey Bub, whud ya thi-*" Joey was back on the far radio and the shooter cut him short with a three-round burst.

The ridiculous helium glove façade floated up and danced behind the scrub bush cover.

Joey drew attention to the near radio: "*Back off Cheetah, before I stomp the thumbs off your feet.*"

While the shooter was delivering three round bursts to each of his nemeses, Joey took a breath of helium. He switched to the far radio where the shooter had just popped one of the gloves.

In a high-pitched helium voice, he screeched: "*Ohhhh... ya got meee...*"

Another burst took out the other glove. Joey tried the center channel and the radio was dead; he switched to the near channel.

"*I'm soooo scaaaarrr'd,*" his trembling voice was still helium pitched.

The expected burst didn't come. He figured there was another half mag volley coming and looked down at his mirror. Something didn't look right: the shooter had a stiff, squared look and his rifle was pointed at the ground.

("The drug must be freakin' him out. Probably best to hit him with another tranq-arrow to be safe.")

Before he nocked an arrow, Joey dropped to his belly to take a proper look. He had a clear view through the break in the forsythia and could see why the shooter looked so square in the mirror. The straight line of the arrow that was stuck through his neck had enhanced his silhouette where it rested on his shoulder pads.

("Can't have any fun with Dad around.")

The shooter's body started to quiver for a few seconds and then it seemed as if his muscles instantly became Jell-O as he crumpled to the ground. Joey laid belly to the earth while his father jogged up to the carcass.

Joe knelt down, removed the helmet, unscrewed his hunting tip, pulled the arrow shaft from the man's body, wiped the shaft with a Kevlar alcohol rag, stowed the shaft, wrapped the hunting tip in the rag, sealed the rag in the Ziploc it came from, made the sign of the cross on the man's forehead; and then stood up. Tending to the dead had taken Joe less than a minute and as he looked about, his furrowed brow revealed his concern: he feared the worst for his son.

"*Pa?*" Joey's voice came over the far radio: "*Pa? I got the gold Pa... The gold Josey and me got from the bank.*"

He switched to the near radio and prattled on with a silly quaver in his voice: "*Tell Ma we lost ole Blooo... They put his tongue in the toaster for humpin' their Chihuahua-*"

"Dammit Little Joe!"

Joey took a breath of helium and came back over the far radio: "*Weeeaaow... Houston, thees ees Mars control... Wee theenk Major Tong's a munkgeee-*"

"Get your ass in here right now," Joe demanded.

Joey pushed his way through the break in the forsythia shrubs and strode up to Joe grinning from ear to ear.

"Wipe that shit-eatin' grin off your face before I knock it off," said Joe, without amusement. "Little Joe-"

He choked on the last word and Joey noted a tear streak on his left cheek... or maybe it was only sweat? Joe grabbed his son in a tight hug. Joey wasn't sure if he was a little frightened- no... confused: he had never known his father to express such emotion.

"I... I thought he got you boy."

"It's OK Dad. I'm fine."

"I know son... and... and I should have known... It's just... It's just that, well, they're burying Grover right now... and Henry Knox, with his little girl... Henry was younger than I am, son..."

Joe silently held his son for nearly a minute. The confusion slowly dissipated from Joey's mind as it became clear to him just how close his father was to the Henrys.

Grandpa Martin had been a friend of Patrick, so Joe had not even started school when he first met teenaged Gerry and Cleve; the camaraderie in kicking around Grover's war stories surely brought them all close. Joe was already security chief at Leatherwood when Virginia Washington Knox was a teenager, so in a sense they all felt like family.

Joe pushed his son to arm's length: "And, you've got blood running down your face."

"No big deal Dad. It was just a stray rock."

"And what if the man had backup nearby?"

"He did; but the guy thought he was just a truck driver. I caught him catchin' some rays on the hood. Yeah: laid back on the windshield, listenin' to the stereo. He's down there huggin' a tree right now."

"You didn't report before moving on them. Haven't heard from your brother either; hope he's alright."

"He is. He got his man. He called me because your phone was out of service; same as it was for me: twice."

"Out of service area? I should have a signal here," Joe declared, as he scooped the phone parts from his pocket. "Well... we've got bodies to take care of. The sad thing is: the dead one will be the easiest to dispose of."

The funeral procession methodically wove its way through St. Albert Cemetery on its pilgrimage to the burial pavilion. The tolling of the bells was right on schedule as programmed into the belfry's automatic tolling mechanism. Cleve had turned a wary eye to the belfry as they passed and was relieved to note a tiny white flag in the shadow of the southeast pillar.

To the south he focused on a man in an overcoat, standing reverently over a headstone in the shade of a gnarled oak tree. In deducing that it was in fact Sheriff Jefferson, he understood that his absence was not a lack of respect and that he had surely been in the vicinity of the funeral services all along. Cleve was reassured with the thought that he had possibly been monitoring the work of Joe's boys and hence backing them up to some degree. Ethan was right to consider the man a trusted ally.

The pallbearers were carrying the dead in a traditional trek all the way to the pavilion on foot. When the caskets were to be removed from the carts in the vestibule, Gerry had suddenly dismissed the hearse and insisted that with his son Pat he would carry his brother to the west coast if necessary. Cleve would probably have talked Gerry down for the sake of the older folks if he had not been delayed inside; as it was, some of them rode in the limousine anyway. When Cleve rejoined the procession, he agreed with their funeral director that they should have a dozen alternates to relieve any of the pallbearers who may lack the endurance to go the distance, or may wish to pass the honor to others who would share the load. Plenty of folks stepped up, including Gil and Pierre. Cleve nodded them in, and though Gerry gave his brother a look: it wasn't the time for questions.

The Frenchmen were the first to step in when a few Knox pallbearers stepped out. Gil stepped in for Monica and Pierre took up a position for Henry: the same fallen they had favored at the visitation. Was it a formulated protocol and they were just being consistent?

Cleve wondered: ("What did he say? They did not partake in Grover's slaughter but would have to live with the Knox incident. Clearly, they played a part at the Knox farm. Perhaps this gesture is actually sincere.")

The caskets were lined up before a podium where Monsignor Lincoln solemnly waited as everyone settled in. The honor guard stood alongside Grover, where the American flag was draped over his casket. The shuffling of feet came to an end with a cloak of silence- but for the soft whisper of a mild breeze and the distant trill of birdsong.

The Monsignor imparted the final blessings of his order, made the sign of the cross over each of the departed, then returned to the podium and bowed his head. After a minute of private thought, Monsignor Abraham Lincoln raised his head and took in a deep breath...

"In final testimony, I would address the patriotic fellowship of our congregation:

"Twelve score and some odd **years ago our fathers brought forth on this continent, a new nation, conceived in Liberty, and dedicated to the proposition that all men are created equal. Now we are engaged in a great civil...** strife, **-testing whether that nation, or any nation so conceived and so dedicated, can long endure... -The world will little note, nor long remember what we say here, but it can never forget what they did here...** They rest here before us: Henry, young Monica, and Grover... guilty of nothing more than exercising their God given rights, in resistance to the forces of tyranny that would deny that freedom. **-It is for us the living, rather, to be dedicated here to the unfinished work which they who fought here have thus far so nobly advanced. It is rather for us to be here dedicated to the great task remaining before us__ that from these honored dead we take increased devotion to that cause for which they gave the last full measure of devotion__ that we here highly resolve that these dead shall not have died in vain__ that this nation, under God, shall have a new birth of freedom- and that government of the people, by the people, for the people, shall not perish from the earth.**[VII] Amen."

"AMEN."

In the distant hills the Martins heard the crack... crack... crack of the final salute in honor of Grover's service to his country. They bowed their heads for a long moment as they visualized a soldier reverently folding the American flag with staunch precision,

then a soldier dropping to one knee and presenting the flag to Sarah
Henry.

11. Allies

George and Martha had sent word around to family and friends that everyone was welcome at the Washington mansion after the funeral. That evening they found that they had far more friends than they knew. It seemed as though the funeral procession had just continued on from St. Albert's parking lot to the Washington estate. Times being what they were: they had expected as much. George didn't know half of their names, though faces were familiar, and there was no telling how many were there on Grover's account.

Sunday morning George had said he'd invite everyone to his place Monday evening and Gerry had expressed his gratitude by offering to take care of the catering. George would have nothing of it, saying it was the least he could do. He knew Gerry would be hard pressed to prepare the counterfeit Henry manor to receive such a large complement of guests on short notice.

The "counterfeit" manor was a façade for a pseudo Leatherwood they'd built along the road. The real Leatherwood had been "off the grid" for nearly two decades. It had been no small feat maintaining a 320-acre wood and glade signature on visual and multispectral band satellite images. Most of the townsfolk knew there was more to Leatherwood than the scene along the road, though few knew the extent of the deception.

Some of the guests were disappointed that this occasion would not resolve their sense of intrigue associated with Leatherwood. For those, the disappointment soon dissipated with the reception and hospitality they experienced at the Washington estate.

Cleve was the last to leave the burial pavilion. Gerry had climbed into the limousine with his mother Sarah, his wife Ann, and daughter Angela. George had led the post-funeral procession to the Washington estate with his wife Martha, his sister Virginia, and the children: John, Eleanor and little Henry. Pat had stayed on with Cleve, browsing epitaphs on his ancestor's tombstones as he waited for his uncle.

Cleve watched the workers lower his brother into the ground then sprinkled a handful of earth on the casket in a gesture that had been all but lost in recent times. He turned from the grave and ambled toward the road.

Gil and Pierre were nonchalantly gazing southeast from alongside an elm tree, but noted Cleve's cue as he casually eyed them. They left their post on a convergent path that brought them together just as Pat made it a party of four. Cleve noticed they both had their wires on, though they had signaled their intent by conspicuously unplugging them as they approached.

"Your man was apparently successful: we get nothing over the air from any of the team," volunteered Gil.

"There was little doubt," Cleve affirmed. "You just move on ahead and meet us at Gino's Café."

Cleve stopped and turned around; standing beside him, Pat understood: that last meeting was meant to appear coincidental. He knew his uncle wasn't a fan of hugging other men, but Cleve was stalling: so, he figured he could get away with giving Uncle Cleve a hug. Cleve surprised him with a warm return. They patted each other on the back, took a last look behind and then headed up the road.

In the car Cleve got a report from Joe and at the café he brought his nephew up to speed on the two strangers. Pat had almost downed his cup of coffee before the Frenchmen arrived; they did have the excuse of not being familiar with the local diners. When the soldiers approached the door, Pat cued Jenny to go distract the boys at the only other occupied table; they were just local schoolboys but Cleve wanted to maintain anonymity. Jenny spilled a little coffee on the floor and bending over to soak it up with a napkin she suddenly looked up with a laugh to catch the boys all goggling her cleavage.

No one had noticed the strangers entering or that the Henrys had exited the room. They escorted the men through Gino's kitchen to a private room upstairs. As the soldiers followed Pat through the door Gil heard the click of a pistol hammer being cocked. Cleve closed the door behind them.

"You can put your gun away Mr. Allen," said Gil. "We are not-well, we *are armed* -but we are not your enemy. If you will relax, we will place our weapons on the table, then we can talk."

"OK, do it."

When they'd each laid two handguns and a knife on the table, Ethan handed Cleve his stainless Python and patted them down.

"Shrewd choice: forty-five with a thirty-two auto for backup," Ethan commented, as he took his Python back and stepped to the opposite side of the table.

"Now, why are you here?"

"Mr. Henry asked us here," Gil replied.

"Yes…" Ethan looked to Cleve and asked: "And how is it that you have come to trust these men, Cleveland?"

"I don't totally trust them, not blindly, though they may well have saved my life, as well as Gerry's," Cleve paused, "That one has not spoken, but I will vouch for this man's sincerity; I've seen it in his eyes."

"Hmm…" Ethan questioned: "Saved you how?"

"He gave up three snipers. Two had been made, but the third… might have got us."

"May have been an elaborate setup to get them inside."

"True… but it's a damn fool setup that sacrifices three men to get two inside."

"Four for two," Pierre cut in.

"What?" Cleve looked to Gil.

Gil rolled his eyes: "There was a driver with the sniper on the knoll, he was just a kid."

Cleve eyed Gil a moment… "Yeah, I heard about 'im."

"Why?" Ethan's eyes toggled between the two soldiers, "Why help us now?"

Pierre answered: "We have always helped you Amareicans ein your quest for freedom. The French fought weith you ein your Revolutionary War and now eit seems you need owaer help again. We were sent here not knowing the UN wanted us to fight against the real Amareicans. We came here only to deiscovaer that the Admeineistration of the United States eis not controlled by Amareicans. Rathaer they are communeists or fasceists or… we don't know- only we know the deisgust we feel when they ordaer the deaths of their own ceiteizens."

"I wondered when you were going to speak up," Cleve offered his hand, "Cleveland Henry."

"Pierre Charles. My Engleish eis not so good: I let Geil do most of the talking."

Gil extended his hand, "Gil Lafayette. What Pierre says is true; the atrocities we have seen performed by this *Executive arm* of your BATFE are disgraceful."

"And what *disgraceful atrocities* have you to tell of Henry and Monica Knox?" Ethan returned to the grilling.

Gil's face became slightly haggard and a shade paler. He glanced to Cleve then back to Ethan.

"Alright... If you must-"

"Ethan," Cleve broke in and looked Ethan in the eye, "You *will* have it out of him, he has agreed to it, but this is not the time for that story. Right now, we have a potential ally behind enemy lines. They will be useless if they lose credibility with their superiors; they'll have to report the loss of their team soon... Ethan?"

Ethan's eyes were smoldering, though they had seemed to cool somewhat as Cleve talked him down.

"Yes... we will proceed," Ethan turned his withering gaze on Gil: "Albeit we have unfinished business, you and I."

"OK," Cleve cleared the air by getting down to the business at hand, "Are today's losses going to put you two under suspicion or are you still clean?"

"We should be alright," said Gil. "We were assigned to this team this morning and were only expected to plant the targeting devices. They slipped us right into this op because we already had knowledge of you and this town from working with Arnold. And, they are short handed after losing Arnold's entire task force to some accident."

Cleve gave Ethan a dirty look when he noted his hand was blocking a smirk from Gil's view.

"Yeah, well his *accident* burned my house to the ground and slaughtered 10-percent of my bison herd," Cleve growled.

"Tell us more. We have not been einformed," said Pierre.

"Another time," Cleve turned back to Gil: "You want to help, here is the plan-"

"First," Gil interrupted, "may I ask the fate of the rest of our team?"

"The BATF agent didn't make it," said Cleve. "The two soldiers and the driver are on ice, we'll keep them in a basement here in town where they'll be zip tied to a dog cage and fed with the animals. Well, they'll get people food and the little old lady taking care of them will probably get a helluva kick out of it; I mean she's usually only got the animals for company. Eventually, I don't know, maybe we'll put 'em in animal shipping crates and FedEx 'em to the Yukon with a little survival gear."

"The kid doesn't have any training, he might not make it back," said Gil.

"Yeah, well ya know, we can't keep taking prisoners anyway; the cost is too high in time, money and risk. The UN soldiers need to understand that they are fighting on the wrong side. If they will not help the American people: they must go home or die."

Cleve shrugged and began again: "OK, back to the plan. You go back to your office boiling mad: *those mongrels got our partners and all the equipment.* You planted your micro-homers and nothing happened. You went looking: all gone without a trace. You tell them that you caught wind of Arnold's story and then get them to tell you their story. Then you want revenge on me and my brother and you get on the next team they send after us."

Gil cut in: "They will probably put us on the next team anyway."

Cleve acquiesced: "Alright, maybe I'm getting a little carried away; play it however you think is right. But if you get on the team, you contact me and we collaborate. What we want is a scheduled assault on the Leatherwood manor while both Gerry and myself are home. Now the manor is right along the highway, downhill of an explosive gas compressor station. We set up a remote-controlled shootout at the house, you hit a target that lights up a gas line on the side of the house, then there's a loaded tanker coming into view from around a switchback above the house and it's remote control with a dummy in the driver seat. A bullet grazes one of your helmets and-"

"Hold on!" Pierre protested, "You want to shoot us ein the head?"

"OK, the plan needs a little work," Cleve went on in one of his unflappable moods, "but it will just be .22 long rifle-"

".22 short," said Pierre.

"That shot won't be coming from the house: it will have to come over the roof from way back in the woods. A short would come in like we lobbed it over the house with a slingshot; no accuracy and it would almost bounce off skin. It has to look like it really did disrupt your aim."

".22 long," Pierre haggled.

"Long rifle or we-" Cleve hesitated and noticed Ethan was shielding his expression with his hand again, apparently near to laughing aloud. "Never mind, we'll work on it. Anyways, somebody puts a wild shot into the windshield and the dummy driver is lost from view, presumed dead. Then the out-of-control tanker runs straight down the hill to where the house is burning. Your team jumps into the SUVs and heads down-mountain ASAP. If the heat doesn't blow the truck, we shoot it. You hear the blast and come creeping back up the hill to find a crater that says we're toast and you leave it for the county to clean up. Gerry and me are chalked up as dead; your assassins stop hounding us."

"You would destroy your brother's home," Gil declared.

"Houses can be replaced, lives cannot," Cleve replied.

"Ha-ha-ha-ha," Ethan released a hearty laugh. "You are one crazy sonofabitch Cleveland Henry."

The dialogue wound down and the Frenchmen were discharged into the alley through the back door. Both parties were upbeat that the rendezvous was the beginning of a lucrative alliance.

Upstairs, Gino tripled the size of the room by sliding a folding curtain to the opposite wall. Tables were pulled together and John Hancock tipped a bottle of black label Jack Daniels to Cleve.

"No thanks, Johnny."

"Hey Patrick: your uncle's got his bodyguard with him this evening, huh."

"Yes sir, Mr. Franklin, it's starting to look like he needs one," answered Pat.

"Hello Cleve… Patrick," said Sheriff Jefferson.

Pat extended his hand: "How ya doin' Mr. Jefferson?"

"Been better. Hard times when you lose good men."

Across the table Cleve was shaking hands with Judge Adams and nodded to Egbert Benson who was quietly sipping a draft beer as he studied the group.

"I half expected William Mason would be listening in with you," said Cleve. "He was at the visitation this morning, but seemed to be absent later on. I didn't expect his mom and dad to make a day of it, but I was disappointed not to see them at all."

Ben spoke up: "Will's sister, Nancy, arrived around midday; I hadn't seen her in years and was headed their way as she spoke with Will. Well, she turned, signed the register and they were gone before I could say: *hey*. George and Mary ain't spring chickens ya know; hope there wasn't an accident or somethin'."

"Hmm… Well," Cleve looked around, "what do you all think? Considering that this morning those UN boys were the enemy: I think it went well."

"Ha…" Ethan's chopped laugh came quickly, "If you didn't scare them off with your action adventure stories."

"Now come on," Cleve urged, "I figured on you to make that trick shot."

"I would skip one off the top of his helmet with a .22-250 round," claimed Ethan, then went on boasting: "Why, I could slap half a dozen on the top of the head, one-two-three, and they'd be so flustered they wouldn't question who put the wild shot into the tanker."

"Now that's the Ethan I'm talkin' about," laughed Cleve.

"Well, you were talking crazy earlier; you are fully aware of what kind of groups you would get with .22 long rifle at that distance. Twenty-five percent chance you would hit the target in the neck, nonetheless, the man quibbles for lesser accuracy in a .22 short. Actually, if your Frenchmen buy into this caper: a silver eagle says that that Pierre character comes to your party wrapped up like a spaceman in full body armor."

"What do you think he'd have said about a varmint round? That guy didn't want me hittin' him with a pea shooter; or maybe he was just practicing up to barter for a new hat at the flea market."

"If you gentlemen are through making fun of our new allies," Judge Adams looked doubtful, "let us leave the Henrys to their own contrivances inasmuch as Cleveland has such grandiose plans. What we all need to discuss is how we shall proceed on a day to day basis."

"Yes," Sheriff Jefferson followed up: "As you all know I haven't got the firepower to stop one of those large task forces. I've only got three men and we can't all be on duty twenty-four/seven. There are only four of us in an emergency: five if Ethan can give us a hand. That's only even money against just one of those BATFE fireteams."

"So, you see gentlemen," Judge Adams finished, "We need to organize if we are to defend our citizens when the next team of federally sponsored assassins comes calling."

"Town hall meeting," proposed Ben. "You know everyone *here* is behind you Sam. What we need is for everyone in the community to make a statement of their stance on the issue. We have families with nary a gun in the household who will welcome militia assistance, rather than have their Fourth Amendment rights extirpated. However, it is not appropriate that we would charge to the aid of a family who would naively open their home to unreasonable search and seizure. ***Those who can give up essential liberty to obtain a little temporary safety deserve neither liberty nor safety.***"[1]

"Well spoken Ben," commended Judge Adams. "Spread the word that everyone should be prepared to make a declaration of his standpoint, so that we may plan accordingly. So be it."

The head count at the Washington's home was well over double the size of the funeral procession and continued to grow. The Washington estate was located at the fringe of the town proper and word of the gathering reached most of those who had attended the morning visitation, plus some. Cleve felt that he should have been there sooner, until they found a line of cars still arriving. Pat parked in a field with the late arrivals and they mingled with the newcomers as they strolled to the manor grounds.

"I suppose George left the invitation open," Cleve noted to Pat, "not that he would have turned anyone away."

At the front porch Cleve glanced around and slipped in behind some shrubberies; Pat just grinned, then walked through the door with some arriving guests. Cleve reappeared shortly amongst the crowd in the back-patio garden area. When George spotted him moving toward the hors d'oeuvres, he started working his way through the crowd in that direction.

George waved his son John over and whispered in his ear: "Go find Gerry and tell him I'm back here with Cleve."

He gave the boy a pat and moved on. George edged his way up behind Cleve and waited for him to turn around. After stuffing another miniature sandwich in his mouth, Cleve spun around with five more ham on ryes in his hand.

"Hrr Gorrj."

"You are getting easy to sneak up on," George teased.

"Orry wnn my mout is full."

"What do you know? Momma's been asking where Cleve's at."

"We had a little rendezvous with the devil and it went fairly well. Anyways, I think so."

The two men backed away from the crush of guests to a quiet clearing in the gardens. When Gerry came around, he abandoned the crowd to make it a threesome. He nodded at George and then removed a ham on rye from the stack between Cleve's thumb and two fingers.

"You're supposed to eat these one at a time, Wildman," said Gerry, biting off a third of the little sandwich. "Ann was worried you were getting her son into trouble."

"No, he was keeping me *out* of trouble; watching my back anyways."

"So, what was that about the devil? Who were the two strangers?" George prodded.

"UN soldiers," replied Cleve. "Yeah, I guess you could call them American sympathizers. They came over to our side when they realized they were puppets of an Administration that wages war on the American public. They're from France and they want to help win us our freedom back like their ancestors did in the eighteenth century. I kinda like 'em."

"What can they do for us?" asked Gerry. "Where are they going to stay? We can't give them the key to the city on their word."

"No-no, they're goin' back in. We'll be using them like double agents until the house of cards comes down. First, we'll have to see how their story holds up when they go home empty handed: no team, no equipment. Or maybe you didn't hear: the Martins cleaned up today."

Cleve related the rest of what he knew of the day's events and went on to explain his plan to fake their deaths.

"You want to blow a tanker of liquid hydrogen?" Gerry protested. "You're going to get somebody killed."

"The idea is for it to look that way," Cleve grinned.

"I'll bet Joe's not too keen on the idea," George observed, "having to move his family and effects from your *pseudo-Leatherwood*."

"Yeah… He doesn't know yet…" Cleve faltered. "But he'll get over it. He was already security when he took the job as caretaker; he knew what he was gettin' into. We'll build another house and he can upgrade the layout."

"You must be aware there are a multitude of legal ramifications to being dead. Do you plan on killing Momma, Ann and our kids as well? Does the town come to our funeral only to find out it's an outrageous joke? Do we wear masks in public or do you think we can hide out indefinitely? And if the task force doesn't buy it: they *will* come looking for us- and they will find Leatherwood. Whether by chance or design, someone will decipher the presence of our visual-band screening eventually; but currently, no one should have cause to scrutinize the satellite images: let's keep it that way. Although, when the USGS publishes the next updated quads: we'll be back on grid anyway; Landsat seven's regime is over, but let's try to remain *out of mind – out of sight* for as long as possible."

Gerry had been a USAF fighter pilot, earning aeronautical and astronautical engineering degrees during his service. Before retiring he worked with NASA and the USGS during the programming phase for Landsat and a whole generation of multispectral landform imagers. Numerous military installations, such as the infamous Area 51, were kept off-grid by a looped program that uploaded seasonally harmonious dummy images with each pass. Gerry had slipped Leatherwood dummies into the loop as well, and though a time of extensive construction at Leatherwood had followed: the next set of updated USGS quads simply lost the old structures, to be replaced by groves and mountain pasture.

Cleve stuffed two more ham on ryes into his mouth and replied: "Rrr-arrr-raar…"

"Heh-ha, go ahead and give him hell Gerr," George chuckled.

Gerry concurred: "Sometimes I think you're like... like a mechanical genius, with your wild inventions that can be *so cool-and yet so commonsensical*. And then you come up with a cockle-brained scheme like this. It's like you've got no horse sense at all."

"Well, I thought it *would* be cool," Cleve began, "but it is nice of you to be so opinionated about this; 'cause I been havin' problems workin' out some of the finer details of the plan."

"I bet you have," George chimed in.

"Glad there was something slowing you down," the relief in Gerry's voice indicated he knew there would be no argument here, "because the gross details of the plan are that the chances of success don't justify scrapping a tanker of hydrogen and a valuable mansion that happens to be a home and operations base for our security chief."

"OK-OK. Discussion closed," Cleve conceded. "We wait for the Frenchman to phone us on the disposable I gave him and we make plans for *our* tribe at that juncture. Tonight, we follow through with the community plan, as Sam and Ben see it. Gentlemen: *our mission, if you should choose to accept it*, is to inform everyone here that he should come to the upcoming town hall meeting prepared to document his standpoint and indicate what aid he may provide the militia in the upcoming… war."

"That message will self-destruct in five seconds."

"Like hell it will," George admonished, "We've got a lot of people to inform and it's not a line you can break the ice with either. Come on boys."

George squeezed back into the crowd while the brothers looked on for a moment.

"Gerry, have you talked with Will or Nancy Mason today?"

"Now there's another sad story to keep the spirits down. *Sally* is here... over there: just this side of the lamppost, short blonde hair... She's going to tell you what she knows anyway, when you visit with her, so I'll leave you to it."

Gerry followed George's route back to the house while Cleve found his way to Sally's side, stopping to speak with several groups along the way. Sally finished what she was saying and turned to see who had approached. When she saw it was Cleve, she fell into his arms and pulled herself close, squeezing him tight for a good while. Cleve had known the Masons since grammar school and had once taken Sally on a date to a rock and roll concert. He knew she had been divorced once, but had never heard if she remarried.

The prolonged hug was giving Cleve time to reminisce: ("That concert was at the river festival, yeah... I was standing behind her thinking her figure was like 90-percent perfect when I lifted her to my shoulders for a better view- and why did we never go out again? Oh yeah, I already had a girl... well: had one on the line anyway. Sally's sister had set us up for a double date with her and- whoever -I had to go for it 'cause Sally was such a knockout. That other doll didn't last long and the next time I saw Sally was a few years later in a wedding. The bridesmaids were wearing those salmon colored silky thin dresses and her figure was like 100-percent perfect by then. Of course, she was married too. Oh well, *ya snooze - ya lose*: that's what her dad told me when I ask him how she was doin'. She still looks too good not to be married. But Gerr indicated she's got a sad story to tell, so clearly this major hugging is not just super solace for losing Grover.")

Sally pulled back to where she could see his eyes but kept her arms around Cleve's waist.

"Are you by yourself Sally? Will and Nancy were around before noon."

"My brothers and sisters are all taking care of legal matters for our parents. I was elected to come home and break the news."

"Was there an accident?"

"No… it wasn't an accident," the tears were welling in Sally's eyes. "They killed them Cleveland. They killed them both."

Sally pressed her face into Cleve's chest and wept quietly. He cupped his hand on the nape of her neck and slid it upward until he felt the soft curls of her hair against his wrist. He held her firmly and far longer than the first time. Cleve was thinking he would hold her for as long as she needed him to, but he was no longer reminiscing: he was planning, scheming, yes- scheming, that's what Gerry had called it.

("They'll be no more tranquilizer wasted on those savages. They don't deserve to be treated like dumb animals. They are not dumb; they are simply wrong. If they will not concede they are wrong and stand down: *then they will die*. They're just going for easy targets now. The Mason's were just a good old couple… Well, they both had some fire left in 'em: I hope they gave 'em hell. Their kids are all good people and sweet Sally… The bastards are gonna pay for this. They're all gonna die.")

The veins were swelling up on Cleve's arms and he was starting to squeeze Sally a little too hard. She had regained her composure and noticed the tension in Cleve's grip. She pulled away and looked into his eyes.

"I'm sorry Cleveland," Sally sympathized, "I'm sorry about Grover… and Mr. Knox and his little girl. That's what this reception is about. I don't mean that Daddy- and Mom -are more important than-"

"Stop Sally: nobody would think anything like that. We've all had time to… to empathize with one another. Your folks… that's a whole new outrage… You just take your time and tell me what happened when you're ready."

Cleve pulled her close again, thinking: ("Have to be gentle with her, she's like a delicate flower.")

She pushed him away and Cleve went off apologizing with a guilty look on his face: "Sorry Sally, I didn't mean to be so forward or, or too rough-"

She cut in, "I just wanted to tell you what I know abou- what do you mean too rough? What? You think I'm *just a delicate woman* that's going to break in your arms, you big galoot."

Sally tipped her head to the side and looked at Cleve with a frown; then wrapped her arms around his chest, squeezed like she was trying to break his ribs, let go and said: "There."

She stepped back and assured him, "If you're too rough with *me*, I'll whack you one on the head."

("That sounded like her mother... but that's OK; I liked Mary because she always reminded me of Momma.")

Folding his arms, Cleve responded with a smirk: "Whatever you say, *Mary*."

Sally slowly broke a smile as she looked into his eyes. She slipped her right hand under his left forearm and gripped his wrist with her left.

"Thanks Cleve; I needed something to... lighten the mood."

Sally took a breath and started her story: "Tom and Liz were riding together because both of their spouses had work or kids to take care of. So they were just stopping in to make sure Daddy was still planning on driving to the funeral; and offer a ride if he wasn't feeling up to it. There were ambulances and police when Tom and Liz arrived. Nancy had previously been contacted when the police found her number in the apartment. They were expecting Nancy and weren't letting Liz into the building. When Tom saw the delay, he parked the car and joined Liz out front. Apparently, Tom made a ruckus and when the officer found out the apartment under investigation belonged to their parents, they were both escorted upstairs to identify them."

Sally had tears running down her cheeks again but continued, "Liz said it was like something from a gangster movie. The door was broken down and the walls were all shot full of holes. There were fi- five covered bodies... and th- and they uncov- it was Ma- it was Mom and Da-"

She was choking on the words and Cleve wrapped his arms around her again as she sobbed against his chest for a while longer. When she had regained her composure again, Sally glanced at him with a long face, then looked to the ground and braced herself to finish.

"Nancy was on the road when she got word on her cell and then she told William. Being an attorney, Nancy has been helping Mom and Dad with financial and legal affairs for years; she would be the one to deal with the authorities. William has always filled in when she was too busy and probably didn't want her going it alone. I was coming here after work and Liz said I should go ahead because somebody needed to."

Sally looked at him with that hurt puppy expression, "That's really all I know, Cleveland."

"Sally, this is really sad news," Cleve began, "You must be proud of your mom and dad for all of their accomplishments. They raised a fine family and were surely a good influence on their grandchildren from all five of your families-"

"Four- four families," Sally corrected. "You knew George Jr. never married, and I have no kids either."

"Sorry, I didn't know-"

"What's to be sorry about? You don't have any kids either," Sally noted.

("So she has kept track of me…")

"I never remarried and nobody even knows how to get in touch with Junior on short notice. He's probably off on a safari somewhere."

"A surfin' safari?"

Sally smiled, "Whatever…"

"Back to your folks: they were the proud epitome of American liberty to the very end. They may be here right now if they had rolled over; but I cannot imagine a Mason living under the lash of political masters. And, they didn't go out with a whimper; they took more than their share with them as an example. I am proud to have known George and Mary as friends of the Henry family."

In silence they shared another semi-intimate hugging. Then Cleve gave her a peck on the cheek and a quarter-smile. He held her at arms length and thought that her expression seemed to say she had been shortchanged.

("Oh no, don't be getting any ideas. There's a war comin'. No time for hanky-panky. Just let it go…")

Cleve started to walk away then stopped and explained tonight's "mission" for the town hall meeting to Sally.

"If you could pass the word, it might be something to clear your mind when conversation gets too, uh… heavy."

Cleve moved off into the crowd and confabulated his way back to the hors d'oeuvres table.

George Washington and Gerry had made more early progress with the mission than Cleve had. Word had gone around to where most of the company was already familiar with the subject when approached. Those who had listened in on the meeting at Gino's had all arrived at some point. Gerry was instructing his son that all who attended that meeting should be informed that he and Cleve were not going to be "blown up".

"Pat, you know your uncle. Sure, he gets carried away sometimes, but if the blueprints don't add up: he'll trash them and make a new plan. So, what did you think of those Frenchmen?"

"I think they were on the level. They didn't want to be actors in Uncle Cleve's movie score anyway," answered Pat.

Gerry gave a nod over Pat's shoulder as Joe Martin Jr. strode up to the two men.

"Everything under control, Joe?" asked Pat.

"Yeah. Dad's going back on the prowl after he caches some captured tech."

"From the overlook?"

"Yeah."

Gerry stood back and watched the two kick it around as he considered what fine young men they had grown into.

Joey continued: "Billy should be here anytime; he's dropping off some packages at Gramma's. Dad said we could stop in while he holds down the fort. He was… saddened to miss the funeral."

Gerry spoke up: "We were thankful that he didn't insist on attending. Grover was like a big brother to him as well."

"You will never know how well I understand that now."

Gerry nodded over Pat's shoulder again and they all watched as Billy Martin limped up to the group.

Joey started in: "Hey little bro. Didn't keep your butt down in a firefight?"

"Back off, *Little* Joe. What's that tape on the side of your skull? Didn't keep your *head* down in a firefight?"

Joey couldn't resist a little more ribbing: "If you want us to start calling you Rooster, or The Duke, we can get you an eye patch to go with that limp."

"Or *you* can wear the patch on the side of your head."

Their ribbings were always good-natured and the Henrys were just looking on waiting for them to finish. Gerry and Pat knew the two were as close as brothers get, though they were both extremely competitive. Gerry always got a kick out of watching them carry on so; it reminded him of his own relationship with Cleve.

Billy was finishing up: "Or you can kiss my ass-"

Joey cut him off: "Hey Bill, take it easy. You did an incredible job at the bell tower. I don't know if I could have pulled that one off with the guy already dug in like that. You did good walking away with not much but a bruise. I got to ya though, so it must have bruised your pride more than your butt anyway."

"Yeah, OK. Thanks Joey. You did good too. Except for getting Dad so pissed off."

"What'd you do Little Joe?" Gerry queried, knowing it had to be one of Joey's pranks.

"It was nothin'," said Joey with a flush, "Tell ya over a beer sometime."

Cleve had stopped to give Momma a hug and explain that they were spreading the plan for the town hall meeting. The word had gotten around pretty well as she had already had several people mention it to her. She thought it was a good idea and was comforted to see the community pulling together when times were hard. Cleve would never say it, but thought Momma looked ten years older tonight. He knew it was the emotional stress of the day that had worn her down more than hard work ever could. He made a mental note to be always mindful of the importance of spiritual health to the maintenance of physical health.

The company had thinned and Martha was getting close to turning lights out as a hint to the holdouts. When the last group remaining included George, she closed the doors, said goodnight and retired to the master bedroom.

Cleve, Gerry, Ben, Judge Adams, John, Ethan, Egbert, Pat and Joey accompanied George as he led them to a large semi-round table in his study. The legs were finely carved African mahogany and the tabletop was a slice from a giant Sequoia redwood. The dark outer bark and every growth ring to the very heart of the tree were clearly visible through a quarter inch of glass polished urethane. The men spread out and sat down around the table.

"We're like Knights of the Round Table now George."

"I wish," George responded. "More like old men that wish we still had your legs, Patrick."

"Heyayy…" growled Cleve, "I resemble that remark."

"So, what are we here for George?" asked Judge Adams.

"You're here to look at my table Samuel," answered George. "And to have a shot of Grand Marnier with me."

As George circled the table, pouring shots, he explained how he had brought the huge redwood disc into the room in three pieces that had separated along natural shrinkage cracks. After mounting the pieces to a sub-structure of aluminum I-beams, he had leveled and polished the wood surface by hand, working each and every end fiber of the grain until he had brought out the finest detail of the ring structure. For Martha the worst part was keeping the room sealed when George brought contractors in to pour, vacuum and cure the polyurethane; then polish the surface to it's glass-like finish. The mahogany legs were a story for another day.

"I'll drink to that," declared Egbert with a chuckle. "It is an awesome table George. Od like ta steeal that one."

"I bet you would. You'd have to cut it up to get it out of the room though."

"I could put a piece of it in the corner of four different rooms and it would still be an awesome set."

George had just poured a shot into Egbert's glass; he knocked it back and continued as George poured another.

"Seriously though George, anyone ever ruins this table: you round up a posse and we'll hang the heathens."

"OK Egg. Can you hold onto that one for a toast?"

"Sure George, sure."

When George had finished pouring shots, he held his up and watched as they all raised a glass.

"To the honored dead: that their memory will live on."

After a moment of silence, John Hancock spoke first: "George, this was a wonderful thing you did here tonight, leaving the invitation open. We didn't have the whole town here, but it was a heck of a start. And Sam, you can go ahead and pick a date for the town hall meeting. I don't think you'll have any problem getting your militia organized. I talked to folks who couldn't wait for the meeting: they wanted to know where to sign up right now."

Ethan agreed: "I myself experienced commensurate enthusiasm, though not always accompanied by the hardware to match such exuberance. One gentleman, I know for a fact, owns no more than the twenty-two squirrel-rifle he inherited from his father; yet he was ready and willing to go to war on a moments notice."

"History has shown that Providence favors our great nation in time of need as goodly men will gravitate to the right," declared Judge Adams. "We now have allies from France; indeed, the two Frenchmen are only a start. But their value is the symbol they represent: that good men, duped by evil in high places, cannot and will not remain loyal to such evil."

George followed with his own proclamation: "Our greatest allies, as we have all found here tonight, have been amongst us all along. Our neighbors, who will raise whatever weapon comes to hand, are our ultimate allies in the fight to preserve the liberty that made this Republic great."

Ben finished with another snippet of wisdom: "These proud Americans will provide aid where aid is needed, for they know that to help your neighbor is to help yourself, and **God helps those who help themselves.**"[1]

12. Back Home

"Wednesday."

"What?"

"Wednesday," repeated Gerry, "nineteen hundred; town hall meeting."

"K."

Cleve finished hosing the mud off a dirt bike leaned up against a quad, then moved on to hosing the quad.

"Had to take her through the mud holes in the bottoms... straight away... didn't you?"

"Not straight away," Cleve contested, "we took quite a tour first."

"Ann almost sent her back out to be hosed off before she let her take a shower."

"She just looked too prim and proper atop that 4-wheeler; like a homecoming queen on a float. I just wanted to make sure she still looked good covered with mud."

"And did she?"

"Yeah... Damn right she did. Actually, she was just laughin' and having a helluva good time."

"Well, that's good. You got her mind off her folks anyway," Gerry surmised. "She *was* a homecoming queen you know."

"Really?"

"You didn't know that? Well, she was a few classes under me and I guess she had graduated by the time you courted her-"

"I didn't *court* her; I only took her on a date."

"Yeah, that's what you said about the rest of them. Then once they got serious: you'd be tearing another heart out."

Cleve repudiated the allegation: "I never broke any of those hearts. Well, maybe a couple. But mostly I never said *I love you*; so if they got broken hearts: it wasn't my fault; they cashed 'em in themselves. Hey, I explained this to Ann a few years back and I got absolution from her."

"Absolution my ass; you might fool Ann, but you can't fool yourself and you sure as hell can't fool me. I don't know if it was the poets or the playwrights that created the ideology that you must *say: I love you* -to make it true. Perhaps a demented interpretation of the same ideology created the culture of saps who believe that if they *hear: I love you* -then it must be true. You know as well as I do that *actions speak louder than words*, but you think when a girl falls in love with you: you can use one of societies silly little ideologies as a *Get Out of Love Free* card."

"I don't make the rules; I just play by 'em. There were only two and a half times in my life that I told a woman I loved her," Cleve calculated.

"You just play by them; so it is just a game to you... Two and a *half*? What the hell is that?"

"The first time I was just a kid and that little girl more or less required it. The second girl... I think I loved her. Then the half... she wanted *something*- so I gave her something like: *I could say I love you, but it would just be rubbish 'cause I won't be doing anything about it, and I'll be leavin' the country soon anyway...* -So that's sorta like half; I mean it was half-ass anyhow."

"You're unbelievable..." Gerry furrowed his brow, "Anyway, back to Sally: Ann says she kinda likes you and we don't want you taking advantage while she's vulnerable-"

"Where is this coming from? You're the one brought her out here."

"Well, Ann did... I mean... why the hell didn't you? Ann just mentioned it as an afterthought; we figured you had already invited her. We wouldn't have let *any* of the Masons stay in a motel, having just lost their folks like that."

"I didn't want her to think I was hittin' on her."

"It's just common courtesy with old friends," replied Gerry. "And you didn't have any qualms about showing her around on the dirt bikes-"

"4-wheeler, she wouldn't ride a bike."

"Same thing, she went dirt riding."

"Not the same thing. A real ma- a real wom- a good- dammit, people oughta ride bikes. Those 4-elers are for farmers."

"We huh-are farmers," laughed Gerry.

"Well, real farmers only use the 4-elers for work. They're just fat tire go-karts for when you're not haulin' a load big enough for a tractor."

"Still keeping a specification list for your perfect woman, huh? I suppose she has to be a snowboarder too."

"No," Cleve countered, "She could ski with Ann if she can't stay up with us. Anyway, you and Pat are skiers, but me and Angie still ride with you, even though you can't stay up in the trees or half foot plus pow."

Gerry ignored the challenge and noted: "So, you've loosened your tolerances in your old age. I don't suppose a girl has to be a scuba diver anymore either. I wonder what ever happened to that one you cut loose because she had an ear-pressure problem; and then it turned out you never had time for a diving trip since. I did notice you're already making snowriding plans for Sally though."

"Knock it off Gerry. You two brought her out here. We've got a war coming; I don't have time for this anyhow."

"That's what we were worried about; because you've never had time… and the hearts kept stacking up. Sally may be a middle-aged woman; that doesn't mean she's not a sweet girl. Just take this as a friendly suggestion from my wife and I: wait until her folks are in the ground a few weeks before you take the Fifth and then *accidently* tear her heart out."

"What makes you think she won't break *my* heart?"

"I hope she does, Cleve. I hope she does."

Tuesday evening Sally spoke with most of her siblings. Visitation for George and Mary Mason was slated for Thursday evening; the funeral would be Friday morning. They had considered burying them at the tiny family plot on the old homestead, but decided not to bring them home. George had served with the U.S. Navy in the Pacific Theater during Word War II; as a veteran of the Solomon Islands campaign, he was a decorated PT boat Commander. The family had agreed that the couple should be laid to rest in a national cemetery.

After Sally had related some of the goings-on in their old hometown, her brothers Will and Tom decided to get out of the big city on Wednesday and sit in on the local town hall meeting. Nancy and Liz would take care of any of the incomplete details for the upcoming funeral. George Mason Jr. was the only one of the six siblings who maintained a local residence, but he was a free-spirited adventurer who was rarely home and he was still incommunicado.

That evening while Gerry was at the computer in the den, a phone in a backpack on the living room floor started ringing. He could see his brother on the stream bank through the great room window. Cleve was putting arrows in a target with the Hoyt bow he had inherited from Grover and Sally was seated in a lawn chair behind him watching the sunset over the lake with a phone to her ear. Gerry slid down the pole to dig through the pack and pulled out the phone he felt vibrating. The disposable cell phone had a strip of tape on it labeled: GL&PC.

"Hello."

"Is this Cleveland?"

"This is his brother."

"Gerry."

"Only one he's got left."

"Yes, he put the number in this phone and you do sound a little like him. I am Gil Lafayette. Is Cleve available?"

"He's outside, so you can talk to me."

"Very good, OK. The attack on your home that Cleve wants us to arrange: we could not arrange it. The bosses at Executive Operations have transferred my partner and I to work another district. We were in meetings all day; we were briefed and debriefed on recent operations. By the end of the day it was determined that no more resources should be wasted on the Henry brothers. The conclusion was that since the Internet is trying to make a folk-hero of Grover Henry: fueling the fire with more martyrs would be a mistake. Also, it will be more cost effective to take the easy targets first. Pierre and I may have nothing more for you with our new assignment, but I will keep this phone, or maybe just the sim card."

"First of all," Gerry began, "Cleve's Leatherwood attack-scam fell through on our end as well. So, we're all good on that count. The rest sounds like good news for us. Just stash that sim chip somewhere and contact us when the roof comes down on you. They will nail you eventually; every innocent life you are inclined to save takes you closer to being busted at- what did you call them -Executive Ops?"

"Yes, and some of them call it the ATF-EO Branch because they work out of the BATFE offices and use some of their equipment. And what you say is correct, for we will not last long in the lion's den. We were only lucky to stumble into alibis on the last two ops and that luck will not last. Thankfully, your men cleaned the slate for us yesterday and prior to that, one of their *easy targets* turned out to be: not so easy."

"That will happen more often than you think," Gerry advised. "We have friends whose elderly parents were just hit by a team that lost three men before taking them down."

"May I ask what was their name?"

"Maybe not. Why?"

"Was it, perhaps: Mason?"

The line was silence for several seconds before Gerry conceded: "It was."

"Mr. and Mrs. Mason were the turning point for me," Gil confessed. "At worst we could have starved them out, but the Executive Ops CO attacked without mercy. My partner and I were sniper backup, and I was ordered to shoot the woman in the back-while she defended her husband. These EO Branch agents have no honor. Watching that old couple defend their home made it clear that it was they who fought for the righteous. Pierre had already made up *his* mind and I do believe that if he had thought I would take that shot: he would have pistol-whipped me and gone his own way alone."

"Well, I'd like to hear more about the Masons, but you've probably been on this phone long enough already. I hope one day you'll get the chance to tell their children what you know," Gerry added.

"Our alibi was that our view was cut off and we missed the firefight. In confidence, tell the family: they should be very proud, for their parents acquitted themselves well."

"I'm glad we had this little talk, because now I better understand why Cleve trusts you."

"It is good to hear that he does," replied Gil. "He impressed me as an honorable man as well."

"Good luck and be careful."

"Au revoir."

Wednesday morning dawn found Sally and Cleve in the south pasture shooting at targets on the east slope. With Cleve's guidance, Sally was perfecting her form and working on accuracy with stock iron sights on a Ruger 10-22 rifle. Cleve had another 10-22 with peep sights leaned against the old tree they were standing under. They would follow up with some handgun practice next; each had a 22-45 Ruger in a holster on the right thigh and Cleve had a Model 59 Smith & Wesson tucked away on his left hip.

Sally wore a loose white linen blouse with the unbuttoned front tails crossed over and tied in a square knot at the small of her back. Her slacks were khaki Wrangler Riggs that seemed to flow from her thin waist over and around her voluptuous hips with a fit expected in Lycra tights. Even the crude cargo pockets had a utilitarian charm; explicitly where her leather holster fit perfectly to the modified garment.

Cleve was considering whether he found the woman more alluring in this rough field attire or the dress she had arrived in. He stood eying her from behind; his thought was that she didn't find trousers at Leatherwood that just happened to enhance her figure to near irresistible. He knew she hadn't bought Riggs off the shelf that fit her figure like that, but wondered why she would pack field garments for a day trip to the Washington estate.

("I don't think Wrangler ever made a woman's cut in their rip stop work wear. Wonder if Sally's the seamstress; she left the rough cut from the knee down, but fit them like a glove from the thigh on. Jordach never made 'em like *that*. Her holster snuggles right into that cargo pocket where it's been re-hemmed for fit. Hot-damn, that Ruger never had it so good; a perfect draw over the arc of her hip… And look at those delectable cheeks: like perfect tear drops… Wait a minute- *those are my pants* -there's that little frayed spot. This is Momma's doings: all those little darts for the perfect fit; I shoulda spotted it right off. Momma could have whipped up clothes from scratch if she wanted to. That's my shirt too; gutted it right down the back so she could tie knots in it. No respect. Then again, that shirt never looked so good.")

Sally had pretty well shot up the first paper target and was ready to move on to the next.

"You're a quick study," commended Cleve, "but then you weren't a greenhorn either."

"Like I said: Mom taught my sisters and I to shoot when we were kids," Sally smiled at the memory, "I thought Mom was like Annie Oakley shooting pests in the barn…"

Sally's expression faded to melancholy for a couple minutes as she watched the sun's rays dancing off the yellow-orange base of the broken cloud cover. It would be another half an hour before the first rays broke over the eastern ridgeline to flood into the dell at Leatherwood. Cleve fully shared her moment as he reminisced on a morning long ago, in the company of his late brother and father.

"Elizabeth always had more tomboy in her than me or Nancy," Sally continued, "and probably shot more birds than Mom did. So, when they moved to the city, Mom gave Liz her little rifle. After they moved away I never visited the old homestead again. Never bought a gun and never did any more plinking."

"Here, see how you like this peep sight," suggested Cleve, handing her the other 10-22.

After Sally had had enough of the rifles, they both put in a good plinking session with the 22-45 Rugers. When they had about used up the .22 ammo, Cleve handed her the Model 59.

"Why don't you go ahead and ring off a few rounds with this nine-millimeter Smith. It's got a little more kick than the twenty-twos, but I think you'll like it."

Sally took her time and after half a dozen shots she was tightening up her group. She stopped at ten rounds and started to hand the gun back to Cleve.

"No: you've got four more rounds, go ahead and empty it. The slide will lock back when you're done."

Sally finished up and then released the magazine. She scrutinized the mags as Cleve swapped her for a full one.

"Fourteen shots; I like that," declared Sally as she clicked the magazine in place.

"Fifteen if you want to start with one in the chamber, but no need for that. Just release the slide and you're good to go."

When she had fired another ten rounds, Cleve told her to leave him a few for the road and returned the tool to its holster.

"We'll head on back and catch breakfast."

After collecting the remains of their paper targets, they walked north along the east tree line. As they approached the lone Quonset hut on the southeast corner of the drive, Sally commented about the artificial trees and shrubberies protruding from the metal structure.

"I noticed all the buildings north of the house have paintings of trees and shrubs all over them, while this one has actual three-dimensional camouflage attached to the arches."

"Well, we try to blend the paintings and the 3-D camo to the live pine trees that are right up against the buildings. From the air the structures look like groves of pine. This one gets special treatment because there's no holography coverage down here to enhance the visual screening. The holographic projectors are most effective in the mist downwind of the fountains; it softens the visual contrast by adding a 3-D edge to the camo paintings."

As they approached the manor grounds, Sally wandered into an unobtrusive clearing in the east wood. She stepped over an irregular rock border onto a carpet of moss surrounding a shallow pool in the small lenticular glade. The elliptical pool appeared to originate at a fabricated grotto of granite block and shrubberies at the southeastern tip of the little clear-cut strip.

"I wouldn't loiter there too long," Cleve warned. "That granite ring you just stepped over is a sort of boundary marker for where you'll get soaked if that fountain kicks on."

"Fountain? I assumed the basin in the grotto was a natural spring feeding the pool."

"No, there's a huge nozzle in that sink and each time it comes on: a load of water gets thrown into the pool as it clears the backfill. In fact, a few years back, it threw young Patrick into the pool from his seat on the lip of the basin."

"Where does the water go?" asked Sally as she stepped from the ring.

"Up on the bluff, where it runs back into the reservoir. This fountain only kicks in when the wind is out of the east; which is rare. The wind direction detectors are not supposed to be sensitive to occasional back gusts and such, but it will surprise you on occasion."

"Leatherwood must stay green and lush all summer long; the air is like just after a spring shower."

"Yeah… but the ice buildup can be a problem in the winter; beautiful –but problematic. And that's a whole 'nother story."

Sally and Cleve circled the manor to find Ann and Sarah seated at the patio table, where they had about finished their breakfast. Cleve noted Sarah eyeing her outfit with a smile as Sally leaned across the round table to snag a slice of coffee cake with a fork. She dropped back into the chair next to Sarah and nibbled a piece of her prize while Cleve sat down across from the two.

"Would any-" Ann started, then answered the ring of her phone: "Yes… mhmm… they're right here. Of course, mhmm… the ants are gone? Good… OK… absolutely." [Click]

"Gerry?" asked Cleve.

"Yes. He was checking the orchards and saw you two headed north. He's on his way in. There's fruit in the covered bowl and donuts under that linen," added Ann as she stood, "I'm going to fry Gerry some bacon and eggs. Would you like anything warm?"

Cleve's face lit up, to which Ann responded: "I know what you want. -Sally?"

"Two eggs, scrambled would be nice, thank you."

Ann headed off to the kitchen and Cleve sat quietly regarding the two across the table.

"You think I didn't recognize your handiwork Momma? You just go ahead and chop up anything you find in that dryer; there's always more where that came from."

"Spare me; as if you don't have enough of those khakis. That's about all you wear."

"No, I've got green ones and black and brown-"

"All the same Wranglers."

"Yeah."

"When Sally said you were taking her shooting today and she needed trousers tough enough to follow you into the bush; finding a pair wasn't hard."

"We were just shooting targets in the pasture."

"After taking her riding through the bottoms yesterday: she figured you would drag her through the briars today, so Mother Nature could rip her pants off for you."

"Momma- you're embarrassing the girl," Cleve scolded, but noticed out the corner of his eye that Sally was actually smiling.

"How clumsy of me: I meant to embarrass *you*," Sarah returned, as she took her coffee and empty plate with her into the house.

Cleve gazed at Sally a moment and with a sly smile admitted: "You do look damn good in those Riggs."

"Oh, I know I do," she confirmed with a grin.

They shared a good laugh as Gerry ambled up and rinsed his hands over a garden fountain nymph.

"What's so funny?" asked Gerry.

Cleve waved his hand to the side- "How are the orchards looking?"

"Look good; I don't think we'll have an insect problem this year."

After some more small talk and breakfast: Gerry suggested they spend the afternoon with a phone book, calling anyone who may not have been informed of the upcoming town hall meeting. Everyone had previously agreed that though a TV announcement would be more efficient than word of mouth, it might draw unwanted visitors to town.

When Gerry had wandered away to check on the animals, Sally looked Cleve in the eye and asked: "Do you know why I wanted to go shooting?"

Cleve gave her a vacant look and waited.

"I want to buy a gun," declared Sally. "I will not willingly watch as someone stomps through my home looking for anything... everything... nothing... I have a small house in the city and I have no neighbors who would- who could -help me...

"When I was young and Daddy would get on a preaching binge about what made the Republic great, his soliloquy would build to a crescendo, and he would conclude with his favorite line: ***If I can only... _leave to my children but a Crust of Bread, & Liberty, I shall die satisfied...***[8] And Mother: I don't remember the occasion- and they weren't team preachers you understand -but I can't ignore the echo of her voice proclaiming: *Americans will not be raped of our liberty.*

"Mom and Dad... they were always such an adorable couple. They had pet names: *hey Ma, yes Pa-*" Sally choked a little at the thought, then stiffened and declared: "I am my Ma and Pa's daughter and I will not be raped in my own home."

Sally dried her eyes on a napkin and looked to Cleve; a final tear dripped from her eye and ran down her left cheek. Cleve's eyes were pinkish, but he was thinking, making plans and doing his best to keep his own eyes from... sweating.

"It will be hard for you to buy a gun without getting in trouble... now that all the legitimate commercial shops have closed their doors," Cleve began slowly; then laid his Model 59 on the table and pushed it to Sally. "Listen, you handled this nine-millimeter very well; you can bor- you can keep it: it's yours. I'll get you a box of ammo and you can take it with you or leave it here: either way, it is yours."

"I can't take your gun Cleveland."

"Sure you can. I only brought that one along to see how well it fit you. In fact, we'll find you a smaller one for backup too, if you'd like."

"Oh, this one is fine. It felt lighter than the twenty-two actually," replied Sally.

"Well, the Smith's an aluminum frame and that 22-45 has a bull barrel. The Ruger is supposed to feel like a forty-five without the kick. Anyway, it's always nice to have something small to tuck away somewhere. You can't hide anything with an outfit like that though, except in your boot."

"They're Ann's boots."

"Whatever…" Cleve gazed off toward the lake for a minute and then continued: "Why don't you sell your place in the city and move back home?"

"I've got a job."

"You ought to be able to last awhile 'til you find something around here. You could fix up the old house on your family farm."

"No: no one kept that old shack up. It's probably nothing but a leaky rattrap by now."

"OK, tear it down and build something new. There are carpenters around here could use the work-"

("And here it comes,") thought Sally.

"-and you could stay here while it was being built," finished Cleve.

("You do want to keep me around, don't you Cleveland.)

"And would you keep harassing me for stealing your clothes?" Sally chided.

"Hah… I don't care about that. I was just harassing Momma for conspiring," replied Cleve, and as he leaned back to sip his coffee went on thinking: ("Conspiring with Ann anyways; everybody loves playing Cupid. Ann thinks she can use child psychology: warning me off and painting Sally as the soft and innocent girl. Then Momma suits her up in a tough, but sexy outfit. They've both heard what I like in a woman and they're trying to bring out that perfect balance of softness and grit in this one. Ya gotta love 'em for it though; only a child or a fool challenges a setup when it's a good setup.")

"Cleveland?"

Cleve was gazing at the waves dancing on the lake when he snapped out of his daydream.

"Yeah?"

"Maybe we could take a look at those other guns now."

"Right. Absolutely. An innocent little thing like you needs all the protection she can get."

"An innocent little thing like me? *I don't know where you get your information bullet-brain.*"

"Heh-heh-heh, come along Princess Leia," chuckled Cleve as he led her away.

13. Town Hall Meeting

"Can we bring this meeting to order?" Judge Samuel Adams called out, then flipped the switch for the microphone and beat on it with his gavel: *Whoump-whoump-whoump.*

"Ahwooooooo…"

"Knock it off Paul- you hooligan," Judge Adams continued, "First order of business is the statements each of you should have dropped into one of these three boxes. The first box was for those of you who want to go it alone and don't want any backup or interference whatsoever. Now anyone who is not present and did not send a statement along with one of you, will be considered to be in that category: unless they personally contact Sheriff Jefferson or myself at a later date. If anyone changes their mind during this meeting: write an overriding statement, label it as such with the date and time, put it in one of these yellow envelopes and drop it in the same box as your original statement. Is that clear?"

"AYE."

"Very good," Judge Adams went on, "The second box was for those of you who will welcome assistance and will hold none of the local militia responsible if things should go awry. I want you to take a good look at the twenty men lined up behind us. One of them will be contacting you in regards to the configuration of your home and your personal requests and/or expectations during a potential incursion. Is that clear?"

"AYE."

"Good. Finally, the third box: those of you who welcome assistance and will join the militia. One of these twenty coordinators will be around to see what you have to offer and to organize five-man teams with whom you will practice. Hopefully, most of you will provide your own firearms, but we will find weapons for those who cannot. There is also plenty of room in the militia for those who wish to help without firing a shot. Is that clear?"

"AYE."

"OK," Judge Adams finished, "If there are no questions for me. I'll pass the mic to Sheriff Jefferson."

The town hall meeting was taking place in the school gymnasium to keep the gathering off the books. Judge Adams and Sheriff Jefferson had chairs behind a small portable podium with their twenty coordinators behind them. The townsfolk were seated in rows of folding chairs and the bleachers along the walls. Aisles remained clear at the base of the bleachers, but groups were standing by the entrance doors and were backed up into the hallways. The PA system was piped to the entire school, so some folks had sat down in classrooms as well.

The sheriff took the podium and spent some time going through the logistics of organizing the teams, when and where they would train, etc.

"The plan is to be prepared for the defense of your homes against a professional assault; whether it be a five-man team or a twenty-five-man task force," Sheriff Jefferson concluded, then stepped down to his chair.

From his seat in the front row, Ethan Allen immediately appeared alongside the podium to take up the microphone and proclaim: "Give me four scrupulously equipped men and I'll bring down three Apache helicopters."

A man in bib overalls and a straw hat hollered: "Wise up Ethan, you couldn't bring down one Black Hawk with your pea-shooters."

"Surely you fathom that you would be obliged to arm my men with *pea-shooters* of exceptional firepower."

"Ahwooooooo…"

"SHADDUP PAUL," shouted the man with the straw hat.

Brrrump-brrrump-brrrump… A row of men started stomping their feet on the bleachers.

Judge Adams leaned forward in his chair and rapped his gavel against the microphone stand, *Whoump*, then took the floor from Ethan: "ORDER! -We don't want you boys having too much fun tonight; the gymnasium was to keep things informal, but I did not foresee this teenage reversion. We still have plenty of folks who would like to speak in a serious mode."

The Judge waited for the crowd to quiet, then announced: "Mr. Lee, you have the floor."

Richard Lee took the microphone and addressed the crowd: "It is high time we mobilized a local militia and I would like to take this opportunity to thank each and every one of you noble souls who dropped a card in that third box. *A militia, when properly formed, are in fact the people themselves... -whereas, to preserve liberty, it is essential that the whole body of the people always possess arms, and be taught alike, especially when young, how to use them...*[12] Looking over this gathering, I am so proud to live in a community of countless young men and women whom I know to have been raised thus."

"RICH-ARD"-*brrrump*-"RICH-ARD"-*brrrump*-"RICH-ARD"-*brrrump*... the bleacher row cheered- followed by a stomp.

"ORDER! Mr. Coxe, you have the floor."

Tench Coxe stepped up to the podium: "As we have come to expect, Richard's words have the ring of truth."

"RICH-ARD"-*brrrump.*

"My friends and countrymen... -the powers of the sword are in the hands of the yeomanry of America from sixteen to sixty... -Congress have no right to disarm the militia. Their swords, and every other terrible implement of the soldier, are the birth-right of an American... -the unlimited power of the sword is not in the hands of either the federal or the state governments, but where I trust in God it will ever remain, in the hands of the people."[13]

"TENCH-TENCH-TENCH"-*brrrump-brrrump-brrrump*... cheered the row of bleacher stompers.

"ORDER! Mr. Webster, you have the floor."

Noah Webster approached the podium, pulled down the microphone and turned on the crowd: "The new socialist Administration has determined that to procure tyrannical rule over these United States: *the people must be disarmed; as they are in almost every kingdom of Europe. The supreme power in America cannot enforce unjust laws by the sword; because the whole body of the people are armed, and constitute a force superior to any bands of regular troops that can be, on any pretense, raised in the United States.*[14] GOD BLESS AMERICA."

"NO-AH"-*brrrump*-"NO-AH"-*brrrump*-"NO-AH"-*brrrump*...

"ORDER! Mr. Paine, the floor is yours."

Thomas Paine gave Noah the thumbs up as he took the microphone and began: "That's a big ten-four Noah-"

"NO-AH"-*brrrump.*

"The Second Amendment must never fall; present company and any sensible man will acknowledge these truths: *the peaceable part of mankind will be continually overrun by the vile and abandoned, while they neglect the means of self defence. The supposed quietude of a good man allures the ruffian; while on the other hand, arms like laws discourage and keep the invader and the plunderer in awe, and preserve order in the world as well as property. The balance of power is the scale of peace... -for while avarice and ambition have a place in the heart of man, the weak will become a prey to the strong. The history of every age and nation establishes these truths, and facts need but little arguments when they prove themselves.*"[15]

"THO-MAS"-*brrrump*-"THO-MAS"-*brrrump*-"THO-MAS"-*brrrump*...

"ORDER! Mr. Washington, you have the floor."

George Washington rose from the second row and waited for the room to go quiet. The big man's voice matched his stature and he addressed the audience from where he stood...

"A free people ought not only to be armed but disciplined; to which end a uniform and well digested plan is requisite:[16] Aye, a local militia is long overdue.

"The time is now near at hand which must probably determine whether Americans are to be freemen or slaves; whether they are to have any property they can call their own; whether their houses and farms are to be pillaged and destroyed, and themselves consigned to a state of wretchedness from which no human efforts will deliver them...[17]

"Lo: our Republic is besieged by *the extreme of Tyranny; and that arbitrary power is most easily established on the ruins of Liberty abused to licentiousness.*"[18]

"LIBERTY!"

"GEORGE"-*brrrump*-

George held his hand overhead and continued: "*The basis of our political systems is the right of the people to make and to alter their Constitutions of Government. __ But the Constitution which at any time exists, 'till changed by an explicit and authentic act of the whole people, is sacredly obligatory upon all.*[VI] My friends: that sacred obligation has been forsaken by the socialist regime that defiles the once venerable halls of the White House. Nonetheless, *We the People* have not- *will not* - abrogate our Constitution or any of the Rights that we hold dear. SO BE IT."

"GEORGE"-*brrrump*-"GEORGE"-*brrrump*-"GEORGE"-*brrrump*…

"ORDER! Is there anyone else?"

Noting Gerry debating with his son as to who would speak for the Henrys, Judge Adams raised his hand: "I have the floor. Thank you Mr. Washington-"

"GEORGE-GEORGE"-*brrrump-brrrump.*

He raised his hand to silence again: "Most of my life I have trusted in Providence that **the said Constitution be never construed to authorize Congress to infringe the just liberty of the press, or the rights of conscience; or to prevent the people of the United States, who are peaceable citizens, from keeping their own arms… -or to subject the people to unreasonable searches and seizures of their persons, papers or possessions.**[19] Yet we are witness to these God given rights being trampled before our very eyes. The time is nigh that the just shall remind the wicked that we do- and always will -hold all the laws of nature to be self-evident."

The Judge had worked himself into a frenzy and clenched his fists overhead as if he held God's Commandments in stone; with eyes wide and blazing his voice built to a crescendo: "*In God We Trust*; the laws of the Republic shall RULE… and this Administration shall *LIVE BY THE RULES OR DIE BY THE RULES.*"

"AHWOOOOOOO…"

"SAM-UEL"-*brrrump*-"SAM-UEL"-*brrrump*-"SAM-UEL"-*brrrump…*

"YEEAAAAAAAH…"

"Alright… ORDER! Mr. Henry, the floor is yours."

Patrick Henry stepped up to the podium and banged the microphone: *Whoump-whoump-* "Thank you Judge Adams."

"SAM-UEL"-*brrrump-brrrump.*

"They tell us, sir, that we are weak- unable to cope with so formidable an adversary. But when shall we be stronger? Will it be the next week, or the next year? Will it be when we are totally disarmed; and when a… United Nations **-guard shall be stationed in every house? Shall we**

gather strength by irresolution and inaction? Shall we acquire the means of effectual resistance by lying supinely on our backs, hugging the delusive phantom of hope until our enemies shall have bound us, hand and foot? Sir, we are not weak, if we make a proper use of those means which the God of nature hath placed in our power... -The battle, sir, is not to the strong alone; it is to the vigilant, the active, the brave... -If we were base enough to desire it, it is now too late to retire from the contest. There is no retreat, but in submission and slavery. Our chains are forged. Their clanking may be heard on the plains... -The war is inevitable- and let it come! I repeat it, sir; let it come... -What is it that gentlemen wish? What would they have? Is life so dear, or peace so sweet, as to be purchased at the price of chains and slavery? Forbid it, Almighty God! I know not what course others may take; but as for me..."

Pat had pulled the wireless microphone from its stand and gripping the mic in his fist, he raised the stainless-steel shaft horizontal overhead as he circled to the front of the podium. Raising his left hand to the microphone, Pat rotated the shaft to vertical as he lowered his hands to waist level. With both fists firmly gripping the mic as if it were the hilt of a sword, the proud young man's demeanor and arms of sculpted sinew made it clear that he would fill the shoes of the Henrys before him. Patrick stood firm and shouted: **"-Give me Liberty, or give me Death!"**[2]

"AHWOOOOOOO..."

"PAT-RICK"-*brrrump*-"PAT-RICK"-*brrrump*-"PAT-RICK"-*brrrump*...

"YEEAAAAAAA..."

"PAT-RICK"-*brrrump-brrrump*-"PAT-RICK"-*brrrump-brrrump*-"ORDER! And thank you Mr. Henry."

Everyone was on their feet and joined the chant: "PAT-RICK-PAT-RICK-PAT-RICK..." while intermittently the bleacher stompers slipped in a: "PAT-PAT-PAT"-*brrrump-brrrump-brrrump*.

"*YEAH-YEAH-YEAH-YEAH-YEAAAAAAAH...*"

"ORDER! If we were having a rock and roll concert we would have invited Ted Nugent."

Someone had jacked into another PA outlet and strummed in with a base guitar: *doo-doo-doo-doo do-do*...

"*WEAAAAAAAAAAAaaohw…*"

"ORDER!" *Whoump-whoump-whoump.*

Pat was stepping down but turned and retrieved the microphone Judge Adams had just whacked with his gavel; the room went quiet: "Thank you everyone. Now let's keep it down. Sam's got a last few words."

"SAM-UEL-SAM-"

"HEYAAA…" Pat growled.

"Thanks Pat."

"PAT-ri…"

Judge Adams' face went stern; he held a hand overhead and continued: "I'm winding this rally down, but anyone who wants to stay on and try to get an interview with the coordinators is welcome. It will save them tracking you down later. I want to thank all of you for coming and God Bless."

Brrrump-brrrump.

After the town hall meeting (or community rally) the gymnasium thinned down to quarter capacity with various size groups staying on until after midnight. Sheriff Jefferson had reprimanded the rock and roller who hacked the PA system while Judge Adams spoke, then told him he and his partner could continue jamming until lock up, as long as they kept it instrumental only and at an acceptable volume. The sheriff figured the background noise might help keep people talking, deliberating and making plans.

Cleve, Gerry, Pat, Angela and Sally had just mustered a group with John Hancock, George and Ben, when Will and Tom Mason joined them.

"Good of you to come," said George.

"Glad we did; that was a most enlightening talk you gave, Mr. Washington," commended Will; and extending his hand to Pat he added: "and I want to shake this man's hand. You must be Gerry's son."

Sally cut in: "Most of you know my brothers: William and Thomson; and yes, this is Patrick and his sister Angela."

"So, you're Patrick's little sister," said Tom.

"Big sister," Angela corrected with mock indignation. "Pat's a year younger than me, but I'm still proud of *little* brother."

Pat just rolled his eyes. No sooner than greetings had been exchanged all around: George Mason Jr. approached the group.

Cleve was the first to pipe up: "Well, the prodigal son is home. Welcome back stranger."

"Wouldn't miss a rally like this; with young Patrick stirring the pot like his grampa used to? That's something to come home for," replied George as he scooped Sally into a hug.

"No question about it Pat, you were impressive," Cleve lauded. "And no one missed the significance of that flamboyant finale. Grover would thank you for the tribute."

The Mason's pulled away from the group for a while to bring George up to speed about their parents. When they rejoined the group, they listened in until there was a lull in the conversation.

"I think I'll try to get on a militia team with Ethan Allen," George Jr. interjected, "Whudda ya think Big George? I'll bet that guy's got one of your *well digested plans*."

"Little George, I would have to say that even you could learn a thing or two from Ethan," George Washington responded with a smile.

"So, you plan to make like you actually live here in town for a change?" John tipped his head back and looked down his nose in disbelief. "Who are you and what have you done with George Mason?"

"Now come on Johnny," protested George, "You know I wouldn't let you down at a time like this."

Ben was standing between the two, though he faced outward from most of the group as he spoke with Will; he turned and put his arm around the adventurer's shoulder: "Good to have you back George."

"Thanks Ben. Listen fellas, I just got in and the next few days is gonna be family time. We'll have time to talk when I come around to visit with each of you next week; right now, I need to have a word with Deadeye over there."

"And making plans for a week down the road... will wonders never cease?" John continued the ribbing.

"Johnny, he's just inviting himself over for some home cooking," Ben followed up.

"Ben likes to razz me too," Cleve cut in, "but then he'll just feed you some possum-innards and grits- Ha-ha... Just kiddin' Benjie. He doesn't eat like he used to, but ole Ben can run a bar-b-que with the best of 'em. Now when you visit Johnny: be sure Dorothy knows you're coming 'cause that girl can cook. She won't let you go till you've put a few pounds on either."

"You've got it all figured out, don't you Cleve?" Gerry interjected. "I guess priorities are different for a single man."

George Jr. was smiling and just shook his head as he strolled away. He approached Ethan, but slowed up and turned a full circle as he surveyed the crowd. He recognized a lot of the older folks and could guess what families some of the younger faces belonged with. Though he had returned home for short periods a few times a year, he rarely contacted anyone and, except for a few local gun club competitions, had not been to a social event in years. Though George returned with the profound sense of loss that came with the news of his parents, the familiar faces, friendly banter, and even the familiarity of the old school, put him at peace with his emotions.

George had always thought of his hometown as a sanctuary, isolated from the corruption of the wide world. Now: there are those who would cut their way into the heart of America to steal a traditional way of life and force their new world order on a free people, perhaps for no more than the sense of power they derive from their evil deeds. Yet here in the country: life goes on, and the community will do whatever is necessary to maintain their way of life. Despite the little changes, despite the years, the traditions that the people hold onto are what make a community... home.

("Home- yes, this is home -and home it must remain,") George was thinking as he noted Ethan's companion departing; he turned and thrust his hand into Ethan's: "You might not remember me Mr. Allen-"

Recognizing the strength in his grip and iron in his eyes, Ethan cut him short: "Surely you jest; between the meticulous consistency of Henry Knox and the lightening reflexes of George Mason Jr., I was never assured the trophy when one of you attended a match."

Neither of them had relaxed their grip as George responded: "Hmm, I never did out shoot you and I didn't think anyone took notice of anything but first place."

"You underestimate yourself my friend; you are an excellent shot, albeit your accuracy was sometimes tempered by your blinding speed of acquisition. Should you have competed regularly, I have no doubt you would have gone home with my trophy on occasion."

"Hmm..." the two men slowly relaxed their grips as George looked away and tried to find words for what he was thinking: "Henry... and Grover... I only just heard... along with word of Mom and Dad. Heartbreaking tales, all of them."

"Sheriff Jefferson claimed you were in Australia. You were incommunicado... in the Outback?"

"No. I did tell Tommy that's where I was headed, but I didn't come straight home from that job. I was on the Okavango Delta."

"Ahh... Travel envy; I should admit: I do listen in when I hear your name. Some folks say the difference in you and Grover Henry was that he told his stories and your life is steeped in mystery."

"Grover was older; I don't imagine he always had time for tales either," George suddenly got a serious look on his face, "Listen: I've got to move on and I wanted to ask if you would consider me for that elite team you were talking about. I can tell you exactly where to hit a Black Hawk to bring it down with one shot, and I'm not talking about a rocket launcher either. I don't know if these dorks will have access to Apaches, but we can figure out the best way to drop one of those as well."

Ethan was grinning from ear to ear: "You're on. Get going; you have got family to take care of. We shall confabulate on the topic later."

Before parting, the two weapon's masters clasp hands in a solid grip that gave both the sense that they had engaged a pact of honor. George headed for the door and home.

At midnight the groups were small and sparse. Judge Adams' coordinators were packing up and the background noise had gone home. Actually, the jam session was quite good for an hour or so. It was when the rock and rollers ran out of material that it devolved into a noise session.

"Shouldn't you have headed out a long time ago Sally?" asked Cleve. "You've got several hours of driving ahead of you."

"The three of us are going to stay with Junior tonight and leave in the morning," she answered. "He said he can make room for us, but that's why we let him go early: so he's got time to shuffle things around and try to make good on his claim."

"OK. We'll see you Friday morning. You be careful driving back."

Sally gave him a good hug and whispered in his ear: "Thanks Cleve. Thanks for everything."

She pulled away then leaned in and gave him a short kiss on the lips.

As the Masons headed for the door Cleve glanced at Gerry and gave him a cool shrug.

14. Gramma's House

Earlier Wednesday evening Gramma Martin was busy grilling up four juicy T-bone steaks and could hear the Irish wolfhound in the basement growling and whining. His whining sounded more like a bull-elk than a dog and he always carried on like that when she was cooking because he'd be getting some scraps after dinner. The woman had already taken the gravy, mashed potatoes and green beans to the basement; when the main course was done she carefully made her way down the stairs with a covered platter. She set the platter on a small circular table and glanced around the room.

"Rrrowww-ow…"

Gramma shook her finger at the big dog: "Now you just quiet down and eat your dog food Bruno. You'll get a little snack for dessert later on."

The little table was located near the center of the room. Extending north, northwest and northeast from the table were three black rubber conveyor belts. When Gramma had distributed steaks, potatoes and green beans on four plates, she laid a plate and drink on each belt. She seated herself at a white lace place setting with the fourth plate. Then she started punching the control buttons that ran the plates out to the three men sitting on classroom desks in heavy steel cages anchored to the north wall.

"If you need anything else boys: just holler," Gramma suggested in a congenial tone.

"Granny, when I get out of here I'm going to twist your arms off and feed them to Bruno here."

"Shut up Dean, the woman just served you a proper meal," snapped the soldier in the center man-cage.

"Just look at her smiling and sweat talking us; she's enjoying it and I'll be damned if she doesn't pay for this," growled Dean.

"Rrrrrrr…" the wolfhound's cage was alongside Dean's and he could sense the malice in the man's voice.

"I'm sorry it's so obvious," apologized Gramma, "but I am enjoying this. I don't usually get this much conversation. Mostly all I get is *rrr* from Bruno and an occasional *yap-yap* from Flossy."

Flossy was lying in the corner and her ears perked up at the sound of her name. She was half toy poodle, half Norfolk terrier and always seemed to be smiling when she looked at you.

"May I have some more steak sauce Gramma?" asked the youngest of the three.

"Of course you may Jimmy," she replied, sending the bottle on the conveyor to the far left cage. "Anyone else."

"I could use some salt," said the center man.

Dean just growled.

"I should have had the boys put you in the far west cell," Gramma chided, "I can't tell you from Bruno with all that growling."

"Yeah Dean, quit acting like an animal. Can't you see the old girl's just doing her job?"

"You idiot; she's got us locked up in dog cages."

"Oh, those are far heavier than dog cages; I had the welders come in and fabricate those cells out of the goodness of my heart," explained Gramma. "I thought we could have dinner together like a family. And I wanted you to be more comfortable when we bring the big screen down for your lessons on the United States Constitution-"

Dean cut her off: "Are you out of your mind?"

"Now young man," Gramma rebuked him, "I could have left you zip tied to that dog cage and be feeding you dog food with a spoon. We can't set you free until you've learned why it's not acceptable for you to shoot honest American citizens. For now, you just calm down and finish your dinner."

Dean knew how to throw a balanced blade but didn't think he could actually take her out with a dull table knife. He just wanted to crack her on the head to hear her yelp. He threw the knife with a quick snap of his wrist, but it toggled between the horizontal bars of the 2-inch square it passed through. Bouncing off the conveyor belt, the knife tumbled into Gramma's glass of milk, tipping it onto her mashed potatoes.

She stood up and reached behind a partition panel to retrieve a cattle prod with a tranquilizer needle on the tip. Stepping up to the cage she poked him in the forearm as he grabbed for the prod. Dean snatched the prod from her grip but had already been dosed. He tried to pull it all the way into the cage to turn it on her and found it was too long. He looked up as Gramma stepped behind the partition.

"DAMN YOU BITCH!"

Bruno was raising hell in the cage next to him, so he tried to shove the prod into the animal. The best he could do was to stick it into the northwest corner of the dog's cage where Bruno latched onto the shaft and tugged, wedging it in position. Dean struggled a while longer before he crumpled to the floor.

Gramma pulled the prod free after encouraging Bruno to let go. She reloaded the needle, poked Dean again to be sure he'd gotten a generous dose and then sat down to finish her dinner.

"This is a delicious steak Gramma," Jimmy complimented her cooking. "It's real lean beef."

"That's bison steak," she specified. "Some of your colleagues were responsible for a recent local surplus of bison meat."

"Oh, they're not really colleagues; I'm just a truck driver they contracted on account of they're short-hand-"

"Zip it mister," commanded the soldier in the center cage. "You don't have to be an asshole like Dean, but don't suck up to her either-ever hear the idiom: name, rank and serial number?"

"Now boys, we don't have to be so formal here," Gramma entreated. "As a point of fact, I don't even know your name Sir."

"My name is Mads," he replied. "We don't want to get too comfortable here: we want out. And yet you'd think the kid here was enjoying dinner at the family supper table with his own grandmother."

"Actually…" Jimmy began, "It's because our Gramma reminds me of my own Grandma back home."

"*Our Gramma*? Listen to yourself, you nut."

"Sorry… but you could lighten up Mads; it's not like she's a Gestapo interrogator."

"Tell us about your grandmother Jimmy," Gramma implored, then hesitated, "Give me a few minutes to start a pot of coffee."

Gramma hurried up the stairs and was back momentarily. She took a small cable hoist into Dean's cage, wrapped a sling under his arms, hooked up the hoist and hauled him off the floor. She stood the little desk up under him, lowered him to the seat, zip tied his ankles and wrists to the desk, removed the hoist, pulled the gate chain tight across the cage door and latched the chain at the end of a 3-foot extension bar that kept the padlock beyond the prisoner's reach.

In the far cage Jimmy was chuckling softly.

"Hey, don't encourage her," Mads whispered, though the humor was contagious and he couldn't keep from smiling.

Gramma hurried upstairs and came back down with the coffee pot and three cups. She let out a sigh as she relaxed in her chair and filled the cups. As the coffee cups moved down the conveyor belt, she scrutinized Dean's lockdown configuration.

"Back in grammar school, I had a couple of fifth-grade students like him. I would have given a week's pay to tie them up like that, just for an hour or so-"

Jimmy broke out laughing and Gramma joined in. Mads wanted to join them but held out; he just smiled and sipped his coffee.

"Will you tell us about your grandmother now?"

"Not much to tell," Jimmy started. "I went to live with her when I was fifteen. I'd lost my parents and when I look back now, I guess Grandma was just too nice. I mean, she could be hardheaded, but she let me get away with anything, probably on account of my folks. So, I got a little wild and dropped out of school. Well, it was Grandma who convinced me to get my GED and that helped a lot. I got my training and became a professional truck driver. Grandma put up the down payment on my rig and I was off and running: a fully independent contract operator. Hauling loads over the road, I was seein' the country and lovin' it. Well, Grandma lost her old caretaker and she asked me to take over running the farm. She wanted me to park the truck and just use it for hauling grain and such. Said if I needed to travel, I could just do it for fun in the off seasons. Well, I thought she was trying to control my life and we had words… I got back on the road and about that time I needed a set of tires; my truck was only half paid for and I hadn't been saving any money. So, I sold the truck and now I just contract driving jobs here and there. I guess I'm as hardheaded as Grandma because we haven't talked in a year. I do miss the old girl…"

"Uuugh…" Dean was coming around.

He licked his lips and rolled his eyes to see what was growling to his left. Bruno was gnawing on the remains of Dean's T-bone steak. As full consciousness returned, the scent of coffee brought awareness of his dry mouth and throat.

"A little of that coffee might ease this pounding in my head," hinted Dean.

"There's a little tube with water clipped to your right collar there," replied Gramma coldly.

He glanced up at two bota bags hanging overhead and sucked up some water without further complaint.

"There's a town hall meeting going on right now, so maybe they'll discuss a long-term plan for you boys," said Gramma reassuringly.

"So, they may let us go?" asked Mads.

"Not for awhile, but it would be easier on everyone if we had a potential timeframe to work with. This is the first time I've come to a first day of class not knowing how many school days that I will have to work with."

("School days? This bitch is crazy,") thought Dean.

Gramma uncovered a homemade apple pie with crumb crust and cut three generous slices.

"Whipped cream?" she asked as she spooned some onto each slice.

She retrieved their coffee cups from the conveyor, topped them up and sent them back with the desserts. Jimmy started wolfing his right down, while in the far cage Dean's nostrils were twitching as he licked his lips.

Mads frowned, then dug in as well: "Sure can't complain about the food."

Dean refused to speak, but every couple minutes he exhaled noisily to remind Gramma he was there. When she'd finished her pie, she scrutinized the man and stared him down while sipping her coffee.

"That left bota contains a superfood slurry that will provide adequate nutrition for as long as is necessary."

Gramma conversed with Jimmy about life on the farm for some time and alluded to the question of how his grandmother would keep the vermin from her chickens when they took her guns. He quietly let Gramma continue on various subjects, but couldn't pull himself from the thought of his own Grandma going it alone. He knew full well that one of the things she was hardheaded about would be her .30-30 Henry rifle. The Henry had been passed down through her family for generations; nobody would take that gun from her.

Gramma was trying to get Mads to open up a little: "You sound Danish, Mads."

"Mm-hmm."

Conversation with Mads remained rather one-sided, while Jimmy went on thinking: ("I never did any hunting- except that fox I got with Grandma's Henry -and I never was much of one for ideologies. When they broke the Second Amendment with that treaty, I thought it was a done deal. What difference if it was me or someone else driving for them; they were just cleaning up anyway. But it's surely not a done deal here; and this little town isn't much different than my own hometown. I've seen firsthand that these EO agents are more like thugs than lawmen and I don't even know if Grandma has someone with her at the farm, or if maybe she had to move to town-")

Jimmy's musings were broken off as Gramma stood and said: "Tomorrow we have breakfast at seven AM and class starts at eight o'clock sharp. We'll be studying the Declaration of Independence first and there will be a quiz every afternoon at four PM. If you fail the quiz: no dessert for you."

"Ooow... *no dessert*... What would I want dessert for? I have a *slurry of adequate nutrition* right here," Dean mocked.

Gramma stacked a pile of dishes and turned to retreat up the stairs.

Dean added softly: "You *will* clip these bonds, so I can use the sanitation bucket tonight..."

"No... I'm afraid you will be shitting in your pants for a while... Smartass."

PART 3

15. Drunken Frenchman

After a few hours at their new assignment, Gil Lafayette and Pierre Charles estimated that their life expectancy as double agents had been halved. The new office was just that: a new acquisition, a new stratagem; the building housed ATF-EO only. As it turned out, many pure BATFE agents (who had not been bought by the Administration) did not approve of Executive Operations. They had been dispensing stumbling blocks for Executive Ops that ranged from organizational indifference to downright gridlock in sanctioning equipment. Gil and Pierre could see that the team commanders were more aggressive under their own budget. The bonus money the COs received for weapons retrieved only encouraged them to take advantage of every asset at their disposal, including pushing their fireteam soldiers into high risk situations.

On Wednesday, the Frenchmen joined their team for exercises at the new training course. It didn't take long to recognize the other two UN soldiers on the team as gung-ho anti-American. They boasted that in their country, they had to fight their way through a wave of UN soldiers volunteering to help take guns away from the "arrogant Americans". They were both Pakistani nationals and introduced themselves as Hamza and Abdul.

"Special Agent Lee has been our commander onward since our arrival," remarked Hamza. "We are of the desire to continue with his assignment. He compliments our maximum performance and shows us honor by requesting that we remain his loyal team."

Only the federal agents were awarded bonuses, but the Pakistanis hinted that performing well for this CO might prove exceptionally rewarding. Hamza and Abdul seemed to want the aggressive assignments and that was what Agent Lee delivered. Gil already had an impression of their CO in his mind's eye, but when he arrived, the Frenchman deleted the image. The man didn't seem so much gung-ho as he did easy-going, friendly and likeable.

"You must be Gil and Pierre," he greeted them both with a warm smile and firm handshake: "Agent Charles Lee; call me Commander or Charlie, I'll answer to either. Formalities don't impress me: only performance."

"Well, that agrees with what we've been hearing from Hamza and Abdul. You have apparently been very busy."

"Yes. We have had a few shakeups; but fortunately, it has been mostly routine. I believe they've kept you hopping too: though you've come through it all as if you live a charmed life."

"We've been in some tight scrapes," Gil dodged, as he scanned for signs of suspicion in Charlie's happy-go-lucky demeanor.

"We'll just send you two in first and nobody'll get hurt, right?" Charlie's smile still didn't give a clue to what he might be thinking.

"I suppose we will find out when we get an assignment," replied Gil nonchalantly.

"Got one; as long as our drills go smoothly today, we move first thing in the morning. Should be an easy hit."

Charlie's team had loaded their SUV and was set to exit the ATF-EO garage at 0530 Thursday. As Charlie climbed into the driver's seat, he glanced at his fireteam seated in the rear van section.

"How about one of you rides shotgun," he suggested. "We aren't making a head on assault from the vehicle and we've got plenty of time too: so you can lose the helmets until we arrive. You know the drill; this guy doesn't leave for work until around oh seven hundred."

Gil moved to the front seat and rode in silence. He hadn't figured out their new CO yet. The fact that the plan was to approach the target in the open told him Agent Lee was not as arrogant as Burr and not as bloodthirsty as Arnold; or maybe he just had more sense.

Gil was thinking: ("He seems friendly enough; maybe he needs the money and thinks this is just a job. Maybe he hasn't hurt anyone yet and thinks he'll never have to as long as he plays it cool.")

They arrived at the target's home where Charlie pulled out a sack of donuts and said: "Now we wait."

("Is this guy cliché or what?")

An hour later the target was spotted approaching his garage from the back walk.

"OK: get into position and come in when I signal you," directed Charlie as he moved in to intercept the target with badge in hand. "Sir, I am Federal Agent Lee. May I have a word with you inside."

The young man looked scared and his hands were shaking as he attempted to push his key into the door lock.

"No sir, in the house please," Charlie demanded cordially, then signaled his team as the man led him to the back door.

The fireteam appeared from four directions and followed them into the house. As the agent and four soldiers filed into the kitchen their target turned and stood up straight, but failed to impress.

In a quavering voice he requested: "Can you show me a search warrant?"

"We have an Executive Order document, but we won't be needing it because you've already invited us inside. Sit down Mr. Brinkman: Theodore Brinkman... may I call you Ted?"

Ted nodded as he seated himself at the head of the kitchen table.

Charlie moved to the opposite end of the table, locked his arms straight and propped himself with his hands on the back of the chair. The soldiers all held SCAR-L rifles, while their CO carried only a handgun strapped down in the holster at his hip. He stared at Ted until the man started to stutter.

"Is-zis-zis this about the g-g-gun. I m-m-meant to turn it in," Ted paused, swallowed hard and steadied himself. "I just heard about the new rule, but I've been w-w-working and I didn't know where to take it."

"Where is it now?"

"It's in m-m-my underwear drawer."

The head of the table was oriented north and Gil was standing directly west of Ted. Abdul was behind Ted to the northeast and Hamza was behind Abdul in the entryway to the living room. West of the table, Pierre was leaned back against the wall with Gil and Charlie on either edge of his peripheral vision; with his eyes shadowed beneath the brim of his hat, he had a perfect view of the Pakistanis as he studied Ted.

"Go get the gun Hamza," Charlie commanded, without removing his eyes from Ted.

Ted was taller than average but was thin as a rail. He had an anemic look to him and was only getting paler under the agent's cold stare. A thud was heard from the ceiling as Hamza dropped a dresser drawer on the floor upstairs. He returned to the kitchen with a full box of .38 Special ammo and a small wooden case. He placed the containers on the table before his CO and backed off to his post behind Abdul. Charlie opened the case and glanced at the contents. Embellished against a blue satin liner was an unloaded revolver with trigger lock latched in place. The two keys for the lock lay on the silken liner next to the fearsome metal club.

"You live here alone," stated Charlie.

"Yes."

"Where are the rest of them?"

"The r-r-rest of what?"

"The rest of the guns. We've got a record of you buying this one, but where are the guns you owned previously?"

"I n-n-never owned a gun before this."

"Come on, *Teddy*, you don't want us to tear this place apart looking for them."

"B-b-but… honest…"

Charlie's intimidating stare was in stark contrast to his friendly demeanor before entering the man's home.

"Fess up you little weasel or we'll string you up by the balls."

From Gil's angle he could see a wet spot spreading at the crotch of Ted's pants. The man did not have the fortitude for deception in the face of these odds and the Frenchmen wanted an end to the abuse, but neither could picture a clear course of action. Gil was scowling at Charlie: there was no honor in totally crushing the harmless kid's spirit; they could take the gun and leave. Pierre remained in his unblinking appraisal mode, noting that Abdul was relishing the torment of this squeamish boy who had failed to come of age.

"Cut his trigger finger off Gil," commanded Charlie.

"What?" Gil's scowl darkened as he scanned the agent for a sign that he was posturing.

"Teddy's right index finger: cut it off. Then we can trade the finger for the rest of his weapons."

The unnerved man's eyes started bugging out and his body was shivering in waves of unmitigated terror. He sprang to his feet and scampered for the back door.

"Nooooooo…"

Charlie put his foot in Ted's path. He tumbled to the floor and crawled to the corner where he curled into a fetal position, whimpering and sobbing uncontrollably.

"Hey Gil: just checking to see how you respond to unscrupulous orders."

Charlie chuckled and turned away, but not before he read the threat in Gil's eyes that revealed he hadn't bought the excuse.

"OK, dump the rest of the drawers and turn over some furniture. See you back in the van," said Charlie as he glanced at his handiwork in the corner and stepped out the door snickering.

The Pakistanis stomped up the stairs to finish making a mess of the place. Gil turned to the innocent child, still curled up and hiding from the world that had turned on him.

Pierre shook his head: "Nothing you can do for heim. He must work heis way through theis alone."

"He hoped I'd do it," whispered Gil.

"I know. Hamza was edgy; he has been ein your shoes. Abdul was amused, even delighted; he would have taken the feingaer."

The Pakistanis were right behind the Frenchmen as they climbed into the back of the SUV. Gil caught Abdul's eye and pointed to the front, but seeing the opening Hamza grabbed the front door handle.

When Charlie was back in traffic, he tipped the rear-view mirror so he could see the men behind him. He reached over and flipped up the lid to a laptop on a stand mounted to the front floorboards.

"Now we go take care of the real target for today."

"But we have not deiscussed the plan," protested Pierre.

"I've got the plan; you just follow orders," said Charlie, pointing to the screen. "He leaves his computer on twenty-four/seven with Skype enabled and no security. His name is Phillip Carrollton and he may look like a regular Joe but he's a real psycho. The search engines have him surfing for every kind of gun, rifle, ammo, explosives, security and weapons systems; our internet profiling programs ID him as a sociopath survivalist researching all the doomsday literature: you name it, he's into it. He's been prescribed a drug that puts him on the high-risk suicide list and you know those nuts always want to take people with them. Profiling has no record of him purchasing any weapons, so I figure he's armed to the gills with black-market equipment. I tried to get an entire task force to take this guy down. But the bosses insisted that would be a frivolous use of manpower for a guy in a one-bedroom apartment; and that we should just walk on eggshells to check him out first."

Gil was watching the target typing away at his computer, oblivious to the surveillance: "He doesn't *look* dangerous and he's got his back to the front door; maybe he's feeding you a data loop."

"Thought of that: we're about to check it out now," answered Charlie as he pulled to a stop. "It's that apartment up there; he's in the northwest first-floor unit. Hamza: go toss a pebble at the southernmost of his west windows and stay out of sight."

They were parked where they could only be seen from the south entrance foyer and the upper floors of the apartment building. Hamza ducked behind some hedges after he'd thrown the rock and the man on their laptop screen responded. He got up and walked off screen to the right; blinds could be heard dropping to the windowsills before he came back into view on the left of the screen. He walked to the door to check through the peephole. The door appeared ordinary, with a deadbolt and security chain. The man sat back down and resumed typing.

"Or maybe he eis a regulair Joe," suggested Pierre.

"Oh no," insisted Charlie, "Everything looks innocent because that's what he wants us to believe. Profiling has got him pegged: he's a psycho all right. And we're not letting him get the jump on us by walking on eggshells."

All five men donned their helmets and Charlie armed himself with an assault rifle this time. As they stepped from the SUV, Charlie instructed Hamza and Abdul to cover the north and west windows.

"Gil and Pierre: you're with me."

Charlie pulled the laptop from the stand then led the Frenchmen across the street and up the walk to the front door. He was carrying on with some friendly banter and held the laptop out so they could see the target hadn't moved from his computer.

"Would you take this monitor Pierre?" requested Charlie, as he checked his helmet strap and held the door open.

Gil followed Pierre into the foyer and Charlie added: "Neither of you move or you get a bullet in the back of the neck. Gil first: slowly place your rifle on the floor- there -then your handguns, then the knife and then take the laptop. Pierre next: same routine, then remove your helmet, then your armor and then take the laptop back. Gil: your helmet and armor."

They commenced following the CO's explicit orders as he elaborated: "The bosses told me to keep an eye on you guys. They made it clear that no one would ask any questions if you should have an accident. Aaron Burr was a friend of mine and you guys don't know what happened to him? Never saw a thing... And then your next team disappears under your noses; couldn't find them anywhere... sure, sure, happens all the time. Well, I'm not waiting to see what you've got in store for us; you're going down. You're going to take the brunt of whatever this psycho's got to offer and if you survive that: I'll blow his whole place and you'll be collateral damage. Now get on down there."

("I knew we never should have let this sonofa-bitch get behind both of us... that laptop distraction did it, or Pierre would have been ready for him as I passed through the door... dammit,") thought Gil as he laid the last of his armor on the pile.

They moved up the west hallway to the target's door. Charlie commanded Gil to stand square at the door with Pierre behind him; then moved past the two and stood with his right shoulder against the wall north of the door.

Pierre was holding the laptop so Charlie could see that Phillip was still oblivious to what was going on in the hall. Pierre was also scrutinizing Charlie for distance, stance, grip and weapon orientation; assembling every detail that would guide his move should an opening arise.

"Eyes straight ahead."

Pierre complied with the command, but his mastery of peripheral observation was a rare asset. In his unblinking mode he was like a coiled serpent in wait.

"OK: knock on the door," said Charlie, "You know the drill."

Gil knocked and Charlie watched on the monitor as Phillip checked through the peephole.

"What do you want?" asked Phillip.

"We would like to have a word with Phillip Carrollton."

"What is this about? And who are you with?"

"We are with Federal Executive Operations and we have an Executive Order to search your apartment," answered Gil, holding up the document in front of the peephole.

Phillip swung the door wide open, stepped back and said: "Come on in."

Charlie had expected they would have to break the door down and then all hell would break loose. When his rubber-duck appeared on the monitor with EO document in hand, Charlie was flabbergasted as Gil stepped inside. Up the hall an apartment door opened and Charlie instinctively glanced behind; he saw the surprise on the resident's face but missed the transformation to fear as she pulled back into her room. Upon spotting the woman he'd recognized his error and jerked his head back around. In that split-second Pierre had tossed the laptop in the air and Charlie's eyes went to the object falling towards his head; the calculating Frenchman's right hand snapped down on the rifle stock while his left slammed the barrel into Charlie's helmet shield. The impact disoriented, but failed to daze the agent as the seasoned soldier drove him to the ground, wrenching the weapon from his grasp in the process.

("Damn those Pakis,") Charlie cursed to himself.

-The night before, he had explained to the Pakistanis that the objective of this operation was to kill three birds with one stone. He went on to explain that he didn't care how many stones (or bullets) it took; he just wanted three dead birds. When the soldiers caught on that he wanted to assassinate the Frenchmen, they had both refused to kill fellow UN soldiers on his word alone. Hamza had pointed out that the proper procedure was military court-martial. Charlie claimed that they were obviously guilty, but circumstantial evidence would not even get them a day in court. He insisted they were risking their own lives by waiting for the turncoats to take them out first. When some blood money exchanged hands, Abdul agreed to back up the CO when he proved guilt, or if the Frenchmen displayed disloyalty. Hamza reluctantly agreed with the understanding that they would not be party to outright murder. Charlie had instructed his two loyal soldiers that when he told them to cover the windows: they should actually circle to the stairwells and be ready to back him up. Now he was thinking they would not help because he had disarmed the Frenchmen, thus setting them up for the psycho.-

As Pierre straightened with Charlie's HK-UMP40 in his hands, Hamza was entering the hallway from the north stairwell, perhaps intending only to stabilize the situation. Pierre had no intention of letting the man *stabilize the situation* as Charlie had; Hamza fell back as a three-round burst cleared his chest by inches and peppered the doorjamb.

When Gil heard the scuffle behind him, he leaned back and glanced up the hall. Spotting Hamza, he immediately spun to the south knowing Abdul would not be outside guarding windows either.

"SIX!" Gil shouted as Abdul leapt from the foyer to center himself in the hallway.

Pierre was already spinning as Gil pulled his head back into the room. Despite his prowess, Pierre failed to complete his turn as Charlie fiercely rolled and clawed into his legs, banging him against the east wall. Gil watched from the doorway as his partner's body lurched into a violent convulsive gyration, while Abdul's full-auto discharge played its funeral hymn. As Pierre's torso rotated past the doorway his upraised hand fell toward Gil, as if to wave him on, or perhaps to say: "*au revoir*."

Gil pulled back while portions of his friend's face flew away to the north. He slammed the door shut and turned on a shocked and frozen Phillip Carrollton, who was standing in the middle of the room between his computer and the door.

"MOVE!"

Spinning Phillip towards the window at the back of the room, he shoved him into action. Gil charged straight at the window and tried to drag him along but Phillip pulled away toward his bedroom. Gil had launched himself into the air, tucking his shoulder to wrap himself in the blinds, so he would crash through the glass in a headlong roll. When his skull slammed against the brick wall behind the blinds he fell back, banging his head on the floor; and everything went from hazy gray to blackness.

The return of Gil's cognizant thought began in a dream: a dream where he had been running in the dark for as long as he could remember; or rather trying to run. He felt he should be running, but his legs were like lead and the sensation was more like slow motion. His left arm was numb, attached to something… someone… holding him back- no, holding him up: controlling his course and speed at a fast stumbling walk.

He felt he should be dead; but this was certainly not heaven and he'd felt worse, so this was not hell: hence he would trust in Providence that he was in good hands. The random flashes of view, like effects from an erratic strobe, were nauseating until he realized his escort was wearing a headlamp; wherefore his focus commenced following the beam. His senses were clearing; they were in a tunnel… a tube- their feet occasionally sloshed through shallow water -a sewer. He noticed it was the curvature of the pipe that propagated his stumbling as his dragging right foot kicked into each coupling joint; wherefore he began high stepping with his right leg. As his gait improved, so did their progress down the off-camber runway. With his expanding awareness came confidence that he was not dreaming, though he was not yet aware as to who, when, where, what, why…

His concentration was improving as the pounding in his head subsided, and his analytical mind started with what he did know: ("OK, I do know my name: I am Gilbert Lafayette. It is springtime-the month of May. I am in the United States. We were on joint-venture ops… We were…")

The image of Pierre's disintegrating face froze in Gil's conscious mind and he stopped in his tracks.

His companion had felt a lightening of the load back where Gil's pace had improved, but he was off-guard for the sudden freeze-up. His momentum rotated him in front of Gil as he released Gil's left wrist to grab his right shoulder. At arms length, the man held Gil lightly with both hands, ready to add support if necessary.

"You alright big guy? You've been on automatic pilot for half an hour. Or it seems like a half-hour; I'm not used to this sort of thing."

The man's headlamp was directed at Gil's eyes; he held them squinted shut and stated: "You are Phillip Carrollton."

Grasping his mistake, Phillip swiveled the light toward the floor: "Yes."

"Go: we can talk on the move. Wherever you are taking us, they will come eventually, if they do not follow behind."

"Maybe. Good thing you were only dazed out of your mind; if I'd had to carry you: our chances would've been slim. Sure you can make it on your own?"

"It will be easier for both of us to walk down the center of the pipe. You lead; try to keep the light steady and on the deck directly in front of you."

Except for the tender, throbbing lumps on his head, Gil felt better as he hiked at a brisk pace under his own steam. The pipe was large enough to stand upright and continued growing as they passed numerous junctions. When his mind felt fully clear, Gil had questions. First, he wanted to know what kind of man he followed; certainly not the psycho Charlie had described.

"You wouldn't have carried me? You'd have done what was necessary to get away…" Gil half questioned, half stated.

"I don't know," Phillip answered honestly. "You saved my life: I owed you one."

"About that: we should be dead and shot full of holes."

"You got that right. About the time you were hittin' the floor from your grandstand play into the wall, they machine-gunned my computer right through the door."

"How did I manage to miss that big picture window?"

"This is a rough part of town. I had it bricked over with a few little glass block windows to peek out through. It made the room feel bigger and was simpler to leave the curtains and blinds as they were.

"So... while they were getting their second wind- probably reloading -I dragged you into my bedroom and locked her down. The bedroom was my bunker; the walls are reinforced concrete block with a vault door. I don't know how long it'll hold up against *your* party though."

"They've got explosives in the truck. But, if you had a safe room and escape route: why didn't you run for it as soon as you ID'd us?"

"Well, your documentation looked legit and you didn't appear to be a thug with a gang; that's all the bunker was for. I didn't have anything to hide; I figured you were looking for guns and I don't have any."

"Our commander had you profiled from your Internet search records as a psychotic survivalist."

"Well... that could be from all the research I do for my book. I am a writer," Phillip added proudly, "I write adventure novels."

"They should have known that," Gil muttered pensively.

"Well, I haven't actually published a book yet. But I'm working on it."

"He said you were on suicidal drugs as well."

"Now I *know* where that shit comes from. They call it the information age; but the information has become like a cancer, with computers as the medium through which its malignant growth mutates as it passes through the grapevine of human data entry. Obsolete information is never trashed anymore: it just becomes more corrupt.

"Sorry, I went off there for a minute. It's just that computers are the quintessential sanction to stereotyping; everyone with a computer program thinks he's a damned genius anymore.

"OK, so a decade ago my sister gets in a car accident and she's pretty busted up, she's in the ER: don't know if she'll make it. We've got the same primary care doctor and he comes out to the waiting room asking how I'm holding up: am I experiencing any depression. Well, yeah Doc, my sister is maybe gonna be dead: I'm feeling a little depressed. So, he comes back out a little later with a little note and it's a prescription for an anti-depressant. So, I pitch it in the trash and finish my coffee. I mean; I'm not taking drugs because my sister's busted up. So, a few years later a colleague mentions the cost of health insurance and hey; we're with the same company, we're both salesman, all the same stats: so why is my rate so much higher? The insurance company tells me it's because I was prescribed a drug for depression and that puts me in the group with a high risk for suicide. Thanks a lot Doc. So that's the game: statistical stereotyping by greedy, arrogant, jackass pseudo-geniuses."

They continued on in silence for some time before Gil asked: "How did we get down here?"

"One of my neighbors is a sort of prepper. He's the Super actually. He wanted a maintenance job where he could prepare for a meltdown- war, asteroid impact, whatever: anything that could result in social disorder. He applied for the job at our building because he had studied the storm sewer maps and wanted to live where he could access an escape route if the city became intolerable to life. He called this his bug-out highway; he was a good source for survival research. And he was right about us being in a bad part of town, so I didn't think it was too paranoid to build a safe room. There's a trap door under my bed and I lowered you to the basement with a sling, then into the pipe. They might not follow us because I left a window unlatched with a stool beneath and planted some fresh scuffmarks on the windowsill. They probably won't go for it if they know about the storm pipes, but the Super, he hid the access pretty well; if they don't know: they'll probably go for a neighborhood search. I think."

"There's light ahead," noted Gil.

"That's the end of the line. We should be ready to go when we step out in the open. I'm going to make for a nearby friend's place and wait for things to cool down. I've got a change of clothes in this pack; they'll be a little small for you, but better than that camo. If your friends are not waiting, we'll take the first ramp to the right then split up at the road. You should take the first bus to anywhere and go from there."

"Never argue with a sound plan. We'll make a run for it."

When Charlie had found the vault door and an empty room he called for explosives, but found his men arguing in the hallway.

"You saw their equipment in the foyer and shot him anyway," Hamza criticized.

"But he tried to kill you."

"If the Frenchman had wanted me dead: I would now be with Allah. He warns me only: do not interfere- a courtesy to fellow soldier."

"Hey... explosives?" interrupted Charlie.

Hamza glanced at him in disgust, then pushed past Abdul and growled: "I will go."

After too long, Charlie sent Abdul to help. Shortly he rushed back into the room.

"Commander, he is gone. The truck is gone!"

"We've got to get into that room," said Charlie; then he suddenly had a revelation about the noises he'd been hearing through the vents, "Hold on, too consistent... it's too consistent! That's a recording: it's a setup, they're not in there anymore."

He ran to the hall and looked both ways, "Find the basement; GO!"

Abdul found his way down first and then met Charlie coming down the steps: "They escaped out the window east."

Charlie phoned the local police demanding an immediate perimeter and search.

The Police Chief responded: "Yes sir. I'll get the whole district right on it."

He handed his dispatcher an address and said: "Have a couple cars do some random passes around that apartment for a while, but tell them not to bother anyone on foot. We've got another one of those ATF-EO assholes down there, barking orders and harassing our citizens."

Gil had changed busses twice before waiting at the central bus station for a ride out of the city. Phillip had bought his clothes with a baggy fit, so they didn't look too bad on Gil. He actually looked like a lumberjack in the dungarees and plaid flannel shirt. On his head he wore a tweed Gatsby cap pulled down over his nasty lumps.

When he was on the road in the back seat of the bus, he dug a sim card from the lining of his wallet and inserted it in the phone. He dialed a number and after a half dozen rings a woman answered.

"Hello."

"Is Cleve there?"

"No."

"Gerry?"

"No."

"May I leave a message?"

"Yes."

"Tell Cleve I will be at the back door where I saw him last, in three to three and a half hours."

"Will do." [Click]

Gil leaned his head against the window thinking the Henry woman was efficient if nothing else…

("Good luck with the book-") he was thinking there was more he could have said to Phillip… and then he dozed off.

When the bus turned east off the highway, Gil sat up and rinsed his eyes with a handful of bottled water. A short while later he was standing in the alley behind Gino's kitchen. There was no one around, so he tapped lightly on the door; the door opened almost immediately.

"Is Cleve-"

A man silently waved him in and led him upstairs. They entered the same room he'd been in on Monday, though it had grown two sizes. Gil counted thirteen men in the room, most of them seated at a line of merged tables Gino had covered for the semblance of a large conference table.

"I didn't expect a town hall meeting," said Gil.

"We had the town hall meeting yesterday," the Judge smiled as he shook Gil's hand, "Samuel Adams."

"Nice to meet you Judge."

"Hmmm." Judge Adams was thinking: ("So, he's not a stranger to research.")

"I didn't expect to see you again so soon," stated Ethan.

"Oh?" Gerry broke in, "I did; a man of moral fiber cannot long endure the company of the impudent."

John Hancock introduced himself with an apology: "I hope you will forgive the fact that most of us here have the advantage of knowing more of you than you of us. We were behind the folding wall when you were being questioned the other night."

"Oh, I knew there was backup behind the curtain: I just didn't know it was the entire Counsel of Elders."

"You may have noted: some of us are quite a bit *elder* than others," Ben interjected.

When Gil had met the entire *counsel,* Ethan asked: "And where is Twenty-two Shorty this evening- your target shy partner?"

"Pierre Charles was shot to death this morning by a teammate loyal to ATF-EO Agent Charlie Lee."

The entire room fell silent for a moment. Ethan was the first to break the silence: he rarely apologized for his arrogance; however, he had put his foot into his mouth this time.

"I am sorry Mr. Lafayette: my jest was not meant to cast aspersions as encomium to your late partner."

"Perhaps it would help if you would relate the chain of events that brings you back," suggested Sheriff Jefferson.

Some time later Gil had brought his tale up to date, having downed several drinks in the process.

"This is not good news," commented Cleve. "So this ATF-EO has an expanded resource base with its own budget now."

"I'm afraid so. Your tyrant is not backing down, nonetheless:

When the government violates the people's rights, insurrection is, for the people and for each portion of the people, the most sacred of the rights and the most indispensible of duties."[20]

John had been filling shot glasses with Black Jack and passing them around; when everyone held a shot, he declared: "Pierre Charles is not the first and will not be the last good man to be lost in the eternal struggle for freedom. He *is* the first of our foreign allies to fall in the current campaign. For that sacrifice we honor and toast the man: to Pierre Charles…"

"TO PIERRE!"

As the company began breaking into numerous dissociated dialogues, Cleve addressed the group: "I've got the tab tonight, so drink up. Gino is keeping an individual tally so we know who will need a ride home. Those of us going to the Mason funeral tomorrow will be leaving early, but don't let that discourage the rest of you. We've a lot to talk about."

Cleve joined Gerry and George Mason Jr. who was saying: "-left this morning and wanted me to come with them, but I just had to get some things done. All I could tell them was that Dad would understand and I will be there for the funeral service."

"I thought you were going with them," said Cleve, "figured you'd ride with Sally. I know she could've used the company."

"You got that right, because she's still at the house. We'll leave real early."

"Glad to see you here though," Cleve added, "I know you're still getting settled back in, and it was short notice. Who called you?"

"Big George."

"You know there were people called your dad Big George after you were born."

"I know, and he was my hero; but Dad wasn't near as *big* as Mr. Washington... Your dad was though; Gerry, your son might even be taller, but hasn't got the bulk yet. Yeah: your dad would have been Big Pat if he were still around. That's one man I wish I was old enough to have known..." George trailed off introspectively.

"Pop was quite a man," Cleve concurred. "Ya know Gerry is not an inch shorter than he was."

"I figured he was close. I always thought Grover looked the most like your dad, but I only yesterday considered that Gerry's silhouette is the spittin' image of Mr. Henry. The picture of him that sticks in my mind is when I was just a little tyke and he picked me up over his head. Dad would pick me up like that, and he was not a small man by any means; but Mr. Henry's hands on my shoulders felt like the jolly Green Giant had me- without the green. And Gerry: he's got those same meaty paws, like a mountain gorilla."

"Hmph-ha-ha," Cleve chuckled, "ain't it the truth?"

"You had best quit talking about me like I'm a monkey who is not standing right here," Gerry beefed.

"Don't get too cocky Monkey-boy, 'cause I can still whoop you and Pat both in an arm wrestle."

His claim was far from an empty boast. Although Cleve was two inches shorter and leaner than Gerry, his physique would not be described as thin, though his muscle texture was accurately described as wiry. In fact, Cleve's arms had more semblance to heavy woven cable than the meaty bulk of the anthropoid.

"Hell, if push comes to shove, I'm just jealous 'cause me an Grover had to let Dad's signet ring pass to you: since you were the only one who had fingers it wouldn't fall off of."

"Speaking of Grover," George cut in, "Big George told me they winched his gun safe through the floor and hauled it away. He had his premier piece locked away in that big safe: pulled it out and showed it to me once. She was the most beautiful piece of bronze sculpture I have ever laid eyes on. Taking the piece was criminal; the inevitable desecration is unforgivable."

"Actually," Cleve responded, "there is some solace there; Grover felt that if there were ever a breakdown of social order: major museums would be the last to fall to the chaos. He donated the piece several months back."

The drinking and discussion continued into the wee hours. Ethan had looked on as Gil described the last stand of George and Mary Mason to their proud son. When most of the company was gone: Gil had approached Ethan with head bowed and offered him the Knox story; prompting Ethan to grip Gil's shoulder at arm's length.

"You have lost a good friend for your day's endeavors, and have miles to go before you rest. We will hold the Knox tragedy au revoir."

A short while later, Gil was riding shotgun in Gomer as Ben made his way down a fire trail in the old south forest. They pulled up to the SUV that Joe Martin had stashed after his son disabled the GPS locators. Cleve had anticipated the possibility of Gil needing a hand and had Joe prepare the unit for that eventuality.

"Now: you drank more than your share tonight son," Ben reminded, "so, you just sleep it off right there in your truck. I know Cleve will have left you some supplies; there'll be food and water for morning and nobody's going to bother you out here. You can make plans tomorrow and take your time about it. I used to camp out here when I was a kid; you can't beat it for riding out a hangover. Good luck and Godspeed."

As Ben drove off, Gil watched until Gomer's taillights vanished into the forest darkness. Then he climbed into the SUV and started taking inventory. He found supplies as Ben had indicated, noting there was two of everything in the way of personal armament.

("They assumed Pierre would still be with me.")

He opened the explosives magazine to see what might be there. He was shocked to see what the team had brought along for the cemetery operation, and that the Henrys had left it for him.

("We hadn't been with them to plan the day, so I suppose they may have had a follow up op for that evening. Hmmm. I've got C-4 and detonators, but no timers and no remotes. Somebody fucked up. Damn.")

Gil sat down and had a snack. He had done so much drinking and talking that evening; he'd forgotten Gino had a kitchen downstairs and now he was ravenous. He was checking the SUV over as he ate. In his drunken state everything he found in the unit seemed to be a sign. Words with hidden meaning were echoing in his head and his rage was mounting with the recollection of each and every offer of condolence he'd received for the loss of Pierre.

("Sidearms, rifles, even my FR-F2 sniper: loaded and ready for action. The LoJack is disabled and they wired a toggle switch so I can transmit an ID at the gates. These guys expect immediate retribution... sure they do. What did Ethan Allen say? *And miles to go before I sleep*; yes Mr. Frost: no rest for me until Pierre is avenged. And Mr. Franklin: *Godspeed*. Yes, of course, I need to move now.")

Gil was soon on the highway speeding north.

("I'll spin through town and load up with those sacks of fertilizer stacked out in front of that lawn and garden shop. I'll need jerry cans for kerosene or diesel. Where am I going to get enough magnesium for a good incendiary burn? Have to get the heat high enough to-")

He spotted the road east into town and swung wide to the left, then tried to slow down in an arc to the right. The SUV went into a 4-wheel slide and Gil cut the wheel back left. He passed his turnoff and found his back tires sliding on the turf right of the highway shoulder as he locked the steering back to the right.

"SHIIIT...

("Fuck it; I don't have time to be steeling shit anyway. I've got to get to the garage before daybreak. I don't need any incendiary device, just need to get those magazines open; sure, that's all...")

Gil engaged the 4-wheel drive and snaked back onto the highway. When his breathing had slowed and he was back in a high-speed cruising mode, he reached into the glove box for the water he'd placed there. He felt an envelope under the bottle.

("What's this? Cash; when those Henrys decide to help, they're not stingy about it. I could have bought those supplies... no, not at this time of night. Probably would have gotten shot by one of the townsfolk either way if I'd tried.")

Gil found himself sticking his head out the window and slapping himself in the face until the lights of the big city pulled him from his tired, drunken stupor. He'd saved a thermos of slightly warm coffee to sharpen his mind for the operation and started downing it as he neared the ATF-EO office.

He set up his FR-F2 in some shrubs straight out from the garage, across the training course. As he drove up to the garage parking lot gate he flipped the toggle switch under the dash and the gate pivoted up.

("They haven't juggled the gate codes anyway. This truck won't have the garage door code for this office though. Looks like the guardhouse is still under construction; this would be a lot tougher if the place wasn't brand new...)

"Wha-"

"Sir, may I see your ID?"

The man had come out of the shadows where he had been sitting on a chair by the unfinished wall of the guardhouse.

"Of course," answered Gil as he held the window button with his right index finger.

As Gil's left hand rose to window level the guard expected to see an ID, but a flick of the wrist sent a knife through his throat to lodge in his number two vertebrae.

("Dammit, there went the covert part of the plan.")

Gil's foot went to the floorboard and he punched it into 4-wheel drive as the SUV leapt forward. He hit the garage door at fifty plus MPH; nevertheless, the vehicle was slowed almost to a standstill as it ripped and tore the steel roll door free of its guide rails. With tires screaming, the SUV pulled free and accelerated into the cage at the back of the shop.

Construction was still under way on the heavy anchors for the finished armory walls and the temporary cage would not hold up to a vehicular attack. The man sitting inside the thin bars jumped up before being crushed along with his splintering desk. Gil jammed the shifter into reverse then forward three times before he had opened an adequate gap in the mangled cage. He rolled out of the driver's door and came to his knees with his SCAR-L pointed at two mechanics who held their hands high: one gripping a boxed-end wrench.

"GO! RUN!" he yelled as they sprinted for the shredded gap in the doorway.

Gil slipped into the cage and pilfered the keys from the dead provisions officer, then started opening explosives magazines. He kept his assault rifle pointed at the fire doors to the front offices as he worked. The near door swung open and his SCAR-L sent a 3-round burst through the door and the agent behind it, who dropped in the doorway. The body was pulled from view and the door glided back closed. Gil shot three more holes in the door each time it started to swing inward. When the last magazine was open, he grabbed the keys for a quad and continued to fire an occasional shot at the door as he backed toward the row of ATVs.

("They'll be coming around the outside any time,") thought Gil as he fired up the quad and shot out of the garage.

He cleared the torn metal curtain with his left hand on the throttle while still firing bursts at the fire doors from the rifle in his right. With his torso rotated ninety degrees and his head one-eighty: he began alternately firing groups in the direction of the doors and aiming for the detonator he had rigged on the back of the SUV.

"DAMN YOU!" Gil cursed himself as he ran out of ammo.

He had failed to set off the explosives that he had risked all to place by the storage magazines. He considered what Pierre would have done to a partner with the impudence to jeopardize an operation handicapped under the influence of alcohol and he immediately pulled the quad into a tight circle that took him back into the frying pan. He watched two agents enter the garage and dive for cover as he slung his rifle aside and pulled his Glock from the holster.

("One shot at a time and I make sure I've got a few rounds left for a kamikaze run if I don't hit the target before I pass the threshold.)

"Ughhh-"

Gil felt a bullet pass his armor and lodge in his left shoulder. He could see the agent that hit him was in position to put him down if he made his run. The shoulder hit had caused him to jerk the quad right, but he jammed the handlebar to put it into a left sweeper and bullets zinged by on either side.

He was headed for cover left of the gap in the door and would have to go back on foot for his final assault- unless... Gil sent two bullets in the direction of his adversary then fired a three-round group at the detonator before passing from view. He saw the flash from behind and jammed his forty-five back into the holster; continuing his turn, he grabbed the handlebars with both hands and twisted the throttle wide open.

Gil was flat-out for the training course when he felt the multi-concussion blast of the magazine detonations lift the quad's rear wheels; then the flashing of the explosions was extinguished by a curtain of darkness that wrapped over the rider as he flew headlong over the handlebars.

16. Saturday in the Park

After the Mason funeral, Cleve found himself at William Mason's home where family and close friends were congregating Friday afternoon. It wasn't a big gathering and although any of the Henrys would have been welcome, the two families had not been close since the Masons had all moved away from the old homestead. Nevertheless, the siblings had all noticed that Sally and Cleve seemed to have some chemistry brewing between them. George had ridden along with Sally for the additional time with his sister, but he intended on going home Friday night by catching a ride with Cleve. That evening, Nancy and Liz were laying a guilt trip on Cleve about taking their little brother away before they'd had enough family time. They were thinking a little more time with Cleve wouldn't be bad for their little sister either. So, George and Cleve agreed to stay over.

Saturday afternoon everyone said their goodbyes and the two men headed south. Sally cruised the cemetery on her way home but found it too depressing and got back into the city traffic. She mopped her eyes with a napkin several times, then turned into the park and climbed out of her car.

Sally found that watching the birds always brightened her mood, so she took along some bread and cake crumbs she had brushed into a baggie while tidying up Will's kitchen. She found a park bench, sprinkled some crumbs out front and waited for the pigeons.

There were plenty of families and joggers passing by, which had given Sally a sense of security while feeding the birds. However, her serenity began to fade as she sensed several individual men were watching her, though they seemed to disappear whenever she took note of their locations. She stood and punched her phone as she began moving towards her car along a route that took her past the most people.

("Traditionally I've had no luck contacting little brother, but he just gave me this new number, and between him, Will, or Tom, I always feel so… invulnerable with Junior around. The same sense I get with Cleve: like I'm in the company of a resolute warrior wearing a happy-go-lucky smile. And they're in the same ride, so I get two for the price of one with this call.")

"This is George."

"Junior, this is Sally. I'm in the park and I think there are men following me."

"What's new? If you weren't my sister, I'd be following you too, Baby."

"Knock it off Junior, I'm serious."

"Hold on Sally. Cleve, can you make that fuel stop ASAP? We might have to turn back."

"Sure."

"Sally, stay with the crowds, don't let them get you alone."

"I'm doing that."

"How far is your car?"

"Not far, I'm almost there."

"Good, stay on the line and let me know if anyone is following you once you're on the road and made a few turns. Cleve's got to gas the car and then we'll be at least an hour back."

When Sally was in the car and moving she said: "I'm in traffic. I'll call you back." [Click]

The men were on the road north when Sally called back.

Her brother answered: "George."

"Junior, I'm not seeing anyone that seems to be following me- but… something just… doesn't feel right."

"If you're really spooked: I'll stay with you for a day and take the bus home tomorrow."

"I'm not *spooked*," Sally didn't want the boys thinking she was being a baby and tried to convince herself that the suspicious men were just doing Saturday in the park, "It was probably nothing. I'm going home and I'll phone you once I'm inside. It'll be all right… Junior… George? Did I lose you?"

When George heard Sally say "*I'm going home*", he cut in: "No Sally; you just keep driving around and we'll scope your six when we get there. If you've got a tail on you, it'll be easier for us to spot them. Then we'll all head to the house together… OK? Sally? You there?"

"You won't get her back for awhile," Cleve advised. "I was day-trading along here once and lost my platform; by the time I'd latched onto the next cell tower the traders had scalped me."

As the cellular reception came and went they tried Sally's phone several times and got no answer. Cleve was already moving too fast for the radar detector to save them from a potential run-in with highway patrol, so he put the pedal to the floor whenever he was clear of traffic. As they approached the city limits, George noticed he had a missed call from Nancy and rang her back.

"George, I'm on the way to the hospital. The police sergeant I dealt with for Mom and Dad said he arrived at Sally's house the same time as EMS. Her place being just up the street from Dad's: the sergeant recognized the name and phoned me."

"What happened?" George queried. "I was just on the phone with her less than an hour ago."

"I don't know; he said he would be at the hospital. Sally is unconscious but stable. Apparently, she has suffered a blow to the head."

There was a moment of silence that Nancy broke: "George?"

"There is nothing we can do for Sally at this juncture. Cleve and I are on the edge of town; we will recon the house and then see you at the hospital. Try to stall the sergeant until we arrive." [Click]

"**P**ull those tactical binocs from the glove box," Cleve directed as he parked against the curb a few houses away from Sally's. "Gimme."

"Hold on; I'm on it," George held onto the little binoculars awhile longer before passing them to Cleve.

There was a black SUV in the drive and a police car parked at the curb. A brawny ATF-EO agent wearing black street clothes was standing on the lawn holding a matte-black shotgun by the pistol grip. His blonde hair was a grease-spiked flattop and he looked like he belonged on an NFL scrimmage line. One of the two policemen facing the agent was pointing at the open doorway and arguing with the man. Cleve continued studying the scene and burned the man's features into memory as he pranced about brandishing his weapon before the local officers.

"See that green engraving on the receiver of his Mossberg?" asked George. "You probably can't read it from here; it's a ZMB Series…

500 Chainsaw it is. I doubt that will be the weapon of choice for most of these EO thugs."

The EO agent suddenly targeted the porch and the near officer's hand went to his sidearm. A magnum 12-gauge slug boomed from the Mossberg and an exquisitely painted bluebird scene of glazed enamel on a hanging vase disintegrated to shards of ceramic and earth, leaving the spider-plant roots dangling from the fishnet webbing that had once supported a beautiful antique vase. The agent threw his head back and laughed as he strolled to the SUV, while the officers stood their ground and watched him go.

"That was my Grandmother's vase. She gave it to Sally because she loved it so," announced George sadly.

Cleve had already convicted the man. He started the engine and grabbed for the shift lever, but found a hand over the knob, holding it in park.

"No Cleve."

Cleve stared into the eyes of a resolute warrior, who reached over and turned the key to off.

"This is not our time. We are outgunned and we have no plan. Sally will be avenged… in time. Let us move on to the hospital and speak with the sergeant."

Cleve's eyes were wide- wild. He took three deep breaths and then relaxed the bone-crushing pressure he had been applying to the hand between his and the shifter knob.

"Just glad you're on my side," observed George as he manipulated his knuckles to see that they all still functioned properly.

Cleve watched as the SUV backed out and drove away in the other direction. He started the engine, did a U-turn and made for the hospital.

Both were silent and Cleve was thinking: ("I always thought of George as a sort of kid; and a wild one at that. But here he is talking sense to me. I guess he's only ten years younger than Sally. Funny, she's the only one that calls him Junior; probably just likes to remind him he's the baby of the family. Damn… I can't believe that big dirt-bag back there got to me. George has loved Sally all his life and he kept his cool. I suppose I should accept that I'm already thinking of Sally as *my* girl; and that's alright, but… the fury… it just snuck up on me this time… maybe guilt… it will not happen again.")

Cleve broke the silence: "This was my fault. I should have spent more time teaching her how to draw… and when."

"Never imagined saying this to you, Iceman: but you are letting emotion get the best of you. We haven't even got the story yet, but you can be sure that asshole back there is responsible."

"Yeah, but I could have held onto the guns until she had become more proficient with them," replied Cleve.

"That Smith and the Walther?"

Cleve glanced questioningly at his companion as he turned a corner and accelerated.

"She left them at my house. She was going to modify some of her clothes with ammo pockets and holsters; and then she planned to come back and practice with them. You should know Sally well enough to know that she makes her own decisions, in fact, I'm sure you did; and you wouldn't have handed her weapons if she was a wishy-washy. You're just feeling sorry for yourself because you weren't there when she needed you; I know, because I am as well."

Cleve parked the car and followed George into the hospital where Nancy explained Sally's condition. She led them to a conference room where Will was chatting with the sergeant. Will had asked him to hold off about Sally until his brother and "Sally's boyfriend" arrived. The sergeant had been filling him in about the problems they were experiencing with the new ATF-EO branch of the BATFE.

"Personally," the sergeant was finishing up as they filed into the room, "I don't believe the federal agents heading up the UN fireteams actually come from the BATFE ranks as they claim. We've worked with enough good ATF agents to know these Executive Ops guys were scraped from the bottom of a barrel somewhere. I think they're mercenaries, foreign and domestic; and I'm not saying all mercenaries are bad, but you get what you pay for. I figure they juggle these Executive Ops agents between BATFE offices to cover the deception, and now they're moving them into their own installations. The west side got a reprieve yesterday when one of their new offices was cratered; I suppose they overlooked some safety concerns when they went straight to work after moving in on the fly."

The sergeant stood to meet the newcomers.

"Glad to meet you Sarge," said Cleve. "So what do you know about Sally?"

"What I know is what I gleaned from the Executive Ops team. I try to be on location whenever there is an event involving this new

ATF-Executive Operations. Most of the time we just get called in to clean up their mess. When they have casualties, they call 911 and we go in with EMS; sometimes we get there in time to see them ruining someone's home, as was the case with Ms. Mason. We always try to get an accurate account for the incident report, but the EO agent often gives us the run around.

"I've got to tell you: over half the teams I've questioned had no respect for their commander; now that tells me a lot, because that is typically rare in chain of command. I had one of those UN boys joking around with me- well, I *was* encouraging him a bit -he tells me: *We're thinking of deep sixing that son-of-a-bitch and catching a flight home…*

"Yeah, it's crazy: Sorry… You want to hear about Ms. Mason; I just wanted to give you a sense of what we have to deal with here."

"No, it's alright Sarge," Cleve reassured him, "It's encouraging to hear that you too find all this to be very wrong. Go on."

"We got there just ahead of EMS and Ms. Mason is out cold on the porch. The UN fireteam was wearing street clothes this time instead of their usual camo and armor; one of them is sitting cross-legged with Ms. Mason's head propped up on a pillow against his chest. Her hair was blood soaked on the left side and the soldier was holding a rag against her head. He said he was trying not to press too hard but had to slow the bleeding. EMS took her from there. The rest of the team was inside ransacking the place. This UN soldier- he and his partner were German -he was clearly disgruntled and ready to talk, but then the Executive Ops agent stormed out the door and said: *I'll take care of these dudes.* Actually, there was no door, I mean, it was on the entry hall floor; he could have taken the key, picked the lock or even kicked the latch free, but no, he had to blast the hinges *and* the latch with his shotgun."

George interrupted: "A Mossberg Chainsaw?"

The sergeant tipped his head to the side for a moment, then nodded: "Yeah, I believe it was… had the top-handle and barrel standoff… You saw the guy? Linebacker with blonde hair?"

"Yeah."

The sergeant continued: "The guy says: *I ordered her to open the door and she pulls a gun on me, so I whacked her with my gun barrel, she tried to dodge, stumbled and hit her head on the porch swing going down. She'll be alright,* he says. The German soldier stood right behind him and- looking me in the eye -slowly shook his head with each lie. Then the soldier waits for the agent to leave and says he can tell me exactly what happened and his partner will back him up. The man says I should record what he's got to say because it's nothing but the truth and he's observed more incidents with this agent that could be deemed war crimes. I've been going over the recording for my report and I quote-"

"Hold on; can we hear the recording?" asked Will.

"Well... I'm not supposed to- well technically... you were supposed to wait until tomorrow for release of the incident report too. But I already broke the rules a little and sometimes rules need breaking... I guess so."

"Appreciate that Sarge," said Cleve.

The sergeant flicked the playback on his recording device and a man's voice with a mild (but choppy) German accent described the incident: "-agent is looking over target's shoulder and she does not pull keys from purse, she pulls canister of pepper-spray. He was right on top of her and could have taken her wrist before she cleared purse. He held shotgun's breacher in his left palm and cracked little doll's skull vith it. Ve were in yard: ve could do nothing. She hit porch floor as he proceeded vith shooting door from frame; a chore he often performs vith relish. My partner was checking girl for pulse and breathing. Agent holds up cellular phone and says: *911 vill take care of that; let's get this job over vith.* I brought pillow from house and held her in position to breathe vithout choking until you arrive." [Click]

"My men stayed there," the sergeant explained: "They will put the door up and tape the entrance until you can get it repaired properly. There's not much more we can do at this juncture, except to pray the little lady comes out of the coma alright."

"We can start a federal lawsuit," asserted Nancy, "That's how much more we can do."

"Yes, yes you can. But I've already heard of folks being targeted for that. Lawsuits don't go far when your life is on hold like Ms. Mason in there."

"They can't bully me," Nancy declared in a huff, "Do you know who I-"

"Hold on Nancy," George interrupted. "Cleve and I are going to leave you to it. Thank you, Sergeant, thank you very much and good luck."

Cleve nodded: "Sarge," and received a return nod as he closed the door behind them.

They moved quickly away down the hall, nevertheless they could still hear Nancy raving on about the percentage of cases her law firm wins.

"Curious, some of the things Dad has said over the years," George related, "We were squirrel hunting- no: rabbit -we hadn't brought a dog along and weren't kickin' anything up and Dad gets real contemplative and says: *Son, take care of your sisters when they need you. Liz can take care of herself and Sally will occasionally need a hand getting wherever it is she wants to be, but there may come a time when you have to save Nancy from herself. I do believe that girl thinks her law degree puts her at the top of the food chain.*"

Cleve tipped his head down and looking up, gave him a crooked quarter-smile.

George grinned: "Hope Dad was not prescient or anything."

17. Freedom

There was a cool evening breeze tousling the bedroom curtains as Gramma slid into her warm feather bed and pulled the sheets snug around her neck. The mild scent of freshly cut bluegrass wafted through the window. It was present to various degrees most of the week as Andy Coxe worked his way up the street mowing one or two lawns each day. She could identify some of the other lawns he mowed by the subtle scents that mingled with the grasses.

Tonight, she detected lemon mint from two houses down, where Andy had cut the lemon balm plants that were spreading into the lawn. She considered it a delicious scent that overwhelmed the distant dogwood blossoms; and her reflections digressed to the lemon-butter fillets she'd served for dinner.

The day had gone very well; after nearly a week of class they had covered and reviewed all the important documents of the Republic. The afternoon quiz and review revealed that Dean had been listening all along, though he had previously refused to acknowledge the fact. Gramma was so delighted with her success that she had removed his bonds as he watched calmly, not even attempting to snatch the clippers and extension pole she used to snip the zip ties.

She had given all three men a change of clothes, soap, a garden hose and a couple hours of privacy to get cleaned up before the evening meal.

("Yes, it was a good day; a day to take pride in,") thought Gramma as she drifted off to a tranquil slumber.

Gramma woke early Wednesday morning feeling refreshed and looking forward to another day of smooth sailing. In the kitchen she started a pot of coffee brewing and then cautiously crept down the basement steps to see if anyone was up yet. She stopped halfway. Something was not right; she should be hearing Bruno pacing and panting at her approach.

Bending down to peek below the rafters, she discovered her Irish wolfhound was standing on his hind legs with his back to Dean's cage. His nose was pointed to the ceiling with tongue hanging from the side of his mouth; tail and forelegs limp. The carcass was hung by the neck with a choker of zip ties, strung together from the clipped ties she had neglected to account for the night before.

Gramma nearly swooned at the sight. She crept back up the stairs and staggered to the kitchen table, where she sat sobbing with her hands over her face.

An hour and several cups of coffee later, Gramma had recovered from the initial trauma of losing her dog. She prepared a tranquilizer needle for the cattle prod and sedated her man. She strapped him to a board and dragged him up the steps with the cable hoist. After loading him onto a transport wheelchair, she leashed Flossy to the chair and shoved it out the back door.

The townsfolk were used to seeing Gramma Martin walking her dogs to the park or around the Square and it was not the first time she had taken someone in a wheelchair out for a stroll. A lethargic man with sunglasses and a hat being pushed along was not an uncommon sight either. She wheeled the unconscious cargo past the bus stop, nodding to the driver.

"Good morning Mrs. Martin," the bus driver smiled, "Taking another senior care resident on a bus tour today?"

"No, I believe we'll give our cabby some business this morning."

Gramma rolled the chair along until they came upon a cab driver reading the paper, leaned back on a sidewalk bench next to his cup of coffee.

"Hello Barney."

"Granny Martin; what brings you out so early?"

"I have a passenger for you who requires some special handling," Gramma ventured.

She sat down and passed him a wad of cash. Barney straightened the bills as he counted them out, while Gramma explained the job. He nodded several times before she handed him an envelope that he slipped into his vest pocket.

"And if that's not enough, you just come by the house when you get back."

"No, I wouldn't do that. This here is a fair contract rate."

"OK, thanks. Now you have a nice trip Barney, and drive careful."

"Don't you worry Granny. I'll take care of him for you," added Barney as he pulled away from the curb.

Gramma padded around the house all morning waiting for her son to arrive. When Joe finally stepped through the back door she ran up and wrapped him in a hug. Billy slipped past them and poured himself a cup of coffee.

"What's this all about Ma? Tell us what happened."

She just pointed at the basement door and sat down in the kitchen. After checking downstairs, the two men returned to sit with her at the table.

"Where's the other one," asked Joe.

She took her time telling the whole story to Joe and Billy. They all sat sipping their coffees for a while until it was clear that Gramma had nothing more to say.

"You should have phoned before you did anything Ma. The Henrys are footing the bill for this little experiment, and they should be included in the decision making."

"They can keep their money if they don't like it. And I want the other two out of here; there is nothing more that I can do for them."

"It's not just the money… but you should have waited. Me and Billy will-"

"Billy and I," the old schoolteacher corrected.

"-Yeah OK… we'll get the dog out of there now and bury him in the country. If you can just take care of your *students* for another day or two or three: we'll work on a plan to get them out of there too."

"I want them out of here now."

"Sorry Mom… guess the whole scene down there will keep reminding you of ole Bruno for a while…"

"Why don't I stay here till we can move 'em; Dad? Would you be OK with that Gramma? You won't have to deal with them at all and I'll clean up downstairs when they're gone."

Gramma silently sipped her coffee another few minutes before she acquiesced: "That will be alright Billy. Thank you."

Late that evening a dusty cab pulled into a lonely commuter parking area in a distant Podunk town. The driver made a 360-degree reconnaissance of the empty lot before climbing from the car. He stretched his arms and legs, rotated his shoulders left and right, did a few deep knee bends and then opened the back door.

Flicking his knife open, he leaned into the vehicle and stabbed the ratchet pawl in the nylon ties at the man's ankles and wrists. As the bonds fell away, Barney stepped back and waited for the man to emerge from the cab.

Firmly planting his boots on the gravel, the man rose cautiously from the back seat as Barney slipped his hand under his vest. He handed the man an envelope, climbed back into his cab and drove away.

The man watched the car disappear in the distance and then opened the envelope. It contained three one-hundred-dollar bills and a letter that read: "*Jimmy: The personal items you arrived with are in your pockets. Your wallet was lean on cash but this should get you home. I wouldn't use that credit card if you don't want an immediate visit from your most recent client. Take care of your grandmother and take care of yourself. Yours sincerely, Gramma.*"

The young man looked up with a gloss on his eyes and cracked a quarter-smile as he marched off in search of a bus depot.

18. Breakfast at Gino's

George Mason Jr. seated himself in a table chair with his back to the corner at Gino's Café. It was the only corner where he didn't feel trapped in a booth seat and still had a view of the entire diner. He couldn't get his mind off his sister Sally all morning and had decided to go for a hot breakfast. Sally was still in a coma and he felt a little guilty for not visiting, although he could not justify the trip since he had four siblings within twenty minutes of the hospital.

When he had finished his biscuits and gravy: he waited for Heidi Jo to bring another green tea. In the meantime, he watched a young man in his late teens scan the room and then charge up to George's table wearing a vibrant smile.

"I knew that was your Z1R out there."

"I hope so; you're the guy that painted her cyber green. Sit down Andy. What? Did you think I was going to save her for a show or something?"

"I just thought you'd be riding one of the newer bikes."

"There are folks consider my *X* an *old* classic as well."

"The ZRX is a classic alright, but it's a sort of retro-Z1R. Where's your Night Rod?"

"The Harley's in the shed. You don't think my butt's big enough to ride two bikes at once, do you? I'm on the *R* today: she's still the quietest muscle bike running on gas… and she's still my best girl."

"You were right about keeping the pinstripes and a half inch of the original silver blue. Looks righteous man."

"Classics always bring a higher bid with original paint, Andy," George coached.

"But you'll never sell that bike."

"Of course not. That's why I diverged from stock. The rest of the '78 Z1Rs are baby blue metallic and now mine's baby green metallic with a streak of the legacy blue. That color not being modern Kaw green and the way it blends right in with the old silver blue: most bike people will just think I bought the silver green one. Oh, the hardcore collectors will remember, but like you say: they'll never get their grubby hands on mine."

Heidi Jo had brought George's tea and was standing beside him waiting for Andy to order.

"I'll just have a coffee Heidi," said Andy, glancing across the table to see that he wasn't becoming a nuisance.

Andy considered George to be the coolest dude in town and felt privileged to have his trust. He kept an eye on the house when the adventurer was away and contracted any small job he could handle; as with the paint job: he often received some tutoring in the process. His high school buddies were mostly intimidated by the mystique of the adventurer and Andy knew they would be impressed if they saw him kicking it around with George at Gino's. He thought George always seemed like a man on a mission and had never seen him so relaxed: so talkative. Andy was worried that he was pushing his luck if he hung with him too long.

"Have some breakfast Andy. You're a growing boy; and the way the grass has been growing you'll probably be working harder than me today. Bring him some bacon and eggs and whatever he wants Heidi Jo."

Andy was taller than George and huffed at the growing boy comment. The man continued as if he hadn't noticed.

"You can afford to grow horizontally a little anyway. And speaking of grass: Do I owe you anything for my lawn? I haven't paid you since last year."

"No sir. I still owe you two mowings. It got real dry last September. But you always pay me so far in advance, I would never complain if you owed me a few."

"I know you wouldn't Andy. That's why I try to keep track."

The two continued kicking small talk around as Andy slowly consumed his meal while speculating that George could have fit right in with the kids of his own generation if he'd been born a couple decades later.

"So, how are things with your babe: Emily Webster?"

"I had to cut her loose," Andy quipped arrogantly.

"Why's that?"

"She wasn't puttin' out."

"You smartass punk. I oughta whack you upside uh the head. That girl's a real sweetheart. I've gathered that from you *and* her father; smart and hard working. What the hell's the matter with you?"

Andy was indignant and embarrassed all at once.

"What did I do? Everybody says *you've* got a woman in every port."

"Don't believe *everything* that *everybody* says. Maybe I've had my share, but maybe none of them were keepers. Anyway, I never condemned a girl because she was saving herself for the one and only. If she can be loyal to a man she has not yet met, chances are: loyalty's in her nature."

"What's loyalty got to do with it?"

"Nothing if you're naught but a ruttin' animal. I suppose you think that's macho."

"Macho is having the power to do whatever you want."

"But are you actually doing what *you* want? Or what you think others will perceive as macho?"

"Well... macho is just power-"

"And what is power? What is the most powerful animal on the planet?"

"I don't know; polar bear maybe..."

"No... the most powerful animal on the planet is man. Polar bear, Kodiak, grizzly: I can put down any one of them, not by the power of primitive instinct, but by the power of intellect. Most of the women who are attracted to hound-dog characteristics see a primitive instinct to be manipulated, a weakness to be exploited; until they get bit and realize they only bedded another horny asshole. I'd bet Emily's idea of macho is a man with brains and potential, with the power to control his own mind; not another guy out for a quickie."

"Yeah... my problem is I think I still love her too."

"Now that's a whole 'nother story. If you are truly in love with the girl and you cashed her in for some fast sex: you're a damned fool. If she's not right for you- maybe it's only puppy love or lust -walk: no regrets. But if she could be the one: you should have sorted that out before you bailed."

"She hasn't got another boyfriend yet."

"There you go, maybe she's giving you a second chance."

"Or maybe she's waiting for me to come crawling back, so she can laugh at me."

"Could be. If you're afraid of being humbled: you're done. You deserve to be laughed at anyway, Andy. Just don't get into one of those vicious torture circles: back together, break up, together, break, together, break, etc. etc. etc. I think too many relationships are based on infatuation or lust; or incompatible couples who think to prove their love by hanging onto a really bad relationship."

"Grandma and Grandpa say there's a lot of hard work in keeping a loving relationship alive."

"Yeah, well, your grandparents have got half a century's experience. They don't mean for you to take those words out of context. People change over the years, the decades, and adjusting to those changes may be hard; but relationships should at least start out easy... *I* think.

"Look, I've had half a dozen girls who I thought I *could* be in love with, but I always played it out until I was sure she was not my soulmate or anything; then a clean break is best. You don't want to be tied down when your one and only does come along."

"So, you're not married because you're still looking for a virgin?"

"I'm gonna whack you one yet. I wouldn't hold it against a girl; but I am not *looking* for a virgin. *You are what you are, not what you were.* We all *grow* into what we are. Though flip-flopping to take advantage of every opportunity is just wicked manipulation..."

George trailed off as he studied one of two strangers seated across the room who stood and ambled over to the men's room. Andy started turning to see what had drawn his attention, but George caught Andy's eye and started back in with a story.

"I had a girl once... well, I didn't have her: I had her attention, because I was over-tipping her. As we got to know each other, she made a point to claim virginity. I figured: maybe so, maybe no. Her performance did not exactly exude virtue. I had to wonder if she had gotten it into her head that I was in the market for a virgin; I don't think it was anything I said, maybe just that I didn't straight away try to get into her pants. For the record: I also don't hold it against a girl for having had more than her share, so long as she has procured a sense of integrity through her journey. However, I will not tolerate a seasoned woman performing the sweet and innocent con on my account."

The stranger had returned to his table. George continued his story as he watched the man drop a couple ones on the table and exit the diner; his companion remained behind to finish his coffee.

"Long story short: I figured if she was as virtuous as she claimed, I would get a read on her sincerity from her response to a calculated piece of prose that painted a picture of a shared moral base in the guise that she was dispensing as the code that had carried her to her twenty-seventh year still single and innocent."

"I have no idea what you just said: but how did you pull that off without freakin' her out?"

"Hey… I'm no Michelangelo, but I painted her a little watercolor card- that was not too corny -and wrote the piece inside. A slight twist on a scheme Benjamin Franklin had for impressing a girl; I didn't have the heart to tell him it never did work- but then knowing ole Ben: he probably wanted the data either way for his statistical analyses…"

George was still monitoring the stranger while keeping Andy's attention by pulling his smartphone from his pocket.

"Here, let me link to my computer and email a dot-doc."

"I can get it right here," said Andy.

The stranger, who had exited, reappeared across the street where George could see him smoking a cigarette by a black SUV. The man still sitting at the table had surveyed the room several times in the last few minutes.

("Good. That will keep Andy busy. Something's about to go down. Don't know what: but something. I can feel it.")

"Got it," said Andy as the text popped up on his screen.

***

For M

We don't… fall in love… too logical for that
Just look at the words… "to fall in love"
Like a trip or a stumble, a mistake of some sort
No… perhaps the poets would have us longing to fall
Hunting, running, searching, chasing, lusting… begging
And for some… the results of self hypnosis is all
For where does the sensation begin in the fallen?
The heart? Or is it rather "to fall in lust" that is so common

But a love that grows with the strength of two hearts…
No fall, no tumble…
Now that is a dream we can get behind
No blast and then crumble…
A blaze, that from a flicker… grows

Ah… but I'm afraid that I must digress
To treat on my own repine, for the state of love and life
For I fear our world has progressed/regressed
To a life of disposable instants…
Instant food, instant drink, instant love and instant gratification
And nothing but disposable empties remains

There's a sad belief that to hop in bed is to fall in love
How long must this fantasy continue?
Just look at the words… "making love"
As if an emotion so… timeless… so eternal…
Can this instant, be created… of nothing more than lust primeval

Not to deny the power of lust, or… your incomparable power to kindle
But in this hi-tech theater, of machines programmed to be impatient
If we play the primitive animal, we surely fit the program standard
But macho… I think not
For what is macho? Strength and power?
Yes… but tempered by strength of mind and moral

And you… the accomplished artist… me the scientist true…
When I gaze into your eyes…
I just know I glimpse your heart
So clear… your eyes… they say
Come on in and look around… nothing here I wish to hide
But performer you are, so forgive the scientist in me
Calculation, probability… the odds are tested and weighed
Will we ever enjoy each other's company?
By the clear blue light of day…

I may just call you M… well, there's Marissa or Mia
Maggie, Muffins, Mags or Macs…
I love the available variety
And if you've been weaving me mystical fantasies
You should know that the ride has been worth it
For reveling in such power is most intriguing indeed…

If I've mostly been writing in nothings
I will try to finish in somethings…
In our lives we may never know… true love
Of that my life may attest…
Myself, I may marry eventually
And I should hope a form of love will be present
But even if there is not really magic
It won't be a marriage for lust or convenience
For better or for worse… she will be… my best… friend
Of that you can be sure…
On that note, this song is good to go
Not to deny the power of lust, but… your friendship will always be precedent.

With L---
George

***

George was watching Heidi Jo at the cash register as the stranger approached. Her eyes nervously shifted from the stranger to the thirty-eight Colt that Gino kept on a shelf beneath the countertop: twice… three times. George was still in his chair but his weight had transferred to his toes.

"So, what happened?" asked Andy, oblivious to the tension in George's anatomy.

"Whudda ya talkin' about kid?" George quipped, glancing at Andy as if he were an annoying child.

"The girl. Was she playing you?"

"Oh. Don't know. It was a dead end anyway: she probably thought I was gay and I probably thought she was. Get out of here Andy; you've got work to do."

Andy was a little confused at the mood change, but was not about to argue with the man when he spoke with such intensity. He thanked George for breakfast and left.

Heidi Jo was busy counting out the stranger's change when he abruptly leaned over the counter to see what the girl was so nervous about.

"FREEZE!" screamed the agent, shoving his badge and handgun in the frightened girl's face.

("Punk,") thought George, as he silently rose with one hand on a Para Ordinance forty-five and the other gripping the Cold Steel Torpedo he intended putting through the man's forearm if the gun's aim drifted from the girl.

Before he had fully straightened, he spotted Sheriff Jefferson through the glass wall, reaching for the door handle. Glancing at George he turned his palm down and made a slow patting motion in a bid to let him handle the situation, then pulled the door open.

The agent yelled "*freeze*" again and glanced to the door, noting the badge on Sheriff Jefferson's vest. His eyes were toggling back and forth as the sheriff advanced.

"What's the problem here son?" asked Sheriff Jefferson.

He strode straight to the agent. His right hand slid along the counter to where his fist closed around a thick glass saltshaker. The agent's eyes locked on the sheriff as he realized his mistake and started to swing his gun around, too late; his wrist was caught in the grip of the sheriff's left hand. A hammer-like blow from the saltshaker fist smashed into his cheek as a knee to his abdomen rode him to the floor.

Sheriff Jefferson's right arm commenced pumping half a dozen hammer blows to the man's head. The agent was propped up against the counter kick plate; his final assessment was that his antagonist's fist and forearm had transformed into a piston and connecting rod running on a crankshaft at just about 120-RPM.

("Now that's something you don't see every day,") thought George, as he dropped back into his seat. ("I'm thinking the stories are true about ole Tommy having a thing for Heidi Jo.")

Sheriff Jefferson came around the corner and turned a scared Heidi towards the kitchen. He reached back, grabbed Gino's Colt and stuffed it into his back pocket. Heidi Jo was moving now and they left by the back door.

George calmly stood and stretched his arms. He walked to door; pulled it half open, then let it go and stepped into the kitchen to find the cooks hiding in the pantry. He opened the door to the stairs and cleared his throat.

"GINO! Better get down here. Your waitress is on leave and you've got garbage on the floor."

George strolled out the front door and fired up his bike. He rode away eyeing the agent across the street, who was calmly speaking into his cell phone.

"The idiot got himself pounded-"

"What do you mean? You were just reconnaissance."

"Listen: I told him to stick to the plan and wait for backup. He was talking crazy and Jefferson wasn't even there yet. I left him to his stupidity. Then I spot him with a gun on the girl and don't know what he's up to. The moron thinks like a cheap alley thug; maybe thought he'd take a hostage. So Jefferson walks in and tears his face off; listen to me, that old dude's one tough cat."

"Where's he at now?"

"Went out the back with the girl. I'd spotted him on a bench down the street when I left the diner and slipped around back to slash both his rear tires, so his tracks'll be easy enough to follow… unless he swaps vehicles. The biker just rode away: he didn't seem too concerned about anything."

"All right, we're at the sheriff's office. He hasn't been back here, so we'll go find out where his tracks lead. There are two more fireteams on the way; they'll be in a white van."

"Listen… we'll have to split up the team that was for meatface. I doubt he makes it; probably got his nasal bones stuck in his brain."

"All right, when your team gets here: take two of his and I'll take the other two when we join up. We'll have six soldiers each for this one."

H eidi Jo was leading as they exited to the alley.
  "Around the corner to the right."
"I know where you park."

Heidi was sprinting out front and Sheriff Jefferson was thinking she could probably outrun him even though he'd always stayed in top shape for his years.

("Wonder if she's got endurance too. I should thank my stars she's not a prima donna with high heal shoes on… although those legs would look real smooth in high heals…")

When she opened the door and hopped into the passenger seat, the sheriff knew somebody had been in his truck. He saw the flat tires as he jogged up; chancing that car bombs were not their style, he fired the engine. It was not far to an intersection with a distant view of the office, where he stopped short of the crosswalk and jumped out to take a look.

Back in the truck, he explained: "There's a team watching the office. We won't make it far before we shuck the rubber and be leaving aluminum stripes wherever we go. I'll have Betty- damn…"

Patting his empty pocket, the sheriff pictured his cell phone lying on the sidewalk bench where he'd watched the stranger leave Gino's.

"We need another vehicle… They can monitor the radio. Have you got a cell Heidi?"

"Gino doesn't want us carrying them at work. It's in my purse in the kitchen- we could go back for my car and purse."

"No, we've got to keep moving. We're incommunicado, we're already outgunned- without even knowing how big their force might be; they could hem us in if we try getting to help…"

Heidi Jo wasn't sure if he was still speaking to her or just thinking aloud. He'd backed up, turned around and was clunking along on the flat tires in the opposite direction.

"No, we're on our own. Have to go south, dump the truck, head into the old forest…

"Bastards got my 10-gauge," he mumbled.

"What was that?" she prompted him to include her in the conversation.

"Aaaah…"

He pulled the snubnose thirty-eight from his pocket, looked over at the girl and handed her the gun.

"Find somewhere to pocket that and practice pulling it out and aiming. Take the bullets out first, so you don't shoot yourself in the foot."

"Hmph. Gino taught me how to shoot it and said I *did very well*."

"Good."

She had removed her apron and he watched curiously as she folded and knotted it into a pseudo-holster.

He started to comment: "Tha-"

Heidi snapped the Colt out and pointed it at his head.

"Didn't Gino teach you to never point a gun at someone you aren't prepared to shoot?"

"You saw me remove the bullets and you told me to practice."

"I kn-"

She pulled it again, aimed at his chest.

"Heidi."

She had drawn again before he had fully voiced her name, aimed at the steering wheel this time. Every time he started a sentence she drew the revolver, aimed at the wheel.

"Alright already," he glanced around shaking his head, though he couldn't suppress a smile. "Load it and put it away.

"There's a pack behind the seat with emergency rations," he leaned his chest against the steering wheel, "Get it out and slip the first aid kit in, plus anything else that makes sense... ammo in the glove box."

Sheriff Jefferson turned left onto the scenic overlook road as Heidi Jo dropped the loaded pack on the seat between them. He was thinking it would be best if he offered the girl some encouragement.

"The best thing we've got going for us back in town is Mason and Gino."

"George? He's nothing but a crazy surfer-"

"Ha-ha. Don't let him fool ya."

"Snowboarder?"

"Heh... Doesn't matter how bad it gets: a little chuckle is always good to clear the cobwebs."

"What's so funny?"

"It's not *that* funny, but if you can't keep your sense of humor: what's it all for?"

He looked over, and realizing he hadn't answered her question, asked: "Did you know George Mason? –His father."

"Never met him, but heard a lot of talk the last week."

"Well, he was a hunting buddy and a good friend. He was a proud American, a respected and honorable man. His son is: well... think younger and edgier version of his father. If he joins up with us at the mine- and if we get hemmed in there, he will come -listen to him and don't get in his way; trust me on this."

"I thought we were going south?"

"Changed my mind. We could hike for days that way. No, between George and Gino, word will get out that we've got trouble after us. We'll drive down to the old mine and hole up there; or if we have enough lead on them: we'll head into the forest from Buzzard Creek and make for Leatherwood."

"*Leatherwood...*"

W hen George left Gino's, he circled to the sheriff's office. Staying out of sight: he noted the stakeout vehicle and no sheriff. He tried calling Ethan Allen while considering what to do: no answer.

("Should I stakeout the stakeout or go on recon?")

His decision was prompted by the black SUV as it drove off. George waited until the SUV made a turn a few blocks away and then made like a drag-bike, braking hard up to his quarry's street. He watched the SUV until it made another turn and then put the old Z1R through the same paces.

His quarry made its way to the side street where the sheriff's truck had been parked. The agent with the other SUV that had been on 1st Avenue was nowhere to be seen; the agent's companion had apparently been left for dead in Gino's.

George had left his bike and was leaning around the corner of a building, watching as his target SUV crept up the lane with a soldier riding the running board. George suddenly stood bolt upright, ran to his bike and shot away.

("They're looking for Tommy's tracks; somebody must have slashed his tires. That's what those stripes were on the road. And... I know exactly where I can get a look inside that van. They'll come right down to the T-intersection at Suzy's Embroidery shop and that's where I'll scope 'em.")

George ripped up an alley and into Suzy's yard. He knocked hard on the back door, carded it open and hollered an apology as he charged in.

"SUZY- sorry, but I've got to get a look at some criminals that are after Sheriff Jefferson."

Suzy pulled the shop's back door open to confront the man charging up her apartment hallway.

"How did you get in here?"

"Carded the door. You should really get a better latch."

"You're the only criminal around here. I never needed a better lock before."

"Sorry Suzy: how 'bought I owe you a steak dinner?" George offered, as he pulled a tiny tactical scope from his pocket and leaned up against the wall.

"What makes you think I'd go out to dinner with you?"

"OK, I'll just pay you for a dinner right now."

"Put your cash away, Georgy. You're not getting off that easy."

"Hold on Suzy; here they come. Turn the lights out."

"That'll cost you a lobster dinner."

George just smiled as he watched the SUV approach. The running boards were free of riders, as the metal wheel tracks on the road had become obvious. Bright reflections off the windshield made it difficult to distinguish soldiers from equipment in the back of the vehicle. As clouds obscured the sun, the view cleared and he counted four soldiers: one fireteam. The piece of intel George found most interesting was revealed as the SUV rounded the corner, when the driver's face was exposed from behind the sun visor and a small green engraving on a shotgun receiver caught his eye in a flicker of sunlight.

"Hello- Judgment day."

"What do you mean by that?" asked Suzy.

"Later. Gotta go."

"Gotta go, gotta go, always gotta go. George: nice to see you back home…"

"Good to be back home, Suzy-Q."

George literally ran out the back door, jumped on his bike and was gone. He was right back on his quarry after two more drag strip like runs along Sheriff Jefferson's aluminum wheel tracks.

After the SUV made another turn he accelerated for a block and then spotted a man ahead waving a rifle like a yellow flag on a track. George pulled the bike down from 60-MPH to stop alongside a tall man in black.

The rifleman was Ethan Allen in his usual colors, except that he wore leather with bandolier bullet slings of .30-30 shells crisscrossing his chest.

"Gino said Tommy had trouble at the café. I made a covert approach on foot and recorded one corpse. Recon from the clock tower disclosed departure of one black SUV to the west and a second abandoning a stakeout at the sheriff's office. Further recon from the street suggests the second SUV is Executive Ops on the trail of these aluminum tracks. Assumption: Tommy's tires were flattened and he was cut off from his office. You: I have observed zipping around town like some kid practicing hole shots. If you were doing that on your Night Rod you would have awakened the dead by now."

"And no doubt the dead would all be asking for a ride on that one. Get on."

George was explaining what he knew as they caught up to their quarry. They were south of town, following the dust trail, just out of sight of the SUV. Tommy's wheel rim tracks were visible in the occasional soft fines of the gravel road. They caught a glimpse of a black vehicle through the dust and George pulled over to give them a lead.

"Undoubtedly his destination is the abandoned mine," said Ethan. "I thought he would conduct them into the old forest. Tommy knows this county well enough to elude them in there, indeed, even should they utilize dogs."

"I had thought so as well, however, I can see his angle. He knows we will come to his aid and that we'd have as much trouble finding him in the forest as they would. In the plant he can find a bunker of sorts where he and Heidi can hide out, or defend, while we whittle them down. Unfortunately, perhaps I should go back for a rifle as it will not be as close as it would have been in the forest."

"Let us first confirm that our friends have attained the sanctuary of the plant. If we had known where this showdown would transpire and had been granted the time: we would both have been appropriately prepared for more than an urban assault."

19. Showdown at the Mine

Ethan Allen and George Mason Jr. stood at the apex of the scenic overlook, gazing off to the southeast where much of the old mine was visible between the partially excavated foothills along Buzzard Creek. Sheriff Jefferson's truck was stuck in the soft earth near the mine barricade where George had left the road. They'd added a few scratches to the old bike's chrome pipe while negotiating the hiking trail to the overlook. George handed Ethan the scope for appraisal of the scene around the black SUV as an Executive Ops agent and four soldiers abandoned the swamped unit.

"I knew we couldn't make it around that water hole on my bike without taking the old girl way down into the woods. That *LOW-WATER CROSSING* sign has been a joke ever since the beavers made it into a small lake. So how many do you think you can get from here Deadeye?"

"They are out of range for a positive shot. I would take them all had I the foresight to arm myself with a thirty-aught-six; regrettably I equipped for the target range of urban ops."

"We don't have the luxury of a portable armory," George quipped. "We've got to start whittling them down and we will take no hostages today. With the first shot, those boys are gonna hightail it for cover behind that first road cut. So, if you're too virtuous to risk maiming these swine: gimme the rifle."

Ethan shouldered the Winchester and cycled the lever action three times in as many seconds. The first target went down but continued crawling and stumbling for cover. The second dropped and stuck: shot through the neck. The third took a solid hit on an armor plate, tumbled to the ground and rolled to his feet running in an erratic evasive pattern. Taking two more shots at his third target, both hits staggered the man without dropping him. Ethan took a deep breath then knocked the stumbling first target to his hands and knees with a solid hit to his armor. A second shot entered beneath the protective plates and ripped through the man's torso as he slid to rest face down. The agent and two soldiers scrambled to cover.

"Sloppy," claimed Ethan. "Seven shells for two kills; damned sloppy."

"Buck up Partner. That's two less to deal with. I'm going to get me one of those rifles and then I'll circle south and into the plant. You cover me 'til the live ones pass beyond the cut; then grab the other SCAR-H and head to the westernmost tailings cone, due east of our twenty."

"I thought I was in command of this team."

"Your team's still in training. And I brought *you* along: so maybe this is *my* team. But if you've got a better plan, speak up, Partner."

"Not at this juncture," Ethan replied as they moved off toward the steeps on the southeast flank of the knoll, then added: "Put your ears on… *Partner.*"

When George arrived at the clean kill, he relieved the body of rifle and ammo then moved to Ethan's first target. The soldier was dead but the rifle slung over his shoulder was out of commission; the receiver had taken a hit.

George spoke into his headset: "Sorry Ethan, you trashed his SCAR-H."

"I was afraid of that. I had descried the flash, but hoped it was a buckle or some other accoutrement."

"And you were right Partner: they're putting these guys in that new armor. I won't be able to get through the ceramic plates with this NATO ammo either."

"No, you won't. Neck, shoulders, waist; target the chinks. I will now proceed to my *assigned* post on the west flank, at an elevation two-thirds the height of the cone."

"Ten-four."

G eorge had made his way across the sand flats southwest of the abandoned processing plant. Jogging along drainage gullies and behind dunes, he had stayed out of sight, though he expected the 3-man EO team was already busy searching the plant. He had concluded that the initial fiasco with Heidi Jo was a rookie mistake or a botched sting; their assigned target must actually be Sheriff Jefferson. They would concentrate on completing the mission before turning their attention to the hunters on their trail.

Ethan's voice came over the headset: "What is your current location?"

"I'm at the edge of the trees south of the structure; ready to make my move. I will scale the exterior shell to access a window into a room at the upper southwest corner. And what is your twenty, Partner?"

"I am located on the mound northwest of the plant, exactly as specified heretofore."

George was scoping the west flank of the cone-shaped tailings mound and spotted Ethan amongst some scattered scrub.

"Did that blind just happen to be growing right where you needed it?"

"Of course not. I hauled it along and set up a pattern. Without it I'd be a manifest target for a helicopter."

"I'm aware of that: but I don't think that agent would have called in a chopper. He didn't know we were trailing them until you took out half his fireteam; and except for Lover's Lookout, there's no cellular signal out here… OK, I'm going to move."

George scrambled for the building's southwest corner. He used brush for cover wherever possible and followed Ethan's advice as they continued conversing over the radios.

"I advise you to make your climb on the western face. Anyone who would fire on you will have to move into my sights and- albeit most of the plant is out of range -I can lob enough bullets that way to keep them dodging."

"We don't want you to give up your twenty, so I will get inside ASAP. However, if they catch me with my pants down, I *will* appreciate the cover fire. You my man."

"I would appreciate you keeping your pants up. Also, I have acquiesced to your previous cowboy references of *partner*; but request you refrain from further role-playing bromides, Sir."

"My apologies Sir. I am not acculturated to utilizing a confederate with your high-handed vein of nobility."

"I am inclined to surmise that I have been cut to the quick, Sir."

"Not at all, Sir. Perhaps I merely attempt to fabricate conversation."

"Perhaps I should put a bullet in your butt, Sir. Perhaps it won't hurt much from this distance."

"Take your best shot, Sir."

"Ha-ha- you are as crazy as Cleveland Henry, my friend."

"I'll take that as a compliment. Speaking of Cleve: I wouldn't mind having the Henry brothers here right now."

"Or Joe Martin and his boys."

"No doubt."

"On another note: I phoned Gino before leaving Lover's Lookout and gave him a progress report to pass along. I told them to hold the rookies for local incursions. They've only trained for urban assault on a local residence and I have no desire to see them stomping into an operation like this."

"Agreed. We're better off only looking out for Number One; followed by Number Two."

"Exactly. George, I'm looking at that elevator on the southeast corner. It's at least as tall as Lover's Lookout; if push comes to shove, I imagine we could get a cell tower signal from there."

"Yeah... I climbed up there when I was a kid... Let's hope nobody shoves that hard 'cause you'd be a sittin' duck to anyone watching."

George had reached the upper level and slipped around the corner into the open window on the south wall. He pushed open the window on the west wall and waved to Ethan.

"You're in. Good. When you're sure they're not waiting to snipe me from the northwest corner, I'll run for an entrance. Or if you think you can drive any of them out into my crossfire: I'll wait."

George lowered his voice: "I'm going to have to cut the chatter in here- shhh... Damn... There's a chopper coming in from the west. We'd best hold 'til they've made their move."

The lone Executive Ops agent who had left his partner in Gino's Café had gotten a call from his office informing him that the two fireteams would not be coming by van. They had loaded into a Black Hawk and would be delivered to him at a rendezvous point west of town. As the helicopter touched down the EO agent waved the soldiers back and climbed in to speak with the pilot.

"We need a ride. Just into the foothills to the east."

"We're only supposed to drop these guys off."

"Listen: the other team was south of town, headed east, when I lost contact. The roads don't go through down there, so they can't be far."

"But Executive Ops is too short-handed, we don't even have a crew-chief with us, he only checked out the helicopter and sent us off. I know how the guns work, but neither me or my copilot have got any experience. They just wanted to get your troops to you quicker. Hey, this is my first assignment and I don't want to screw up."

"Listen Rookie: you don't get this boat off the ground right now, you *are* screwing up. You won't be needing the guns. Now this is an order: you'll make the drop, then back off to a safe distance, then put her down and wait."

The pilot grumbled under his breath as he lifted off and proceeded eastward.

"Echo-Oscar Base: this is Black Hawk Foxtrot-Tango-Five-Seven-Niner," the copilot radioed in, "We are proceeding to secondary drop-point and additional standby. Over... Over... Echo-Oscar Base... do you copy? That's odd... I'm not-"

The EO agent cut him off: "There's their truck in that swamp-hole. I'll be... Damn me to hell. Look at that. He's down two men already. Listen: I warned him that sheriff is no slacker."

"Where do you want to put down?" asked the pilot, surveying the scene nervously.

"As close in as you can get us; the sooner we make it to cover the better. We'll rap to the ground all at once and run for the structure. Now tune your radio to their comm channel and let's see if we're close enough to get them on the wire."

A broken transmission immediately crackled in over the cabin speakers: "-aker, breaker. Alpha Team to gunship- identify yourself. Breaker-brea-"

"Shut up and listen, Buffalo-brain. I told you Jefferson wasn't wearing kid gloves and you already lost two of your boys."

"Back off, Slade. There's somebody else out here. We followed Jefferson's tracks into the plant on the north side and he's still got the girl with him; now get in here and we'll finish this."

"We're on our way."

The nine men dropped their ropes and bailed out of the Black Hawk simultaneously. Before they tagged earth, a bullet cracked against the airframe adjacent to the greenhorn pilot's face.

George and Ethan watched as the Black Hawk wump-wump-wump'd its way in and hovered over the clearing west of the plant. As eight men in camo and one in black bailed out on static rappelling ropes, George casually reported to Ethan as he targeted the pilot.

"I can't drop the bird from this angle- not clean anyway -so, I'll try shaking up the pilot and see if he'll dump his load in a heap. Looks like we've got two fireteams and only one EO agent; they must be having trouble finding enough traitors and low-life mercenaries who are willing to kill American citizens."

"When they touch ground: take out as many as you can with the SCAR-H. As long as you place your shots between the primary ceramics, those seven-sixty-two NATO rounds should go through. Work on the easternmost soldiers first to drive them this way. My lesser firepower necessitates superior precision; hence I will not give away my location until they are in range."

"Ten-four."

When George took his first shot with the SCAR-H the weapon jammed. He had cleared the dirt from the receiver when he retrieved the rifle, but couldn't properly clean it or silently test it. He immediately pulled his Para Ordinance and banged a 3-round group of .45 slugs off the windshield.

George was amazed and delighted with the effect his feeble display had on the pilot. The helicopter pulled up and away then dropped back down as the pilot realized he had jerked his cargo of soldiers around like puppets on strings. Several of the men had tagged earth twice before he dropped lower and dragged them all through the brush. With tangled ropes, they were all down; the copilot released the entire string and they sailed off south.

No sooner than the group of slugs was off, the forty-five was back in George's holster. He released the magazine from the SCAR-H, popped a few shells into his palm, banged the mag on the wooden window sill, wiped the shells on his shirt, shoved them back into the mag, cleared the jammed cartridge with his knife, cut a few wads from his shirt, swabbed the chamber and receiver, blew a wad through the barrel, popped the mag back in and cycled the bolt.

He immediately took a single shot at the foot of a soldier on the southeastern edge of the group; and the bolt cycled without a jam. He didn't know if the bullet had penetrated, but the man danced off to the north as a 9-round burst spurred the rest of the group into putting distance between themselves and the shooter. The runners erratically dodged their way toward the northwest corner of the plant.

Targeting the joints in their armor, George began killing soldiers in earnest. Even with the 7.62 NATO cartridges he averaged several rounds per kill, plus strafing fire to herd them towards Ethan.

There were three soldiers down and out when the SCAR-H jammed again. He dropped the weapon and crept away from the window.

"Ethan: they're all yours. That damned NATO rifle jammed again and I've got to move before the boys in here zero my twenty."

"I wasn't aware it had jammed previously as your timing was exquisite: had you fired on them sooner, mayhap they'd have high-tailed it to the west. Albeit I was curious as to what had possessed you to pull a handgun on a Black Hawk."

"Hey, one hit and the pilot panicked: I reckoned a slap in the face couldn't hurt... Anyway, once I got the SCAR-H back online, the only soldier I got with a single round was a headshot. They've got the new tactical helmets, but I think once they're in range, your thirty-thirty will punch through as well. Don't let the one with the scoped sniper get away or we might regret it later. I got to go silent running now. Have fun..."

"Watch your six... Partner."

("I might get ole Slick to loosen up yet,") George mused, as he pulled himself through a hole in the ceiling.

All nine men rappelling from the Black Hawk were caught off guard when it abruptly yanked them upward and then dropped them back down as they were violently jerked westward, dragged and dumped in the brush. When they were up and running they moved north until the gunfire from the southeast ceased; then they began arcing toward the northwest corner of the plant. The only obviously open entry along the west wall of the enormous structure was back toward the enemy fire that had taken down three of their companions. They hoped to find open access around the corner.

"Hey, any of you boys still got your wires on, this is your CO. Sorry about that landing; could have been-"

"What the hell's goin' on out there Slade?"

"Shut up. We got our hands full. Listen: you just stop that sniper on the southwest corner."

"We're still huntin' for Jefferson and we don't have time to babysit you."

"Listen: you better find him before he finds you; now get off our channel...

"So, none of our girls opened their little purses to buy a one-piece radio for their shiny new helmets, huh? You're all content getting your standard issue wires ripped from your pockets. Probably think getting drug through the bushes was my fault…"

"Flip to our channel and quit talking to yourself Slade."

"Fuck you-"

Slade was bringing up the rear, following the zig-zag pattern of the soldiers when the man in front of the one he followed dropped to his knees with a hole punched through his helmet.

The soldier between Slade and the dead man started swinging his weapon to his left at the sound of the shot and had discharged a full auto burst before the corpse fell to horizontal. He continued peppering the tailings mound with 3-round bursts in the vicinity of the bushwhacker's blind.

("Hate to leave that Mk-20 behind,") thought Slade as a bullet over his head sent him charging past the downed soldier and after the leaders yelling: "GO, GO, RUN… Too many of them- listen to me! Our target is inside."

Slade and the three soldiers were soon running along the north wall of the plant; on their left a row of overlapping tailings mounds extended east beyond the rust-stained structure. Between their guardian's 3-round bursts, bullets impacted or ricocheted off steel and concrete. An open entrance was visible in the distance, but when a bullet thumped the lead soldier square on an armor plate: they all turned left and scrambled up the bank of mineral tailings.

After dispatching the soldier carrying the scoped Mk-20, Ethan cycled his lever-action Winchester and… dived to his belly: firing wild as he dropped to the sandy surface. He rolled down and away as the last two bullets of a dozen round burst whistled by overhead.

Ethan knew the soldier now had his rifle shouldered and would not provide a warning arc of sand geysers on replay. He stood and fired: wide this time, as the mineral sands continued moving beneath his feet and he was forced to drop back down as a 3-round burst passed overhead.

("Why did I listen to crazy George and set up on this sand pile? OK, it was the closest venue with any semblance of cover. Nevertheless, I can't belly up for a shot, because instead of the sand catching bullets, I will. Got to keep moving random, stay around back, then stand up and shoot while I'm still sliding downhill. No other way.")

Ethan stood and fired another round: and overcompensated a little wide the other way. While analyzing his predicament, he continued his random showings, up and down the tailings cone.

("The sand slippage is apparently an exponential deceleration that varies across the cone surface; nonetheless, drift at each locale results in a mathematical progression that I shall attempt to calibrate to my windage and elevation corrections… if I am not shot first. Unfortunately, I'm going to have to start targeting the runners before they make it into the building. I'll have to herd them in behind that first mound. They won't know I'm hemming them in until they realize the second cone is enough bigger that they can't even go east without moving into my sights. Of course, they're pushing the limits of my range now, but they won't chance continuing down the line if I deprive them of the cover fire that's keeping me off balance. Either I'll get their savior before they reach cover, or they'll pin me down while he runs to join them.")

Ethan had already skipped a dozen bullets off the north wall, spattering them with concrete chips, before he hit the lead runner hard in the back. When the four runners hooked left for cover, he concentrated on their rear point man. On the shifting sands, Ethan couldn't risk pausing for a sure shot because his adversary on point was very good, and had solid footing with full-auto firepower. To keep the soldier wasting ammo, he continued popping up with a wild shot here and there.

On the occasion that a 2-round burst passed overhead: Ethan immediately stood back up and took aim on the soldier below, who was cycling a fresh magazine into his weapon. The drift of the mineral sands underfoot slowed to a predictable rate as the soldier's rifle reached his shoulder and a .30-30 slug passed through his brain.

("Damned waste,") thought Ethan. ("Probably a good soldier: misguided, but a good man… He gave his life for his comrades.")

Scanning the opposing tailings mound, he noted a sand slide halfway up the south flank. After letting a group of bullets fly over the slide area, he ducked back into surveillance mode and waited for an actual target.

With no target forthcoming: Ethan decided to shake things up on the other mound. He started skipping bullets off the sand up and down the north and south flanks to discourage his opponents from bellying up for a shot.

"George: I got two soldiers and have four pinned down. I haven't been stingy with my ammo; so perhaps they think there are a number of us and we are well armed. On the other hand: if they do make a run for it, I will not get them all because they are out of range again. My point is: we could certainly use some backup."

He wasn't sure if it was the wind that replied or a whispered: "OK."

When the soldiers leading him up the tailings mound turned to station themselves with their sights on their point man's target area, Slade said: "Yeah, good move boys. Let's get him out of there. Listen-"

The three soldiers had planted themselves in a vertical line along the south flank; each had settled in with his right knee on the sand. They were set to take over the point man's cover fire when their CO moved up next to the bottom man and initiated a minor slide that quickly escalated. One after another the men slid into a steep bowl that formed where the cascading sand was flowing into a cavity beneath the slide area. The last soldier to slip from view helplessly watched the scene down on the flats, as his teammate fell.

Before the shifting sands were on the ebb, the lead soldier was tramping his way back up the mound. The others followed him to where the saddle between the overlapping cones had been weathered by the wind and rain to form a shallow depression the size of a small patio. Slade had tried peeking over the edge of the slide area and ducked as a barrage of bullets skipped overhead, sprinkling him with sand. He was checking out the plant to the south as he sidestepped into the shallow sand patio.

"Listen: That s-"

Slade was turning towards the others when his left foot was kicked from under him; his weapon was yanked from his grasp as he fell to his knees. Then a heavy boot thumped against his armor, bowling him over.

"Get over there, swine," the lead soldier commanded in a mild German accent.

Slade eased himself to a sitting position against the berm on the east edge of nature's little sand patio. He was seated next to the only soldier left alive from his own team; the man had been disarmed as well. He eyed the two German soldiers leaned back on the opposite berm: the lead German sat with his SCAR-H where Slade could see straight down the barrel. The other German lit up two cigarettes and passed one to his partner as he adjusted the rifle across his knee to target Slade's soldier at chest level. The lead German took in a deep puff; then regarded his partner curiously from the corner of his eye as he considered that a group of 7.62 NATO would still penetrate this super armor at point blank range *and* kick like an ox in the process.

"Listen-"

"Shut up," the lead German wiggled his trigger finger as he continued puffing on his cigarette.

George heard Ethan's request for backup from between the third floor and the second floor hung-ceiling in the southeast corner of the plant. He'd covered the offices on all three floors along the south wall and was planning to cross the hallway on the third floor to search the other half of the southern office block. Unless the EO agent or his team gave away their location, he planned to methodically search the entire plant in hopes of running across Sheriff Jefferson and Heidi Jo first.

He considered the possibility of acquiring another SCAR-H from one of the soldiers already inside: a long shot, time consuming and too risky. He could go back for the weapon he had discarded and attempt another cleaning, but that rifle had already proven itself unreliable.

("Lastly and most importantly: the quarry now knows I am inside. Should I attempt to cover Ethan from the north wall, it would be as risky for me as it would for him to make a run for the building without cover fire. No, I'll have to make the climb.")

Moments later he was making his way up the old elevator. He climbed out on top and looked up at the rusty radio tower that continued from the center of the circular roof. He checked his phone for signal strength to find one bar flashing on intermittently.

"Ethan, I'm atop the southeast elevator and I'm not getting enough signal."

"I caught a glimpse of you as you first came over the edge. Albeit I don't believe my crew on the next mound east had the angle. Have you got them in sight?"

"I was watching for them and I've got my scope on them right now: they're in the saddle."

"What are they doing? I knew they could not slip away, although I have not seen or heard from them since their initial ascent."

"They're just sitting there like Boy Scouts around a campfire- wait a minute -the boys on the west have their guns on the agent and the other soldier. I think we might have another couple American sympathizers."

"Or they may just be infuriated at the moron for dumping them all in our crossfire."

"They wouldn't blame the other soldier for that though."

"He may be hands down loyal to his CO."

"Well, this phone call is too important to make with a choppy connection. I'm pretty sure the top of that tower will get me a good signal."

"You don't have to risk it, George. A full-auto burst from a SCAR-H in the hands of a child could finish you from here. I will detain them as long as I can and then circle north to enter the plant from the east."

"That's as many as seven marks for me, until you make it inside."

"Don't count Tommy out."

"Right. How much ammo you got left?"

"I have twenty-six rounds of .30-30 and twenty-four rounds for my 1911."

"Twenty-six, huh? No doubt you'll save the forty-five for inside: from where you're sittin' they'd just laugh if you started tossing lead spitballs."

"Of course."

"I'm going to chance it, my friend," said George as he started climbing. "Here's what I'm gonna do though: I won't commit myself right away. I'll climb five feet and then wave to them. If they go for the snipe: I'll try to jump before they can get me. If they ignore me: I'll go the distance and make the call."

Ethan watched George climb on after a short delay at the appointed interval.

"What is your prognosis?"

"I believe I got the OK."

"You believe? And what effectuates this belief?"

"Smoke signals."

"Smoke signals… George: working with you is like playing checkers at a picnic table while hoping the tornado in the neighbor's yard does not turn your way… Good luck."

S lade had been silent for a spell, then began again: "Lis-"

"Do not speak," the barrel of the lead German's rifle began to quiver as if he was itching to shoot.

Slade complied, then watched as both soldiers removed their helmets and replaced them with camo caps. He scowled, then leaned his forearms on his knees and watched a beetle struggling in the sand.

The lead German felt a light nudge from his silent partner, who glanced southeast. He leaned back to observe a climber at the far end of the plant who gave him a little double wave. The man was likely one of those who had killed his teammates and he considered emptying a magazine on him immediately. However, the man had also had the opportunity to shoot first and wave later, but did not.

They were in a foreign country and would have to trust someone eventually, now that they had turned on ATF Executive Ops. He glanced at his partner and shook his head very slightly, once.

The silent German raised his left arm overhead and stretched. When Slade had glanced up, then back down at his beetle: the soldier drew a circle with his cigarette, followed by a check mark.

The sky had been clearing all morning and the sun was baking the dark mineral sand as it climbed toward the mid-day zenith. The little patio-like depression was becoming a solar oven.

"May I?" Slade's soldier pointed to a camo cap clipped to his pack.

The lead German nodded. He watched the sweat drip from beneath Slade's helmet and assumed the man's ego wouldn't allow him to request a reprieve. He assumed correct, though Slade was also listening for some tidbit about what was transpiring inside.

Slade kept his mouth shut for over an hour. Spike hailed him twice but Slade couldn't get him to recognize an irregular cough or sniffle as code. When he could stand it no longer, Slade flipped his face shield open and held up his hands.

He blurted out: "So what is this? Listen: this is mutiny. You'll be labeled traitors. Why don't we just forget the whole thing and get on with the op?"

"Ve are not traitors. You are traitor. Ve were duped into helping your Executive Ops. After Adolf Hitler's Third Reich: Germans do not take well to being manipulated by tyrants."

Slade glanced at the soldier beside him: "So you turn on your teammate as well?"

"He is not teammate. That one is dog; must be one of yours. The rest of our team is face down, out there."

The German pointed his cigarette over his shoulder to the southwest then blew a full breath of smoke straight overhead. When the smoke passed the crest of the mound: a bullet skipped off the peak, whistled through the little cloud and stirred dust on the next mound east; while a light spray of sand rained down on the party. A moment later six shots rang out in half as many seconds. From the German's vantage point, an arc of tiny sand geysers erupted on the next mound, from eight o'clock through four o'clock. They had already witnessed two identical displays in the past hour.

Slade was quiet for another good spell before starting back in.

"Listen: we've got to move before they come for us."

"It is just one man out there," the German clarified. "He warns us there is no safe path away from here."

"OK, then let's show him there is. We can cover each other as we run for the building. Listen: we're closer now, if we just come off this sand pile right down there to the southeast, we're good to go. Man, what if that other guy sets up a turret on this end of the building? And there's a whole town over there: they could have backup coming."

"Ehhhxcellent. Ve vill wait for Americans to bring us supper. Maybe they roast a hog in our honor."

"Roast a hog? You're losing your mind: do you know it? Listen to me: they'll kill you in a heartbeat. And we've got an agent inside that needs our help-"

"Spike-headed bastard needs knife in gut. Ve told command ve won't work vith that one. They send us on mission vithout orders. Expect us to follow imbeciles like you. You have experience only for crashing parties in city. Do not ask for our experience: ask for sacrifice at your stupidity. You force unskilled pilot to land beneath gun-turret at front door; your only orders are: *RUN*. You lose most of your men; think all is well. You are less than swine; you are filthy swine. Also, when spike-headed dog is gutted and skinned: ve cheer loss of war criminal."

Slade's face had flushed to a rosy red. He turned to the building and yelled.

"Did you get all that Spike?"

"Yeah… don't get yourself shot before I can zero the Kraut. My first slug is gonna shove that cigarette down his throat. I never did-"

"Remove helmet," the lead German commanded.

Slade thumbed the channel selector as he pulled the helmet off. He threw it in the sand laughing while the silent German destroyed it with a 3-round burst.

"Fool: should have checked radio first."

20. Sojourn at Leatherwood

If a person hiked into the foothills east of the mine and continued to climb to where the ridges grew steep: he would come upon a dammed gorge. The waters flowing from the dam eventually merge with Buzzard Creek and various other tributaries to form a greater river far to the south. The dam itself is host to an array of turbines, fed by a deep canal and linked to the power grid at Leatherwood. Should a person follow that canal into the dell at Leatherwood and mingle with the inhabitants there, he would currently find the attitude was overwhelmingly: "business as usual".

On this day, the usual population at Leatherwood was augmented by a couple of schoolboys that Nancy Anne Morris had deposited there. Gouvér had been called out to the coast for a corporate conference and had a notion to take his wife along for an additional day of rest and relaxation. He correctly assumed that the Henrys would enjoy the company of his two sons for a couple days, as a welcome diversion from their recent losses. Sarah had expressed a fondness for the spirited boys and had previously offered to take care of them on short notice. She warned Nancy Anne that she would put them to work, but that they would find it fun as well as educational.

Cleve had been out and about early that morning and had come back in for a late brunch with Sarah and the boys.

"A feed like that oughta keep you guys going all day," said Cleve. "Momma, would you mind if I hijack Gouvér Jr. for the afternoon? Then you *and* his little brother can teach him a thing or two about beekeeping tomorrow."

"Of course. What did you have in mind for the young man?"

"Oh, we need to change the media in the pre-filters to the Hydrogen Hut. I thought I could teach the big guy about industrial safety while he plays go'fer for me. Anyways, it couldn't hurt to split these rascals up for the day."

Gouvér Jr. pulled away as Cleve waggled his hand in the boy's shaggy hair. The boy watched his brother and Sarah disappear through the garden shrubs and then turned back to nervously watch his new teacher pour another cup of coffee. Cleve leaned back, sipped his coffee, looked down his nose at the boy and cocked his lips to one side in a smirk that said: *"me genius, you punk..."* Then he set his cup down and laughed.

"Lighten up Junior-Goov; they'll be no quiz or report card tonight. So... just tell me what you think is the first thing we'll do to make sure we don't get blown up today?"

The boy's eyes opened wide before he looked down at his feet; then he looked up and confidently stated: "We'll crack the door and sniff for the odor of gas."

"That's good thinking Goov, very good. Your parents have taught you to recognize the odor of a natural gas leak in your home. That scent is added to natural gas so you will recognize it. However, today you will learn about two industrial gases: hydrogen and oxygen. They are being produced here in their pure form and have no odor. Before we approach the Hydrogen Hut, we'll pick up a couple monitors that will warn us if the air becomes enriched with either gas."

"And since we breathe oxygen, only the hydrogen is dangerous..."

"Actually, only about one-fifth of the air we breathe is oxygen, but it doesn't take a much higher percentage of oxygen to be as dangerous as the hydrogen, or worse. In an enriched environment: oxygen allows the oils in your skin to burn like a fuel soaked rag; it would be a horrible thing to see. You were basically correct in that we should check for dangerous gas. And now you know what gases we may encounter, and what makes them dangerous."

"Dad says that me and my brother should always ask a lot of questions when we are out here. When he takes us out of school for a day, he says it's a field trip: not a vacation. He says teaching is not your job, but if we ask the right questions: you can teach us more in a day than we can learn in a week at school."

"Does he now?"

"Yes. He says your family always manages to run profitable businesses, even though some of your methods appear to be oxymorons. He says you and your brother have got savvy."

"Savvy huh?" Cleve smiled at the young man, who seemed to have grown more sophisticated in the absence of his sibling. "It takes more than savvy. Sometimes it takes a lot of hard work: like you're going to see when we crack open that first bank of filters."

"Dad says you make a lot of money selling that gas."

"Well, not so much as we did at first. There were tax incentives to get folks like us into the business. We knew they'd soon drop the incentives, but that wasn't enough for the government: they had to start squeezing us for more and more tax. If the Pinks weren't so greedy: we would have expanded and built more production facilities instead of going into a research and storage mode."

"We learned in school that energy taxes have to be increased, because the energy companies make too much money and we need the government to distribute all that excess money properly. They call it *Trickle-Down Economics* if the government *gives* all the profits to greedy businesses."

"And do you believe all this financial wisdom the Pinks have imparted upon you, child?"

Gouvér huffed: "Who are these Pinks?"

"They are socialists and communists, such as those who pump innocent children full of propaganda… which suggests they are motivated by nefarious ulterior motives, or at the very best: by pure naiveté.

"The naive hold the self-righteous attitude that they are helping the less fortunate by forcing their will on everyone; when in fact they only serve their own interests, just as surely as the nefarious. Such travesty of the Robin Hood ideal is naught but crony perversion: ***-to the end that the lesson should be constantly enforced that, though the people support the government, the government should not support the people…***"[21]

"But my teacher said we should trust our leaders because most of them are intellectuals with high IQs."

"Ha… My problem with *intellectuals* is that most of them are oblivious fools."

"Isn't that an oxymoron, Sir?"

"You like that word… Perhaps I'm referring to those *intellectuals* who *are* morons- minus the oxy. I'm thinking with respect to common sense they have the mentality of an 8-year old anyway; actually most 8-year olds have more common sense than many adults. But I diverge from my point: The typical *intellectual* is good with numbers and is a storehouse of information; he knows the answers to all the questions on the test. The arrogant *intellectual* is a speed-reader who absorbs all that he reads without stopping to analyze, question, and consciously decipher any and all subjective data woven within the facts. The speed-reader's vulnerability to propaganda is mind-boggling; in his thirst for knowledge, he should use care when subjecting his mind to this form of self-inflicted brainwashing.

"Back to my problem with *intellectuals*- seems to me: so many of them are the arrogant sort who think objective science is for peons. So often in his own private reality: he believes the questionable data or downright lies- that keep the funding coming -thinking he knows all the facts. He's got the world by the tail: results don't really matter, because he's a genius who thinks he's doing the right thing. He'll fix the mycelium fibers in the fungus on the veins in the leaves of the trees… while the forest dies. The Pinks have carefully pumped him with their socialist propaganda and he believes he can fix our way of life… and that one is an arrogant fool."

"Father says we must take our studies beyond the classroom to understand why the world is not ready for socialism. But we study enough in school already and all that matters is answering the test questions like the teacher wants, in order to get good grades."

"Are you listening to me? Or did I bore you to death with that little spiel?"

"No Sir- I mean: yes Sir, no Sir. I was just giving you a perspective from the schoolyard."

"OhhKay: excuse accepted with reservations noted. Knowledge and wisdom are more important than grades, Little-Goov. You can answer questions on the test like the teacher wants; but don't be brainwashed with hogwash. Know the difference and question anything that doesn't make good sense, beforehand, during class. Remember: *a rose is a rose* and socialism by any other pretext is still socialism.

"Here's my take on socialism Goov: A green Socialist is just a Communist Light; but in time, via the malignant tendrils of cronyism: socialism inevitably devolves to nothing more than tag-team fascism. They're all too pink for me."

"Father once said that a pure form of socialism may some day unite the universe; but not to hold my breath waiting."

"Ha- that's your pop. Hey, your father is a sharp cookie. My dad always said *no matter how long you live, never kill the child inside you*; and that's Big-Goov for ya: he'll always hold on to that utopian romantic inside. And I respect him for that; but believe me: your dad is a laissez-faire capitalist and knows full well why it works."

"Why do you say that, Sir?"

"Well… Do you remember a decade back when your dad brought you up onto a big oilrig where I showed you some drill cuttings under my microscope? I flipped a switch and the samples glowed greenish-yellow…"

"I remember a big drill with pipes and hoses all around…"

"You were just a little tyke; I guess you were too overwhelmed with the drill rig to care about my rock cuttings."

"I remember a big pipe turning in the floor and a man in greasy coveralls telling me if I fell into his pit he would suck me up and pump me thousands of feet below the ground."

"Yeah, well, ole Digger always did have a flare for the dramatic. Anyways, that well was a deep wildcat- OK, it wasn't much over a mile down; the big dogs wouldn't call that deep, but it was the deepest ever drilled up there in Montgomery County. It was my prospect: I did all the geology work, leased the acreage, then organized all the contractors to drill and complete the well. Our wildcat target was a Silurian reef, which we did not find. I say *WE* because I sold shares of that well to numerous people and your father was one of them. That's why you were allowed on the drill rig that day: because you had a stake in the project. Senior-Goov risked about ten grand of your family's money, which might have earned a million in the following years. Unfortunately, we all lost most of our investment, as the well only provided minimal production from a shallower oil horizon.

"OK Junior-Goov, now let's put that risk into perspective; keeping in mind that if the well had hit big, we could have made one hundred times our investment: your family would have been one of those *energy companies who make too much money* and your pink government would want a big tax on your oil production so they could *distribute all that excess money properly*.

"Now, everyone must decide for themselves what is acceptable risk and acceptable return. Let's suppose that you invested in a bunch of wildcats and only one hit? You might still make a good lick; but since your pink government has slapped a big tax on that oil- *because you energy companies make too much money already* -you might not break even for all your risk.

"So maybe you just sit on your money: you don't make any oil and the government doesn't get any tax money. Or: what happens when the government does get ahold of tax money? Of course, your pink media put the spin on it, but here's where your *Trickle-Down*

Economics kick in. The government takes 50-percent of the take and passes it to their cronies across the board, then 30-percent goes to corrupt administration costs, then 20-percent to the various agencies for which it was intended, where half of that is lost to incompetence and the final 10-percent trickles into the economy."

"That is an extremely cynical assessment, Sir."

"Heh-heh... Now that's what I'm talkin' about. You are a sharp cookie yourself, Sir; and I salute you for challenging my specious statistics. Touché. You catch my drift anyway: laissez-faire capitalism is not *Trickle-Down Economics* and I don't know who could fall for that spin.

"When we risked our time and money to drill that well, we lost big-time; but that money was not wasted and it did not trickle anywhere. It poured into the accounts of all of our contractors who worked on the well. Drillers, loggers, cementers, perforators, materials suppliers, acidizing, hydraulic fracturing, trucking, etc, etc, etc...

"The big oilrig had been parked all that year because exploratory drilling had been on a downturn. The drill crews had been swapping out part-time between their little rigs and workover rigs. We spudded the well in December and all those men had good paychecks at Christmas. I can remember walking out to the road just before shift change and seeing the wife of a roughneck waiting patiently in the car; three kids in the back seat- all younger than your little brother - waiting for Dad to get off work. At that moment I realized that, hit or miss: all those folks were making money because we took the risk. And that's why capitalism works: no government middleman, no corrupt manipulation of funds, just honest Americans working together to get the job done."

"So, you lost Dad's money?"

"I do believe I said that several times, Goov. In fact, he lost three-quarters of his investment. But don't you fret about it, because he made a righteous killing on another prospect a couple years later. Now that one wa-"

Cleve's phone was buzzing against his leg and he held his hand up to Gouvér as he pulled it out.

"This is Cleve."

"George Mason here. I am currently balanced at the top of the tri-bar antennae on the southeast elevator at the old mine- hoping a couple UN soldiers don't decide to machinegun my lights out. Let me just give you a full rundown of the situation."

When George had laid out their predicament, he asked if they might enlist the aid of the Martins as well.

"Not currently... although I could fill in for Joe, if you'd rather I send him."

"Cleve: ZMB Flattop is here-"

"Me and Gerry will be there within an hour." [Click]

He motioned Gouvér to follow as he jogged off with his phone back to his ear.

"Gerry, meet me at the garage ASAP: duty calls."

Cleve broke to a walk and mellowed his voice when he realized he was barking orders at young Gouvér. He finished up with the boy as they circled the manor house to the overhead door entry to the garage.

"OK: you go find Momma- probably still decking out your brother so he doesn't get stung; they'd be in Number Two. You'll have to work with them today. Sorry Junior-Goov: maybe we can do the filters tomorrow. Either way, I do expect you back this summer and I've got an assignment for you in the meantime: you'll have plenty of spare time for online research after school's out.

"I want you to note the definition of a *Ponzi scheme* and then research the cases of such schemes that have sent men to jail. Then determine what the Federal Reserve actually does, not by definition of the Fed, but by action. Rather, by policy and results. Scrutinize the progression of the dollar's value in the century before the Fed, in contrast to the century after the Fed. If you find the Fed's policy to have been a reversible, perhaps justifiable scheme in its infancy: consider that, perhaps arrogance gave way to corruption when the gold standard was abolished.

"To your allegation of my own cynicism, I plea: *guilty as charged.* However, if we include the Federal Reserve in the category of *cronies* and/or *corrupt administrations*, I submit to you: my propaganda is not so far from the truth.

"Now, go find the beekeepers. If they're not in the big barn: come back to the house and Ann will help you find them. Stay cool Goov."

Cleve was strapping boots on over the calves of dark green lightly armored riding Kevlars when Gerry jogged into the garage. As Cleve went into detail about the situation at the mine, Gerry began strapping on flat black tactical armor.

"You're not wearing full armor, Wildman?"

"Those H-rifles'll cut through that too."

"These plates won't take a *square* hit: no. But that chicken-shit stuff will only turn a steep angle ricochet."

"And that's all they'll have to turn," replied Cleve as he pulled on a matching green jersey with lime green chevrons across the surface.

The Kevlar and soft armor jersey had fingerless gloves that were one-piece continuous with the sleeves. There were numerous Velcro latch down points at the waist and shoulders, so the entire jersey fit his torso like a glove. A flexible nylon guide rail ran from one wrist to the other centered on his shoulder blades as it crossed his back. Seven tiny servos ran a chain in a continuous loop thru the rail, dragging a little trolley to any point along the guide. Gerry recognized the mechanism as an upgraded version of one of his brother's experimental fabrications.

"You're not going into battle wearing an experiment?" Gerry stated questioningly, while looking around for the Dyneema composite shield that he knew Cleve would be latching onto the mechanism.

The shield resembled a shallow stir-fry pan of exceptional size and thickness. The outer face was dark green with a lime green star at the center and lime green chevrons radiating from the star.

"The experiments are over: she's ready for action. And my shield will turn more than your armor, while giving me more freedom of movement."

"*IF* you can keep it between you and the bullets. Whoa, don't put that shield on until we get out of the truck."

"What are ya talkin' about? I'm gettin' on the bike."

"What are you thinking?"

"I'm thinking we head down to the south gorge and turn west at the dam."

"When was the last time you rode a bike over that ridge west of the gorge?"

"Never."

"Eggs-zactly. You've got to follow the east bank of the gorge way south before you can tack west; and I'm talking dead battery south. No. You back that Lincoln in here and we'll bike it from the ridge west of Buzzard Creek."

Cleve couldn't argue with Gerry's knowledge of the trails around Leatherwood. They loaded up the Navigator as Cleve related the rest of George's story.

21. Back at the Old Mine

("Looks like the same scene George described,") thought Cleve as he scoped the party of four from his bike. ("Which means Ethan will still be covering them from the other side of that mound, maybe with a slingshot by now.")

Cleve was stopped on the haul road above the highwall; the soldiers were south-southeast and Ethan was southwest. They had left the Lincoln northeast of his location; it was about a mile up the shallow valley that ran into Buzzard Creek just above the mine ramp. He didn't risk coming in any closer, even though the big Allison purred like a kitten with the exhaust cutouts closed.

To his southeast, Cleve noted Gerry's track arcing up and across the ramp as his bike slowed to a crawl; Gerry hopped off to carefully walk it into the vines and creek bank overgrowth on the south side of the ramp.

As his brother crept off into the bush, Cleve speculated: ("Gerr must have spotted something down there or he would have continued to the oxbow and climbed the bluff like he planned.")

As for Ethan's little campaign: the game remained the same; though Cleve would have to get ammo to him if he was to hold his position. Apparently, George's silent agreement with the soldiers still held. The black-garbed agent below was waving his hands and appeared to be railing at his captors as Cleve's serenity was disrupted by the crack of a .30-30 round, followed by another half dozen that stirred up a semi-circle of dust down in the mineral tailings.

("Hell, Ethan's not even down to his handgun yet. Unless George told him I'd be on time and that was his finale. That joker on the mound is definitely not ZMB Flattop, so I gotta get inside… And here I come…")

Cleve swooped down onto the little flat above the highwall, kicked it into 4th gear, and then 5th. He held his velocity to a few MPH slower than he had for his previous encounter with the sand pile. Speeding toward the drainage notch that targeted him just left of the mound's peak; his plan was to give the motor all the juice he could muster a moment before touchdown on the far side of the cone. Landing near the peak would minimize his downward velocity and max dig with the rear wheel should lighten his front-wheel touchdown enough to keep him from burying the bike this time.

Cleve launched from the lip of the highwall and knew his timing and form were flawless as he sailed to a perfect touchdown, which floated his front wheel to the surface where he... cut hard to the right as Ethan dove down the hill. He ripped past Ethan's former position, arcing off to the right.

After tumbling through several twisting rolls, Ethan slowed to a feet first slide on his knees- still clenching his Winchester. He looked up to watch the bike cut a sharp switchback as Cleve tried to avoid the full-grown bushes that had popped up since his last visit. As the bike came back for a second pass, Ethan fought the sliding sands and scrambled upward from Cleve's path; but the bike came up short as the bushes wedged the front wheel, shifting its momentum into a downside roll.

Cleve tucked in to ride it out as the bike rotated over him and stuck on the left side- pointing southeast. He was still in the saddle, covered with sand, as he squinted at Ethan with a frown.

"Where the hell did these shrubberies come from?" growled Cleve.

He spun his tire, grinding up a bush as he ejected branches to the rear and down the flank of the cone. Then he tugged the bush free of his front wheel and tossed it down the slope.

"Jesus Christ, save us from our sinners. My Winchester has been compromised with sand and look at what you've done to my blind."

"You were outa ammo anyways," said Cleve as he began unstrapping a rifle case from the side of his bike.

"I've got a few rounds left... What, pray tell, is that turtle doing crawling down your arm?"

"Huh? Oh, that's my shield."

Cleve had worn the disc centered on his back for the jump, and during the rollover he had inadvertently activated the servos that were dragging the shield to his left forearm.

"Captain Greenhorn, I presume?"

Ethan was busy cleaning his rifle when Cleve tossed the sealed case to the sand.

"Well, if you can get it cleaned up, there's two boxes of .30-30 in there. Have fun…"

Cleve had righted the bike and was off, digging and sliding his way down the tailings mound. Ethan watched the shield crawl its way back toward his shoulder, centering itself on Cleve's left bicep before he was down on the sand flats and heading due south.

Grabbing the rifle case, Ethan turned toward what was left of his blind: shaking his head as he leaned into the climb.

"I pray I am not alone in my failure to find the *fun* in the harvesting of human beings."

He half expected George to respond to the prayer he'd whispered to the wind, but noted that he had lost his radio in the tumble.

("No time to dig around in the sand; George has probably turned his off by now anyway,") Ethan justified.

He continued checking for movement on the other mound as he stacked and fluffed the remaining scrub materials for his blind. He heard one 3-round burst but saw nothing. Then he moved back to his post where he had previously dug out numerous shallow notches: each to provide firmer footing as he alternated positions during the next exchange. Unfortunately, Cleve had obliterated all but one of them.

He set up at the remaining locale and opened the rifle case. A scoped Model 700 Remington was embedded in the fitted padding.

("Three hundred Ultra Mag… I could hug you Cleveland -if you were not so ugly.")

He scooped four cartridges from the box, slipping one in the chamber and three in the magazine. Ethan failed to notice the grin on his own face as he began shoving the other sixteen rounds into one of his empty bandoliers; leaving an empty pocket after each shell that he forced into an undersized loop. He was barely started when the boom of a 12-gauge magnum load snapped him upright, followed closely by the crack of a NATO round.

Ethan still had no indication of movement on the mound. The magnum 12-gauge round had a different ring to it and not just the difference in the ballistics; he was certain that first shot had come from the plant. It had to be the EO agent who had left the SUV in the waterhole.

Ethan was scanning the broken upper deck windows when he glimpsed some movement. Then he scrutinized the window through the riflescope. The tip of a barrel arced upward from the base of the window and back out of sight behind the window frame.

("He's there alright.")

Spike had suspected Slade was having problems when he hadn't heard anything meaningful from his radio for an hour. He didn't care because he was keeping radio silence himself while he and his men searched the shops in the northeast corner of the plant. When they found egress on the east wall, they slipped outside.

Slade had not responded to hails on either channel, so Spike determined that if they were to get any help from the backup crew he would have to find out what was holding them up. He had sent one of his soldiers north: to circle west. The other was to continue searching inside: covering all the buildings on the east end and moving south.

Spike was back inside, silently moving west along the north wall when Slade broke the silence. The German's voice was activating Slade's auto-mic as well and Spike stopped in a crouch beneath a piece of machinery. He sat down to listen in and think.

("That dimwit Slade has lost control of the team, and from the sound of the shots outside, they must be pinned down as well. And this other guy's inside somewhere, so I've gotta watch my own six or he'll zero me. Don't know if that damned Slade's even worth saving: it'll only get me him and maybe one more soldier... Then again, it'll be worth the trouble just to grease that wiseass Kraut.")

He crawled over to the north door where they'd first entered, but the big tailings mounds were too close to see anything. Growling a curse, he crawled back to cover and continued his slow trek through the unfamiliar landscape of machinery. When he heard the light tapping of irregular footsteps: he froze.

The metallic sound came from the top of machinery to the south. Spike was crouching beside a shaker unit that's deck was five feet above the floor. He dropped to his knees and started to move forward when he realized the steps had moved to the unit just on the other side of the shaker. He tucked under the edge, leaning his shoulder up against the surface, and felt a body's weight jar the unit as it landed atop the shaker.

The EO agent held his breathe as he rolled onto his back, pushed his shotgun's pistol grip against the floor, and directed the barrel straight up. His eyes were snapping up and down from one end of the unit to the other as the light tread slowly approached the north edge of the table. Spike watched in disgrace as a white-haired nose sniffed its way to where two golden eyes were staring straight down into his.

"Goats... damned goats," whispered Spike.

Zigzagging and backtracking to stay behind cover, Spike gradually worked his way toward the northwest corner, eventually slipping into an enclosed stairwell.

Breathing a sigh of relief, he pulled his helmet off and set it on the steps. Then he sat down next to the helmet and pulled out a pack of medicinal cigarettes. He lit up and drew in a deep hit...

("This should relieve some of the pain and anguish I could suffer... wasting these damned criminals...")

He released the breath real slow...

"-And then the cold hard cash on payday will relieve the rest of my pain... Heh-heh, ha-ha, ho-ha-ha, ohh yeah..."

When Slade's voice came back over the radio: Spike stood up a little too quick and swayed toward the staircase.

("The damned weasel is just begging for another chance now.")

He listened in and slowly climbed the stairs, toking on the last of his cigarette. At the 3rd floor he dropped the roach and searched the offices for a blown window with a view. The German was really starting to rile him with his disrespect for Spike's heroic accomplishments. He ignored a clatter from inside the plant.

"Damned feral goats."

Realizing he'd found the room with the best view he was going to get, he watched as Slade looked up and spoke directly to him. Spike flipped his mic back on and his venomous response was cut short as Slade removed his helmet. Then through the window came the sound of a 3-round burst.

Looking up at the scene outside: his view of Slade and the German was torso only; the two beyond them were only just visible camo hats. Spike leaned up against the wall and took aim on the German... and waited.

("They're gonna have to take care of the other one themselves, but it won't do me any good if this one nails Slade; actually, it won't help to lose the stooge either, but he's just hardware: there's more where he came from.")

The German kept glancing nervously from Slade to the building and finally stood to scan the broken windows. Spike hit him below his right eye with a magnum 12-gauge slug that spun him into the bank of sand. The German's partner swung his rifle toward the window as the other soldier dove into him- and a NATO round sailed clear of the building.

"Thanks Dude," mumbled Spike as he pumped another magnum cartridge into the chamber; he took aim but the wrestling soldiers had dropped beyond his view.

Slade had dived to his belly at the first sign of trouble. He got to his knees, scrambled forward to retrieve a handgun and stood up to put three bullets in the struggling German's head. Then he turned and desecrated the other dead German's body with a superfluous shot through the forehead.

"You're a worm Slade," Spike whispered to himself.

Ethan had the 700 Remington leveled at the office window with the crosshairs on the shooter's likely post. He heard three cracks of a handgun, and then a fourth; the breacher tip of the shooter's ZMB Chainsaw arced into view and back inside at the window's base.

("Come on… come on… take aim… and leeean out there this time… hold on: he's done. They already got them; they got our sympathizers.")

Before Ethan had completed the thought, he had shifted the crosshairs to where he estimated the shooter would still be standing and fired a round through the building. He cycled the bolt action, aimed a yard deeper and lower then… slid the safety on.

("Can't keep firing blind. One was risky enough- chances are: it went out the other side of the building. George could be creeping up on that guy right now and I don't know where Gerry's at, or Tommy for that matter; we can't afford any friendly-fire incidents. At least I am now familiar with my gun's scope and ballistics.")

He went back to shoveling ammo from the boxes to his bandolier slings. After he finished with the .300 Ultra Mag, he topped up his Winchester and loaded the rest of the .30-30 shells into the other empty bandolier. He was again ready to move on a moments notice.

The next time Ethan stood to check on his quarry: he ducked as a 3-round burst plugged the sand in an arc toward his position. The EO agent was running for the open doorway and the cover fire had come from the base of the mound, a hundred yards northwest of the door.

Ethan wanted to kick himself for letting another soldier get the drop on him with a rapid-fire weapon. Now that he was in the sights of a SCAR-H, Ethan knew he was not quick enough with a scope to target the running man: not without dying. However, his current locale was the only solid footing he had to work with, and he was determined to stay put.

He grabbed his Winchester, stood and put a .30-30 slug between the runner's shoulder blades. Slade took the bullet square on an armor plate and staggered without slowing down, while Ethan ducked another 3-round burst. He started to stand and dropped back down as he heard the burst come prematurely; then another three before he had moved again.

("He was baiting me... I'm being too consistent.")

He popped his head up and dropped under a 3-round burst, then another burst, and another.

("Now *he* is being consistent. The agent will be inside any second and he knows I've got to stop him now.")

Ethan wanted to try once more for the head shot, but waited... and the bullets passed overhead right on time.

("Mhmm... He brought one of the other rifles along to throw me off on the mag change. Damn him.")

He waited four seconds to pop his head up and found the soldier in full sprint. The EO agent was standing in the doorway with a rifle in either hand. Ethan dropped to cover, just glimpsing the flash from Slade's left hip as sand scattered left and right overhead.

("Thankfully this one's a wild shot...")

Bullets screamed by for two seconds of full-auto fire.

("And a moron: that's one down...")

He tossed an empty ammo box in the air and the deluge of bullets resumed.

("Lord: he's naught but an idiot.")

Ethan had the Remington in his hands and was rising before the second rifle was empty. The agent stepped back into the building as Ethan zeroed the crosshairs on the doorjamb at head level. He could see the tip of the man's boot on the threshold and as Slade leaned forward to peek out: a bullet passed through his eye and blew out the back of his skull.

The sprinting soldier had twenty yards to go when he saw the back of his CO's head fly away. His stride broke to a walk, and in a few steps, he stopped with his back to Ethan. The soldier had recognized the difference in the report that accompanied the .300 Ultra Mag projectile: his armor would not save him.

Ethan counted a full seven seconds before the man spun on his right foot, swinging his weapon a hundred and sixty degrees before one clean bullet passed through his heart.

Ethan transferred the Remington to his left hand and stood, crossed himself, pulled his Winchester from the case with his right and hiked off to the west.

His track arced to the north where he intersected the old haul road. He followed the road to where it turned back northwest and then he continued east beyond the highwall, noting the two Germans lying in the sand saddle as he passed.

"Poor devils... Got righteous; too little, too late..."

Cleve rode south, intentionally weaving an erratic pattern through the scrub out on the sand flats. He traveled two-thirds of the north-south width of the plant, then turned east when he was square with the only open entrance along the west face of the building.

The entrance was one of a series of 30X30 foot doors, each composed of two sliding panels meeting at the center. The opening was at a single panel that had fallen inward, most likely at the coaxing of vandals.

As Cleve wove his way toward the opening, his shield motored its way down to his left forearm where he slipped his fingers through a handgrip near the inner edge of the disc, then re-established his hold on the handlebars. The enemy knew that George was inside, so they would not shoot from the main chamber where they could find themselves under fire. That left only three windows on the north end from which they could guard the door, accepting George's assertion that he would have cleared the south half of the plant by mid-day. Cleve's intel indicated that the hit men didn't have the manpower to cover ingress; nevertheless, he tried to keep the shield between him and those windows. He shot through the opening and bounced over the fallen door; glancing right, he darted for cover behind a short stack of haul truck tires as he scanned the huge enclosure for danger.

The three floors of offices on the north and south walls were the only component rooms to the peripheral structure, with the north offices extending only a short distance down the length of the north wall. The rest of the shops, separators and machinery rooms were independent constructs within the peripheral shell, which gave the eastern interior the look of a miniature city covered in the dust of ages.

Except for entryways, the lower thirty feet of the shell was sheathed in steel siding. The north and south walls rose another ten feet above the top of the 3rd floor offices, admitting daylight through translucent fiberglass siding up to the edge of the pitched tin-roof. From there the north and south pitched-roof sections rose to meet another 10-foot vertical wall of fiberglass that also ran the east-west length of the structure.

The gable walls were fiberglass from thirty feet upward, although much of the siding was missing down the center of the west face, where the fiberglass had been sun baked in the afternoon heat then blown out by storms and the prevailing southwest wind.

Linked to the concrete exterior pillars on the north and south walls: a line of interior pillars rose to the edge of the center pitched-roof section. The foundation of pillars shouldered the support framework for the building and the huge I-beam that ran the length of the central peak, which topped out over eighty feet from the floor.

Fifteen feet below the main beam, a steel and wood plank deck ran the length of the building. Steel hooks hung from numerous 8-wheel trolleys on the central I-beam, some of which still hosted extension cables or chain hoists that passed to the ground floor via a 4-inch slot down the center of the upper deck. Most of the chain hoists remained on the lesser north-south I-beams at the 65-foot level.

There was a labyrinth of conveyor belts and steel catwalks crisscrossing on either side of the centerline. Several of the conveyors disappeared into chimneys to the roof where more belts extended to exterior elevators.

Cleve was lost in thought: considering whether to leave the bike now and creep into the darker reaches, or start with the high ground out here. The problem with climbing was that he would be visible from below until he reached the upper deck, because the stairs and catwalks were all bar grating and bolted steel: which made for an easy target and a squeaky racket at the very least. Although bullets would pass through the 3X12 inch planks on the deck as well: at least the enemy would be shooting blind. Cleve considered his options for climbing to the upper deck while he dug out his hunter's hearing aids.

("OK, I could run up that staircase: noisy and too slow. I could ride the bike up: noisier and a little faster, provided I can wheelie and pivot every flight without a hitch. Either way I'd have to disconnect my shield, so I could quickly switch arms as I round the corner at each flight of stairs, and that won't happen on the bike-)

("What's that? Somebody's speaking... can't make it out, but I believe it's coming from a northwest third floor office. I gotta get the high ground on that sucker before he comes out.")

Cleve looked around and spotted a shaker screen panel leaned against a shaker deck at a 30-degree angle. He maneuvered the bike onto the screen and powered it to the top where... he dropped into the rectangular funnel that emptied to the conveyor belt beneath. Unfortunately, his ramp screen was the one that belonged in the shaker.

He cussed himself for not checking before he signaled his presence with all the metallic clanging. He heard gunfire outside... As he dragged the screen up onto the shaker there was a shot from inside the office block, and then another outside. He lapped the screen up over the input conveyor... more shots outside. Then he lined his bike up on the screen and launched up onto the conveyor belt. He recognized the distant crack of his Remington as a high-power projectile entered the plant from the office block: banging its way past catwalks and conveyors to exit through the east wall.

("Hope Ethan's keeping things under control out there.")

Clear of the loose shaker screen, he slowed to a mid-range speed as he rode the belt toward a roof chimney. Cleve was so intent on staying centered on the belt that he didn't consider the proximity of the material conveyor's support cables until he steered left to hop an easy two feet onto the upper deck: and caught his shield.

He spun counterclockwise to tumble across the oak planks, while the bike's front tire tracked to the centerline and into the 4-inch slot, twisting the forks when the tail end whipped counterclockwise to a violent rebound. The encounter with the support cable had snapped the tiny chain that had been moving Cleve's shield along the guide rail on his jersey, so he stripped it out of the servos and then twisted the shield free of the little trolley at his wrist.

("That mistake could have cost me big time if I'da been caught before I was over the deck.")

He was snapped from his reverie as a 12-gauge slug ruined the steering stem and handlebars of his bike. The boom of three more magnum shells followed the first as splintering wood sprayed upward from the points of a triangle around the downed machine.

Cleve picked up an abandoned wheel chock as he rolled to his feet and tossed it at the ruined motorcycle; then he bolted across the deck as four more slugs ripped through the planks on the far side of the bike.

"Hmpf..."

Leaning over the north edge of the deck, Cleve stared down into the eyes of his antagonist: ZMB Flattop.

("A worm and a weasel Slade,") thought Spike as he leaned away from the window.

Then he jerked his chin back as a .300 Ultra Mag slug passed under his nose, splattering him with plaster from the wall.

("And you're on your own.")

He fell backwards, rolled to his feet and dove from the room. He charged to the stairs and down to the ground floor; slipping through the door he flattened against the wall, scanning for where the sound of scurrying goats was coming from.

The crunchy clunking as Cleve passed over each set of belt rollers was barely audible over the pinging of debris bouncing off equipment on the floor below. Spike glanced up when he noted the dust filtering down through the air.

("What? Are they on the catwalks or convey- What the...")

He spotted the bike just as Cleve was passing from view above the south edge of the upper deck. All consideration for stealth vanished as Spike charged out in the open, raising his shotgun overhead. Weaving his way through the machinery (trying to decide where to shoot) he recognized the motorcycle wheel hanging through the deck. Halfway to the centerline driveway, Spike cut loose with his Mossberg.

After four rounds he waited for movement- or blood. He heard a *ker-plunk*, the wheel shifted, and he sent four more slugs through the deck: this time splintering oak in a pattern northeast of the bike.

He continued scanning the deck as his fingers scrabbled for more magnum cartridges. Almost directly overhead: Spike watched a face appear... followed by the flash of shiny Titanium Gold as he found himself peering up the barrel of a custom MRI Desert Eagle.

Spike tipped his head forward and dove for cover; he arched his neck and back as he dropped to hands and knees: scrambling for shelter beneath heavy machinery. On his way down, a .50 caliber AE slug hammered his left shoulder plate; then another hammered at his spine. He kicked forward to slide under the edge of a shaker; someone rang the bell and he thought he detected a sledgehammer impacting the top of his skull as the lights went out.

Cleve swung his Desert Eagle in line with the man's head and hesitated as he considered the possibility of riding a chain hoist down, disarming him, then beating him senseless. Sally was still in a coma and he questioned whether this animal deserved a merciful death.

In a split-second Spike dove for cover as Cleve cut loose, hammering him as he slid to safety. He'd tossed his shotgun ahead as he scrambled, but it came up short and the Mossberg's bright green engraving was still visible beyond the edge of the shaker. Cleve took deliberate aim at the ZMB emblem and fired a bullet through the receiver.

("Damn that armor is tough; don't know if I put him down or not.")

Cleve was immediately scanning the deck for materials he could work with. He moved to the bike and pried up one of the deck planks so he could keep an eye on Spike's locale. Pulling the front wheel free of the slot, he laid it over and assessed the damage: only the front end was ruined; the motor and batteries had not been hit.

The throttle cable had been severed halfway to the rheostat, activating a kill switch by default. He pulled the lower throttle sheathing from the inner cable and opened the bike's tool kit. Then he disabled the kill switch, flipped the main power back on and gave the cable a light tug; the rear wheel kicked: so far so good…

("This job is gonna be all green lights from here.")

Cleve had the bike set where he had a view while he worked; he still had his hunter's ears in, but had not heard a thing from Spike. He had been hearing gunfire outside and then came the rat-tat-tat of full-auto fire from just outside the north door. He couldn't see anyone around the entry partition, but then a body hit the floor after the crack of a .300 Ultra Mag- with ricochets through the floor machinery. The follow-up round a few moments later had a ring of finality: and Cleve suspected Ethan's campaign on the north side was complete.

Under the bike's side cover, Cleve bypassed the rheostat and reversed the polarity from the batteries. He picked up a 20-foot handler's hook and pulled three of the big 8-wheel I-beam trolleys in line over the bike, juggled cables and hoists, attached a chain hoist from the easternmost trolley to the bike frame at the steering head and hoisted the ruined front end a few inches off the ground. Then he carried a two-hundred-pound scrap cover plate over and dropped it by the bike; keeping a wandering eye on Spike's hideout all the while.

Cleve was kneeling down, bolting a length of chain to the scrap iron when he felt a slight shift in the deck- nearly imperceptible, but there it was again... His eyes were locked on Spike's position when he rolled left, bringing his gun up between his legs, aimed directly behind his former position.

"Dammit Gerry. Warn me before sneaking up like that."

Cleve turned back to his work and the stakeout.

"I was trying to find cover before you spun around and shot me."

"Like I almost *did*. Where'd you come from anyways?"

"Down the chimney."

"Thought you were coming in the back way..."

"Decided to take the high ground and have a look-see first."

"Well, I've got one pinned down- or dead -under that shaker there... You've got to get some of that new armor Gerr: if you're going to keep wearing that heavy shit. That boy was shaking off bullets like they were flies."

"Yes: but that stuff is special order..."

"Anyways, I haven't heard a peep out of ZMB there- and I won't while we're talkin' -so keep your eyes peeled. I can see you've got your ears in."

"You could have finished him off right through that steel panel if you hadn't left the Ultra Mags with Ethan."

"Iron plate *and* the super armor? Maybe not. You recognized the seven-hundred, huh?"

"I was coming down the belt from the northeast elevator when he packed up and headed west."

"I figger'd he got the last one."

"I couldn't see them below the roofline, but they gave Ethan hell: before he finished them off."

"OK, we haven't seen George; he must be down there in the east end with the last two-"

"One. I exterminated one out back."

Without asking if he'd used up the entire can of pesticide: Cleve eyed his little brother casually. He had sparred with Gerry enough over the years to know the man could be deadly with any weapon, from his feet upward.

"Oh...K-"

"Shh…" Gerry held up his hand and cocked his head.

There was a sub-metallic tapping coming from below: obviously from Spike's vicinity.

"Yeah, I guess he's still kickin'. You keep an eye out, while I finish with this bike."

"And what are you about?"

"I'm *about* to knock down a Black Hawk."

"I thought George said it went home."

"Actually, he said it went south. When I climbed the ridge from the truck- way up there -I scoped the chopper way south on the flats, in the shade of that little copse of trees; you know the one…
Anyways, now that we've got *them* outnumbered: it's just a matter of time before these boys call in the big guns."

"You *are* probably right; but I can see this is another of your hair-brained schemes that won't work. If we stay here: that gunship could come in and hang about twenty or thirty yards from the gable wall-with his guns just about head level -and this bike here: will maybe launch high enough to hit the windshield; *maybe*. If we work together we can take out this character below us easy enough, and then without a spotter inside, the gunship wouldn't know where to shoot. But this is all moot, because Ethan has probably got the chopper under his crosshairs right now."

Cleve tipped his head to the side and looked up with one eye closed, "Ethan doesn't know about the chopper."

"You didn't tell him…"

"I was busy, and I was in a hurry."

"Oh, I bet you were. Busy shaking sand off your ass again."

"Hey… we'll talk about that later."

"First thing: the bike is going to drive right out of that groove."

"No. I'm tying this hunk of iron on right in front of the tire-actually behind the tire since it'll be goin' backwards -so we'll drop the weight through the deck and it'll keep the tire *in* the groove."

"It's still not going to do much more than distract the pilot; or piss him off if you scratch his paint job."

"You're not seeing the big picture here. Just grab that other handler's hook and help me with this-"

"Whoa… look," said Gerry, pointing down at the shaker.

They'd both heard the *clink-scrape* as a dented helmet slid out from under the machine. Cleve immediately complied with Spike's request by blasting a hole through it, which popped the helmet into the air as the bullet impacted the concrete.

"I don't know about super armor, but it is a super helmet that takes two rounds of .50 caliber AE to penetrate."

"I was only loaded for tonight's target practice and we didn't lose any time gettin' on the road. And-"

"Second time you've used that *in a hurry* excuse in the last five minutes."

"-And: you see that notch out of the shaker? I lost a bit of energy on the one that banged his helmet."

"And why didn't you take the head shot first?"

"Well... maybe I wanted to punish him a little... first."

"Your assignment for tonight is to study the maxims: *teamwork, be prepared* and... *it wasn't meant to BE a GAME!*"

"Yes Mother. I may have overlooked a little intel *teamwork* with Ethan, but I'm sure he was happy to find that I would *be prepared* to hand over my Ultra Mag firepower when he needed it."

Gerry had drawn a Model 500 Smith & Wesson and when Cleve finished speaking he fired two .50 Magnum rounds at the thick steel plate that Spike was under. With the first boom a deep crater appeared; the second round put a hole through it.

"You've just got to quit using that cheap ammo Cleveland. If I had an extra fifty rounds along, I'd make Swiss cheese of those panels: probably wind up chasing your boy around the shaker and back to where he started. He'd probably already moved before he tossed that helmet-"

Cleve put his hand up: "He's talkin'..."

"-that fuckin' bird in the air, or I will track you down and shoot your ass myself. I'm taking fire here... And see if that *worm* Slade is still cowering on the north sand pile; he should have come through the door by now."

"You heard that; now let's get this job done," said Cleve, continuing as they worked, "We want as much speed as possible, but I'm thinking we'll burn the motor if I just flip it on in high gear. The tire's fat enough it won't fall through or even wedge in that slot; but it's gonna get max traction with that pig iron plate holding it in there. I'm thinking we'll walk the chain out to about 45-degrees, then hold the wheel up and get the whole train moving before we drop it in there hot. What do you think: fourth or fifth gear?"

"I was thinking third or fourth."

"Fourth it is."

"But I still think it might flip if it gets to hopping."

"Always got to make things difficult? OK, go get that 2-wheel dolly."

Cleve grabbed one of the trolley handler's and shot the hook off; the bullet went through the deck, ricocheted off machinery and out the front of the building. Then he shot the axle in half on the dolly, shoved one half into the long shaft and crushed it against the axle. Next, he slid it through the bike frame alongside the footpegs, attached the other wheel and centralized the shaft with duct tape. He looked up at Gerry.

"Happy?"

"I'll be happy if you don't hit us with a ricochet. Yes, it might keep it up until it stabilizes."

"Those training wheels will probably never touch the ground. Think I'll give our rat a last reminder to stay in his hole 'til trouble arrives."

Cleve drew his sidearm and fired a .50 AE round into a panel on either side of the shaker. The impacts left pockmarks on the surface.

"Uh-huh, you better leave that plinking ammo at home next time."

"Just get on the other side of the bike and be ready."

The pilot of the Black Hawk was munching a Snickers bar while his copilot sipped coffee from a thermos cup. It was going on three hours since they'd put the helicopter down in the shade and the sun had come around to bake them from behind. The copilot had lost all contact with their ATF-EO base and expressed his concern at 15-minute intervals on the hour.

"I'm telling you: something is seriously wrong, Luke. We need to return to base and find out what. We were supposed to return immediately; they may need us there."

"I know. But our last orders came from the field agent and we can't leave without him releasing us or having his orders overridden by Command. We shouldn't have to deal with either of them; we should have a crew chief onboard for this."

"This *fast-track* to our own S-70 has quickly become the fast-track to a bad deal; we never should have let them dazzle us into this *promotion* to Executive Ops."

"At first I was imp-"

"Hold on: one of them is calling in... It's the other guy: Spike."

"Breaker, gunship, Black Hawk up, uhh... FT-five-seventy-nine: get it up, get it in here," Spike ordered in a raspy whisper.

The pilot fired the engine as his copilot responded: "This is Black Hawk Foxtrot-Tango-Five-Seven-Niner, what exactly are your orders Sir? Over."

"My orders are for you to move on that west wall and air it out on the top quarter of the building."

"You want us to jump out onto the building? Over."

"No, you idiot... There's a deck below that I-beam sticking out from the central peak. I want you to machinegun everything between that deck and the I-beam."

The pilot broke in: "We will retrieve your teams when your operation is complete, but we have not been authorized to fire the guns. Over."

"Then you call in and get authorization."

"Unfortunately, we have lost all communication with the base. Over."

"Then *I* am giving you authorization."

The Black Hawk pilots were kicking around what to say or do when Spike began raising his voice to abuse and threaten them. Luke frowned and continued warming up the engine; after serious consideration he lifted off and the helicopter sailed north. The copilot grumbled a bit then took command as he prepared the starboard minigun.

"-and this fast-track gets worse all the time... We will swing west and then attack on a 90-degree azimuth. Move in at one hundred knots, bring your airframe to a 60-degree azimuth and decelerate, hover with your rotor perimeter approximately twenty meters from the gable wall, while my minigun cleans up."

"No. We'd be taking fire the whole way in. I'm taking her in on a 0-degree azimuth and you will fire square off the starboard as we move into position."

"I became crew chief when I became gunner. I want to see what we are getting into before we get there. You won't be taking fire, Luke, because I'll be taking their gunner out."

"Think I trust you on that? Davey, you don't have experience on those guns any more than I do. I'm pilot and you are my rookie gunner."

"What's to experience? Aim and pull trigger. Luke, we have no military rank: we're both contract pilots. So, follow chain-of-command protocol; you're on the fast-track to mutiny."

"Drop the *fast-track* crap, dammit. We left the base with me in command and that's how it stays."

They were on final approach to the plant; too late to change Luke's mind, so Davey just grumbled to himself.

"Damned fast-track to a bad idea…"

"Spike's orders were to take out the whole upper deck, so you start firing through the gable wall when we reach that step to the upper roof. You can start choosing targets at the open section."

"Yeah-yeah: I got this."

When they'd cleared the step to the central pitched roof section, Davey began blasting the wall to splinters and powder like it was… fiberglass. Through the dust of disintegrating fiberglass, he thought he saw men diving from the deck, and then the view cleared as they hovered alongside the window.

His eyes were drawn to a large projectile hurtling toward the cockpit on a catapult-like monorail system. Davey instinctively tracked after the motorcycle with the minigun, blowing chunks of the wood deck away in a roaring blaze. He recognized the inverted bike attached to a chain hoist trolley before he caught the target with the minigun.

When Luke spotted the machine accelerating toward his helicopter's fuselage, he had no idea if it could swing high enough to do any serious damage, but he didn't want to risk any damage at all.

"RAILGUN!" Luke yelled to Davey, who was busy obliterating the deck behind the self-propelled projectile.

He banked the Black Hawk out and away from the building as the bike was taking air off the end of the deck. When the gunship lurched westward, Davey fought to bring his weapon to bear on the bike as it swung upward through 45-degrees of arc and slammed against the immobile trolleys that were stacked at the I-beam end-stop.

Davey caught the swinging motorcycle and chain halfway through the arc: chewing up the tubular frame under the stream of bullets and spewing LFP battery debris as he strove to deflect the scrap iron from the gunship. When the crude projectile failed to release: the momentum of the swing held the tri-trolley stack from rebounding off the end-stop; and both pilots felt a wave of relief as remains of the bike disintegrated under Davey's minigun fire.

In several heartbeats the imminent threat of the motorcycle as massive projectile had given way to nolo contendere. In the following few heartbeats the Black Hawk banked away from the gable wall as pilot and gunner watched a pair of massive steel hooks swing up past the rotor blades.

"Holy shit…"

The loop of cable slipped from the westernmost trolley hook and a 70-foot steel noose sailed toward the main rotor. In those few heartbeats the value of the motorcycle as mass driver had become clear.

Luke knew they would not escape the noose and hollered: "Hold on to your seat Davey- we're goin' down."

With a *whack-whack-whack-crunch* the tail rotor was relieved of its duty along with three of the main rotor blades.

"Dammit Luke, we're on the fast-track ta hell now."

When Spike's senses were returning his first thought was to play dead since that's how he felt anyway: like his body was concrete; except for the back of his head: which felt like Jell-O under a blow torch. He figured if anyone could see him, they hadn't shot him yet, so he would be safer not trying to move until he was actually sure he could.

As his mind cleared and he brought his conscious reality up to date, he began assessing his immediate surroundings to determine he was in fact beneath the shaker he dove for while taking fire. When he decided to make his move, he hauled himself to his knees. Glancing around he noted his predicament looked much the same as when the goat had embarrassed him earlier.

("Damned goat. I'd feel better if it was just him kickin' me in the head right now… How long have I been out? Surely Slade's in here by now.")

He carefully slipped his helmet off and felt the back of his head.

("Doesn't hurt so bad with this bucket off. Really creased the bitch though; and I just about left it on the steps.")

Most of the bullet's energy was transferred to his armor when he arched his cervical spine and turtled the helmet into his shoulder pads. The slug had glanced off the helmet and then the armor, but it still left its mark on his scalp.

He carved some of the padding from the helmet and tried to hammer the dent out with the butt of his knife, then tried it on.

Between the lump on his head and the ridge inside the helmet, any protection it provided was offset by the pain it also provided. He drank some water then removed his radio from the useless helmet, which he slid past his ruined shotgun to test for a shooter.

("No respect: shootin' a man's gun like that.")

When the helmet popped into the air: he ducked the concrete spatter and radioed the Black Hawk. Then he ate a PowerBar and waited.

When his gunship's minigun cut loose, Spike figured a few seconds was all it would take for the enemy to lose interest in him altogether. With his sidearm in hand, he sprang to his feet to find two men had leapt from the south edge of the upper deck and were now swinging on chains in diverging arcs to the east and west.

He was raising his Glock 27 to take aim when the torrent of minigun fire slashed through the deck and arced across the driveway into the steel machinery. Spike turned and sprinted for all he was worth. He ducked behind a heavy machine as the clatter of fiercely ricocheting bullets arced past and continued west into the office block.

Thinking the gunner was out of control Spike was back up and weaving his way northeast. He heard the steady *wump-wump-wump* of the helicopter mis-beat and follow up with the *whack-whack-whack-crunch* that preceded its impact with the earth. Spike felt the reverberation through the concrete slab along with the thunder of the crash, but didn't look back. Noticing scraps of Slade's skull on the doorjamb ahead, he chose not to find out if the north side was safe for travel. Instead, he hooked east through the plant to backtrack the same path he'd taken to the west end when the team split up.

("These hooligans have got no respect at all: I don't know how they managed to take out that Black Hawk, but they're not supposed to *do* that.")

Using the handling hook, Gerry had drawn in the pulley chains for each of their chosen chain hoists and hung them for quick access. When they had completed the launch of their Macgyvered mass driver, they dove from the deck with chains in hand.

Cleve's hoist trolley was blocked in place on a north-south I-beam to his left. If the I-beam were a minute hand pointing to six o'clock on the deck: he left the deck at four o'clock and swung in a broad counterclockwise spiral to the floor. He took a fat delay, then locked the brakes and dropped to the concrete at eight o'clock. Cleve's feet hit the floor running on a northeasterly track through the machinery: shadowing his quarry for intercept. The minigun fire had all passed overhead and he had lost all concern for the gunship when he heard the extension cable find its mark.

The brothers' flying descents were implemented with manual chain hoists by gripping the ascending and descending loops of the continuous loop pulley chain. The load chain and hook were best left undisturbed, hanging vertically from the hoist. By allowing the ascending loop of the pulley chain to slip through one hand, a man's descent proceeded for as long as he delayed before adding friction to slow down, or firmly gripping both loops to lock the brakes.

Gerry had not been so lucky as his brother. His descent was meant to be a mirror image of Cleve's, but his hoist trolley rolled south with him and when it stopped solid against a block: the load chain swung past the pulley chain, wrapped around, tangled, hooked and locked the mechanism. Gerry's timing and target were forfeit; he spiraled in below the hoist. Sliding on both loops of the chain until his gloves started to burn, he lowered himself hand over hand for the last few yards.

Gerry ran straight for the west entrance and charged the broken helicopter before the gunner could regain his bearings. The man was hanging in his harness, rubbing his neck.

"Where is your copilot?" demanded Gerry as he checked for tracks around the wreck.

"Here… We don't have a crew chief," mumbled Davey.

Gerry checked the pilot, who was still in his seat, bleeding from a nasty impact to his left cheek. He patted him down and checked around for weapons; Gerry's 500 Smith & Wesson was still directed at the copilot.

"OK: Get up," said Gerry, and then patted him down. "Now get up there and take care of your pilot."

Gerry broke out the first-aid kit and tossed it to Davey.

"Better bandage that wound and keep the bleeding under control."

He holstered his gun and stood with one foot on the gunner's seat and both hands resting on ceiling handles. Gerry's imposing frame had Davey feeling like a child seated before his father after being a bad boy; only he knew the threat was more than a spanking this time.

"We're just contract pilots," Davey started.

"I can see that."

"They said we wouldn't have to use the guns when we took the job."

"Oh? You took to it like a duck to water though, didn't you?"

"It was Spike: he demanded that we help him…"

"Yes… we did catch the end of that conversation."

"I was hoping I wouldn't actually hit anyone. I never fired a minigun before-"

"Obviously. *I* would have taken out that makeshift railgun fifty meters up the track. And you might not know it, but you almost cut your boy in half as he bolted. I had a ringside seat as you cut that swath through the plant chasing the dirtbike; that's what it was you know."

"Yeah, I could see that as I stopped it. And then the cable… In a way, it was kind of graceful the way it sailed right up there like that."

"I'll bet your pilot was shittin' his pants."

"Luke tried to drop under it right at the last… Hope he's alright," added Davey as he checked the bandage. "I told him to come in from the west right from the start."

"Did you? Perhaps there's hope for you yet: maybe in the commercial crop dusting service. OK, I'm going to leave you two here, but you will not step beyond the airframe."

"But it might catch fire; I thought we'd be leaving any min-"

"Don't try to bullshit me, Son. You weren't ten meters from the deck when you attained free-fall. This old girl can do more than twice that without coughing up any fuel. We'll be right inside there; you leave the chopper before EMS arrives: You die. Trust me on this."

"When will EMS arrive?"

"I don't know; just take care of your friend and you'll be alright. And take this experience to heart: whom you work for is far more important than what you are paid."

Gerry had already put a bullet through the black-box and ripped the wiring from the radio. Removing the bolt assembly from the minigun as they spoke: he tossed it in the sand and jogged back to the building. Davey noted the precision in his forceful stride and considered the sincerity he'd sensed in the big man's voice: he decided they would wait for EMS in the ruins of their S-70 Black Hawk.

As Spike approached the complex of constructs on the east end, he attempted to re-establish contact with his team.

"Status report… status? Give me a click if you can't talk."

He clicked his own mic off and on twice.

"Come on. One of ya's… Damn."

As he neared the east wall he started working his way south in hopes of running across his inside man. He knew they had become the minority, but all he needed to know was that the target was dead, then he could disappear into the woods. There would be no bonus if they did not complete the mission.

("And what about that bozo I sent north: he should be back inside by now too. They should have reported in a long time ago: but I didn't check in either, maybe they were too busy. Maybe they're in a tight spot, ready to pounce, turned the radio off so they wouldn't be made. Or maybe they got Jefferson and headed out. No, they'd have headed back to the truck and still be in radio range. Unless they headed for the chopper way down there, or maybe they were on the chopper? No, the pilots would have said something. You're losin' it Roy. They would have radioed before getting out of range and would have clicked if they were here… Must be the blow to the head: reality denial. They're done. You're on your own. Fuck Jefferson, *and* the bonus: I gotta get the hell outa here. But first I've got to get this dude that's tracking me; he didn't even care that I knew, before we got into this maze of buildings and pipes; out there in the machinery he was just taunting me, wanted me to *know* I was being hunted: damn him- he'll *die* for that. And he's still tracking me; no… he's shadowing me, out there, to the west- There it is again: just a light brush, a drag of the foot; damn him: he wants me to know he's out there. He's still taunting me; waiting to take me out on his own terms…")

Spike froze, backed up a few steps and tucked into a doorway.

("This is crazy. He could be on top of this wall, around the next corner, inside this room behind me… I gotta make him come to *me*.")

He crept across the walkway between the buildings, which had the feel of an alley between garage workshops in a little town. The shop he checked had a door, which might work for shooting someone through, but it was a transfer terminal full of manifolds and pipes: he didn't like it.

He slipped in and out of the next two doors, which opened to the same room that was chock-full of electric motors of all sizes; a mounted armature waited for rewind and half a dozen heavy wood tables hosted disassembled motors that would never run again. Slots in the ceiling allowed the larger motors to be brought in on chain hoists through a removable partition in the front wall: no good.

The next shop had no door; it had storage shelves along the left wall with a small storage nook between the left wall and a short entry hallway; it had two lathes in the main room and the glass wall across the front was covered in a buildup of oil from the lathes and dust from the plant. Spike would have to choose soon, so this would have to be it.

("A perfectly obvious place for an ambush and that son of a bitch is just cocky enough to think he can outsmart me.")

Spike had carefully paced one step into the room to check it out. He turned to the left, took a step backwards and carefully ground his heel in the dust; then he walked forward and into the storage nook.

("He'll have no idea which side I'm on, so he'll know the odds are against him if we shoot it out through the walls. No. He'll dive into the room thinking he can out shoot me on the slide: and he'll die right there on the floor.")

Sheriff Jefferson and Heidi Jo sat on the floor with their backs against a concrete wall. They were in the largest of the interior structures; it was constructed mostly of concrete that supported a maze of interlaced piping. Their hideout was in a basement chamber where mineral slurries were combined or separated through manifolds that linked a multitude of pipes to the boiler rooms through the wall at their backs.

The sheriff had chosen it because the concrete provided the best protection from stray bullets and their specific location could only be fired upon down the line of pipes they were sitting between. Halfway to the manifolds was a concrete support block that would provide solid cover if they were found; and ricochet shots should mostly follow the pipes into the wall. Unfortunately, the floor was wet and smelled like rat dung: a fact that Heidi had not ceased pointing out.

"I don't like it here. It's wet and cold and it stinks."

"Not the best place for a first date, huh?"

"I'm not kidding Tommy."

"Yeah, I know. But I don't think we can find any place safer. You heard the gunfire: I told you they would come. We should just wait it out here."

They were both quiet for a while and Heidi leaned her head against his shoulder. Eventually she brought up another sore subject.

"I have *got* to go to the bathroom Tommy."

"I know; me too. But I'll piss in my pants before I'll risk your life out there. Just go piss over there by that slab."

"That's just nasty Tommy. This place smells bad enough as it is, and you said if someone starts shooting we're going to lie down up there. We haven't heard any shots for a while; maybe it's time to crawl out of our hole," she wrapped her arms around his bicep, "Get some fresh air?" and gave him a peck on the cheek, "Have a look-see? Hmm?"

She was snuggling against his neck and gave him a lick. He was becoming aroused and silently berated himself.

("What am I a horny kid? Getting a hard-on in this disgusting pit; next thing you know I'll be slurping on her face and she'll throw up. I guess she's right: we better get some air.)

"Alright: stay behind me. Keep the thirty-eight in your hand; you only have six rounds so remember: shoot for the face; anywhere else is a waste of ammo," he stopped before they climbed from the basement, "When we get to the top of the steps, we'll move into the control room- with all the solenoid breakers -and you can use the bathroom on the south wall while I watch the door," he stepped to a corner and relieved himself, "We'll decide from there if we should crawl back into our rat hole."

"You couldn't wait 'til we got upstairs?"

"I couldn't wait and have you get shot, while I had my hands full."

"Hmf."

The control room had numerous holes in the hung ceiling with tangles of wiring hanging down onto several of the tables and operator's panels. The sheriff turned toward the west exit and she rounded the corner to the right, stopping when she saw the "MEN" sign over the short hallway. She looked around to see if he had found her reflexive hesitation humorous, but he was leaning into the doorway with his Colt Python in hand, carefully surveying the next room, which opened to a foyer and the building's west entrance.

Sheriff Jefferson was standing at ninety degrees to the doorway looking toward the far entrance over his right shoulder when Heidi Jo returned to the room. He glanced at her and back at the front entrance twice, slipped his three-fifty-seven into the holster, then turned toward her with his palms up.

"Heidi, I'm sorry about dragging you into all this filth; and I know housekeeping hasn't been taking care of that bathroom either; and-"

"It's not your fault Tommy. I know that…"

"And I know that too, but it's been so disgusting for you here; and I know I've been a little too crude; and I just think a man should be treating you like a lady; and I thought maybe when we get out of this: maybe I can make up for it, a little, by taking you out someplace real nice?"

"Maybe…"

("Well, that's something.")

Sheriff Jefferson was wearing a half smile and Heidi Jo was looking at her feet to hide her own humor at how long it had taken him to ask her out. The snubnose was in her hand at her side as she looked up and then snapped it up with her left hand under the grip; her aim went high then dropped to his right shoulder.

"Hei-" he commenced a reproach, then noting her lack of mirth, he simultaneously felt: a blow against his shoulder; a jolt against his holster; an impact against the floor; and a knife against his throat, as Heidi watched a soldier drop from above.

The soldier had removed his helmet and armor in order to silently negotiate the crawlspace above the hung ceiling, so he would have to keep his human shield alive until he had disarmed the woman pointing a gun his way.

"If you just set that gun down, little lady, no one here will get hurt."

Her expression had become frantic as her pistol wavered between the sheriff's shoulder and the soldier's forehead.

"Just calm down Heidi and everything will be all right," cooed Sheriff Jefferson and then he silently mouthed the word: "*Shoot.*"

He was slowly edging his left hand towards the knife at his neck and he tensed his right arm as he prepared to grab the hand that gripped his revolver. He mouthed: "*shoot*" again. Her vision was blurring through the welling tears when she pulled the trigger and shot the sheriff in the shoulder.

What happened next was like a perfectly choreographed scene that transpired in an instant, and yet to her: time seemed to flow like a slow-motion dream with intermittent jolts of shocking reality. Heidi Jo fell back in shock, trying to bring her gun back on target, but her body was frozen with the fear that she would do more harm than good.

The soldier raked his blade across her friend's neck: opening his throat from trachea to jugular, and she felt the horror of that moment would never end...

Beyond the scope of her senses, the assassin's other hand had concurrently drawn the Colt Python from the dead man's holster and fired a shot. Heidi registered the flash and instantly found her back against the wall with a bullet through her own right shoulder; and she unjustly felt her failure had come full circle as she watched Tommy's corpse slip to the floor.

Her anatomy seemed frozen again, this time from the shock of *being* shot and in her dreamlike daze: a curious, strangely humorous scene unfolded. She watched a thick antenna appear on the assassin's head. The man straightened and Heidi imagined he was standing guard over a sleeping animal... her dreamlike fantasy continued:

("He's a unicorn man, that's what he is. That's not an antenna: that's his little horn...")

Her dizzy delusion slowly drifted back to stiff reality as the man crumpled and another man dropped from the ceiling; pulled the Cold Steel Torpedo from the assassin's skull and wiped the blood on his shirt.

She realized the man was George Mason Jr. as he reverently lifted Tommy to lay him on a tabletop. Heidi began sobbing uncontrollably as she slid to the floor. George immediately scooped up the pack by the door and knelt by the girl to tend her wound. The primary threat to her life would be loss of blood. Sheriff Jefferson kept a few packets of Bleed-X powder in his first aid kit and George dumped one each into the entrance and exit wounds, while she continued sobbing as he worked.

"OK, Heidi, here's what we're gonna do-"

"I shot him. I shot Tommy-"

"Heidi: don't worry about that now."

"But he's dead- Tommy's dead..."

"Heidi-"

"No-no-NO-NO-" she cried out in ascending volume.

They had both been speaking in whispers, but Heidi was wracked with sobs as she continued getting louder. George cupped his left palm under her right cheek and clapped her left cheek with his right hand. The slap in the face shocked and silenced her.

"You've got to hold it together Heidi. The time to mourn is later; Tommy gave his life protecting you: don't waste that life. He was only shot in the shoulder, same as you; it was the enemy who killed him. They will be drawn to the gunfire, so we have got to move. I know it hurts, but we have to find you a safe hideout, then I have to get back to work. We will get you to the hospital as soon as the plant is clear."

As he helped her to her feet she whispered: "Basement, the pipes, Tommy said it was the best place."

"Good girl; just show me where."

She put her arm over George's shoulder and he helped her down the steps. She continued to point the way, though George could see their prints in the dust where they had come out. He would cover their tracks on his way out as Tommy had apparently done on the way in.

"Smells like rat-shit in here," said George.

"That's what I said. We were in here for ages. I thought the shooting was over when we came out."

"That fella was probably waiting for you almost as long as you were in here. I found his armor and assault rifle where he entered the crawlspace and I followed him. Before I go back to work, I will go get that SCAR-H and- the rifle -and bring it back here."

Now that they were out of sight, George completed his first aid on Heidi's shoulder; particularly the exit wound where he poured the third packet of clotting agent and packed the wound with gauze.

She thought his wording was odd; twice he had mentioned going "*back to work*" and she thought of what Tommy had said about trusting the man. George was trying to keep her mind occupied and continued talking about whatever he had a notion to.

"Actually, it's more like an attic above those hung ceilings; there's room to duck walk and there are some joists, but not many, and they're not uniform; you are safest staying on the walls, which don't extend through to the roof; technically hung ceilings are hung below the walls in individual rooms. Some of these buildings don't even have roofs; apparently, they lowered stuff right in. OK, so I was following him, but staying behind the big ventilation tubes as much as possible to try and get in close enough to make my move. Then he dropped in… and by the time I reached the gap… I was… too late…"

George hadn't meant to go there and Heidi started sobbing again.

"Sorry Heidi, so sorry…"

"Tommy said this was the safest place in the plant… *sniff*… He wanted to stay… but it's so revolting- *sniff*… and then it was so sweet when he asked me out… *sniff*- I've been waiting years for him to do that- *sniff*…"

"Don't take the long wait personally Heidi. Nobody thought Tommy would ever get over losing his wife."

"I didn't ever know he was married."

He lost Martha to pancreatic cancer at a young age and then he lost himself between work and helping the local kids, mostly through the Boy Scouts: that's where I first met him; later Dad and I would do out-of-state hunting trips with him. He was scoutmaster for the longest time and was still teaching for merit badges and organizing most of the campouts. Tommy was a lot younger than Dad, but he was always like an uncle to me… and a good friend-," George choked off the last word.

"Thought he was always a bachelor- *sniff*."

"I don't think he ever looked at another woman until…"

George had finished taping her up. He took her hand and gave it a squeeze.

"You're gonna be alright. OK? I'm going to get that rifle now and be right back. I'll tap the pipe seven times; that will be the signal: ding ding-ding-ding ding ding-ding. Anyone pokes their head around that corner without the signal: shoot first and ask questions later."

George did a quick recon, retrieved the SCAR-H and returned to Heidi's side. He gave her some quick instructions and encouragement.

"There's nobody else in this building yet; that's a good sign. OK, here's the short course. First, you probably want to leave this setting right here, it'll be just like your handgun: one round at a time. In this next position, each time you pull the trigger you will deliver a 3-round burst; it would be harder for you to handle with your sore shoulder: on the other hand, you will be shooting with your left and it would give you three chances to score for your pain. Do not put it in this last position; this is full-auto: this setting is mostly for… well; it's mostly for fools, unless you've got belt feed or a drum clip at the very least. You'd use your ammo up before you realized your shoulder was hurting. OK… You're set kiddo."

"Uh… Oh- I don't feel so good."

"No, I don't imagine you do. There are smelling salts in the first aid kit; do your best to stay alert. Just hang in there and we'll be back in a flash to get you out of here."

"We?"

"You felt that minor shock wave that rolled through here while I was away: that was the enemy's helicopter going down. I don't know how we managed it: but that was a grand slam for the home team. The plant may already be clear; I'm about to go check it out. Eight taps this time: ding ding-ding-ding ding ding-ding ding. Be looking for Cleveland or Gerry Henry, Ethan Allen or me."

On his way back through the control room George removed what was left of his own shirt and covered Sheriff Jefferson. Saying a brief prayer, he made the sign of the cross over him three times and backed away.

"Rest in peace… Uncle Tommy…"

Cleve had been shadowing Spike through the east end *ghost town*; he planned to move on him farther south where the layout of pipes, catwalks and conveyors converged into a tight maze. There was actually a sequential and systematic arrangement to the entire processing plant, which Cleve had recognized through exploration of the entire facility in his youth. The logistics of the layout was coming back to him as he moved past the various constructs, reviewing the workings and contents of each in his mind's eye.

He was drawn from his musings when his quarry was overdue passing a checkpoint. Cleve backtracked and moved in to check tracks: the quarry had not returned the way he had come. Checking around the corner through the periscope option on his tactical scope, the alley was all clear to the south.

("Alright: ZMB slipped through one of those five doors. The far door is a mill and steel scrap; the next is lathes and scrap; next two: motors and repair; this end: junction block, but his tracks are in and out of this one for sure. And in the motor room… and… out the other… door. In the next one… in, and… from here… I… can't tell if he came out.")

Circling to the missed checkpoint he looked north up the alley.

("Alright: no footprints visiting the antique milling machine museum. And no prints back out of the lathe museum: so our boy is setting up shop in there.")

Cleve checked the alley behind the lathe shop to confirm no exit. Except for slots along the top, for ventilation and lighting, the rear wall was continuous. He circled back, slipped through a shop on the west side of the alley, crossed the street and stepped silently into the entrance to Spike's trap. Standing in the short entry hall with the Desert Eagle in his right hand and his backup Ruger P89 in his left: Cleve knew it was an ambush.

His breath came slow and steady; Cleve's mind and senses were totally focused on the present as he meticulously surveyed the scene. The footprints before him were obvious: obviously devised to force him into a choice, or to leave him no choice at all. At the upper periphery of his vision, he noted the ceiling panel was missing from the entry hall. Cleve silently backed off and moved up the alley.

Moments later he was back in the entry hall. Bending his knees to thirty degrees, with the backs of his hands against his shoulders; focusing tension through his entire body: Cleve sprang squarely upward, quietly launching two 40-pound motors like massive shot-put over the walls to come crashing through the hung ceiling on both sides of the entrance.

Spike bounded from the storage nook, rotating right to see what was coming through the ceiling. As Spike's handgun came into view, Cleve's fists came together like a bolt cutter. The butt of his left fist banged down on the radius bone at Spike's wrist: fracturing the carpus; the butt of his right fist popped the Glock from the hand: tearing ulnocarpal ligaments in Spike's broken wrist.

As Cleve's right fist snapped upward past the tumbling Glock, his left fist rebounded to follow his right. He blocked Spike's knife arm with his right forearm, and in a divergent flash: Cleve's left elbow smashed into Spike's face.

With his cheek fractured from the left eye socket to his shattered nose, Spike fell back and kicked at his adversary: driving himself to the floor and propelling Cleve into the room.

Cleve drew his Desert Eagle and retrieved Spike's Glock as the Executive Ops mercenary scrambled to his feet. He tossed the Glock's magazine over his shoulder, then removed the slide and pitched it out the door, dropping the remains in the scrap heap.

The blood began running from Spike's nose to drip from his chin.

"Hurts... Doesn't it? Traitor... Looks like that helmet messed up your punk-ass hairdo Butterboy. Turn around and let's see if my bullet left a part in those cute little butter-spikes."

"I'll turn around to walk away from your bloody carcass after I tear your arms off. You're the criminals here. I work for the Administration."

"Your Administration is defunct. Led by a socialist tyrant who subverts the Constitution and attacks American citizens in their homes. He is a traitor by definition. You were an American citizen; you know this to be true. You and all who follow this Administration are traitors as defined in the Constitution of the United States."

"Fuck you."

"You are filth. You turn on your countrymen for money…"

"Fuck you. Real big man, aren't you? Bringing a gun to a knife fight."

"Oh, you want some of this Buck?" growled Cleve as he pulled his Intrepid-XL from the sheath.

Spike growled back: "Fuck you. I'm gonna slice you up and rip you apart little man."

"You're a big boy, Butter-spike, bigger than my little brother. Let's just see how much easier it is to cut you down to size."

Spike snarled at his antagonist and moved out in the open as Cleve stowed the magazine and set his sidearm on the lathe to his left. Spike was still holding his tactical blade in his left hand; his damaged wrist didn't look any better than his broken nose.

"Or we could settle this like real men: hand to hand," growled Spike.

Cleve tipped his head to the side and looked at the crooked hand; Spike grit his teeth, straightened it and wiggled his fingers as if it was fine.

"You must be a glutton for punishment, Buttercup, but if that's what you want: *we aim ta please*."

Spike bent down and slid his knife away. Cleve had already set his knife on the lathe when Spike made a move for his backup P238; the Sig Sauer was on Spike's right ankle and he went for it with his left hand. Cleve snatched the Buck back up, but thought better of trying to put it through Spike's head before being hit by a .380 ACP slug. He grabbed the lathe and jerked himself to the floor, sliding behind the machine in the dust.

("And now *he's* got the gun at the knife fight,") thought Cleve, rolling to his back with blade in hand as he clawed for the Ruger on his calf.

Cleve heard a *whump-thud-crump-dunk*; and rolled to his knees to peek around the corner with his little periscope. He attempted to bring the view into focus and speculated as he adjusted from one extreme to the other.

("Looks like sorghum after the frost. Hmm. Oh- too close -it's just Spike-head.")

Cleve slid his scope to the upper edge of the lathe. Spike was face down on the floor with a lumpy burlap sack lying across his shoulders and a few pieces of brick by his head where they'd fallen from the sack. Noting boots at Spike's side, he panned upward past flat-black armor and a hands on the hips "Superman" stance, to Gerry's frowning face.

"What are you doing?"

"Hey Gerr... Just checking to see what I missed out there."

"No: I mean why is this sadistic bastard still alive? I suppose you felt the need to tell him you were Sally's avenging angel?"

"No. That would give him something to taunt me with."

"You'll be pulling wings off of flies next... I hope this is an isolated incident: you can't take such risks in every battle. What if you'd busted your trigger finger? How are you going to shoot straight? The war may have just begun."

"Yes Mother."

Cleve had slapped the mag back into his gun, holstered it and was standing by Gerry, watching the door with one foot on Spike's ankle.

"It's like this Gerr. First: I've got six good trigger fingers- well, four good and two more: fair. And second: well, second... well OK, I was toying with him. But, I was teaching him about the Constitution... and maybe Gramma Martin could teach him some more while he heals up and then maybe Little George would have a chance to teach him something else."

"Always playing the wise guy; you know Gramma is doubly retired after that reform school experiment. Unfortunately, some of these UN soldiers who died today were probably good men, but the laws of our Republic are no secret, and it was their duty to understand those laws before setting foot on American soil. However, these Executive Ops mercenaries: they know exactly what they do. Their crimes are unconscionable. For them, death comes quickly: no sympathy and no regrets. And this one was despicable: heinous garbage. Just finish him and move on-"

Cleve felt a slight vibration underfoot as they heard the crunch of cartilage and bone shattering behind them. They turned simultaneously as George dropped a piece of 2X4 alongside another that was wedged beneath Spike's broken neck; his head was twisted to an impossible angle.

"We're finished here," said George, stepping outside.

"I didn't even hear him slip in here," whispered Gerry.

Gerry looked at Cleve and Cleve looked around at the holes in the ceiling.

"He's like a spider…"

"Would've made a helluva rock fighter when we were kids…"

George was scoping the scene in every direction as the brothers joined him in the alley.

"You two were kickin' it around in there like that one wrapped it up; I took one soldier inside the facility: there was another-"

"Done."

"And Ethan's charge?"

"Done."

"ETHAN? ETHAN ALLEN… ALL CLEAR…"

Following George's broadcast, a not so distant response came in a sarcastic tone: "*COMING SIR.*"

Moments later Ethan rounded the corner to their north and jogged up to the group. He glanced at the body beyond the doorway.

"So, the last soldier is down as well? I passed the remains of one back there in Buzzard Creek."

Cleve tweaked one eye toward his brother with an admonishing expression: as if he suspected Gerry had chewed the man's arms off.

George glanced at the .300 Ultra Mag cartridges in Ethan's bandolier and cracked a quarter-smile.

Ethan's eyes toggled back and forth questioningly.

"No one has found our reluctant campers as yet?"

"We've lost Tommy," George answered softly.

All heads were bowed as George allowed them their moment of silence.

"But Heidi's been shot through the shoulder; we must get her medical attention immediately."

Cleve was first to respond: "Gerry, you get the girl; I'll get the bike and shoot her to the hospital-"

Gerry cut in: "No. I'm the better rider: I'll take her."

Generally, Cleve would have challenged Gerry's claim, but in this case, he knew it to be true. Gerry's greater mass to total load ratio gave him a distinct advantage and he had more passenger experience from riding with his wife.

"OK: You bring the bike around to the north door and I'll meet you there with the girl. Ethan: If they send another Black Hawk it will come to the first one's black-box-"

"Oh, hold on," Gerry held up his hand, "There are two commercial pilots waiting in the wreck for EMS and its black-box is dead; but reinforcements would still come here first."

Cleve was looking down his nose at Gerry with squinted eyes and a wise guy smirk.

"They were just kids... Maybe you'll want to teach *them* about the Constitution."

"OK: once Gerry is off, I will jog up into the woods for my truck and come back down here for you guys. Anyways, in the meantime we don't want a chopper going after Gerry. So Ethan: can you and George take out another Black Hawk?"

"*I will lay my life on it, that with fifteen hundred men, and a proper train of artillery, I will take Montreal...*"[22]

Cleve looked Gerry in the eye for a short moment then they simultaneously turned to George who was grinning ear to ear. All eyes returned to Ethan...

"Uh... Oh... sorry guys. I got a little over-exuberant there; I suppose that would be rather ambitious..."

Cleve held a hand out, palm up: "The Blackhawk?"

"Heh-ha-ha," George chuckled, "We'll take care of it- GO."

Cleve was in the basement and knew exactly where George was talking about; he actually felt a little guilty he had not thought to tell him to look there first, but then that might have gotten George killed first: second guessing never helped anyone. He tapped the pipe: *ding ding-ding-ding ding ding-ding ding...*

"Heidi? It's Cleve Henry... Are you alright?"

He peeked around the corner; she was unconscious. Cleve moved in close and tried to rouse her to no avail. He picked her up and started working his way out through the pipes. Once he reached the steps it was easy going and they made good time to the north door.

Cleve thought he had beaten Gerry there, but found the bike parked another five yards west. Gerry was busy removing the armor from his torso.

"Ethan made a real mess of that door."

"Hmm. You have any clotting agent?"

"No."

"Probably just as well; George bandaged her up pretty good and there's no gauze left in their kit. We should probably fold up some T-shirt and-"

"Duct tape," they echoed at once and then both pulled a flattened partial roll from a pocket.

"OK, three wraps on the over-bandage; then we use the rest to tape her to your back."

"She's out cold, huh?"

"Yeah, well she moaned a couple times on the way out, but never opened her eyes."

Cleve put a number of wraps around their torsos then taped Heidi Jo's head loosely against his shoulder. Gerry pulled her arms around his waist and held her hands together for two wraps of tape.

"You can stand up on the pegs if you have to, but it won't do Heidi any good and you better be careful you don't mash her legs when you sit back down. Let me get her ankles then you're ready to go. Just don't crash."

"Hey, that's why *I'm* riding. Didn't want you jumping off some cliff and rolling her in the sand," Gerry retorted as Cleve finished taping her ankles against the outside of his calves.

"OK, get out of here."

Cleve watched them round the northwest corner of the building and then jogged off toward Buzzard Creek.

Gerry kept his speed up except when the riding got rough. He eased his way through the edge of the woods to avoid the water hole with the abandoned SUV and was surprised to see the Sheriff's truck at the barricade. Noting the ruined wheels, he understood why they had continued on foot from so far out. On the gravel Gerry ran the bike near flat out; then approaching town he spotted vehicles across the road... military vehicles.

22. The Party's Over

The Cessna Citation Mustang that Gerry had chartered for dispatching Gramma Martin's two UN students was experiencing noticeable turbulence as the aircraft continued descending to a landing pattern altitude. With a jolt, Mads woke as his head thumped against the window. He was belted in, but immediately began stretching his arms and legs when he noted he was no longer bound like a hog on a spit. He glanced around then rubbed his eyes.

"Where's Dean?"

"Already dropped him," answered the pilot.

"In the ocean?"

"No."

While studying the landscape below, Mads repeated: "Where?"

"Exactly where I was paid to deliver him."

"Where are *we*?"

"We're a little southeast of Hanstholm."

"Denmark? You're taking me home?"

"Not quite; I'm dropping you at Thisted Airport. Sorry, I don't make the plans: I'm just the delivery boy."

Gerry slowed as he approached the roadblock then stopped a few yards from the vehicle. A soldier approached the bike from an angle, eyeing his strange cargo.

("Regular Army troops,") thought Gerry and proceeded explaining his rush: "I have a wounded girl here who needs medical attention, Sir."

The soldier's eyes opened wide in recognition and he saluted: "Colonel Henry, Sir. I didn't recognize you."

"*Retired* colonel: no need to salute, Corporal. Randolph, isn't it?"

"Yes Sir. Dad always had a lot of respect- he… he always calls you Colonel. Sir, we can take the girl to the hospital."

"I'm almost there; better that she goes straight into the ER when they cut her free. Call ahead and have them waiting at the emergency entrance."

"Will do; and I'll send an escort ahead."

"My brother will be coming along in a badass Lincoln-"

"I know the rig, Sir; we'll let him through. Dad says if Mr. Henry were still around: Cleveland would be drivin' him to drinkin'."

"You got that right," replied Gerry as he rode away.

When Cleve got his Navigator rolling he picked his way down the valley to Buzzard Creek. When he cleared the creek onto the ramp, he opened the exhaust cutouts and ripped past the tailings mounds, crossing it up to the left and then back right into the sand flats. He spun a donut to a stop, and then looked over Ethan's former post on the west mound.

They weren't there, so he scanned from the building down to the wreck on his right; there were four men standing by the downed Black Hawk. Luke had come around but was being partially supported by Davey.

Cleve shot off toward the wreck, pulling the front wheels a couple feet in the air over a little mound of brush. He spun a clockwise one-eighty to land next to the group.

"Christ, you're a madman, Cleveland. May I postulate that clandestine overwhelms you with boredom?"

"Just get in the truck Ethan."

When they were all loaded, Cleve roared off to the west, spraying sand as he fishtailed left and right exiting the yard.

"DO YOU THINK YOU COULD CLOSE THOSE HEADER DUMPS SO WE CAN TALK- back here? Thank you. There's an SUV stuck in the waterhole up here; you might want to find a way around-"

"Hold on to your seats; the snorkel's up."

Cleve closed the intake cutout so the engine would breath from the snorkel at roof level. He nailed the throttle at the last road cut and the Lincoln launched into the water hole at seventy plus MPH. They didn't touch bottom until near halfway; hammer down, they passed south of the other SUV with the Goodyears digging their way to shallow water on the far shore. In minutes they were tearing up the gravel, heading for town.

"What's your rush Cleveland? These boys are far from critical," noted Ethan, who was keeping an eye on the pilots.

"Just wanted to get clear as quick as possible, so if any more choppers show up, they won't figure us to be leavin' the party."

George was riding shotgun and laughed: "These tractor tires just left a wake out of there like an interstate highway from the air."

"There's nothing coming from our base; we haven't heard from Executive Ops in hours," Davey volunteered (and got a dirty look from Luke).

"All right you spoilsports, I'll ease her into town real quiet-like. Aw-oh… looks like we're stoppin' anyways."

"Those are regular troops: U.S. Army," said George.

A soldier waved them around the truck in the road and another waved them down on the other side. He approached George's window and Cleve called over to him.

"Afternoon Corporal; anything we can do for you?"

"Yes Mr. Henry, I have a message for you. Major Wilson would like to have a word with Colonel Henry after he's done at the hospital. If you just bring him back here, we'll inform the major."

"I'll tell you what: we've got a couple boys here that you could take off our hands and we'll tell you about it after we pick up Ge- uh- *Colonel* Henry."

Ethan nudged the pilots out the back and closed the door.

"But- what is this- who-"

"They misplaced a Black Hawk and need a ride…"

Cleve started driving away.

"Hold on Sir-"

"It's alright: the Colonel will tell you all abou-" Cleve cut himself off by opening the header cutouts, blasted some raw exhaust as he took off, then closed them up for silent running into town.

"What have you found out?"
Gerry had assured them that the doctors had Heidi Jo out of danger and now he wanted answers as they drove back to see Major Wilson.

"Nothing," replied Cleve, "I was just happy to get rid of those two corndogs you left in the chopper. Figured we'd let the *COLONEL* ask the questions."

"I *told* Corporal Randolph I was retired… That was Edmund's boy you know; apparently they're trying to send soldiers to their own hometowns to take the edge off of local confrontations during this campaign."

"So you do know something."

"Only that they are not here to cause trouble."

"We'll see…"

Cleve pulled over in the weeds opposite the roadblock and the four men climbed out. Corporal Randolph offered a smile and then directed them to a field encampment. Some of the off-duty soldiers watched the four men suspiciously as they strode toward Major Wilson's command tent.

Cleve and Gerry carried their .50 caliber handguns holstered on a thigh and a tactical knife sheathed on the opposite hip.

Ethan wore his forty-five on his left hip and carried his Winchester in his right hand; he wore one bandolier over his shoulder which he had repacked with .30-30 shells in Cleve's SUV.

George was the only sleeper in the group: at average stature, he looked relatively innocuous from the front; though his tattered T-shirt exposed the impressive musculature of his torso and the forty-five at the small of his back. Beneath his trousers, his calves were still strapped with throwing knives and torpedoes.

The major stood and shook his head as they approached.

"Now here's a motley looking crew if I've ever seen one."

Cleve looked over his partners, not having considered just how filthy they'd become in the dark mineral dust of the mine. He looked down his nose at the major and grinned.

"We resemble that remark, Sir."

"You certainly do. You must be Cleveland Henry," he offered his hand as introduction: "Major James Wilson."

"Nice to meet you, Major; this is my brother Gerry."

"Of course. Good afternoon Colonel."

"Major… Meet Ethan Allen and George Mason Jr."

"Nice to meet you all. I must admit I find you rather presumptuous to assume I would find it appropriate that you walk into my camp armed as you are."

Ethan answered first: "Pardon my candor, Sir; we *assume* nothing. Quite frankly my man, we don't give a damn what you consider appropriate. We have just lost our sheriff- our friend: assassinated by an Executive Ops task force. The fact that you have requested an audience with Gerry Henry, rather than sending soldiers to assassinate more of our countrymen, indicates you are an honorable man. Hence, we meet you on the field to parley."

"Pardon me, Sir. I meant no offence. In truth, I find your bold approach invigorating. We are in fact on the same side of the field, so to speak. The task force you speak of is surely a constituent of the very same division we are here to- ahh -collect. My men are at the hospital questioning those two pilots right now and I was hoping you could shed some light on the situation in the meantime."

"Yes we can," said Cleve, "I got a call that there were bodies down at the processing plant for the old mine. So the four of us got together and found Sheriff Jefferson with his throat slit and sweet little Heidi Jo from Gino's Café with a bullet hole through her shoulder. I carried the girl out to Gerry's bike and he took her to the hospital. We found a couple live ones in the chopper and dropped them off with Corporal Randolph. That's about it."

"Mhmm... Has anyone else got anything to add?"

The major got the stonewall and added: "We've got a copter looking for that downed S-70; maybe you all can take me to that mine entrance before you go home."

"Sure can, just follow me," said Cleve, turning away.

"Colonel, would you stay on a minute?"

When the other three men were out of earshot, Major Wilson spoke softly: "Sir, between you and me, I don't care what went on down there. Executive Operations was cobbled together with mercs and rogue agents; and the way they've been using the UN soldiers is an embarrassment for the United States. But shit happens in war and they obviously made a war zone of your town. We just want to clean this mess up."

"There are two soldiers along the entry drive; five in the west yard; two between the first and second tailings mound north of the facility; a soldier and an agent at the north door; an agent, a soldier and the sheriff in the east end shops; and one soldier in the creek east of the facility. Fifteen casualties total; we will appreciate you delivering Sheriff Jefferson's body to the County Morgue."

"Thank you, Sir."

Cleve was vigilantly eying the side mirror and every piece of vegetation that offered any cover as he led the major's modest staff car down the gravel road. Gerry flipped his phone shut, mentioning it was Ann, as he watched Cleve rubbernecking every nubbin of scrub along the roadside.

"Will you just chill; you're giving me the willies. I'm relatively confident that there's not a herd of tanks out here; it's difficult to hide an M1A3 Abrams in 4-foot scrub. And it seems that this war may be winding down early. Ann says she's recording a- how did she word it? -a *shockingly monumental* State of the Union address. I told her to drop the file on my Inbox and I can pick it up on your laptop here, right?"

"You could if my modem wasn't back at the house."

"You can get it on my smart phone," said George, "Gimme your email and then you can put your password in."

"Gerry-dot-Elbridge-dot-Henry at Leatherwood55-dot-com."

"Actually, I just lost the tower; but we can get it up on Lover's Lookout when we go for my *R*." George turned to Ethan, "*Frankly my man, I don't give a damn?*"

Ethan flushed slightly, "Hey, that's just between us…"

"You're gettin' to be almost human, Partner."

When they pulled through the parking area Major Wilson waved them clear as he climbed from his car to wait at the mine barricade for the heavy-duty vehicles. Cleve wound on up the trail to the scenic overlook and the four men climbed out.

They checked the scene to the southeast where Army soldiers were in the waterhole attaching a winch hook to the stranded SUV and a UH-60 hovered over the S-70 crash site. One by one they turned their backs on the cleanup to take in the view to the northwest. The town looked as tranquil as the first time each of them had climbed the overlook as young boys.

"OK George, gimme the file and I'll pipe it into the big screen."

Cleve backed the Lincoln up to the park bench and hung a super thin 50-inch monitor at the back door.

"How 'bout a cold one?" offered Cleve as he pulled a bottled water and a grapefruit juice from the cooler.

"Is that all you've got?"

"No: I've got pineapple, orange and grape juice as well."

George frowned, "I guess it ain't time ta celebrate until the state of the Union sees some improvement."

"It's improving already with the good guys home," returned Gerry, tossing his head southward.

"OK boys; let's have some quiet. Here it comes."

"**A** dmiral, Sir: We are rolling; you are on the air…"
"Ladies and gentleman, fellow citizens of these United States: The first imperial President in the history of the Republic has been dethroned; he and a portion of the Cabinet are now in military custody. The remainder of the Cabinet, the Joint Chiefs of Staff, both Houses of Congress and the Supreme Court are, and shall remain, under house arrest until Article 32 hearings have determined who shall be referred to general court-martial under the Uniform Code of Military Justice.

"I have been appointed acting Commander in Chief of the United States Department of Defense, and spokesman for the *Combatant Command Campaign*, by unanimous approval of the current Combatant Commanders of the ten Unified Combatant Commands. This appointment and the Article 32 detentions are not intended to cast aspersions on the offices of the Executive, Judicial, or Legislative Branches of our government. Numerous cases of individual treason against the United States have been previously identified within these agencies, first and foremost: the imperial Presidency. Cronyism between the President and at least one member of the Joint Chiefs of Staff has established the Unified Combatant Commands as the highest level of command, within the Department of Defense, not currently under investigation for treason.

"This unprecedented Combatant Command Campaign will continue until all civil servants referred to general courts-martial for treason, as defined in Article III, Section 3 of the Constitution, are tried as prisoners of war insomuch as they collaborated with the Administration in levying war against the citizens of the United States of America.

"Bear with me as I outline some critical objections to ratification of the Constitution by a handful of our nation's Founding Fathers: objections not to the intended *spirit* of the document itself, but to the loopholes that have led to the ultimate degradation of the *spirit* of the document two and a half centuries hence.

"Patrick Henry refused to attend the Constitutional Convention of 1787; fearing a presidency would lead to a monarchy, and he later pressed for *amendments* to protect individual rights. Rhode Island refused to send delegates to said convention and delayed three years to ratify the Constitution with the reservation that a *bill of rights* be included. Of those attending the signing ceremony at said convention, three delegates refused to sign: Elbridge Gerry and George Mason would require a bill of rights; Edmund Randolph found the document lacking in *checks and balances*.

"Thomas Jefferson did not attend the convention, but his writings include volumes on the importance of *term limits*, in the spirit of transient honorable service: whereas a lucrative profession in politics may devolve to abuse.

"And to conclude my introductory history lesson, George Washington, the symbolic father of our country and the finest example of what an American politician was mean to be: a man who did not seek office, but served through sense of duty when called... Upon leaving office, in Washington's Farewell Address[VI] he delivers a warning against faction and the *dangers of Parties*: which has now become the apocalyptic bane of this Republic.

"In framing the Constitution,[IV] the overwhelming majority of our Founding Fathers considered a bill of rights naught but a frivolous pursuit: veritably a display of arrogance to grant God-given rights previously acknowledged in the Declaration of Independence.[III] Recent history has proven that these inalienable rights would be challenged regardless of their unambiguous delineation in the Bill of Rights.[V]

"This solidarity of Combatant Commanders, *in order to form a more perfect Union*, has formulated additional checks and balances to preserve the spirit of the Constitution and the sovereignty of the Republic. These amendments to the Constitution will be honed and ratified in convention by newly elected Executive and Legislative officials. Said Constitutional Convention shall remain in session until Amendments Eleven through Twenty-nine have been reviewed and voted by three-fourths majority to remain in force.

"After a three-day recess, or at which time those Supreme Court Justices convicted of perjury against their oaths have been removed from office: the President and the Senate shall reconvene; at which time the Senate will confirm, only by two-thirds majority vote, those incumbent Justices who have been faithful to their oaths. The President's new appointments will be confirmed only by Senate two-thirds majority vote, and there will be an amendment as such for all future confirmations of *ALL* Presidential appointments.

"U.S. Navy JAG shall provide courts-martial and Article 32 investigations for the President and Congress. U.S. Air Force JAG shall provide the same for the Supreme Court and shall carry out the Supreme Court's secondary duties during this interim campaign. U.S. Army JAG shall provide courts-martial and Article 32 investigations for all lesser officials, officers and federal employees.

"In the interest of brevity, I will outline only crucial changes this campaign shall implement. An unabridged document will be available for download tomorrow after zero eight hundred hours, under the title of: *Declaration for the Combatant Command Campaign*, at www-dot-usa-dot-gov-slash-Topics-slash-Reference-Shelf-slash-Documents-dot-shtml.

"The Election Assistance Commission- the EAC -will create a database into which an eligible candidate for office shall enter his or her qualifications and his policy on a dozen relevant contemporary issues. Candidates will be prioritized and he who has served previously shall have his qualifications updated to include how many times he voted contrary to his claimed policies. The database of candidates will be available online and at libraries, Post Offices and various other government offices; hardcopy will be mailed by request in hardship cases; twenty-eight days prior to the *general election* a mandatory hardcopy mailing will post to all registered voters.

"It is your moral duty to research the candidates. You may vote for a candidate that you were asked, told, or paid to vote for; but it is your civil duty to place that vote with full knowledge of that candidate's policies. This is the information age: avail yourself of the information provided by said EAC database. And vote not as an avenue to the acquisition of personal perks; vote as an honorable investment in the future of America. **And so, my fellow Americans: Ask not what your country can do for you; ask what you can do for your country.**[23]

"The new Congress shall frame an amendment for a two-term limit in the Senate and a three-term limit in the House. Cronyism and faction must be suppressed. The Supreme Court is free of term limits; but the Senate shall reconfirm each Justice's appointment every four years, only by two-thirds majority vote.

"Congress shall frame an amendment to suppress formal political parties in the Republic. This is not to say that party members shall be hunted down: fascism is the foe, not the goal. The spirit of party shall never be stifled in those who live by the crony code. Nevertheless, the sanctioning of a two-party system by the federal government shall end. The EAC shall identify independent candidates by stated policy and individual voting records.

"Election of the President and V-P shall be as per Article II, Section 1, Clause 3 of the Constitution; notwithstanding later amendments to the contrary, which shall be abrogated. Candidates shall run for President independently; runner-up for the Presidency shall be Vice-President; no party platform: no partisan faction. There shall be no votes *wasted* on an independent, because all political candidates shall be independent. *The party is over...*

"Make no mistake: This *is* a military coup. Scholars will protest that there is no provision in the Constitution for military coup. I can attest that this is ironclad fact; indeed, one of the greatest fears of our Founding Fathers was that a tyrant could use a powerful military to the ruins of liberty. Sadly, it has been politicians, justices and a multitude of other civil servants who have broken their oaths to *support and defend* the Constitution. Perhaps it is the very fact that our men and women in uniform risk their lives regularly to defend the freedom of Americans and allies alike which hones the *honor* that runs as pure in their veins as the blood of our forefathers, who gave their lives to win and preserve our proud American heritage.

"Though the Founding Fathers did their best to include safeguards to protect their young Republic, they hoped the people would never allow cronyism and faction to penetrate so deeply as to threaten our national liberty, and they failed to include provisions to purge the corruption; but in their wisdom, they included Article VI, Clause 3: requiring all civil servants to take their oath to support said Constitution. To justify our own application of military justice against this rampant corruption that subverts the Constitution, we embrace the American values defined by the Declaration of Independence.

"And it is my oath to you, the free citizens of these United States of America, that when the Combatant Command Campaign is complete and an honorable Administration has been instated: I shall step down. And you have the guarantee of the other nine Combatant Commanders as well as every other member of the U.S. Military in union with the proud American citizens who shall never yield liberty to the hand of tyranny. -*And for the support of this Declaration, with a firm reliance on the protection of divine Providence, we mutually pledge to each other our Lives, our Fortunes and our sacred Honor.*"[III]

Somewhere on the frozen tundra north of the Arctic Circle a UN soldier garbed in Arctic white camo sat up and squinted. Inventory of his pockets revealed that, excepting his original sage and brown camo and any trace of firearms, all of his gear was accounted for. He wrapped his fingers around the hilt of his Ka-Bar Big Brother, pulled it from the sheath and smiled.

Rolling to his hands and knees he noted two bota bags and a long rod lay just beyond where his head had rested. The reeling soldier gripped the 12-foot single tipped spear and staggered to his feet. The fog was slowly clearing from his mind as he rocked foot to foot, rotating a 360-degree circle around the spear. His eyes were leveled on the horizon, registering nothing but endless frozen wasteland.

Equilibrium returned to his stance and he lifted the shaft from the tundra, noting the precision machining, the balance and weight: titanium... The butt end was engraved with red anodized calligraphic script: "*Yours sincerely, Gramma.*" He turned his face to the wind, threw back his head, and like the Arctic wolf: howled to the moon...

"DAMN YOU BITCH!"

APPENDICES I

1 Quotes attributed to Benjamin Franklin; circa latter-18th century:

"It is the working man who is the happy man. It is the idle man who is the miserable man."

"Tricks and treachery are the practice of fools that don't have enough brains to be honest."

"Rebellion to Tyrants is Obedience to God." _Benjamin Franklin's proposed motto for the Great Seal of the United States.

"Half a truth is often a great lie."

"Those who can give up essential liberty to obtain a little temporary safety deserve neither liberty nor safety."

"God helps those who help themselves."

2 "They tell us, sir, that we are weak- unable to cope with so formidable an adversary. But when shall we be stronger? Will it be the next week, or the next year? Will it be when we are totally disarmed; and when a British guard shall be stationed in every house? Shall we gather strength by irresolution and inaction? Shall we acquire the means of effectual resistance by lying supinely on our backs, hugging the delusive phantom of hope until our enemies shall have bound us, hand and foot? Sir, we are not weak, if we make a proper use of those means which the God of nature hath placed in our power. Three millions of people, armed in the holy cause of liberty, and in such a country as that which we possess, are invincible by any force which our enemy can send against us. Besides, sir, we shall not fight our battles alone. There is a just God who presides over the destinies of nations; and who will raise up friends to fight our battles for us. The battle, sir, is not to the strong alone; it is to the vigilant, the active, the brave. Besides, sir, we have no election. If we were base enough to desire it, it is now too late to retire from the contest. There is no retreat, but in submission and slavery. Our chains are forged. Their clanking may be heard on the plains of Boston. The war is inevitable- and let it come. I repeat it, sir; let it come! It is in vain, sir, to extenuate the matter. Gentlemen may cry, peace, peace- but there is no peace. The war is actually begun. The next gale that sweeps from the north will bring to our ears the clash of resounding arms. Our brethren are already in the field. Why stand we here idle? What is it that gentlemen wish? What would they have? Is life so dear, or peace so sweet, as to be

purchased at the price of chains and slavery? Forbid it, Almighty God! I know not what course others may take; but as for me: Give me Liberty, or give me Death!" _Patrick Henry – March 23, 1775; in an 1817 William Wirt reconstruction of George Tucker's recollections of Mr. Henry's speech to the Second Virginia Revolutionary Convention at St. Johns Church, House of Burgesses, Richmond, Virginia.

3 "What signify a few lives lost in a century or two? The tree of liberty must from time to time be refreshed with the blood of patriots and tyrants. It is its natural manure." _Thomas Jefferson – November 13, 1787; in a letter to William S. Smith, concerning Shays' Rebellion.

4 "And what country can preserve its liberties, if the rulers are not warned from time to time, that this people preserve the spirit of resistance? Let them take arms." _Thomas Jefferson – 1787; in a letter to William S. Smith.

5 In the Constitution for the United States of America - [See APPENDICES IV for complete text]: Article. II. Section.1. The executive Power shall be vested in a President of the United States of America… -Before he enter on the Execution of his Office, he shall take the following Oath or Affirmation: - "I do solemnly swear (or affirm) that I will faithfully execute the Office of President of the United States, and will to the best of my Ability, preserve, protect and defend the Constitution of the United States." Article. III. Section.3. Treason against the United States, shall consist only in levying War against them, or in adhering to their Enemies, giving them Aid and Comfort…

6 "Societies exist under three forms sufficiently distinguishable. 1. Without government, as among our Indians. 2. Under governments wherein the will of every one has a just influence, as is the case in England in a slight degree, and in our states in a great one. 3. Under governments of force: as is the case in all other monarchies and in most of the other republics. To have an idea of the curse of existence under these last, they must be seen. It is a government of wolves over sheep. It is a problem, not clear in my mind, that the 1st. condition is not the best. But I believe it to be inconsistent with any great degree of population. The second state has a great deal of good in it. The mass of mankind under that enjoys a precious degree of liberty and happiness. It has its evils too: the principal of which is the

turbulence to which it is subject. But weigh this against the oppressions of monarchy, and it becomes nothing. Malo periculosam, libertatem quam quietam servitutem. [*I prefer the tumult of liberty to the quiet of servitude.*] Even this evil is productive of good. It prevents the degeneracy of government, and nourishes a general attention to the public affairs. I hold it that a little rebellion now and then is a good thing, and as necessary in the political world as storms in the physical. Unsucceful rebellions indeed generally establish the incroachments on the rights of the people which have produced them. An observation of this truth should render honest republican governors so mild in their punishment of rebellions, as not to discourage them too much. It is a medecine necessary for the sound health of government." _Thomas Jefferson – January 30, 1787; in a letter to James Madison.

7   Quotes attributed to Aaron Burr; circa 1800:

"Never do today what you can do tomorrow. Something may occur to make you regret your premature action."
"Law is whatever is boldly asserted and plausibly maintained."
"Slander has slain more than the sword."

8   "-but if I can only live to see the American union firmly fixed, and free Governments well established in our western world, and can leave to my children but a Crust of Bread, & Liberty, I shall die satisfied..." _George Mason – October 2, 1778; in a letter written at Gunston-Hall, Virginia.

9   "-when the resolution of enslaving America was formed in Great-Britain, the British Parliament was advised by an artful man, who was governor of Pennsylvania, to disarm the people. That it was the best and most effectual way to enslave them; but that they should not do it openly; but weaken them and let them sink gradually..." _George Mason – June 14, 1788; in a Debate in the Virginia Ratifying Convention.

10   "That the freedom of the press is one of the great bulwarks of liberty and can never be restrained but by despotic governments." _George Mason – 1778; SEC.12, in the Virginia Declaration of Rights.

11 "Our All is at Stake, & the little Conveniencys & Comforts of Life, when set in Competition with our Liberty, ought to be rejected not with reluctance but with Pleasure." _George Mason – April 5, 1769; in a letter to George Washington.

12 "A militia, when properly formed, are in fact the people themselves... -whereas, to preserve liberty, it is essential that the whole body of the people always possess arms, and be taught alike, especially when young, how to use them; nor does it follow from this, that all promiscuously must go into actual service on every occasion. The mind that aims at a select militia, must be influenced by a truly anti-republican principle; and when we see many men disposed to practice upon it, whenever they can prevail, no wonder true republicans are for carefully guarding against it." _Richard Henry Lee and/or Melancton Smith – January 25, 1788; in Letters from the Federal Farmer to the Republican, Letter XVIII, Poughkeepsie County Journal, New York.

13 "The powers of the sword, say the minority of Pennsylvania, is in the hands of Congress. My friends and countrymen, it is not so, for the powers of the sword are in the hands of the yeomanry of America from sixteen to sixty. The militia of these free commonwealths, entitled and accustomed to their arms, when compared with any possible army, must be tremendous and irresistible. Who are the militia? Are they not ourselves? Is it feared then, that we shall turn our arms each man against his own bosom? Congress have no right to disarm the militia. Their swords, and every other terrible implement of the soldier, are the birth-right of an American... -the unlimited power of the sword is not in the hands of either the federal or the state governments, but where I trust in God it will ever remain, in the hands of the people." _Tench Coxe – February 20, 1788; in The Pennsylvania Gazette.

14 "Before a standing army can rule, the people must be disarmed; as they are in almost every kingdom of Europe. The supreme power in America cannot enforce unjust laws by the sword; because the whole body of the people are armed, and constitute a force superior to any bands of regular troops that can be, on any pretense, raised in the United States." _Noah Webster – October 17, 1787; alias "A Citizen of America" in An Examination Into the Leading Principles of the Federal Constitution, Philadelphia.

15 "COULD the peaceable principle of the Quakers be universally established, arms and the art of war would be wholly extirpated: But we live not in a world of angels. The reign of Satan is not ended; neither are we to expect to be defended by miracles... -Thus the peaceable part of mankind will be continually overrun by the vile and abandoned, while they neglect the means of self defence. The supposed quietude of a good man allures the ruffian; while on the other hand, arms like laws discourage and keep the invader and the plunderer in awe, and preserve order in the world as well as property. The balance of power is the scale of peace. The same balance would be preserved were all the world destitute of arms, for all would be alike; but since some *will not*, others *dare not* lay them aside. And while a single nation refuses to lay them down, it is proper that all should keep them up. Horrid mischief would ensue were one half the world deprived of the use of them; for while avarice and ambition have a place in the heart of man, the weak will become a prey to the strong. The history of every age and nation establishes these truths, and facts need but little arguments when they prove themselves."
_Thomas Paine – July, 1775; Thoughts On Defensive War, in the Pennsylvania Magazine.

16 "Among the many interesting objects, which will engage your attention, that of providing for the common defence will merit particular regard._ To be prepared for War is one of the most effectual means of preserving peace._ A free people ought not only to be armed but disciplined;_ to which end a uniform and well digested plan is requisite: And their safety and interest require that they should promote such manufactories, as tend to render them independent on others for essential, particularly for military supplies..." _George Washington – January 8, 1790; in a Speech of the President of the United States to both Houses of Congress.

17 "The time is now near at hand which must probably determine whether Americans are to be freemen or slaves; whether they are to have any property they can call their own; whether their houses and farms are to be pillaged and destroyed, and themselves consigned to a state of wretchedness from which no human efforts will deliver them. The fate of unborn millions will now depend, under God, on the courage and conduct of this army. Our cruel and unrelenting enemy leaves us only the choice of brave resistance, or the most abject submission. We have, therefore, to resolve to conquer or die." _George

Washington – August 27, 1776; Address to the Continental Army, before the Battle of Long Island.

18 "The Treaties of the European Powers with the United States of America, will have no validity on a dissolution of the Union. We shall be left nearly in a state of Nature, or we may find by our own unhappy experience, that there is a natural and necessary progression, from the extreme of anarchy to the extreme of Tyranny; and that arbitrary power is most easily established on the ruins of Liberty abused to licentiousness." _George Washington – June 8, 1783; in a Circular to the States.

19 "-the said Constitution be never construed to authorize Congress to infringe the just liberty of the press, or the rights of conscience; or to prevent the people of the United States, who are peaceable citizens, from keeping their own arms; or to raise standing armies, except when necessary for the defense of the United States, or of some one or more of them; or to prevent the people from petitioning, in a peaceable and orderly manner, the federal legislature for a redress of grievances; or to subject the people to unreasonable searches and seizures of their persons, papers or possessions." _Samuel Adams – February 6, 1788; in The Massachusetts Convention.

20 "When the government violates the people's rights, insurrection is, for the people and for each portion of the people, the most sacred of the rights and the most indispensible of duties." _Marie Jean Paul Joseph Roche Yves Gilbert du Motier, Marquis de La Fayette – 1790; Speech to the French National Constituent Assembly. Also; Article 35 of the French political document: Declaration of the Rights of Man and Citizen of 1793.

21 "To the House of Representatives:_ I return without my approval House bill number ten thousand two hundred and three, entitled "An Act to enable the Commissioner of Agriculture to make a special distribution of seeds in drought-stricken counties of Texas, and making an appropriation therefor."_ It is represented that a long-continued and extensive drought has existed in certain portions of the State of Texas, resulting in a failure of crops and consequent distress and destitution._ Though there has been some difference in statements concerning the extent of the people's needs in the localities thus affected, there seems to be no doubt that there has

existed a condition calling for relief; and I am willing to believe that, notwithstanding the aid already furnished, a donation of seed-grain to the farmers located in this region, to enable them to put in new crops, would serve to avert a continuance or return of an unfortunate blight._ And yet I feel obliged to withhold my approval of the plan as proposed by this bill, to indulge a benevolent and charitable sentiment through the appropriation of public funds for that purpose._ I can find no warrant for such an appropriation in the Constitution, and I do not believe that the power and duty of the general government ought to be extended to the relief of individual suffering which is in no manner properly related to the public service or benefit. A prevalent tendency to disregard the limited mission of this power and duty should, I think, be steadfastly resisted, to the end that the lesson should be constantly enforced that, though the people support the government, the government should not support the people._ The friendliness and charity of our countrymen can always be relied upon to relieve their fellow-citizens in misfortune. This has been repeatedly and quite lately demonstrated. Federal aid in such cases encourages the expectation of paternal care on the part of the government and weakens the sturdiness of our national character, while it prevents the indulgence among our people of that kindly sentiment and conduct which strengthens the bonds of a common brotherhood._ It is within my personal knowledge that individual aid has, to some extent, already been extended to the sufferers mentioned in this bill. The failure of the proposed appropriation of ten thousand dollars additional, to meet their remaining wants, will not necessarily result in continued distress if the emergency is fully made known to the people of the country._ It is here suggested that the Commissioner of Agriculture is annually directed to expend a large sum of money for the purchase, propagation, and distribution of seeds and other things of this description, two-thirds of which are, upon the request of senators, representatives, and delegates in Congress, supplied to them for distribution among their constituents._ The appropriation of the current year for this purpose is one hundred thousand dollars, and it will probably be no less in the appropriation for the ensuing year. I understand that a large quantity of grain is furnished for such distribution, and it is supposed that this free apportionment among their neighbors is a privilege which may be waived by our senators and representatives._ If sufficient of them should request the Commissioner of Agriculture to send their shares of the grain thus allowed them, to the suffering farmers of Texas, they might be enabled to sow their crops; the constituents, for whom in theory this grain is intended, could well bear the temporary deprivation, and the donors would experience the satisfaction attending deeds of charity." _Stephen Grover Cleveland – February 16, 1887; Veto of the Texas Seed Bill.

22 "A vast continent must now sink to slavery, poverty, horrour, and bondage, or rise to unconquerable freedom, immense wealth, inexpressible felicity, and immortal fame._ I will lay my life on it, that with fifteen hundred men, and a proper train of artillery, I will take Montreal. Provided I could thus be furnished, and if an Army could command the field, it would be no insuperable difficulty to take Quebeck." _Ethan Allen – July 2, 1775, Crown Point; in a letter to the Provincial Congress of New York.

23 "In the long history of the world, only a few generations have been granted the role of defending freedom in its hour of maximum danger. I do not shrink from this responsibility: I welcome it. I do not believe that any of us would exchange places with any other people or any other generation. The energy, the faith, the devotion which we bring to this endeavor will light our country and all who serve it, and the glow from that fire can truly light the world._ And so, my fellow Americans: Ask not what your country can do for you; ask what you can do for your country._ My fellow citizens of the world: Ask not what America will do for you, but what together we can do for the freedom of man._ Finally, whether you are citizens of America or citizens of the world, ask of us here the same high standards of strength and sacrifice which we ask of you. With a good conscience our only sure reward, with history the final judge of our deeds, let us go forth to lead the land we love, asking His blessing and His help, but knowing that here on earth, God's work must truly be our own." _John F. Kennedy – January 20, 1961; in the Inaugural Address, United States Capitol, Washington, D.C.

APPENDICES II

THE DECLARATION OF PATRIOTISM
(A declaration by the fictional character "Grover T. Henry"
in "Treaties, Traitors and Patriots" by G.A.Crews)
***

DECLARATION OF PATRIOTISM TO THE REPUBLIC

IN GRASSROOTS.

By Declaration of the free patriots of the United States of America,

When in the Course of human events, it becomes necessary for a patriotic people to reject the heinous demands of a political regime intent on fracturing the very foundations of the Republic in their contempt for the ideals set forth by the Founding Fathers in the Constitution for the United States of America, and to assume among the powers of the earth, the Freedom guaranteed by said Constitution, and all Freedoms to which the Laws of Nature and of Nature's God entitle them; a decent respect for the opinions of mankind requires that they should declare the causes which impel them to disregard the unconstitutional demands and illegitimate laws presented by the Executive traitors, Judicial perjurers and Legislative incompetents.

We hold these truths to be self-evident, that all men are created equal, that they are endowed by their Creator with certain unalienable Rights, that among these are Life, Liberty and the pursuit of Happiness.— That to secure these rights, Governments are instituted among Men, deriving their just powers from the consent of the governed,— That whenever any Form of Government becomes destructive of these ends, it is the Right of the People to alter or to abolish it,— Or, in the case of the Republic, to re-establish The Constitution as "the law of the land", and to remove those whom have attained office through perjury in a conspiracy to subvert the national sovereignty of the Republic. Prudence, indeed, will dictate that Governments long established should not be abolished for light and transient causes; and accordingly all experience hath shown, that mankind are more disposed to suffer, while evils are sufferable, than to right themselves by abolishing the forms to which they have been pacified. But when a long train of abuses and usurpations, pursuing invariably a new world order based in Socialism and Communism, evinces a design to reduce the Republic under absolute Despotism.— It is their right, it is their duty, to throw off such Government, and to provide the old Guards for their future security.— Such has been the patient sufferance of these United States; and such is now the necessity which constrains the Patriots who live by the Laws of the Republic, to oust the traitors who would make war on the peaceable citizens of this great Nation in defiance of the 2nd Amendment to the Constitution for the United States of America.

The history of the current President of the United States is a history of repeated injuries and usurpations, all having in direct object the destruction of the sovereignty of these United States.

To prove this, let Facts be submitted to a candid world:

> He has excited domestic insurrections amongst us, is guilty of sedition by inciting class and racial bigotry; and by attacking our right to bear arms has endeavored to bring on the inhabitants of our cities, the merciless criminal element, whose known rule of warfare is to prey on the weak.
> *(Amendment II. A well regulated Militia, being necessary to the security of a free State, the right of the people to keep and bear Arms, shall not be infringed. _US Constitution)*

> He has attacked and invaded our homes, depriving us in many cases, the benefits of Trial by Jury.
> *(Amendment IV. The right of the people to be secure in their persons, houses, papers, and effects, against unreasonable searches and seizures, shall not be violated, and no Warrants shall issue, but upon probable cause, supported by Oath or affirmation, and particularly describing the place to be searched, and the persons or things to be seized. Amendment V. ...nor shall any person be subject for the same offence to be twice put in jeopardy of life or limb, nor shall be compelled in any criminal case to be a witness against himself, nor be deprived of life, liberty, or property, without due process of law... Amendment VI. In all criminal prosecutions, the accused shall enjoy the right to a speedy and public trial, by an impartial jury of the State and district wherein the crime shall have been committed... _US Constitution)*

> He has instituted multitudes of Agencies, and sent hither swarms of Officers to harass our people, and eat out their substance.
> *(Amendment IX. The enumeration in the Constitution of certain rights shall not be construed to deny or disparage others retained by the people. Amendment X. The powers not delegated to the United States by the Constitution, nor prohibited by it to the States, are reserved to the States respectively, or to the people. _US Constitution)*

308 G.A.CREWS

He has combined with the United Nations to subject us to a jurisdiction foreign to our Constitution, and unacknowledged by our laws; by enacting International gun treaties and giving his Assent to their Acts of pretended Legislation: he thereby levies war against us. *(Article. III. [Section 3.] Treason against the United States shall consist only in levying War against them... Article. II. [Section 1.] The executive Power shall be vested in a President of the United States of America... Before he enter on the Execution of his Office, he shall take the following Oath or Affirmation: -- "I do solemnly swear (or affirm) that I will faithfully execute the Office of President of the United States, and will to the best of my Ability, preserve, protect and defend the Constitution of the United States." Article. II. [Section 4.] The President, Vice President and all civil Officers of the United States, shall be removed from Office on Impeachment for, and Conviction of, Treason, Bribery, or other high Crimes and Misdemeanors. _US Constitution)*

He has affected to render our Military, Federal and Local Police independent of and superior to the Civil power, in contempt of his Oath, by Executive Action and usurpation of the 2nd Amendment, he has constrained our fellow Citizens to become the executioners of their friends and Brethren, or to fall themselves by their Hands;

If and when they too are deaf to the voice of justice, and we have conjured them by the ties of our common kindred to disavow these usurpations: We must, therefore, acquiesce in the necessity to hold them, as we hold the rest of mankind, Enemies in War, in Peace: Friends.

We, therefore, the Patriots of the United States of America, in Grassroots, Internet, appealing to the Supreme Judge of the world for the rectitude of our intentions, do, in the Name, and by Authority of the good People of these States, solemnly publish and declare: That these United States are, and of Right ought to be Free and Independent States; that they are Absolved from all Allegiance to the current President's treasonous regime, and that all political connection between them and said regime, is and ought to be totally dissolved; and that as Free and Independent States, if the US Senate fails in its duty to impeach all officials party to the treachery delineated hereto, they have full Power to levy War, conclude Peace and replace the traitors with elected officials whom in good faith do not perjure their oath to uphold The Constitution, and to do all other Acts and Things which Independent States may of right do. And for the support of this Declaration, with a firm reliance on the protection of divine Providence, we mutually pledge to each other our Lives, our Fortunes and our sacred Honor.

APPENDICES III

THE DECLARATION OF INDEPENDENCE
(As transcribed by Greg Crews from
photocopy of the handwritten text)
✳✳✳

IN CONGRESS, JULY 4, 1776.

The unanimous Declaration of the thirteen united States of America,

When in the Course of human events, it becomes necessary for one people to dissolve the political bands which have connected them with another, and to assume among the powers of the earth, the separate and equal station to which the Laws of Nature and of Nature's God entitle them, a decent respect to the opinions of mankind requires that they should declare the causes which impel them to the separation._____ We hold these truths to be self-evident, that all men are created equal, that they are endowed by their Creator with certain unalienable Rights, that among these are Life, Liberty and the pursuit of Happiness.___ That to secure these rights, Governments are instituted among Men, deriving their just powers from the consent of the governed,__ That whenever any Form of Government becomes destructive of these ends, it is the Right of the People to alter or to abolish it, and to institute new Government, laying its foundation on such principles and organizing its powers in such form, as to them shall seem most likely to effect their Safety and Happiness. Prudence, indeed, will dictate that Governments long established should not be changed for light and transient causes; and accordingly all experience hath shewn, that mankind are more disposed to suffer, while evils are sufferable, than to right themselves by abolishing the forms to which they are accustomed. But when a long train of abuses and usurpations, pursuing invariably the same Object evinces a design to reduce them under absolute Despotism, it is their right, it is their duty, to throw off such Government, and to provide new Guards for their future security.__ Such has been the patient sufferance of these Colonies; and such is now the necessity which constrains them to alter their former Systems of Government. The history of the present King of Great Britain is a history of repeated injuries and usurpations, all having in direct object the establishment of an absolute Tyranny over these States. To prove this, let Facts be submitted to a candid world._____ He has refused his Assent to Laws, the most wholesome and necessary for the public good._____ He has forbidden his Governors to pass Laws of immediate and pressing importance, unless suspended in their operation till his Assent should be obtained; and when so suspended, he has utterly neglected to attend to them._____ He has refused to pass other Laws for the accommodation of large districts of people, unless those people would relinquish the right of Representation in the Legislature, a right inestimable to them and formidable to tyrants only._____ He has called together legislative bodies at places unusual, uncomfortable, and distant from the depository of their public Records, for the sole purpose of fatiguing them into compliance with his measures._____ He has dissolved Representative Houses repeatedly, for opposing with manly firmness his invasions on the rights of the people._____ He has refused for a long time, after such dissolutions, to cause others to be elected; whereby the Legislative powers incapable of Annihilation, have returned to the People at large for their exercise; the State remaining in the mean time exposed to all the dangers of invasion from without, and convulsions within._____ He has endeavoured to prevent the population of these States; for that purpose obstructing the Laws for Naturalization of Foreigners; refusing to pass others to encourage their migrations hither, and raising the conditions of new Appropriations of Lands._____ He has obstructed the Administration of Justice, by refusing his Assent to Laws for establishing Judiciary powers._____ He has made Judges dependent on his Will alone, for the tenure of their offices, and the amount and payment of their salaries._____ He has erected a multitude of New Offices, and sent hither swarms of Officers to harrass our people, and eat out their substance.____ He has kept among us, in times of peace, Standing Armies without the Consent of our legislatures._____ He has affected to render the Military independent of and superior to the Civil power.____ He has combined with others to subject us to a jurisdiction foreign to our constitution, and unacknowledged by our laws; giving his Assent to their Acts of pretended Legislation:___ For Quartering large bodies of armed troops among us:__ For protecting them, by a mock Trial, from punishment for any Murders which they should commit on the Inhabitants of these States:___ For cutting off our Trade with all parts of the world:___ For imposing Taxes on us without our Consent:___ For depriving us in many cases, of the benefits of Trial by Jury:___ For transporting us beyond Seas to be tried for pretended offences:____For abolishing the free System of English Laws in a neighbouring Province, establishing therein an Arbitrary government, and enlarging its Boundaries so as to render it at once an example and fit instrument for introducing the same absolute rule into these Colonies:____ For taking away our Charters, abolishing our most valuable Laws, and altering fundamentally the Forms of our Governments:___ For suspending our own Legislatures, and declaring themselves invested with power to legislate for us in all cases whatsoever.___ He has abdicated Government here, by declaring us out of his Protection and waging War against us.____ He has plundered our seas, ravaged our Coasts, burnt our towns, and destroyed the lives of our people.____ He is at this time transporting large Armies of foreign Mercenaries to compleat the works of death, desolation and tyranny, already begun with circumstances of Cruelty & perfidy scarcely paralleled in the most barbarous ages, and totally unworthy of the Head of a civilized nation.____ He has constrained our fellow Citizens taken Captive on the high Seas to bear Arms against their Country, to become the executioners of their friends and Brethren, or to fall themselves by their Hands.___ He has excited domestic insurrections amongst us, and has endeavoured to bring on the inhabitants of our frontiers, the merciless Indian Savages, whose known rule of warfare, is an undistinguished destruction of all ages, sexes and conditions. **In** every stage of these Oppressions We have Petitioned for Redress in the most humble terms: Our repeated Petitions have been answered only by repeated injury. A Prince whose character is thus marked by every act which may define a Tyrant, is unfit to be the ruler of a free people.   Nor have We been wanting in attentions to our Brittish brethren. We have warned them from time to time of attempts by their legislature to extend an unwarrantable jurisdiction over us. We have reminded them of the circumstances of our emigration and settlement here. We have appealed to their native justice and magnanimity, and we have conjured them by the ties of our common kindred to disavow these usurpations, which, would inevitably interrupt our connections and correspondence They too have been deaf to the voice of justice and of consanguinity. We must, therefore, acquiesce in the necessity, which denounces our Separation, and hold them, as we hold the rest of mankind, Enemies in War, in Peace Friends.____

We, therefore, the Representatives of the **united States of America,** in General Congress, Assembled, appealing to the Supreme Judge of the world for the rectitude of our intentions, do, in the Name, and by Authority of the good People of these Colonies, solemnly publish and declare, That these United Colonies are, and of Right ought to be **Free and Independent States;** that they are Absolved from all Allegiance to the British Crown, and that all political connection between them and the State of Great Britain, is and ought to be totally dissolved; and that as Free and Independent States, they have full Power to levy War, conclude Peace, contract Alliances, establish Commerce, and to do all other Acts and Things which Independent States may of right do.____ And for the support of this Declaration, with a firm reliance on the protection of divine Providence, we mutually pledge to each other our Lives, our Fortunes and our sacred Honor.

John Hancock

Button Gwinnett	Wm Hooper		Rob Morris	Wm Floyd	Josiah Bartlett
Lyman Hall	Joseph Hewes,		Benjamin Rush	Phil. Livingston	Wm. Whipple
Geo Walton.	John Penn	Samuel Chase	Benj. Franklin	Faans. Lewis	Sam Adams
		Wm. Paca	John Morton	Lewis Morris	John Adams
		Thos. Stone	Geo Clymer		Rob Treat Paine
		Charles Carroll of	Jas. Smith.		Elbridge Gerry
	Edward Rutledge /.	Carrollton	Geo. Taylor		Step. Hopkins
			James Wilson	Rich Stockton	William Ellery
	Thos Heyward Junr.	George Wythe	Geo. Ross	Jns Witherspoon	Roger Sherman
	Thomas Lynch Junr.	Richard Henry Lee	Caesar Rodney	Fras. Hopkinson	Sam Huntington
	Arthur Middleton	Th Jefferson	Geo Read	John Hart	Wm. Williams
		Benj Harrison	Tho McKean	Abra Clark	Oliver Wolcott
		Thos Nelson jr.			Matthew Thornton
		Francis Lightfoot Lee			
		Carter Braxton			

***

LEGEND TO THE SIGNATURES ON THE DECLARATION OF INDEPENDENCE

(GEORGIA)
Button Gwinnett
Lyman Hall
George Walton

(NORTH CAROLINA)
William Hooper
Joseph Hewes
John Penn

(SOUTH CAROLINA)
Edward Rutledge
Thomas Heyward, Jr.
Thomas Lynch, Jr.
Arthur Middleton

(MASSACHUSETTS)
John Hancock

(MARYLAND)
Samuel Chase
William Paca
Thomas Stone
Charles Carroll of
Carrollton

(VIRGINIA)
George Wythe
Richard Henry Lee
Thomas Jefferson
Benjamin Harrison
Thomas Nelson, Jr.
Francis Lightfoot Lee
Carter Braxton

(PENNSYLVANIA)
Robert Morris
Benjamin Rush
Benjamin Franklin
John Morton
George Clymer
James Smith
George Taylor
James Wilson
George Ross

(DELAWARE)
Caesar Rodney
George Read
Thomas McKean

(NEW YORK)
William Floyd
Philip Livingston
Francis Lewis
Lewis Morris

(NEW JERSEY)
Richard Stockton
John Witherspoon
Francis Hopkinson
John Hart
Abraham Clark

(NEW HAMPSHIRE)
Josiah Bartlett
William Whipple

(MASSACHUSETTS)
Samuel Adams
John Adams
Robert Treat Paine
Elbridge Gerry

(RHODE ISLAND)
Stephen Hopkins
William Ellery

(CONNECTICUT)
Roger Sherman
Samuel Huntington
William Williams
Oliver Wolcott

(NEW HAMPSHIRE)
Matthew Thornton

APPENDICES IV

THE CONSTITUTION FOR THE UNITED STATES OF AMERICA
(As transcribed by Greg Crews from
photocopy of the handwritten text)
***

We the People of the United States, in Order to form a more perfect Union, establish Justice, insure domestic Tranquility, provide for the common defence, promote the general Welfare, and secure the Blessings of Liberty to ourselves and our Posterity, **do** ordain and establish this Constitution for the United States of America.

Article. I.

Section.1. All legislative Powers herein granted shall be vested in a Congress of the United States, which shall consist of a Senate and House of Representatives.

Section.2. The House of Representatives shall be composed of Members chosen every second Year by the People of the several States, and the Electors in each State shall have (the) Qualifications requisite for Electors of the most numerous Branch of the State Legislature.

No Person shall be a Representative who shall not have attained to the Age of twenty five Years, and been seven Years a Citizen of the United States, and who shall not, when elected, be an Inhabitant of that State in which he shall be chosen.

Representatives and direct Taxes shall be apportioned among the several States which may be included within this Union, according to their respective Numbers, which shall be determined by adding to the whole Number of free Persons, including those bound to Service for a Term of Years, and excluding Indians not taxed, three fifths of all other Persons. The actual Enumeration shall be made within three Years after the first Meeting of the Congress of the United States, and within every subsequent Term of ten Years, in such Manner as they shall by Law direct. The Number of Representatives shall not exceed one for every (Thirty) Thousand, but each State shall have at Least one Representative; and until such enumeration shall be made, the State of New Hampshire shall be entitled to chuse three, Massachusetts eight, Rhode-Island and Providence Plantations one, Connecticut five, New-York six, New Jersey four, Pennsylvania eight, Delaware one, Maryland six, Virginia ten, North Carolina five, South Carolina five, and Georgia three.

When vacancies happen in the Representation from any State, the Executive Authority thereof shall issue Writs of Election to fill such Vacancies.

The House of Representatives shall chuse their Speaker and other Officers; and shall have the sole Power of Impeachment.

Section.3. The Senate of the United States shall be composed of two Senators from each State, chosen by the Legislature thereof, for six Years; and each Senator shall have one Vote.

Immediately after they shall be assembled in Consequence of the first Election, they shall be divided as equally as may be into three Classes. The Seats of the Senators of the first Class shall be vacated at the Expiration of the second Year, of the second Class at the Expiration of the fourth Year, and of the third Class at the Expiration of the sixth Year, so that one third may be chosen every second Year; and if Vacancies happen by Resignation, or otherwise, during the Recess of the Legislature of any State, the Executive thereof may make temporary Appointments until the next Meeting of the Legislature, which shall then fill such Vacancies.

No Person shall be a Senator who shall not have attained to the Age of thirty Years, and been nine Years a Citizen of the United States, and who shall not, when elected, be an Inhabitant of that State for which he shall be chosen.

The Vice President of the United States shall be President of the Senate, but shall have no Vote, unless they be equally divided.

The Senate shall chuse their other Officers, and also a President pro tempore, in the Absence of the Vice President, or when he shall exercise the Office of President of the United States.

The Senate shall have the sole Power to try all Impeachments. When sitting for that Purpose, they shall be on Oath or Affirmation. When the President of the United States (is tried,) the Chief Justice shall preside: And no Person shall be convicted without the Concurrence of two thirds of the Members present.

Judgment in Cases of Impeachment shall not extend further than to removal from Office, and disqualification to hold and enjoy any Office of honor, Trust or Profit under the United States: but the Party convicted shall nevertheless be liable and subject to Indictment, Trial, Judgment and Punishment, according to Law.

Section.4. The Times, Places and Manner of holding Elections for Senators and Representatives, shall be prescribed in each State by the Legislature thereof; but the Congress may at any time by Law make or alter such Regulations, except as to the Places of chusing Senators.

The Congress shall assemble at least once in every Year, and such Meeting shall be on the first Monday in December, unless they shall by Law appoint a different Day.

Section.5. Each House shall be the Judge of the Elections, Returns and Qualifications of its own Members, and a Majority of each shall constitute a Quorum to do Business; but a smaller Number may adjourn from day to day, and may be authorized to compel the Attendance of absent Members, in such Manner, and under such Penalties as each House may provide.

Each House may determine the Rules of its Proceedings, punish its Members for disorderly Behaviour, and, with the Concurrence of two thirds, expel a Member.

Each House shall keep a Journal of its Proceedings, and from time to time publish the same, excepting such Parts as may in their Judgment require Secrecy; and the Yeas and Nays of the Members of either House on any question shall, at the Desire of one fifth of those Present, be entered on the Journal.

Neither House, during the Session of Congress, shall, without the Consent of the other, adjourn for more than three days, nor to any other Place than that in which the two Houses shall be sitting.

Section.6. The Senators and Representatives shall receive a Compensation for their Services, to be ascertained by Law, and paid out of the Treasury of the United States. They shall in all Cases, except Treason, Felony and Breach of the Peace, be privileged from Arrest during their Attendance at the Session of their respective Houses, and in going to and returning from the same; and for any Speech or Debate in either House, they shall not be questioned in any other Place.

No Senator or Representative shall, during the Time for which he was elected, be appointed to any civil Office under the Authority of the United States, which shall have been created, or the Emoluments whereof shall have been encreased during such time; and no Person holding any Office under the United States, shall be a Member of either House during his Continuance in Office.

Section.7. All Bills for raising Revenue shall originate in the House of Representatives; but the Senate may propose or concur with Amendments as on other Bills.

Every Bill which shall have passed the House of Representatives and the Senate, shall, before it become a Law, be presented to the President of the

[BEGIN PAGE 2 OF 4]

United States; If he approve he shall sign it, but if not he shall return it, with his Objections to that House in which it shall have originated, who shall enter the Objections at large on their Journal, and proceed to reconsider it. If after such Reconsideration two thirds of that House shall agree to pass the Bill, it shall be sent, together with the Objections, to the other House, by which it shall likewise be reconsidered, and if approved by two thirds of that House, it shall become a Law. But in all such Cases the Votes of both Houses shall be determined by yeas and Nays, and the Names of the Persons voting for and against the Bill shall be entered on the Journal of each House respectively. If any Bill shall not be returned by the President within ten Days (Sundays excepted) after it shall have been presented to him, the Same shall be a Law; in like Manner as if he had signed it, unless the Congress by their Adjournment prevent its Return, in which Case it shall not be a Law.

Every Order, Resolution, or Vote to which the Concurrence of the Senate and House of Representatives may be necessary (except on a question of Adjournment) shall be presented to the President of the United States; and before the Same shall take Effect, shall be approved by him, or being disapproved by him, shall be repassed by two thirds of the Senate and House of Representatives, according to the Rules and Limitations prescribed in the Case of a Bill.

Section.8. The Congress shall have Power To lay and collect Taxes, Duties, Imposts and Excises, to pay the Debts and provide for the common Defence and general Welfare of the United States; but all Duties, Imposts and Excises shall be uniform throughout the United States;

To borrow Money on the credit of the United States;

To regulate Commerce with foreign Nations, and among the several States, and with the Indian Tribes;

To establish an uniform Rule of Naturalization, and uniform Laws on the subject of Bankruptcies throughout the United States;

To coin Money, regulate the Value thereof, and of foreign Coin, and fix the Standard of Weights and Measures;

To provide for the Punishment of counterfeiting the Securities and current Coin of the United States;

To establish Post Offices and post Roads;

To promote the Progress of Science and useful Arts, by securing for limited Times to Authors and Inventors the exclusive Right to their respective Writings and Discoveries;

To constitute Tribunals inferior to the supreme Court;

To define and punish Piracies and Felonies committed on the high Seas, and Offences against the Law of Nations;

To declare War, grant Letters of Marque and Reprisal, and make Rules concerning Captures on Land and Water;

To raise and support Armies, but no Appropriation of Money to that Use shall be for a longer Term than two Years;

To provide and maintain a Navy;

To make Rules for the Government and Regulation of the land and naval Forces;

To provide for calling forth the Militia to execute the Laws of the Union, suppress Insurrections and repel Invasions;

To provide for organizing, arming, and disciplining, the Militia, and for governing such Part of them as may be employed in the Service of the United States, reserving to the States respectively, the Appointment of the Officers, and the Authority of training the Militia according to the discipline prescribed by Congress;

To exercise exclusive Legislation in all Cases whatsoever, over such District (not exceeding ten Miles square) as may, by Cession of particular States, and the Acceptance of Congress, become the Seat of the Government of the United States, and to exercise like Authority over all Places purchased by the Consent of the Legislature of the State in which the Same shall be, for the Erection of Forts, Magazines, Arsenals, dock-Yards, and other needful Buildings;_____ And

To make all Laws which shall be necessary and proper for carrying into Execution the foregoing Powers, and all other Powers vested by this Constitution in the Government of the United States, or in any Department or Officer thereof.

Section.9. The Migration or Importation of such Persons as any of the States now existing shall think proper to admit, shall not be prohibited by the Congress prior to the Year one thousand eight hundred and eight, but a Tax or duty may be imposed on such Importation, not exceeding ten dollars for each Person.

The Privilege of the Writ of Habeas Corpus shall not be suspended, unless when in Cases of Rebellion or Invasion the public Safety may require it.

No Bill of Attainder or ex post facto Law shall be passed.

No Capitation, or other direct, Tax shall be laid, unless in Proportion to the Census or Enumeration herein before directed to be taken.

No Tax or Duty shall be laid on Articles exported from any State.

No Preference shall be given by any Regulation of Commerce or Revenue to the Ports of one State over those of another; nor shall Vessels bound to, or from, one State, be obliged to enter, clear, or pay Duties in another.

No Money shall be drawn from the Treasury, but in Consequence of Appropriations made by Law; and a regular Statement and Account of the Receipts and Expenditures of all public Money shall be published from time to time.

No Title of Nobility shall be granted by the United States: And no Person holding any Office of Profit or Trust under them, shall, without the Consent of the Congress, accept of any present, Emolument, Office, or Title, of any kind whatever, from any King, Prince, or foreign State.

Section.10. No State shall enter into any Treaty, Alliance, or Confederation; grant Letters of Marque and Reprisal; coin Money; emit Bills of Credit; make any Thing but gold and silver Coin a Tender in Payment of Debts; pass any Bill of Attainder, ex post facto Law, or Law impairing the Obligation of Contracts, or grant any Title of Nobility.

No State shall, without the Consent of (the) Congress, lay any Imposts or Duties on Imports or Exports, except what may be absolutely necessary for executing it's inspection Laws: and the net Produce of all Duties and Imposts, laid by any State on Imports or Exports, shall be for the Use of the Treasury of the United States; and all such Laws shall be subject to the Revision and Controul of (the) Congress.

No State shall, without the Consent of Congress, lay any Duty of Tonnage, keep Troops, or Ships of War in time of Peace, enter into any Agreement or Compact with another State, or with a foreign Power, or engage in War, unless actually invaded, or in such imminent Danger as will not admit of delay.

Article. II.

Section.1. The executive Power shall be vested in a President of the United States of America. He shall hold his Office during the Term of four Years, and, together with the Vice President, chosen for the same Term, be elected, as follows

Each State shall appoint, in such Manner as the Legislature thereof may direct, a Number of Electors, equal to the whole Number of Senators and Representatives to which the State may be entitled in the Congress: but no Senator or Representative, or Person holding an Office of Trust or Profit under the United States, shall be appointed an Elector.

The Electors shall meet in their respective States, and vote by Ballot for two Persons, of whom one at least shall not be an Inhabitant of

[BEGIN PAGE 3 OF 4]

the same State with themselves. And they shall make a List of all the Persons voted for, and of the Number of Votes for each; which List they shall sign and certify, and transmit sealed to the Seat of the Government of the United States, directed to the President of the Senate. The President of the Senate shall, in the Presence of the Senate and House of Representatives, open all the Certificates, and the Votes shall then be counted. The Person having the greatest Number of Votes shall be the President, if such Number be a Majority of the whole Number of Electors appointed; and if there be more than one who have such Majority, and have an equal Number of Votes, then the House of Representatives shall immediately chuse by Ballot one of them for President; and if no Person have a Majority, then from the five highest on the List the said House shall in like Manner chuse the President. But in chusing the President, the Votes shall be taken by States, the Representation from each State having one Vote; a quorum for this Purpose shall consist of a Member or Members from two thirds of the States, and a Majority of all the States shall be necessary to a Choice. In every Case, after the Choice of the President, the Person having the greatest Number of Votes of the Electors shall be the Vice President. But if there should remain two or more who have equal Votes, the Senate shall chuse from them by Ballot the Vice President.

The Congress may determine the Time of chusing the Electors, and the Day on which they shall give their Votes; which Day shall be the same throughout the United States.

No Person except a natural born Citizen, or a Citizen of the United States, at the time of the Adoption of this Constitution, shall be eligible to the Office of President; neither shall any Person be eligible to that Office who shall not have attained to the Age of thirty five Years, and been fourteen Years a Resident within the United States.

In Case of the Removal of the President from Office, or of his Death, Resignation, or Inability to discharge the Powers and Duties of the said Office, the Same shall devolve on the Vice President, and the Congress may by Law provide for the Case of Removal, Death, Resignation or Inability, both of the President and Vice President, declaring what Officer shall then act as President, and such Officer shall act accordingly, until the Disability be removed, or a President shall be elected.

The President shall, at stated Times, receive for his Services, a Compensation, which shall neither be increased nor diminished during the Period for which he shall have been elected, and he shall not receive within that Period any other Emolument from the United States, or any of them.

Before he enter on the Execution of his Office, he shall take the following Oath or Affirmation: -- "I do solemnly swear (or affirm) that I will faithfully execute the Office of President of the United States, and will to the best of my Ability, preserve, protect and defend the Constitution of the United States."

Section.2. The President shall be Commander in Chief of the Army and Navy of the United States, and of the Militia of the several States, when called into the actual Service of the United States; he may require the Opinion, in writing, of the principal Officer in each of the executive Departments, upon any Subject relating to the Duties of their respective Offices, and he shall have Power to grant Reprieves and Pardons for Offences against the United States, except in Cases of Impeachment.

He shall have Power, by and with the Advice and Consent of the Senate, to make Treaties, provided two thirds of the Senators present concur; and he shall nominate, and by and with the Advice and Consent of the Senate, shall appoint Ambassadors, other public Ministers and Consuls, Judges of the supreme Court, and all other Officers of the United States, whose Appointments are not herein otherwise provided for, and which shall be established by Law: but the Congress may by Law vest the Appointment of such inferior Officers, as they think proper, in the President alone, in the Courts of Law, or in the Heads of Departments.

The President shall have Power to fill up all Vacancies that may happen during the Recess of the Senate, by granting Commissions which shall expire at the End of their next Session.

Section.3. He shall from time to time give to the Congress Information of the State of the Union, and recommend to their Consideration such Measures as he shall judge necessary and expedient; he may, on extraordinary Occasions, convene both Houses, or either of them, and in Case of Disagreement between them, with Respect to the Time of Adjournment, he may adjourn them to such Time as he shall think proper; he shall receive Ambassadors and other public Ministers; he shall take Care that the Laws be faithfully executed, and shall Commission all the Officers of the United States.

Section.4. The President, Vice President and all civil Officers of the United States, shall be removed from Office on Impeachment for, and Conviction of, Treason, Bribery, or other high Crimes and Misdemeanors.

Article. III.

Section.1. The judicial Power of the United States, shall be vested in one supreme Court, and in such inferior Courts as the Congress may from time to time ordain and establish. The Judges, both of the supreme and inferior Courts, shall hold their Offices during good Behaviour, and shall, at stated Times, receive for their Services, a Compensation, which shall not be diminished during their Continuance in Office.

Section.2. The judicial Power shall extend to all Cases, in Law and Equity, arising under this Constitution, the Laws of the United States, and Treaties made, or which shall be made, under their Authority;___ to all Cases affecting Ambassadors, other public Ministers and Consuls;___ to all Cases of admiralty and maritime Jurisdiction;___ to Controversies to which the United States shall be a Party;___ to Controversies between two or more States;_between a State and Citizens of another State,___ between Citizens of different States,___ between Citizens of the same State claiming Lands under Grants of different States, and between a State, or the Citizens thereof, and foreign States, Citizens or Subjects.

In all Cases affecting Ambassadors, other public Ministers and Consuls, and those in which a State shall be Party, the supreme Court shall have original Jurisdiction. In all the other Cases before mentioned, the supreme Court shall have appellate Jurisdiction, both as to Law and Fact, with such Exceptions, and under such Regulations as the Congress shall make.

The Trial of all Crimes, except in Cases of Impeachment, shall be by Jury; and such Trial shall be held in the State where the said Crimes shall have been committed; but when not committed within any State, the Trial shall be at such Place or Places as the Congress may by Law have directed.

Section.3. Treason against the United States, shall consist only in levying War against them, or in adhering to their Enemies, giving them Aid and Comfort. No Person shall be convicted of Treason unless on the Testimony of two Witnesses to the same overt Act, or on Confession in open Court.

The Congress shall have Power to declare the Punishment of Treason, but no Attainder of Treason shall work Corruption of Blood, or Forfeiture except during the Life of the Person attainted.

Article. IV.

Section.1. Full Faith and Credit shall be given in each State to the public Acts, Records, and judicial Proceedings of every other State. And the

[BEGIN PAGE 4 OF 4]

Congress may by general Laws prescribe the Manner in which such Acts, Records and Proceedings shall be proved, and the Effect thereof.

Section.2. The Citizens of each State shall be entitled to all Privileges and Immunities of Citizens in the several States.

A Person charged in any State with Treason, Felony, or other Crime, who shall flee from Justice, and be found in another State, shall on Demand of the executive Authority of the State from which he fled, be delivered up, to be removed to the State having Jurisdiction of the Crime.

No Person held to Service or Labour in one State, under the Laws thereof, escaping into another, shall, in Consequence of any Law or Regulation therein, be discharged from such Service or Labour, but shall be delivered up on Claim of the Party to whom such Service or Labour may be due.

Section.3. New States may be admitted by the Congress into this Union; but no new State shall be formed or erected within the Jurisdiction of any other State; nor any State be formed by the Junction of two or more States, or Parts of States, without the Consent of the Legislatures of the States concerned as well as of the Congress.

The Congress shall have Power to dispose of and make all needful Rules and Regulations respecting the Territory or other Property belonging to the United States; and nothing in this Constitution shall be so construed as to Prejudice any Claims of the United States, or of any particular State.

Section.4. The United States shall guarantee to every State in this Union a Republican Form of Government, and shall protect each of them against Invasion; and on Application of the Legislature, or of the Executive (when the Legislature cannot be convened), against domestic Violence.

Article. V.

The Congress, whenever two thirds of both Houses shall deem it necessary, shall propose Amendments to this Constitution, or, on the Application of the Legislatures of two thirds of the several States, shall call a Convention for proposing Amendments, which, in either Case, shall be valid to all Intents and Purposes, as Part of this Constitution, when ratified by the Legislatures of three fourths of the several States, or by Conventions in three fourths thereof, as the one or the other Mode of Ratification may be proposed by the Congress; Provided that no Amendment which may be made prior to the Year One thousand eight hundred and eight shall in any Manner affect the first and fourth Clauses in the Ninth Section of the first Article; and that no State, without its Consent, shall be deprived of its equal Suffrage in the Senate.

Article. VI.

All Debts contracted and Engagements entered into, before the Adoption of this Constitution, shall be as valid against the United States under this Constitution, as under the Confederation.

This Constitution, and the Laws of the United States which shall be made in Pursuance thereof; and all Treaties made, or which shall be made, under the Authority of the United States, shall be the supreme Law of the Land; and the Judges in every State shall be bound thereby, any Thing in the Constitution or Laws of any State to the Contrary notwithstanding.

The Senators and Representatives before mentioned, and the Members of the several State Legislatures, and all executive and judicial Officers, both of the United States and of the several States, shall be bound by Oath or Affirmation, to support this Constitution; but no religious Test shall ever be required as a Qualification to any Office or public Trust under the United States.

Article. VII.

The Ratification of the Conventions of nine States, shall be sufficient for the Establishment of this Constitution between the States so ratifying the Same.

The Word, "the," being interlined between the seventh and eighth Lines of the first Page, The Word "Thirty" being partly written on an Erazure in the fifteenth Line of the first Page, The Words "is tried" being interlined between the thirty second and thirty third Lines of the first Page and the Word "the" being interlined between the forty third and forty fourth Lines of the second Page.
Attest William Jackson Secretary

done in Convention by the Unanimous Consent of the States present the Seventeenth Day of September in the Year of our Lord one thousand seven hundred and Eighty seven and of the Independence of the United States of America the Twelfth

In witness whereof

We have hereunto subscribed our Names,

Go.Washington_Presidt.
and deputy from Virginia

Delaware	Geo: Read, Gunning Bedford junr, John Dickinson, Richard Bassett, Jaco: Broom
Maryland	James McHenry, Dan of St Thos. Jenifer, Danl Carroll
Virginia	John Blair __, James Madison Jr.
North Carolina	Wm. Blount, Richd. Dobbs Spaight., Hu Williamson
South Carolina	J. Rutledge, Charles Cotesworth Pinckney, Charles Pinckney, Pierce Butler
Georgia	William Few, Abr Baldwin

New Hampshire	John Langdon, Nicholas Gilman
Massachusetts	Nathaniel Gorham, Rufus King
Connecticut	Wm. Saml. Johnson, Roger Sherman
New York	... Alexander Hamilton
New Jersey	Wil: Livingston, David Brearley., Wm. Paterson., Jona: Dayton
Pennsylvania	B Franklin, Thomas Mifflin, Robt Morris, Geo. Clymer, Thos. Fitz Simons, Jared Ingersoll, James Wilson, Gouv Morris

APPENDICES V

THE BILL OF RIGHTS
***

Congress approved the original document on September 25, 1789. Article the third through Article the twelfth were ratified by the several State Legislatures on December 15, 1791; these ten articles became Amendment I through Amendment X. Article the first was never ratified; Article the second was ratified on May 7, 1992 as Amendment XXVII.

***

(As transcribed by Greg Crews from photocopy of the handwritten text)
***

Congress OF THE United States
begun and held at the City of New York, on
Wednesday the fourth of March, one thousand seven hundred and eighty nine.

THE Conventions of a number of the States, having at the time of their adopting the Constitution expressed a desire, in order to prevent misconstruction or abuse of its powers, that further declaratory and restrictive clauses should be added: And as extending the ground of public confidence in the Government, will best ensure the beneficent ends of its institution.

RESOLVED by the Senate and House of Representatives of the Unite States of America, in Congress assembled, two thirds of both Houses concurring, that the following Articles be proposed to the Legislatures of the several States, as Amendments to the Constitution of the United States, all, or any of which Articles, when ratified by three fourths of the said Legislatures, to be valid to all intents and purposes, as part of the said Constitution: viz.

ARTICLES in addition to, and Amendment of the Constitution of the United States of America, proposed by Congress and ratified by the Legislatures of the several States, pursuant to the firth Article of the original Constitution.

Article the first..........After the first enumeration required by the first Article of the Constitution, there shall be one Representative for every thirty thousand, until the number shall amount to one hundred, after which, the proportion shall be so regulated by Congress, that there shall be not less than one hundred Representatives, nor less than one Representative for every forty thousand persons, until the number of Representatives shall amount to two hundred, after which the proportion shall be so regulated by Congress, that there shall not be less than two hundred Representatives, nor more than one Representative for every fifty thousand persons.

Article the second.....No law, varying the compensation for the services of the Senators and Representatives, shall take effect, until an election of Representatives shall have intervened.

Article the third........Congress shall make no law respecting an establishment of religion, or prohibiting the free exercise thereof; or abridging the freedom of speech, or of the press, or the right of the people peaceably to assemble, and to petition the Government for a redress of grievances.

Article the fourth......A well regulated Militia, being necessary to the security of a free State, the right of the people to keep and bear Arms, shall not be infringed.

Article the fifth.........No Soldier shall, in time of peace be quartered in any house, without the consent of the Owner, nor in time of war, but in a manner to be prescribed by law.

Article the sixth........The right of the people to be secure in their persons, houses, papers, and effects, against unreasonable searches and seizures, shall not be violated, and no Warrants shall issue, but upon probable cause, supported by Oath or affirmation, and particularly describing the place to be searched, and the persons or things to be seized.

Article the seventh....No person shall be held to answer for a capital, or otherwise infamous crime, unless on a presentment or indictment of a Grand Jury, except in cases arising in the land or naval forces, or in the Militia, when in actual service in time of War or public danger; nor shall any person be subject for the same offence to be twice put in jeopardy of life or limb, nor shall be compelled in any criminal case to be a witness against himself, nor be deprived of life, liberty, or property, without due process of law; nor shall private property be taken for public use, without just compensation.

Article the eighth......In all criminal prosecutions, the accused shall enjoy the right to a speedy and public trial, by an impartial jury of the State and district wherein the crime shall have been committed; which district shall have been previously ascertained by law, and to be informed of the nature and cause of the accusation; to be confronted with the witnesses against him; to have compulsory process for obtaining Witnesses in his favor, and to have the Assistance of Counsel for his defence.

Article the ninth........In suits at common law, where the value in controversy shall exceed twenty dollars, the right of trial by jury shall be preserved, and no fact tried by a jury shall be otherwise re-examined in any Court of the United States, than according to the rules of the common law.

Article the tenth........Excessive bail shall not be required, nor excessive fines imposed, nor cruel and unusual punishments inflicted.

Article the eleventh...The enumeration in the Constitution of certain rights shall not be construed to deny or disparage others retained by the people.

Article the twelfth......The powers not delegated to the United States by the Constitution, nor prohibited by it to the States, are reserved to the States respectively, or to the people.

ATTEST,   Frederick Augustus Muhlenberg   Speaker of the House of Representatives
                   John Adams,   Vice-President of the United States, and
                                                        President of the Senate

John Beckley,   Clerk of the House of Representatives.
Sam. A. Otis   Secretary of the Senate

APPENDICES VI

WASHINGTON'S FAREWELL ADDRESS
(As transcribed by Greg Crews from
photocopy of the handwritten text)
***

(1

Friends & Fellow-Citizens

The period for a new election of a citizen to administer the executive government of the United States, being not far distant, and the time actually arrived, when your thoughts must be employed in designating the person, who is to be clothed with that important trust, it appears to me proper, especially as it may conduce to a more distinct expression of the public voice, that I should now apprise you of the resolution I have formed, to decline being considered amid the number of those, out of whom a choice is to be made. ____

I beg you, at the same time, to do me the justice to be assured, that this resolution has not been taken, without a strict regard to all the considerations appertaining to the relation, which binds a dutiful citizen to his country ___and that, in withdrawing the tender of service which silence in my situation might imply, I am influenced by no diminution of zeal for your future interests, no deficiency of grateful respect for your past kindness; but am supported by a full conviction

2)

conviction that the step is compatible with both.

The acceptance of, & continuance hitherto in, the office to which your suffrages have twice called me, have been a uniform sacrifice of inclination to the opinion of duty, and to a deference for what appeared to be your desire. __I constantly hoped, that it would have been much earlier in my power, consistently with motives, which I was not at liberty to disregard, to return to that retirement, from which I had been reluctantly drawn. _____The strength of my inclination to do this, previous to the last election, had even led to the preparation of an address to declare it to you; but mature reflection on the then perplexed & critical posture of our affairs with foreign nations, and the unanimous advice of persons entitled to my confidence, impelled me to abandon the idea. __

I rejoice, that the state of your concerns, external as well as internal, no longer renders the pursuit of inclination incompatible with the sentiment of duty, or propriety; & am persuaded, whatever partiality may be retained for my services, that in the present circumstances of our country, you will not disapprove my determination to retire. __

The impressions, with which, I first undertook the arduous trust, were explained on the proper occasion. __In the discharge of this trust, I will only say, that I have, with good intentions, contributed towards the or ganization

(3

ganization and administration of the government, the best exertions of which a very fallible judgment was capable.___ Not unconscious, in the outset, of the inferiority of my qualifications, experience in my own eyes, perhaps still more in the eyes of others, has strengthened the motives to diffidence of myself; and every day the encreasing weight of years admonishes me more and more, that the shade of retirement is as necessary to me as it will be welcome. __ Satisfied that if any circumstances have given peculiar value to my services, they were temporary, I have the consolation to believe, that while choice and prudence invite me to quit the political scene, patriotism does not forbid it. __

In looking forward to the moment, which is intended to terminate the career of my public life, my feelings do not permit me to suspend the deep acknowledgment of that debt of gratitude w-^{ch} I owe to my beloved country,_ for the many honors it has conferred upon me; still more for the stead

fast

4)

fast confidence with which it has supported me and for the opportunities I have thence enjoyed of manifesting my inviolable attachment, by services faithful & persevering, though in usefulness unequal to my zeal. _ If benefits have resulted to our country from these services, let it always be remembered to your praise, and as an instructive example in our annals, that under circumstances in which the passions agitated in every direction were liable to mislead, amidst appearances sometimes dubious, _ viscissitudes of fortune often discouraging, _ in situations in which not unfrequently want of success has countenanced the spirit of criticism, the constancy of your support was the essential prop of the efforts, and a guarantee of the plans by which they were effected. __ Profoundly penetrated with this idea, I shall carry it with me to my grave, as a strong incitement to unceasing vows in that Heaven may continue to you the choicest tokens of its beneficence _ that your union & brotherly affection may be perpetual _ that the free constitution, which is the work of your hands, may be sacredly maintained _ that its administration in every department may be stamped with wisdom and virtue _ that, in fine, the happiness of the people of these states, under the auspices of liberty, may be made complete, by so careful a preservation and so prudent a use of this blessing as will acquire to them the glory of recommending it to the

applause

(5

applause, the affection- and adoption of every nation which is yet a stranger to it. Here, perhaps, I ought to stop. But a solicitude for your welfare, which cannot end but with my life, and the apprehension of danger, natural to that solicitude, urge me on an occasion like the present, to offer to your solemn contemplation, and to recommend to your frequent review, some sentiments; which are the result of much reflection, of no inconsiderable observation, and which appear to me all important to the permanency of your felicity as a people. __ These will be offered to you with the more freedom, as you can only see in them the disinterested warnings of a parting friend, who can possibly have no personal motive to biass his counsel. ·)

·) Nor can I forget, as an encouragement to it, your indulgent reception of my sentiments on a former and not dissimilar occasion.

Interwoven as is the love of liberty with every ligament of your hearts, no recommendation of mine is necessary to fortify or confirm the attachment. __

The unity of government which constitutes you one people is also now dear to you. __It is justly so; __ for it is a main pillar in the edifice of your real independence, the support of your tranquility at home; your peace abroad; of your safety; __of your prosperity; __ of that very Liberty which you so highly prize. _ But as it is easy to foresee, that from different

causes

6)
causes & from different quarters, much pains will be taken, many artifices employed, to weaken in your minds the conviction of this truth; _as this is the point in your political fortress against which the batteries of internal & external enemies will be most constantly and actively (though often covertly & insidiously) directed, it is of infinite moment, that you should properly estimate the immense value of your national union to your collective & individual happiness; ___that you should cherish a cordial, habitual & immovable attachment to it; accustoming yourselves to think and speak of it as of the palladium of your political safety and prosperity; watching for its preservation with jealous anxiety; discountenancing whatever may suggest even a suspicion that it can in any event be abandoned, and indignantly frowning upon the first dawning of every attempt to alienate any portion of our Country from the rest, or to enfeeble the sacred ties which now link together the various parts. __

For this you have every inducement of sympathy and interest. __ Citizens by birth or choice, of our common country, that country has a right to concentrate your affections. ___ The name of <u>American</u>, which belongs to you, in your national capacity, must always exalt the just pride of patriotism, more than any appellation derived from local dis
criminations

(7
criminations. __ With slight shades of difference, you have the same Religeon, Manners, Habits & political principles. __ You have in a common cause fought & triumphed together _ The independence & liberty you possess are the work of joint councils, and joint efforts _ of common dangers, sufferings and successes. _

But these considerations, however powerfully they address themselves to your sensibility are greatly outweighed by those which apply more immediately to your interest. __ Here every portion of our country finds the most commanding motives for carefully guarding & preserving the union of the whole.

The <u>North</u>, in an unrestrained intercourse with the <u>South</u>, protected by the equal Laws of a common government, finds in the productions of the latter, great additional resources of maratime & commercial enterprise and precious materials of manufacturing industry. __ The <u>South</u> in the same intercourse, benefitting by the agency of the <u>North</u>, sees its agriculture grow & its commerce expand. Turning partly into its own channels the seamen of the <u>North</u>, it finds its particular navigation envigorated; _and while it contributes, in different ways, to nourish & increase the general mass of the national navigation, it looks forward to the protection of a maratime strength, to which itself is unequally adapted. ___ The <u>East</u>, in a like intercourse with the <u>West</u>, already finds, and
in

8)
in the progressive improvement of interior communications, by land & water, will more & more find a valuable vent for the commodities which it brings from abroad, or manufactures at home. ___ The <u>West</u> derives from the <u>East</u> supplies requisite to its growth & comfort, ___ and what is perhaps of still greater consequence, it must of necessity owe the <u>secure</u> enjoyment of indispensable <u>outlets</u> for its own productions to the weight, influence, and the future maritime strength of the Atlantic side of the Union, directed by an indissoluble community of interest as <u>one nation</u>. __ Any other tenure by which the <u>West</u> can hold this essential advantage, whether derived from its own separate strength, or from an apostate & unnatural connection with any foreign power, must be intrinsically precarious. __

While then every part of our country thus feels an immediate & particular interest in union, all the parts combined cannot fail to find in the united mass of means & efforts greater strength, greater resource, proportionably greater security from external danger, a less frequent interruption of their Peace by foreign nations; _ and, what is of inestimable value! they must derive from union an exemption from those broils and wars between themselves, which

(9

so frequently afflict neighboring countries, not tied together by the same government; which their own rivalships alone would be sufficient to produce, but which opposite foreign alliances, attachments & intrigues would stimulate & imbitter. __ Hence likewise they will avoid the necessity of those overgrown military establishments, which under any form of government are inauspicious to liberty, and which are to be regarded as particularly hostile to Republican Liberty: In this sense it is, that your union ought to be considered as a main prop of your liberty, and that the love of the one ought to endear to you the preservation of the other. __

These considerations speak a persuasive language to every reflecting & virtuous mind; and exhibit the continuance of the Union as a primary object of Patriotic desire. __ Is there a doubt, whether a common government can embrace so large a sphere? ___Let experience solve it. __ To listen to mere speculation in such a case were criminal. __ We are authorized to hope that a proper organization of the whole, with the auxiliary agency of governments for the respective subdivisions, will afford a happy issue to the experiment. __ 'Tis well worth a fair and full experiment

10)

With such powerful and obvious motives to union, affecting all parts of our country, while experience shall not have demonstrated its impracticability, there will always be reason, to distrust the patriotism of those, who in any quarter may endeavor to weaken its bands. __

(11

In contemplating the causes w-^{ch} may disturb our union, it occurs as matter of serious concern that any ground should have been furnished for characterizing parties by Geographical discriminations __ Northern and Southern __ Atlantic and Western; whence designing men may endeavour to excite a belief that there is a real Respect for local interests and views.

12)

One of the expedients of party to acquire influence, within particular districts, is to misrepresent the opinions & aims of other districts. __ You cannot shield yourselves too much against the jealousies & heart burnings which spring from these misrepresentations. ___ They tend to render alien to each other those who ought to be bound together by fraternal affection. __ The inhabitants of our Western country have lately had a useful lesson on this head. __ They have seen, in the negotiation by the Executive, and in the unanimous ratification by the Senate, of the Treaty with Spain, and in the universal satisfaction at that event, throughout the United States, a decisive proof how unfounded were the suspicions propagated among them of a policy in the General Government and in the Atlantic states unfriendly to their interests in regard to the Mississippi. __ They have been witnesses to the formation of two Treaties, that with G. Britain and that with Spain, which secure to them everything they could desire, in respect to our Foreign Relations, towards confirming their prosperity. __ Will it not be their wisdom to rely for the preservation of_ of these advantages on the Union by w-^{ch} they were procured? __ Will they not henceforth be deaf to those

advisers, if such there are, who would sever them from their Brethren and connect them with aliens? __
To

(13

To the efficacy and permanency of your Union, a government for the whole is indispensable. __ No alliances however strict between the parts can be an adequate substitute. __ They must inevitably experience the infractions & interruptions which all alliances in all times have experienced. __ Sensible of this momentous truth, you have improved upon your first essay, by the adoption of a Constitution of Government, better calculated than your former for an intimate Union, and for the efficacious management of your common concerns. __ This government, the offspring of our own choice uninfluenced and unawed, adopted upon full investigation & mature deliberation, completely free in its principles, in the distribution of its powers, uniting security with energy, and containing within itself a provision for its own amendment, has a just claim to your confidence and your support. __ Respect for its authority, compliance with its Laws, acquiescence in its measures, are duties enjoined by the fundamental maxims of true Liberty. __ The basis of our political systems is the right of the people to make and to alter their Constitutions of Government. __ But the Constitution which at any time exists, 'till changed by an explicit and authentic act of the whole people, is sacredly obligatory upon all. __ The very idea of the power and the right of the people to establish Government presupposes the duty of every individual

14)

individual to obey the established Government.

All obstructions to the execution of the Laws, all combinations and associations, under whatever plausible character, with the real design to direct, controul counteract, or awe the regular deliberation and action of the Constituted authorities are destructive of this fundamental principle and of fatal tendency. __ They serve to organize faction, to give it an artificial and extraordinary force – to put in the place of the delegated will of the Nation, the will of a party,__ often a small but artful and enterprising minority of the Community; _ and, according to the alternate triumphs of different parties, to make the public administration the mirror of the ill concerted and incongruous projects of faction, rather than the Organ of consistent and wholesome plans digested by common councils and modified by mutual interests. ___ However combinations or associations of the above description may now & then answer popular ends, they are likely, in the course of time and things, to become potent engines, by which cunning, ambitious and unprincipled men will be enabled to subvert the power of the People, & to usurp for themselves the reins of Government; destroying afterwards the very engines which have lifted them to unjust dominion. __
Towards the preservation of your
Government

(15

Government and the permanency of your present happy state, it is requisite, not only that you steadily discountenance irregular oppositions to its acknowledged authority, but also that you resist with care the spirit of innovation upon its principles however specious the pretexts. ___ One method of assault may be to effect, in the forms of the Constitution, alterations which will impair the energy of the system, and thus to undermine what cannot be directly overthrown. ___ In all the changes to which you may be invited, remember that time and habit are at least as necessary to fix the true character of Governments, as of other human institutions __ that experience is the surest standard, by which to test the real tendency of the existing Constitution of a Country __ that facility in changes upon the credit of mere hypotheses & opinion exposes to perpetual change, from the endless variety of hypotheses and opinion: _and remember, especially, that for the efficient management of your common interests, in a country so extensive as ours, a Government of as much vigour as is consistent with the perfect security of Liberty is indispensable __Liberty itself will find in such a Government, with powers properly distributed and adjusted, its surest Guardian. __ It is indeed little else than a name, where the Government is too feeble to withstand the enterprises of faction, to confine in a mass the bane-of the society, within the

16)

the limits prescribed by the laws & to maintain all in the secure & tranquil enjoyment of the rights of person & property. __

I have already intimated to you the danger of Parties in the state, with particular reference to the founding of them on Geographical discriminations. __Let me now take a more comprehensive view, & warn you in the most solemn manner against the baneful effects of the Spirit of Party, generally

This spirit, unfortunately, is inseparable from our nature, having its root in the strongest passions of the human mind. ___It exists under different shapes in all Governments, more or less stifled, controlled, or repressed; but in those of the popular form it is seen in its greatest rankness and is truly their worst enemy. __

(17

The alternate domination of one faction over another, sharpened by the spirit of revenge natural to party dissension, which in different ages & countries has perpetrated the most horrid enormities, is itself a frightful despotism. ___ But this leads at length to a more formal and permanent despotism. ___ The disorders & miseries, which result, gradually incline the minds of men to seek security & repose in the absolute power of an Individual: and sooner or later the chief of some prevailing faction more able or more fortunate than his competitors, turns this disposition to the purposes of his own elevation, on the ruins of Public Liberty. __

Without looking forward to an extremity of this kind (which nevertheless ought not to be entirely out of sight) the common & continual mischiefs of the spirit of Party are sufficient to make it the interest and the duty of a wise People to discourage and restrain it. __

It

18)

It serves always to distract the Public councils and enfeeble the Public administration. __ It agitates the community with ill founded jealousies and false alarms, kindles the animosity of one part against another, foments occasionally riot & insurrection. __It opens the door to foreign influence & corruption, which find a facilitated access to the government itself through the channels of party passions. Thus the policy and and the will of one country, are subjected to the policy and will of another. __

There is an opinion that parties in free countries are useful checks upon the administration of the Government and serve to keep alive the Spirit of Liberty. __ This within certain limits is probably true __ and in governments of a monarchical cast patriotism may look with indulgence, if not with favour, upon the spirit of party. __ But in those of the popular character, in Governments purely elective, it is a spirit not to be encouraged. __ From their natural tendency, it is

certain there will always be enough of that Spirit for every salutary purpose. ___ And there being constant danger of excess, the effort ought to be by force of public opinion to mitigate & assuage it. __A fire not to be quenched; it demands a uniform vigilance to prevent its bursting into a flame, lest instead of warming it should consume. __
It

(19

It is important, likewise, that the habits of thinking in a free country should inspire caution in those entrusted with its administration, to confine themselves within their respective Constitutional Spheres, avoiding in the exercise of the powers of one department to encroach upon another. __ The spirit of encroachment tends to consolidate the Powers of all the departments in one, and thus to create whatever the form of government, a real despotism. __ A just estimate of that love of power, and proneness to abuse it, which predominates in the human heart is sufficient to satisfy us of the truth of this position. __The necessity of reciprocal checks in the exercise of political power; by dividing and distributing it into different depositories, & constituting each the Guardian of the Public Weal against invasions by the others, has been evinced by experiments ancient & modern; _some of them in our country & under our own eyes. ___To preserve them must be as necessary as to institute them. __If in the opinion of the People, the distribution or modification of the Constitutional powers be in any particular wrong, let it be corrected by an amendment in the way which the Constitution designates. __But let there be no change by usurpation; for though this, in one instance, may be the instrument of good, it is the customary weapon by which free governments are destroyed. __ The precedent must always greatly overbalance in permanent
evil

20)
evil any partial or transient benefit which the use can at any time yield. __

Of all the dispositions and habits which lead to political prosperity, Religion and morality are indispensable supports. __ In vain would that man claim the tribute of Patriotism, who should labour to subvert these great Pillars of human happiness, these firmest props of the duties of men & citizens. __ The mere Politician, equally with the pious man ought to respect & to cherish them. __A volume could not trace all their connections with private & public felicity. __ Let it simply be asked where is the security for property, for reputation, for life, if the sense of religious obligation desert the oaths, which are the instruments of investigation in Courts of Justice? __ And let us with caution indulge the supposition, that morality can be maintained without religion. __Whatever may be conceded to the influence of refined education on minds of peculiar structure __ reason & experience both forbid us to expect that national morality can prevail in exclusion of religious principle. __

'Tis substantially true, that virtue or morality is a necessary spring of popular government. __The rule indeed extends with more or less force to every species of free Government. __ Who that is a sincere friend to it, can look with indifference upon attempts to shake the foundation of the fabric

(21

Promote then as an object of primary importance, Institutions for the general diffusion of knowledge. __ In proportion as the structure of a government gives force to public opinion, it is essential that public opinion should be enlightened.

As a very important source of strength & security, cherish public credit. __One method of preserving it is to use it as sparingly as possible: __avoiding occasions of expense by cultivating peace, but remembering also that timely disbursements to prepare for danger frequently prevent much greater disbursements to repel it __avoiding likewise the accumulation of debt, not only by shunning occasions of expense, but by vigorous exertions in time of Peace to discharge the Debts which unavoidable wars may have occasioned, not ungenerously throwing upon posterity the burden which we ourselves ought to bear. __The execution of these maxims belongs to your Representatives, but it is necessary that public opinion should cooperate. To facilitate to them the performance of their duty, it is essential that you should practically bear in mind, that towards the payment of debts there must be Revenue __that

to

22)

to have Revenue there must be taxes _ that no taxes can be devised which are not more or less inconvenient & unpleasant __ that the intrinsic embarrassment inseparable from the selection of the proper objects (which is always a choice of difficulties) ought to be a decisive motive for a candid construction of the conduct of the Government in making it, and for a spirit of acquiescence in the measures for obtaining Revenue which the public exigencies may at any time dictate. __

Observe good faith & justice towards all Nations. Cultivate peace and harmony with all __Religion & morality enjoin this conduct; and can it be that good policy does not equally enjoin it? _ It will be worthy of a free, enlightened, and, at no distant period, a great nation, to give to mankind the magnanimous and too novel example of a People always guided by an exalted justice & benevolence. __ Who can doubt that in the course of time and things the fruits of such a plan would richly repay any temporary advantages w.ch might be lost by a steady adherence to it? Can it be, that Providence has not connected the permanent felicity of a Nation with its virtue? __The experiment, at least, is recommended by every sentiment which ennobles human nature. __ Alas! is it rendered impossible by its vices?

In

(23

In the execution of such a plan nothing is more essential than that permanent, inveterate antipathies against particular nations and passionate attachments for others should be excluded; _and that in place of them just & amicable feelings towards all should be cultivated. ___The Nation which indulges towards another an habitual hatred, or an habitual fondness, is in some degree a slave. __It is a slave to its animosity or to its affection, either of which is sufficient to lead it astray from its duty and its interest. __ Antipathy in one Nation against another _disposes each more readily to offer insult and injury, to lay hold of slight causes of umbrage, and to be haughty and intractable, when accidental or trifling occasions of dispute occur. __ Hence frequent collisions, obstinate envenomed and bloody contests. __ The Nation, prompted by ill will & resentment sometimes impels to war the Government, contrary to the best calculations of policy. __ The Government sometimes participates in the national propensity, and adopts through passion what reason would reject; _ at other times, it makes the animosity of the Nation subservient to projects of hostility instigated by pride, ambition and other sinister & pernicious motives. __ The peace often, sometimes perhaps the Liberty, of Nations has been the victim. __

So

24)
So likewise, a passionate attachment of one Nation for another produces a variety of evils. __ Sympathy for the favourite nation, facilitating the illusion of an imaginary common interest, in cases where no real common interest exists, and infusing into one the enmities of the other, betrays the former into a participation in the quarrels & wars of the latter, without adequate inducement or justification: _It leads also to concessions to the favourite nation of privileges denied to others, which is apt doubly to injure the Nation making the concessions, __ by unnecessarily parting with what ought to have been retained _& by exciting jealousy, ill will, and a disposition to retaliate, in the parties from whom eq.l privileges are withheld: And it gives to ambitious, corrupted, or deluded citizens (who devote themselves to the favourite Nation) facility to betray, or sacrifice the interests of their own country, without odium, sometimes even with popularity; _ gilding with the appearances of a virtuous sense of obligation a commendable deference for public opinion, or a laudable zeal for public good, the base or foolish compliances of ambition, corruption or infatuation. __

As avenues to foreign influence in innumerable ways, such attachments are particularly alarming to the truly enlightened and independent Patriot. __ How many opportunities do they afford to tam

per

(25

per with domestic factions, to practice the arts of seduction, to mislead public opinion, to influence or awe the public councils! __Such an attachment of a small or weak, towards a great & powerful nation, dooms the former to be the satellite of the latter. _

Against the insidious wiles of foreign influence, (I conjure you to believe me fellow citizens,) the jealousy of a free people ought to be <u>constantly</u> awake, since history and experience prove that foreign influence is one of the most baneful foes of Republican Government. _ But that jealousy to be useful must be impartial; else it becomes the instrument: of the very influence to be avoided, instead of a defense against it. __ Excessive partiality for one foreign nation and excessive dislike of another, cause those whom they actuate to see danger only on one side, and serve to veil and even second the arts of influence on the other. _ Real Patriots, who may resist the intriegues of the favourite, are liable to become suspected and odious; while its tools and dupes usurp the applause & confidence of the people, to surrender their interests. ___

The great rule of conduct for us, in regard to foreign Nations is in extending our comercial relations to have with them as little <u>political</u> connection as possible. __ So far as we have already formed engagements let them be fulfilled,

with

26)
with perfect good faith. __ Here let us stop.

Europe has a set of primary interests, which to us have none, or a very remote relation. __Hence she must be engaged in frequent controversies, the causes of which are essentially foreign to our concerns. ___ Hence therefore it must be unwise in us to implicate ourselves, by artificial ties, in the ordinary vicissitudes of her politics, or the ordinary combinations & collisions of her friendships, or enmities: __

Our detached & distant situation invites and enables us to pursue a different course. ___ If we remain one People, under an efficient government, the period is not far off, when we may defy material injury from external annoyance; __when we may take such an attitude as will cause the neutrality we may at any time resolve upon to be scrupulously respected; __when belligerent nations, under the impossibility of making acquisitions upon us, will not lightly hazard the giving us provocation; _when we may choose peace or war, as our interest guided by justice shall counsel. __

Why forgo the advantages of so peculiar a situation? _ Why quit our own to stand upon foreign ground? __ Why, by interweaving our destiny with that of any part of Europe, entangle our peace and

prosperity

(27

prosperity in the toils of European ambition, Rivalship, Interest, Humor or Caprice? __

'Tis our true policy to steer clear of permanent alliances, with any portion of the foreign world __ so far, I mean, as we are now at liberty to do it_ for let me not be understood as capable of patronizing infidelity to existing engagements (I hold the maxim no less applicable to public than to private affairs, that honesty is always the best policy). __ I repeat it therefore, let those engagements be observed in their genuine sense. __But in my opinion, it is unnecessary and would be unwise to extend them. __

Taking care always to keep ourselves, by suitable establishments, on a respectably defensive posture, we may safely trust to temporary alliances for extraordinary emergencies. __

Harmony, liberal intercourse with all nations, are recommended by policy, humanity and interest. __ But even our commercial policy should hold an equal and impartial hand: _ neither seeking nor granting exclusive favours or preferences; _consulting the natural course of things; _diffusing & diversifying by gentle means the streams of commerce, but forcing nothing; __establishing with powers so disposed _ in order to give to trade a stable course, to define the rights of our merchants, and to enable the Government to support them _ conventional rules of inter

course

28)

course, the best that present circumstances and mutual opinion will permit, but temporary, & liable to be from time to time abandoned or varied, as experience and circumstances shall dictate; constantly keeping in view; that 'tis folly in one nation to look for disinterested favor from another__ that it must pay with a portion of its Independence for whatever it may accept under that character __ that by such acceptance, it may place itself in the condition of having given equivalents for nominal favours and yet of being reproached with ingratitude for not giving more. __ There can be no greater error than to expect, or calculate upon real favours from Nation to Nation. __'Tis an illusion which experience must cure, which a just pride ought to discard. __

In offering to you, my Countrymen, these counsels of an old and affectionate friend, I dare not hope they will make the strong and lasting impression, I could wish __that they will control the usual current of the passions, or prevent our Nation from running the course which has hitherto marked the Destiny of Nations. _ But if I may even flatter myself, that they may be productive of some partial benefit, some occasional good; that they may now & then recur to moderate the fury of party spirit, to warn against the mischiefs of foreign Intriegue, to guard against the

Impostures

(29

Impostures of pretended patriotism _ this hope will be a full recompense for the solicitude for your welfare, by which they have been dictated. __

How far in the discharge of my official duties, I have been guided by the principles which have been delineated, the public Records and other evidences of my conduct must witness to You and to the world. __To myself, the assurance of my own conscience is, that I have at least believed myself to be guided by them.

In relation to the still subsisting war in Europe, my Proclamation of the 22^d of April 1793 is the index to my Plan. __ Sanctioned by your approving voice and by that of Your Representatives in both Houses of Congress, the spirit of that measure has continually governed me; _ uninfluenced by any attempts to deter or divert me from it. __

After deliberate examination with the aid of the best lights I could obtain I was well satisfied that our Country, under all the circumstances of the case, had a right to take, and was bound in duty and interest, to take a neutral position. __ Having taken it, I determined, as far as should depend upon me, to maintain it, with moderation, perseverence & firmness. __

The

30)

The considerations which respect the right to hold this conduct, it is not necessary on this occasion to detail. __I will only observe, that according to my understanding of the matter, that right, so far from being denied by any of the Belligerent Powers has been virtually admitted by all. __

The duty of holding a neutral conduct may be inferred, without anything more, from the obligation which justice and humanity impose on every Nation, in cases in which it is free to act, to maintain inviolate the relations of Peace and amity towards other Nations. _

The inducements of interest for observing that conduct will best be referred to your own reflections & experience. __With me, a predominant motive has been to endeavor to gain time to our country to settle & mature its yet recent institutions, and to progress without interruption, to that degree of strength & consistency, which is necessary to give it, humanly speaking, the command of its own fortunes. __

Though in reviewing the incidents of my administration, I am unconscious of intentional error_ I am nevertheless too sensible of my defects not to think it probable that I may have committed many errors. __ Whatever they may be I fervently beseech the Almighty to avert or mitigate the evils to which they may tend. ___ I shall also carry with me the hope that my Country will never cease to view them with indulgence; and that after forty five years of my life dedicated to its service, with an upright zeal, the faults of incompetent abilities will be consigned to oblivion, as myself must soon be to the mansions of rest.

Relying

32

Relying on its kindness in this as in other things, and actuated by that fervent love towards it, which is so natural to a man, who views in it the native soil of himself and his progenitors for several Generations;__ I anticipate with pleasing expectation that retreat, in which I promise myself to realize, without alloy, the sweet enjoyment of partaking, in the midst of my fellow Citizens, the benign influence of good Laws under a free Government __ the ever favourite object of my heart, and the happy reward, as I trust, of our mutual cares, labours and dangers.

United States,   G^{eo.}Washington
19th September, 1996

APPENDICES VII

THE GETTYSBURG ADDRESS
Everett Copy
(As transcribed by Greg Crews from
photocopy of the handwritten text)
***

Address delivered at the dedication of the Cemetery at Gettysburg.

Four score and seven years ago our fathers brought forth on this continent, a new nation, conceived in Liberty, and dedicated to the proposition that all men are created equal.
 Now we are engaged in a great civil war, testing whether that nation, or any nation so conceived and so dedicated, can long endure. We are met on a great battle-field of that war. We have come to dedicate a portion of that field, as a final resting place for those who here gave their lives that that nation might live. It is altogether fitting and proper that we should do this.
 But, in a larger sense, we can not dedicate__ we can not consecrate__ we can not hallow__ this ground. The brave men, living and dead, who struggled here, have consecrated it, far above our poor power to add or detract. The world will little note, nor long remember what we say here, but it can never forget what they did here. It is for us the living, rather, to be dedicated here to the unfinished work which they who fought here have thus far so nobly advanced. It is rather for us to be here dedicated to the great task remaining before us__ that from these honored dead we take increased devotion to that cause for which they gave the last full measure of devotion__ that we here highly resolve that these dead shall not have died in vain__ that this nation, under God, shall have a new birth of freedom- and that government of the people, by the people, for the people, shall not perish from the earth.

Abraham Lincoln.

November 19. 1863

ABOUT THE AUTHOR

G.A.Crews holds a Master of Science degree in Geology and Geophysics from the University of Missouri-Rolla. He is owner/operator of Thunderbore LLC. As contractor: he has provided services in oil, coal and mineral exploration in the USA (17 states), Australia (6 states), Canada, India, Botswana and South Africa; as operator: oil well promotion, drilling and completion. He is an AIPG Certified Professional Geologist; an Illinois Licensed Professional Geologist; a US Patent recipient; an FAA licensed Private Pilot; a master sculptor of the finest bronze sculpture; a rock climber who has solo summited the Devils Tower; an expert snowboarder; a motorcycle enthusiast; a PADI certified scuba diver; and a Missouri spelunker. He is a member of: the American Association of Petroleum Geologists, Sigma XI, the National Rifle Association, the Illinois State Rifle Association, Gun Owners of America, the National Association for Gun Rights, the BlueRibbon Coalition, the National Space Society, the Planetary Society, and the Illinois Sheriffs' Association.

"Treaties, Traitors and Patriots" is a tale that expounds the response of traditional America to a revolutionary coup by a socialist Administration. When the foundations of the Republic are threatened by unconstitutional Executive Orders, the forces of tyranny find the spirit of liberty alive and well. The tale is a drama of treachery and tragedy, allegiance and honor, compassion and humor.

Character dialogue is laced with pertinent historical quotes that are fully credited in the several appendices. While providing an entertaining piece of reality fiction, the author uses the medium to revive some real US history; perhaps enticing those who may balk at the prospect of reviewing the writings of our Founding Fathers, from documents, letters and speeches that should have been studied in school.

Made in the USA
Columbia, SC
09 June 2018